'He tried to speak, to babble something - gratitude perhaps, or last words, or an eager yell for more - but there was only silence. His lungs were like two casts of plaster and bonemeal, each filled to brimming with hot liquid rubber. His muscles heaved against the taut liquid bags like two fists clenching two tennis balls, and his ears roared, and things went black. Suddenly he could hear his heart straining to beat, *thud-thud, thud-thud*, each concessive shock of the ventricles passing through his liquid-filled lungs with booming subaqueous clarity.

And then the beat stopped too.'

Bruce Sterling was born in 1954 in Brownsville, Texas. His grandfather was a rancher, his father an engineer. Sterling, purportedly a novelist by trade, actually spends most of his time aimlessly messing with computers, modems, and fax machines. He and his wife Nancy have a daughter Amy, born in 1987. They live in Austin.

Sterling sold his first science fiction story in 1976. His solo novels include *Involution Ocean*, *The Artificial Kid*, *Schismatrix* and *Islands In The Net* and his first collection of short stories was *Cystal Express*. He also writes non-fiction (including *The Hacker Crackdown: Law and Disorder on the Electronic Frontier*) and SF criticism for *Science Fiction Eye* and *Monad*, in addition to regular columns for *Interzone* and *The Magazine of Fantasy and Science Fiction*.

Globalhead

'Sterling is a brilliant and dangerous short-story writer - you can't go wrong there' *Science Fiction Eye*.

'Sterling has long been associated with the sub-genre known as cyberpunk, which posits a fast-paced future dominated by computers and the public and private forces that control them. But as this collection shows, there's a lot more to Mr Sterling than cyberpunk... A lively and always provocative writer' *New York Times Review of Books*

'One of the most powerful and innovative talents to enter SF' *Gardner Dozois*

'A prophet of hyper-realist SF, fiction devoted to headlong change... But Sterling's mastery of SF extends well beyond [a] single vision of the future... Enthralling and subversive' *SF Commentary*

Heavy Weather

BRUCE STERLING

PHŒNIX

A PHOENIX PAPERBACK

First published in Great Britain by Millennium in 1994
This paperback edition published in 1995 by Phoenix,
a division of Orion Books Ltd,
Orion House, 5 Upper St Martin's Lane, London WC2H 9EA

Copyright © Bruce Sterling 1994

The right of Bruce Sterling to be identified as the author of
this work has been asserted by him in accordance with the
Copyright, Designs and Patents Act 1988

A CIP catalogue record for this book is available
from the British Library.

ISBN: 1 85799 299 7

Printed and bound in Great Britain by
The Guernsey Press Co. Ltd, Guernsey, C.I.

CHAPTER

1

Smart machines lurked about the suite, their power lights in the shuttered dimness like the small red eyes of bats. The machines crouched in niches in white walls of Mexican stucco: an ionizer, a television, a smoke alarm, a squad of motion sensors. A vaporizer hissed and bubbled gently in the corner, emitting a potent reek of oil, ginseng, and eucalpytus.

Alex lay propped on silk-cased pillows, his feet and knees denting the starched cotton sheets. His flesh felt like wet clay, something greased and damp and utterly inert. Since morning he had been huffing at the black neoprene mask of his bedside inhaler, and now his fingertips, gone pale as wax and lightly trembling, seemed to be melting into the mask. Alex thought briefly of hanging the mask from its stainless-steel hook at the bedside medical rack. He rejected the idea. It was too much of a hassle to have the tasty mask out of reach.

The pain in his lungs and throat had not really gone away. Such a miracle was perhaps too much to ask, even of a Mexican black-market medical clinic. Nevertheless, after two weeks of treatment in the *clínica*, his pain had assumed a new subtlety. The scorched inflammation had dwindled to an interestingly novel feeling, something thin and rather theoretical. The suite was as chilly as a fishbowl and Alex felt as cozy and as torpid as a carp. He lay collapsed in semidarkness, eyes blinking grainily, as a deeper texture of his illness languorously revealed itself. Beneath his starched sheets, Alex began to feel warm. Then light-headed. Then slightly nauseous, a customary progression of symptoms. He felt the dark rush build within his chest.

Then it poured through him. He felt his spine melting. He seemed to percolate into the mattress.

These spells had been coming more often lately, and with more power behind them. On the other hand, their dark currents were taking Alex into some interesting places. Alex, not breathing, swam along pleasantly under the rim of unconsciousness for a long moment.

Then, without his will, breath came again. His mind broke delirium's surface. When his eyes reopened, the suite around him seemed intensely surreal. Crawling walls of white stucco, swirling white stucco ceiling, thick wormy carpet of chemical aqua blue. Bulbous pottery lamps squatted unlit on elaborate wicker tables. The chest of drawers, and the bureau, the wooden bedframe, were all marked with the same creepy conspiracy of aqua-blue octagons . . . Iron-hinged wooden shutters guarded the putty-sealed windows. A dying tropical houseplant, the gaunt rubber-leafed monster that had become his most faithful companion here, stood in its terracotta pot, gently poisoned by the constant darkness, and the medicated vaporous damp . . .

A sharp buzz sounded alongside his bed. Alex twisted his matted head on the pillow. The machine buzzed again. Then, yet again.

Alex realized with vague surprise that the machine was a telephone. He had never received any calls on the telephone in his suite. He did not even know that he had one. The elderly, humble machine had been sitting there among its fellow machines, much overshadowed.

Alex examined the phone's antique, poorly designed push-button interface for a long groggy moment. The phone buzzed again, insistently. He dropped the inhaler mask and leaned across the bed, with a twist, and a rustle, and a pop, and a groan. He pressed the tiny button denominated *ESPKR*.

'*Hola*,' he puffed. His gummy larynx crackled and shrieked, bringing sudden tears to his eyes.

'*¿Quien es?*' the phone replied.

'Nobody,' Alex rasped in English. 'Get lost.' He wiped at one eye and glared at the phone. He had no idea how to hang up.

'Alex!' the phone said in English. 'Is that you?'

2

Alex blinked. Blood was rushing through his numbed flesh. Beneath the sheet, his calves and toes began to tingle resentfully.

'I want to speak to Alex Unger!' the phone insisted sharply. '¿Dónde está?'

'Who is this?' Alex said.

'It's Jane! Juanita Unger, your sister!'

'Janey?' Alex said, stunned. 'Gosh, is this Christmas? I'm sorry, Janey . . .'

'What!' the phone shouted. 'It's *May the ninth*! Jesus, you sound really trashed!'

'Hey . . .' Alex said weakly. He'd never known his sister to phone him up, except at Christmas. There was an ominous silence. Alex blearily studied the cryptic buttons on the speakerphone. *RDIAL, FLAS, PROGMA*. No clue how to hang up. The open phone line sat there eavesdropping on him, a torment demanding response. 'I'm okay,' he protested at last. 'How're you, Janey?'

'Do you even know what *year* this is?' the phone demanded. 'Or where you *are*?'

'Umm . . . Sure . . . ' Vague guilty panic penetrated his medicated haze. Getting along with his older sister had never been Alex's strong suit even in the best of times, and now he felt far too weak and dazed to defend himself. 'Janey, I'm not up for this right now . . . Lemme call you back . . . '

'Don't you dare hang up on me, you little weasel!' the phone shrieked. 'What the hell are they doing to you in there? Do you have any idea what these *bills* look like?'

'They're helping me here,' Alex said. 'I'm in treatment. . . . Go away.'

'They're a bunch of con-artist quacks! They'll take you for every cent you have! And then kill you! And bury you in some goddamned toxic waste dump on the border!'

Juanita's shrill assaultive words swarmed through his head like hornets. Alex slumped back into his pillow heap and gazed at the slowly turning ceiling fan, trying to gather his strength. 'How'd you find me here?'

'It wasn't easy, that's for sure!'

Alex grunted. 'Good . . .'

'And getting this phone line was no picnic either!'

Alex drew a slow deep breath, relaxed, exhaled. Something viscous gurgled nastily, deep within him.

'Goddamn it, Alex! You just can't do this! I spent three weeks tracking you down! Even Dad's people couldn't track you down this time.'

'Well, yeah,' Alex muttered. 'That's why I did it that way.'

When his sister spoke again, her voice was full of grim resolve. 'Get packed, Alejandro. You're getting out of there.'

'Don't bother me. Let me be.'

'I'm your *sister*! Dad's written you off – don't you get that yet? You're grown up now, and you've hurt him too many times. I'm the only one left who cares.'

'Don't be so stupid,' Alex croaked wearily. 'Take it easy.'

'I know where you are. And I'm coming to get you. And anybody who tries to stop me – you included – is gonna regret it a lot!'

'You can't do anything,' Alex told her. 'I signed all the clinic papers . . . they've got lawyers.' He cleared his throat, with a long rasping ache. Returning to full alertness was far from pleasant; various parts of his carcass – upper spine, ankles, sinuses, diaphragm – registered sharp aching protests and a deep reluctance to function. 'I want to sleep,' he said. 'I came here to rest.'

'You can't kid me, Alejandro! If you want to drop dead, then go ahead! But don't blow family money on that pack of thieves.'

'You're always so goddamned stubborn,' Alex said. 'You've gone and woke me up now, and I feel like hell!' He sat up straight. 'It's my money, and it's my life! I'll do whatever I want with it! Go back to art school.' He reached across the bed, grabbed the phone lead, and yanked it free, snapping its plastic clip.

Alex picked the dead phone up, examined it, then stuffed it securely under the pillows. His throat hurt. He reached back to the bedside table, dipped his fingers into a tray of hammered Mexican silver, and came up with a narcotic lozenge. He unwrapped it and crunched it sweetly between his molars.

Sleep was far away now. His mind was working again, and required numbing. Alex slid out of the bed onto his hands and knees and searched around on the thick, plush, ugly carpet. His head swam and pounded with the effort. Alex persisted, being used to this.

The TV's remote control, with the foxlike cunning of all

4

important inanimate objects, had gone to earth in a collapsing heap of Mexican true-crime *fotonovelas*. Alex noted that his bed's iron springs, after three weeks of constant humidity, were gently but thoroughly going to rust.

Alex rose to his knees, clutching his prize, and slid with arthritic languor beneath the sheets again. He caught his breath, blew his nose, neatly placed two cold drops of medicated saline against the surface of each eyeball, then began combing the clinic's cable service with minimal twitches of his thumb. Weepy Mexican melodramas. A word-game show. Kids chasing robot dinosaurs in some massive underground mall. The ever-present Thai pop music.

And some English-language happytalk news. Spanish happytalk news. Japanese happytalk news. Alex, born in 2010, had watched the news grow steadily more glossy and cheerful for all of his twenty-one years. As a mere tot, he'd witnessed hundreds of hours of raw bloodstained footage: plagues, mass death, desperate riot, ghastly military wreckage, all against a panicky backdrop of ominous and unrelenting environmental decline. All that stuff was still out there, just as every aspect of modern reality had its mirrored shadow in the Net somewhere, but nowadays you had to hunt hard to find it, and the people discussing it didn't seem to have much in the way of budgets. Somewhere along the line, the entire global village had slipped into neurotic denial.

Today, as an adult, Alex found the glass pipelines of the Net chockablock with jet-set glamour weddings and cute dog stories. Perky heroines and square-jawed heroes were still, somehow, getting rich quick. Starlets won lotteries and lottery winners became starlets. Little children, with their heads sealed in virtuality helmets, mimed delighted surprise as they waved their tiny gloved hands at enormous hallucinations. Alex had never been that big a fan of current events anyway, but he had now come to feel that the world's cheerful shiny-toothed bullshitters were the primal source of all true evil.

Alex collided and stuck in a Mexican docudrama about UFOs; they were known as *los OVNIS* in Spanish, and on 9 de mayo, 2031, a large fraction of the Latin American populace seemed afflicted with spectacular attacks of *ovnimanía*. Long minutes of Alex's life seeped idly away as the screen pumped images at him: monster fireballs by night, puffball-headed dwarfs in jumpsuits of silver lamé, and a video prophecy from some interstellar Virgen de Guadalupe with her own Internet address and a toll-free phone number . . .

The day nurse tapped at the door and bustled in. The day nurse was named Concepción. She was a hefty, no-nonsense, fortyish individual with a taste for liposuction, face-lifts, and breast augmentation.

'¿*Ya le hicieron la prueba de la sangre?*' she said.

Alex turned off the television. 'The blood test? Yeah, I had one this morning.'

'¿*Le duele todavía el pecho como anoche?*'

'Pretty bad last night,' Alex admitted. 'Lots better, though, since I started using the mask.'

'*Un catarro atroz, complicado con una alergia,*' Concepción sympathized.

'No problem with pain, at least,' Alex said. 'I'm getting the best of treatment.'

Concepción sighed and gestured him up. '*Todavía no acabamos, muchacho, le falta la enema de los pulmones.*'

'A *lung* enema?' Alex said, puzzled.

'*Sí.*'

'Today? Right now? ¿*Ahora?*'

She nodded.

'Do I have to?'

Concepción looked stern. '¡*El doctor Mirabi le recetó! Fue muy claro. "Cuidado con una pulmonía." El nuevo tipo de pulmonía es peor que el SIDA, han muerto ya centenares de personas.*'

'Okay, okay,' Alex said. 'Sure, no problem. I'm doing lots better lately, though. I don't even need the chair.'

Concepción nodded and helped him out of bed, shoving her solid shoulder under his armpit. The two of them made it out the door of the suite and a good ten meters down the carpeted hall before Alex's knees buckled. The wheelchair, a machine of limited but highly specialized intelligence, was right behind Alex as he stumbled. He gave up the struggle gracefully and sat within the chrome-and-leather machine.

Concepción left Alex in the treatment room to wait for Dr Mirabi. Alex was quite sure that Dr Mirabi was doing nothing of consequence. Having Alex wait alone in a closed room was simply medical etiquette, a way to establish whose time was more important. Though Dr Mirabi's employees were kept on the hustle – especially the hardworking retail pharmacists – Dr Mirabi himself hardly seemed oppressed by his duties. As far as Alex could deduce from the staff schedules, there were only four long-term patients in the whole *clínica*. Alex was pretty sure that most of the *clínica's* income came from yanquis on day trips down from Laredo. Before he himself had checked in last April, he'd seen a line of Americans halfway down the block, eagerly picking up Mexican megadosage nostrums for the new ultraresistant strains of TB.

Dr Mirabi's treatment room was long and rectangular and full of tall canvas-shrouded machinery. Like every place else in the *clínica*, it was air-conditioned to a deathly chill, and smelled of sharp and potent disinfectant. Alex wished that he had thought to snag a *fotonovela* on the way out of his room. Alex pretended distaste for the *novelas'* clumsy and violence-soaked porn, but their comically distorted gutter-level Spanish was of a lot of philological interest.

Concepción opened the door and stepped in. Behind her, Dr Mirabi arrived, his ever-present notepad in hand. Despite his vaguely Islamic surname, Alex suspected strongly that Dr Mirabi was, in fact, Hungarian.

Dr Mirabi tapped the glass face of his notepad with a neat black stylus and examined the result. 'Well, Alex,' he said briskly in accented English, 'we seem to have defeated that dirty streptococcus once for all.'

'That's right,' Alex said. 'Haven't had a night sweat in ages.'

'That's quite a good step, quite good,' Dr Mirabi encouraged. 'Of course, that infection was only the crisis symptom of your syndrome. The next stage of your cure' – he examined the notepad – 'is the chronic mucus congestion! We must deal with that chronic mucus, Alex. It might have been protective mucus at first, but now is your metabolic burden. Once the chronic mucus is gone, and the tubercles are entirely cleansed – cleaned . . . ' He paused. 'Is it "cleaned," or "cleansed"?'

'Either one works,' Alex said.

'Thank you,' the doctor said. 'Once the chronic mucus is scrubbed away from the lung surfaces, then we can treat the membranes

directly. There is membrane damage in your lungs, of course, deep
cellular damage, but we cannot get to the damaged surfaces until the
mucus is removed.' He looked at Alex seriously, over his glasses.
'Your chronic mucus is full of many contaminations, you know!
Years of bad gases and particles you have inhaled. Environmental
polutions, allergic pollens, smoke particles, virus and bacteria. They
have all adhered to the chronic mucus. When your lungs are
scrubbed clean with the enema, the lungs will be as the lungs of a
newborn child!' He smiled.

Alex nodded silently.

'It won't be pleasant at first, but afterward you will feel quite
lovely.'

'Do you have to knock me out again?' Alex said.

'No, Alex. It's important that you breathe properly during the
procedure. The detergent has to reach the very bottom of the lungs.
You understand?' He paused, tapping his notepad. 'Are you a good
swimmer, Alex?'

'No,' Alex said.

'Then you know that sensation when you swallow water down the
wrong pipe,' said the doctor, nodding triumphantly. 'That choking
reflex. You see, Alex, the reason Mother Nature makes you choke on
water, is because there is no proper oxygen in water for your lungs.
The enema liquid, though, which will be filling your lungs, is not
water, Alex. It is a dense silicone fluid. It carries much oxygen
dissolved inside it, plenty of oxygen.' Dr Mirabi chuckled. 'If you lie
still without breathing, you can live half an hour on the oxygen in a
single lungful of enema fluid! It has so much oxygen that at first you
will feel hyperventilated.'

'I have to inhale this stuff somehow, is that it?'

'Not quite. It's too dense to be inhaled. In any case, we don't want
it to enter your sinuses.' He frowned. 'We have to decant the fluid
into your lungs, gently.'

'I see.'

'We fit a thin tube through your mouth and down past the
epiglottis. The end of the tube will have a local anesthetic, so you
should not feel the pain in the epiglottis very long . . . You must
remain quite still during the procedure, try to relax fully, and
breathe only on my order.'

Alex nodded.

'The sensations are very unusual, but they are not dangerous. You must make up your mind to accept the procedure. If you choke up the fluid, then we have to begin again.'

'Doctor,' Alex said, 'you don't have to go on persuading me. I'm not afraid. You can trust me. I don't stop. I never stop. If I stopped at things, I wouldn't be here now, would I?'

'There will be some discomfort.'

'That's not new. I'm not afraid of that, either.'

'Very well, Alex.' Dr Mirabi patted Alex's shoulder. 'Then we will begin. Take your place on the manipulation table, please.'

Concepción helped Alex to lie on the jointed leather table. She touched her foot to a floor pedal. A worm gear whined beneath the floor. The table bent at Alex's hips and rose beneath his back, to a sharp angle. Alex coughed twice.

Dr Mirabi drew on a pair of translucent gloves, deftly unwrapped one of his canvas-bound machines, and busied himself at the switches. He opened a cabinet, retrieved a pair of matched, bright yellow aerosol tanks, and inserted both tanks into sockets at the top of the machine. He attached clear plastic tubing to the taps on the tanks and opened both the taps, with brief pneumatic hisses. The machine hummed and sizzled a bit and gave off a hot waft of electrical resistance.

'We will set the liquid to blood heat,' Dr Mirabi explained. 'That way there is no thermal shock to the tubercles. Also heat will dissolve the chronic mucus more effectively. Efficiently? Is it "efficiently" or "effectively"?'

'They're synonyms,' Alex said. 'Do you think I might throw up? These are my favorite pajamas.'

Concepción stripped the pajamas off, then wrapped him briskly in a paper medical gown. She strapped him against the table with a pair of fabric belts. Dr Mirabi approached him with the soft plastic nozzle of the insert, smeared with a pink paste. 'Open widely, don't taste the anesthetic,' he warned. Alex nevertheless got a generous smear of the paste against the root of his tongue, which immediately went as numb as a severed beef tongue on a butcher's block.

The nozzle slid its way down a narrow road of pain along his throat. Alex felt the fleshy valve within his chest leap and flap as the tube touched and penetrated. Then the numbness struck, and a great core of meat behind his heart simply lost sensation, went into nothingness, like a core mechanically punched from an apple.

His eyes filled with tears. He heard, more than saw, Dr Mirabi touching taps. Then the heat came.

He'd never known that blood was so hot. The fluid was hotter than blood, and much, much heavier, like fizzing, creamy, molten lead. He could see the fluid moving into him through the tube. It was chemical-colored, aqua blue. 'Breathe!' Dr Mirabi shouted.

Alex heaved for air. A bizarre reverberating belch tore free from the back of his throat, something like the cry of a monster bullfrog. For an instant he tried to laugh; his diaphragm heaved futilely at the liquid weight within him, and went still.

'*El niño tiene un bulto en la garganta,*' said Concepción, conversationally. She placed her latex-gloved hand against his forehead. '*Muy doloroso.*'

'*Poco a poco,*' Dr Mirabi said, gesturing. The worm gear rustled beneath the table and Alex rose in place, liquid shifting within him with the gut-bulging inertia of a nine-course meal. Air popped in bursts from his clamped lips and a hot gummy froth rose against his upper palate.

'Good,' said Dr Mirabi. 'Breathe!'

Alex tried again, his eyes bulging. His spine popped audibly and he felt another pair of great loathsome bubbles come up, stinking ancient bubbles like something from the bottom of LaBrea.

Then suddenly the oxygen hit his brain. An orgasmic blush ran up his neck, his cheeks. For a supreme moment he forgot what it was to be sick. He felt lovely. He felt free. He felt without constraint. He felt pretty sure that he was about to die.

He tried to speak, to babble something – gratitude perhaps, or last words, or an eager yell for more – but there was only silence. His lungs were like two casts of plaster and bonemeal, each filled to brimming with hot liquid rubber. His muscles heaved against the taut liquid bags like two fists clenching two tennis balls, and his ears roared, and things went black. Suddenly he could hear his heart straining to beat, *thud-thud, thud-thud,* each concussive shock of the ventricles passing through his liquid-filled lungs with booming subaqueous clarity.

And then the beat stopped too.

ON THE EVENING of May 10, Jane Unger made a reconnaissance of her target, on the pretext of buying heroin. She spent half an hour in line outside the clinic with desolate, wheezing Yankees from over the border. The customers lined outside the clinic were the seediest, creepiest, most desperate people she'd ever seen who were not actual criminals. Jane was familiar with the look of actual criminals, because the vast network of former Texas prisons had been emptied of felons and retrofitted as medical quarantine centers and emergency weather shelters. The former inhabitants of the Texan gulag, the actual criminals, were confined by software nowadays. Convicted criminals, in their tamper-proof parole cuffs, couldn't make it down to Nuevo Laredo, because they'd be marooned on the far side of the Rio Grande by their government tracking software. Nobody in the clinic line wore a parole cuff. But they were clearly the kind of people who had many good friends wearing them.

All of the American customers, without exception, wore sinister breathing masks. Presumably to avoid contracting an infection. Or to avoid spreading an infection that they already had. Or probably just to conceal their identities while they bought drugs.

The older customers wore plain ribbed breathing masks in antiseptic medical white. The younger folks were into elaborate knobby strap-ons with vivid designer colors.

The line of Americans snaked along steadily, helped by the presence of a pair of Mexican cops, who kept the local street hustlers off the backs of the paying clientele. Jane patiently made her way up the clinic steps, through the double doors, and to the barred and bulletproof glass of the pharmacy windows.

There Jane discovered that the clinic didn't sell any 'brown Mexican heroin.' Apparently they had no 'heroin' at all in stock, there being little demand for this legendary substance among people with respiratory illnesses.

Jane slid a private-currency card through the slit beneath the window. The pharmacist swiped Jane's card through a reader, studied the results on the network link, and began to show real interest. Jane was politely abstracted from the line and introduced to the pharmacist's superior, who escorted her up to his office. There he showed her a vial of a more modern analgesic, a designer endorphin a thousand times more potent than morphine. Jane turned down his offer of a free trial injection.

When Jane haltingly brought up the subject of bribery, the supervisor's face clouded. He called a big private-security thug, and Jane was shown out the clinic's back entrance, and told not to return.

Keep It Simple, Stupid. The famous KISS acronym had always been Jane's favorite design principle. If you need access, keep it simple. Bribing the staff of the clinic sounded like the simplest solution to her problem. But it wasn't.

At least one of the staff seemed happy enough to take her bribe money. Over a long-distance phone line from Texas, Jane had managed to subvert the clinic's receptionist. The receptionist was delighted to take Jane's electronic funds in exchange for ten minutes' free run on the clinic's internal phone system.

And accessing the clinic's floor plans had been pretty simple too; they'd turned out to be Mexican public records. It had been useful, too, to sneak into the building under the simple pretext of a drug buy. That had confirmed Jane's ideas of the clinic's internal layout.

Nothing about Alex was ever simple, though. Having talked to her brother on the phone, Jane now knew that Alex, who should have been her ally inside the enemy gates, was, as usual, worse than useless.

Carol and Greg – Jane's favorite confidants within the Storm Troupe – had urged her to stay as simple as possible. Forget any romantic ninja break-and-enter muscle stuff. That kind of stunt hardly ever worked, even when the U.S. Army tried it. It was smarter just to show up in Nuevo Laredo in person, whip out a nicely untraceable electronic debit card, and tell the night guard that it was Alejandro Unger out the door, or *No hay dinero*. Chances were that the guard would spring Alex in exchange for, say, three months' salary, local rates. Everybody could pretend later that the kid had escaped the building under his own power. That scheme was nice and straightforward. It was pretty hard to prosecute criminally. And if it ended up in a complete collapse and débâcle and embarrassment, then it would look a lot better, later.

By stark contrast, breaking into a Mexican black-market clinic and kidnapping a patient was the sort of overly complex maneuver that almost never looked better later.

There'd been a time in Jane Unger's life when she'd cared a lot about 'later.' But that time was gone, and 'later' had lost all its charm. She had traveled twelve hundred kilometers in a day, and now she was on foot, alone, in a dark alley at night in a foreign country, preparing to assault a hospital single-handed. And unless they caught her on the spot, she was pretty sure that she was going to get away with it.

This was an area of Nuevo Laredo the locals aptly called 'Salsipuedes,' or 'Leave-if-you-can.' Besides Alex's slick but modest clinic, it had two other thriving private hospitals stuffed with gullible gringos, as well as a monster public hospital, a big septic killing zone very poorly managed by the remains of the Mexican government. Jane watched a beat-up robot truck rumble past, marked with a peeling red cross. Then she watched her hands trembling. Her unpainted fingertips were ivory pale and full of nervous jitter. Just like the jitter she had before a storm chase. Jane was glad to see that jitter, the fear and the energy racing along her nerves. She knew that the jitter would melt off like dry ice once the action started. She had learned that about herself in the past year. It was a good thing to know.

Jane made a final check of her equipment. Glue gun, jigsaw, penlight, cellular phone, ceramic crowbar – all hooked and holstered to her webbing belt, hidden inside her baggy paper refugee suit. Equipment check was a calming ritual. She zipped the paper suit up to the neck, over her denim shorts and cotton T-shirt. She strapped on a plain white antiseptic mask.

Then she cut off the clinic's electrical power.

Thermite sizzled briefly on the power pole overhead, and half the city block went dark. Jane swore briefly inside her mask. Clearly there had been some changes made lately in the Nuevo Laredo municipal power grid. Jane Unger's first terrorist structure hit had turned out to be less than surgical.

'Not my fault,' she muttered. Mexican power engineers were always hacking around; and people stole city power, too, all kinds of illegal network linkups around here . . . They called the hookups *diablitos*, 'little devils,' another pretty apt name, considering that the world was well on its way to hell . . . Anyway, it wouldn't kill them to repair one little outrage.

Greg's thermite bomb had really worked. Every other week or so, Greg would drop macho hints about his military background doing structure hits. Jane had never quite believed him, before this.

Jane tied a pair of paper decontamination covers over her trail boots. She cinched and knotted the boot covers tightly at the ankles, then ghosted across the blacked-out street, puddles gleaming damply underfoot. She stepped up three stone stairs, entered the now pitch-black alcove at the clinic's rear exit, and checked the street behind her. No cars, no people, no visible witnesses . . . Jane pulled a translucent rain hood over her head, cinched and knotted it. Then she peeled open a paper pack and pulled on a pair of tough plastic surgical gloves.

She slapped the steel doorframe with the flat of her hand.

The clinic's door opened with a shudder.

Jane had structure-hit the door earlier, on her way out of the clinic. She'd distracted her security escort for two vital seconds and craftily jammed the exit's elaborate keypad lock with a quick, secret gush of glue. Alex had palmed the aerosol glue can, a tiny thing not much bigger than a shotgun cartridge. Glue spray was one of Carol's favorite tricks, something Carol had taught her. Carol could do things with glue spray that were halfway to witchcraft.

Despite the power outage, the door's keypad lock was still alive on its battery backup – but the door mistakenly thought it was working. Smart machines were smart enough to make some really dumb blunders.

Jane closed the door gently behind her. It was chilly inside the building, pitch-black and silent and sepulchral. A good thing, because she'd immediately begun to sweat like crazy in the stifling gloves, hood, overalls, mask, and boots. Her armpits prickled with terror sweat as if she were being tattooed there. Cops – or worse yet, private-industry investigators – could do plenty with the tiniest bits of evidence these days. Fingerprints, shoeprints, stray hairs, a speck of clothing fiber, one lousy wisp of DNA . . .

Jane reached inside her paper suit through a slit behind its hip pocket. She unclipped the penlight from her webbing belt. The little light clicked faithfully under her thumb and a reddish glow lit the hall. Jane took a step down the hall, two, three, and then the fear left her completely, and she began to glide across the ceramic tiling, skid-dancing in her damp paper boot covers.

She hadn't expected burglary to be such a visceral thrill. She'd been inside plenty of ruined buildings – just like everyone else from her generation – but she'd never broken her way into a live one. A rush of wicked pleasure touched her like a long cold kiss on the back of the neck.

Jane tried the first door to her left. The knob slid beneath her latexed fingers – locked. Jane had a handheld power jigsaw on the webbing belt that would slice through interior door locks like a knife through a wedding cake, and for a moment her left hand worked inside the paper suit and she touched the jigsaw's lovely checkered rubber grip. But she stopped. She wisely resisted the urge to break into the room just for the thrill of it. Would they be locking Alex into a room at night? Not likely. Not night-owl Alex. Stubborn, mean-tempered, night-owl Alex. Even at death's door, Alex wouldn't put up with that.

Next door. Unlocked. Room empty.

Next door. It was unlocked too. Some kind of janitor's supply, rags and jugs and paper. A good place to start a diversionary fire if you needed to.

Next door. Unlocked. The room stank. Like cough medicine cut with absinthe. Little red-eyed machines on the walls and floor, still alive on their battery backup. Jane's dim red light played over a big empty bed, then on a startling knot of hideous shadow – some kind of half-wilted monster houseplant.

She hadn't found her brother yet, but she could sense his presence. She slipped through the door, closed it gently, leaned her back against it. The reek in the room pried at her sinuses like the bouquet off a shot of cheap whiskey. Jane held her breath, playing the penlight around. A television. Some kind of huge clothes hanger like an outsized trouser press . . . a wardrobe . . . scattered tape cassettes and paper magazines . . .

Something was dripping. Thick oily dripping, down at floor level. It was coming from the big trouser-press contraption. Jane stepped toward the machine and played her light across the floor. Some kind of bedpan there.

Jane half knelt. It was a white ceramic pot, half-full of a dark nasty liquid, some kind of dense chemical oil. Grainy stuff like fine coffee grounds had sunk to the bottom, with a nasty white organic scum threading the top, just like a vile egg-drop soup . . . As Jane watched, a sudden thin drool of the stuff plummeted into the pot.

Her light went up. It discovered two racks of white human teeth. A human mouth there, with tight-drawn white lips and a stiff blue tongue. The head was swaddled in bandages, a thick padded strap at the forehead. Some kind of soft rubber harness bar was jammed into the gaping jaws . . .

They had him strapped to a rack, head down. Both his shoulders strapped, both his wrists cuffed at his sides, his chest strapped down against the padded surface. His knees were bound, his ankles cuffed. The whole rack was tilted skyward on a set of chromed springs and hinges. Up at the very top, his pale bare feet were like two skinned animals. Down at the bottom, his strap-swaddled head was just above the floor.

They were draining him.

Jane took two quick steps back and slapped her plastic-gloved hand against the mask at her mouth.

She fought the fear for a moment and she crushed it. And then she fought the disgust, and she crushed that too.

Jane stepped back to the rack, deliberately, and put her gloved hand at the side of Alex's neck. It was fever-hot and slick with his sweat.

He was alive.

Jane examined the rack for a while, her eyes narrowing hotly. The fear and disgust were gone now, but she couldn't stop her sudden hot surge of hatred. This was probably a fairly easy machine to manage, for the sons of bitches who were used to using it. Jane didn't have time to learn.

She undid the stop locks on the casters at the bottom, shoved the whole contraption to the side of the big bed, and toppled it, and Alex, onto the mattress, with one strong angry heave.

The straps on his chest were easy. Just Velcro. The padded latches on his wrists and ankles were harder: elaborate bad-design flip-top lock-down nonsense. Jane yanked her jigsaw and went through all four of the evil things in ten seconds each. There was bad noise – a whine and a muted chatter – with a sharp stench of chewed and molten plastic. Not too much noise, really, but it sounded pretty damned loud inside a blacked-out building. Someone might come to investigate. Jane patted the glue pistol in its holster at the back of her webbing belt.

When the last strap went, Alex tumbled off the rack into her lap. She rolled her brother faceup and checked his eyeballs. Cold, cold as a mackerel, even while his fevered skin was as hot as the shaved hide of a lab rabbit . . . She'd have to carry him out.

Well, Alex had been pretty easy to carry the last time she had tried it. When he'd been five years old, and she'd been ten. Jane knelt on the bed and methodically clipped her jigsaw back onto her belt, inside her paper suit. And then she thought somberly about the strength that it would take to do this thing.

Jane rolled off the bed onto her feet, grabbed her brother by both his slender wrists, and heaved.

He slid across the sheets like an empty husk. Jane jammed her left shoulder under his midriff and hoisted him in a fireman's carry, flinging her left arm across the backs of his knees . . . The moment she had him up, she realized that she was strong enough – more than strong enough. There was nothing left of her brother but birdbone and gristle.

Fluid gurgled loudly out of him and spattered the backs of her legs.

Jane staggered through the door and into the hall. She heard footsteps overhead, somewhere up on the second floor, and a distant mutter of puzzled voices . . . She lurched down the hall toward the exit and pulled the jimmied door open, right-handed. Her brother's lolling head cracked against the jamb as she stumbled through.

She pulled the door shut behind her, then sank to her knees on the cool pavement of the alcove. Alex sprawled bonelessly over her in his backless medical gown. She slid Alex aside onto the chill stone paving.

Breathing hard, Jane felt at the webbing belt and yanked out her cellular phone. She pushed little glowing yellow numbers with her thumb.

'Hello,' her car recited cheerfully. 'I am Storm Pursuit Vehicle Charlie. There's no one aboard me right now, but if you have an ID, you can give me verbal orders. Otherwise, leave a message at the beep.'

Jane pressed the digits 56033.

'Hello, Juanita,' the car replied.

'Come get me,' Jane panted. 'You know where. Come quick.'

SHE'D FORGOTTEN HOW fast Charlie could move when there were no human beings aboard it. Freed from the burden of protecting human flesh from g-forces, the robot car moved like a demented flea.

Charlie landed on the street in front of her with a sharp hiss of pneumatics, at the far end of a twenty-meter leap. It then began noisily walking sideways, up and across the pavement.

'Stop walking sideways,' Jane ordered it. 'Open your doors.' She braced herself against the wall of the alcove, squat-lifted Alex onto her unused and un-aching right shoulder, and made it down the stairs. 'Turn around,' she puffed.

Charlie spun around with microprocessed precision, its pistoned wheel spokes wriggling.

Jane heaved and shoved her brother into the passenger seat, closed the door, and stepped back, panting. Her knees trembled so badly that she felt too tired to walk.

'Turn around again!' she ordered. Charlie spun neatly in place, on the damp and darkened street. Jane clambered shakily into the driver's seat. 'Go fast!'

'Not until you're strapped in.'

'All right, go at a conventional pace while I am strapping us in,' Jane grated. 'And stop using Jerry's verbal interface at me.'

'I have to use Jerry's verbal interface when I'm out of range of the Troupe's uplink and in conventional mode,' the car said, rolling daintily down the street.

Jane struggled to strap her unresisting brother into the vehicle harness. His blond head lolled like a daisy at the end of a stalk and his floppy arms were like two bags of wax. It was just too cramped inside the car, no use.

Jane lurched back into her own seat, frustrated. 'Well, can you run my interface if you segue into unconventional mode?' she said.

'UHMMMMMMM . . .' the car temporized, for a full fifteen seconds. 'I think I can do that, if we pull over and I reboot.'

'No, no!' Jane said. 'God, no! Don't reboot! Just get us out of town on the route that you have in memory.'

'Okay, Juanita, will do.'

'Jesus,' Jane said. She folded up the steering wheel to make more room and succeeded in wedging her brother upright against the passenger door. He coughed then, twice, blue drool appearing at his lips.

Jane peeled her plastic gloves off, then whipped the rain hood from her hair. Her hair was sweat-caked to her scalp – she tugged at it with damp sweaty fingers. She'd been doing okay until she'd had to manage heavy lifting.

She yanked the paper covers from off her trail boots, then peeled and shrugged her way out of the paper suit, down to her shirt and shorts, much to the bemusement of passing night-owl pedestrians on the Avenida Guerrero.

Jane methodically stuffed the boot covers, and the gloves, and the paper suit, all into the rain hood. She drew the hood's drawstring tight and repeatedly stomped the evidence into a small wad. She eighty-sixed the saw blade – incriminating traces of plastic on it now – and, just for luck, the glue canister too. If they were mad enough about the break-in to hire a good PI, then they might trace the glue batch. Jane hated to throw away good hardware, but on mature consideration, it was a lot less troublesome than getting clamped into a Mexican electronic bail cuff, down at the *juzgado*.

She detached all her tools from the webbing belt, carefully set the tools and the belt into the metal kit box in back.

The car crossed before the Mercado Maclovia Herrera, heading toward the old international bridge. She hoped nobody was in the mood to take any special notice of Charlie. On a dark night, the car could pass for a standard smuggler's vehicle, a vehicle rather too common to notice in towns either side of the border.

Jane pulled into the darkest corner of a parking lot, beside a gigantic, thriving supermarket tobacconist's. Even at midnight, rings of Yankee addicts were steadily packing their lungs with smoke. Jane yanked another paper refugee suit from the U.S. government carton, and in a seven-minute determined struggle, she crammed Alex's arms and legs into the suit and zipped him up to the neck. She didn't have any shoes for Alex. She should have thought about the god-damned shoes.

When they crossed the flood-swollen Rio Grande, Jane grabbed the car's roll bar, stood up in her seat, and flung all the criminal evidence over the railing. Let them arrest her for littering. Or maybe for illegal discharge into an aquifer.

Jane pulled over at a U.S. Customs booth. An elderly customs officer emerged, with long snow-white hair, a walrus mustache, and a hand-carved mahogany cane. He tottered over to her car.

When Jane saw how proudly and carefully the old gentleman had darned and brushed his U.S. Customs jacket, she took an instant liking to him.

'Nice car,' he drawled.

'Thank you, sir.'

The officer tapped one of Charlie's spring-mounted antennas with his cane. 'Ex-military stuff?'

'Yeah!' Jane told him brightly. 'Actually it's a knockoff of an American Special Forces all-terrain vehicle.' Jane paused. 'It's been kind of modified.'

'Looks that way . . . ' He nodded, moving spryly around it. There wasn't room inside Charlie for any serious amount of contraband. Unlike the usual smuggler's vehicle, Charlie didn't have a trunk. It had a short flatbed, now empty, and the car's engine was grafted into the axles, spokes, and hubs. Charlie basically resembled a double glass coffin mounted onto a wheeled spider.

'You're letting this car drive itself tonight, miss?'

The old man had actually called her 'Miss.' Jane couldn't recall anyone calling her 'miss' since she'd turned twelve years old. She was charmed by the customs man's stately anachronism. She smiled at him.

'It's got a license,' Jane said. 'Want to see it?'

'That's okay,' he grumbled. 'What's with Junior here?'

'Big party in town,' Jane said. 'He overdid it tonight, and he's passed out. You know how it is with kids these days.'

The customs officer looked at her with pity. 'You don't mean to tell me that, did you, miss? You meant to tell me the truth, and say that he's sick, didn't you?'

Jane felt her face go stiff.

The old man frowned. 'Miss, I can recognize this situation. God knows we see it often enough, down here. Your friend there is sick, and he's wasted, too, on who-knows-what . . . We don't allow that kind of goings-on here on American soil. . . . And there's some dang good reasons why it's not allowed up here . . .'

Jane said nothing.

'I'm not telling you this just to hear myself chatter, y'know.'

'Look Officer,' Jane said. 'We're American citizens. We're not criminals.' She held up her bare wrist. 'If you want to turn us back from here, then we'll go back to Mexico. But if I had anything I really wanted to hide from you, then I wouldn't even stop here at all, would I? I wouldn't even take the road. This is an *all-terrain vehicle*, okay? I can ford the river anywhere I want, and be in San Antonio in two hours.'

The customs officer tapped the toe of his polished shoe with his cane.

'If you want to lecture me, Officer, okay, that's fine. I'm listening. I even agree with you. But get real.'

He stared briefly into her eyes, then looked aside and rubbed his mustache. 'It floats, too, huh?'

'Of course this car floats. It swims! I know it looks like solid steel, but that's all foamed metal there. Without the batteries, the whole car only weighs ninety kilos. I can deadlift this car all by myself!'

Jane stopped. The old man seemed so crushed that she felt quite sorry for him. 'Come on, Officer. I can't be telling you anything new here, right? Haven't you ever *caught* one of these things before?'

'To tell you the truth, miss, we don't even bother catching 'em nowadays. Not cost-effective.' He peeled off an adhesive sticker and attached it to Charlie's front roll bar. 'Y'all take care now.' He waved them on.

Jane let the car drive. They were through Laredo and onto the highway in short order. Even with the prospect of a ten-hour drive in darkness, Jane felt far too wired to sleep. She knew from experience that she was about to pull another all-nighter. She'd be up and jumping till 8:00 a.m., then grab maybe three hours' doze, and be back up and after it again, with nothing to show for it but a sharpened temper. She'd never been much good at sleeping, and life around Jerry Mulcahey's people had only wound her up tighter.

As the city lights of Laredo faded behind her, stars poured out overhead. It was a clear spring night, a little mare's-tail cirrus on the western horizon. She'd once heard Jerry say that it bothered him to ride a car in complete darkness. Jerry was thirty-two, and he could remember when people did most of their own driving, and even the robots always left their headlights on. Jane, by contrast, found the darkness soothing. If there was anything really boring about the experience of driving at night, it was that grim chore of gripping a wheel with your own hands and staring stiff-necked for hours into a narrow cone of glare. In darkness you could see the open sky. The big dark Texas sky, that great abyss.

And you could hear. Except for the steady rush of wind, Charlie was almost silent; a faint whir of tough plastic tread lightly kissing the highway, the frictionless skid of diamond axles. Jane had taped or glued everything on the car that would rattle. Jane did not permit her machines to rattle.

Jane heard Alex gurgling as he breathed. She turned on a small interior light and checked her brother again. In the feeble amber glow he looked very bad. At his best, Alex was not an attractive young man: gaunt, hollow-chested, pop-eyed, with a thin bladelike nose and clever narrow bird-claw hands. But she'd never seen him look this supremely awful. Alex had become a repulsive physical presence, a collapsed little goblin. His matted blond hair stood up in tufts across his skull, and he stank. Not just sweat reek – Jane was used to people who stank of sweat and camp smoke. A light but definite chemical stench emanated from her brother's flesh. They'd been marinating him in narcotics.

She touched his cheek. His skin was chilly and damp now, like the skin on a tapioca pudding. The paper refugee suit, still fresh from the carton but already badly wadded, made him look like a storm victim in deep shock, someone freshly yanked from wreckage. The kind of person whose demand for your help and attention was utter, total, immediate – and probably more than you could bear.

Jane turned on the radio, heard a great deal of encrypted traffic from banks, navigation beacons, and hams, and turned it off again. Funny what had happened to the broadcast radio spectrum. She turned on the car's music box. It held every piece of music that had ever meant anything to her, including stuff from her early childhood that she'd never managed to erase. Even with sixteen-digit digital precision, everything she'd ever recorded took up only a few hundred megabytes, the merest sliver in the cavernous memory of a modern music box.

Jane played some Thai pop music, cheerful energetic bonging and strumming. There'd been a time, back in design school, when Thai pop music had meant a lot to her. When it seemed that a few dozen wild kids in Bangkok were the last people on earth who really knew what it meant to have some honest fun. She'd never figured out why this lovely burst of creativity had happened in Bangkok. With AIDS still methodically eating its way into the vast human carcass of Asia, Bangkok certainly wasn't any happier than most other places. Apparently the late 2020s had just somehow been Bangkok's global moment to shine. It was genuinely happy music, bright, clever music, like a gift to the world. It felt so new and fresh, and she'd listened to it and felt in her bones what it meant to be a woman of the 2020s, alive inside, and aware inside.

It was 2031 now. The music was distant now, like a whiff of good rice wine at the bottom of an empty bottle. It still touched something inside her, but it didn't touch all of her. It didn't touch all the new parts.

ALEX WOKE IN wind and darkness. Rapid warbling music was creeping up his shins. The music oozed like syrup into his skull and its beat gently pummeled him into full consciousness. With awareness came recognition: Thai pop gibberish. No other noise had quite that kind of high-pitched paralyzing sweetness.

Alex turned his head – with a painless squeaking deep in the vertebrae of his neck – and he saw, without much real surprise, his sister. Barely lit by the tiny amber glow of a map light, Juanita sat perched in the driver's seat. Her head was thrown back, her elbows were propped on her bare, hairy knees, and she was munching government-issue granola from a paper bag.

The sky above them was a great black colander of stars.

Alex closed his eyes again and took a slow deep breath. His lungs felt truly marvelous. Normally his lungs were two wadded tissues of pain, two blood-soaked sponges, his life's two premier burdens. But now they had somehow transmuted into two spotless clean-room bags, two crisp high-tech sacs of oiled wax paper, two glorious life-giving organs. Alex had a savage cramp in his lower back, and his feet and hands were so chilled by the whipping night wind that they felt like the feet and hands of a wax dummy, but that didn't matter. That was beside the point.

He couldn't believe how wonderful it felt just to sit there breathing.

Even his nose was clear. His sinuses. His sinuses felt as if they'd been steam-cleaned. He could smell the wind. There was sage in it, the fervent bitter reek of a ten-thousand-year-old Texas desert gone mad with repeated heavy rains. He could even smell the sweet reek of federally subsidized dietary sucrose on Juanita's munching teeth. Everything smelled so lovely.

Except for himself.

Alex shifted in the seat and stretched. His spine popped in four places, and blood began to tingle back into his numbed bare feet. He coughed. Dense liquid shifted tidally, deep within his chest. He coughed again, twice. Dregs of goo heaved and fizzed within his tubercles. The sensation was truly bizarre, and remarkably interesting. The slime they'd pumped into him tasted pretty bad, oiling the back of his tongue with a thick bitter nastiness, but its effect on his lungs and throat was ambrosial. He wiped happy tears from his eyes with the back of his wrist.

He was wearing a paper refugee suit. He'd never actually worn one before, but he'd certainly seen plenty of them. Paper suits were the basic native garb of the planet's derelict population. A modern American paper refugee suit, though utterly worthless and disposable, was a very high-tech creation. Alex could tell, just by stirring around inside it, that the suit's design had absorbed the full creative intelligence of dozens of federal emergency-management experts. Whole man-years, and untold trillions of CAD-CAM cycles, had vanished into the suit's design, from the microscopic scale of its vapor-breathing little paper pores, up to the cunning human ergonomics of its accordioned shoulder seams. The paper suit was light and airy, and though it flapped a little in the night wind, it kept him surprisingly warm. It worked far better than paper clothing had any natural right to work.

But, of course, it was still paper clothing, and it still didn't work all that well.

'Nice fashion choice,' Alex said. His larynx had gone slick with oil, and his voice was a garbled croon.

Juanita leaned forward, turned up the interior lights, and shut off her music.

'You're awake now, huh?'

Alex nodded.

Juanita touched another button at the dash. Fabric burst from a fat slot above the windshield and flung itself above their heads. The fabric hissed, flopped, sealed itself, and became a roof of bubbled membrane. A sunburned dome of stiff ribbed fabric that looked as dry and brown and tough as the shell of a desert tortoise.

Juanita turned to him in the sudden bright windless silence inside the car. 'How d'you feel?'

'I've been worse,' Alex whispered gluily, and grinned a little. 'Yeah. I feel pretty good.'

'I'm glad to hear that, Alex. 'Cause it's no picnic, where we're going.'

Alex tried to clear his throat. Blood-hot oil clung to his vocal cords. 'Where are we?'

'Highway 83, West Texas. We just passed Junction, headed toward San Angelo. I'm taking you where I live.' Juanita stared at him, as if expecting him to crumble to pieces on the spot. 'Actually I don't live anywhere, anymore. But I'm taking you to the people I stay with.'

'Nice of you to ask permission, Janey.'

She said nothing.

This was a different kind of silence from his sister. Not irritated silence. And not barely controlled fury. A deep, steely silence.

Alex was nonplussed. He'd never been on good terms with his sister, but in the past he'd always been able to come in under her radar. He'd always been able to get at her. Even when worse came to worst, he could always successfully catch some piece of her in his teeth, and twist.

'You shouldn't be doing this, you know,' he said. 'They were helping me.'

Silence.

'You can't stop me from going back there if I want to.'

'I don't think you're gonna want to go back,' Juanita told him. 'That clinic won't be happy to see you again. I had to break you out. I structure-hit the building and I glue-gunned a guard.'

'You *what?*'

'Ever seen a guy get glue-gunned? It's not pretty. Especially when he takes it right in the face.' Juanita knocked back a palmful of granola. 'He'd have yelled, though, if I hadn't glued him,' she said, munching deliberately. 'I had to clear his nose with acetone, once I had him pinned. Otherwise he'd have smothered to death right there on the spot.' She swallowed, and laughed. 'I'd bet good money he's still stuck to the wall.'

'You're kidding, right?'

She shook her head. 'Look, you're sitting here, aren't you? How do you think you got into this car? Did you think those hustlers were just gonna let you go? When I broke into your clinic room, you were upside down, naked, unconscious, and strapped to a metal rack.'

'Jesus,' Alex said. He ran his hand through his hair, and shivered. His hair was filthy – he was filthy all over, a mess of fever sweat and human grease. 'You're telling me *you* broke me out of the clinic? Personally? Jesus, Janey, couldn't you have sued them or something?'

'I'm a busy woman now, Alex. I don't have time for law-suits.' Juanita pulled her feet out of her trail boots, dropping the boots onto the floorboard and crossing her sock-clad legs in the seat. She looked at him, her hazel eyes narrowing. 'I guess there might be some trouble if you went back and informed against me to the local authorities.'

'No way,' he said.

'You wouldn't sue me or anything?'

'Well, I wouldn't rule out a lawsuit completely,' Alex said, 'not considering Dad's idea of family finances . . . But there's no way I need Mexican police to deal with my own sister.' He rubbed his greasy, stubbled chin. 'At least, I never did *before*. What the hell has got into you?'

'Plenty. A lot.' she nodded. 'You'll see.'

'What did you do to your hair?'

She laughed.

'You gave up dyeing it,' he concluded. 'That's its natural color, right? Brownish. Did you stop paying people to cut it?'

He'd struck home. 'Oh, that's really good, coming from you,

Alejandro. Yeah, I look like a derelict, don't I? I look like a displaced person! You know what *you* look like, handsome? You look like you washed up five days after a hurricane surge. You look like a goddamn cadaver.' Her voice rose. 'I just dragged you back from the brink of the grave! I'm dressed up for committing a felony, you moron!'

'You used to dress for the couture circuit, Janey.'

'Once,' she said. 'I did a few designs, one season. Boy, you never forget.'

'Your hair's been red ever since I can remember.'

'Yeah? Well, maybe I needed red hair once. Back when I was into identity crisis.'

Juanita picked at her hair for a bit, then frowned. 'Let's get something straight right now. I know you can go back over the border if you want to. I know all about your scene, and I know all I wanna know about your creep-ass little dope-smuggler friends. I can't stop you. I don't even much want to stop you.' She snorted. 'It's just that before you check back into the hospital-from-hell and elaborately croak yourself, I want to show you something. Okay? I want you to see exactly what's happened to me since the last time we met.'

Alex considered this proposal at length. Then he spoke up. 'Oh yeah?'

'Yeah! This car is going to take us into camp, and I'm going to show you the people that I live with. They're probably going to really hate your guts. They didn't much like me, either – not at first.' Jane shrugged. 'But they're alive inside, Alex. They have something to do that's really worth doing. They're good people, they really are. They're the only people I've ever met that I really respect.'

Alex mulled over this bizarre news. 'They're not *religious*, are they?'

She sighed. 'No, they're not religious.'

'This is some kind of cult thing, though, isn't it? I can tell from the way you're talking. You're way too happy about this.'

'No, I'm not in a goddamned cult! Well, okay then – yes, I am. The Troupe's a cult. Kind of. But I'm not brainwashed. That's not the story.'

Alex parsed this statement and filed it away. 'So what's the story, then?'

'I'm in love.' Juanita dug into her bag of granola. 'So there's a big difference. Supposedly.'

'You're in love, Janey? Really?'

'Yeah. I really am.'

'*You*?'

'Yes, goddamn it, of course me!'

'Okay, okay, sorry.' Alex spread his hands. 'It's coming clear to me now. I'm starting to get it. New boyfriend doesn't like red hair?'

'I just stopped doing red hair. A year ago. It didn't fit anymore.'

'So what *does* boyfriend like? Besides you, presumably.'

'Boyfriend likes really big tornadoes.'

Alex sank into his seat.

'His people are called the Storm Troupe. We hack heavy weather. And that's where I'm taking you now.'

Alex gazed out to his left. Dawn was smearing the horizon. The eastern stars were bleaching out, and lumps of dark poisonous gray green – cedar and juniper brush – were emerging from roadside darkness. Alex looked back at his sister. 'You're serious about this?'

'Yep! Been hacking storms quite some time now.' She offered him her paper bag. 'Have some granola.'

Alex took the bag, dipped into it, and ate. He was hungry, and he had no prejudice against government-issue chow. It had the complete recommended dietary allowances and the stuff was so bland that it had never irritated any of his various allergies. 'So that's really what you're doing, huh? You chase thunderstorms for a living these days?'

'Oh, not for a living,' she said. She reached down and clicked off the map light, then stretched, briskly tapping her fingernails against the fabric roof. She wore a short-sleeved shirt of undyed cotton, and Alex noted with vague alarm that her freckled arms were lithe with muscle. 'That's for TV crews, or labcoat types. With us, it doesn't pay. That's the cool thing about it. If you're in the Troupe, you just *do storms*.'

'Damn, Janey!'

'I like doing storms. I like it a whole lot. I feel like that's what I'm for!' Juanita laughed, long and high-pitched and twitchy. Alex had never heard her laugh like that before. It sounded like the kind of laugh you had to learn from someone else.

'Does Papa know about this?'

'Papa knows. Papa can sue me. You can sue me, too, little brother. If you boys don't like how I'm living, then you can both kiss my ass!'

He grinned. 'Damn, Janey.'

'I took a big risk to do this for you,' she told him. 'So I just want you to know' – she placed her hand against the side of his head and looked into his eyes – 'I'm not doing this for you because I think you're cute. You're not cute, Alex. And if you screw things up between me and my Troupe, then I'm finished with you, once and for all.'

'I never asked you to do any of this!'

'I know you didn't ask me, but nevertheless, if you mess with me and Jerry, then I'm gonna break both your legs and leave you at the side of the road!'

Alex found it hard to take this wild threat seriously, though she was clearly very sincere. It was the old story. As far as Alex figured it, all the trouble he'd had with his sister in the past was entirely her own doing. She'd always been the one barging into his room to bend his arms, break his toys, and bark out orders. Sooner or later all their encounters ended with him prying her fingers from his throat.

He, on the other hand, almost never tried to inferfere in the near hysteria that Juanita called her daily life. Just watching his sister go at life, repeatedly cracking brick walls with her head, made him feel tired. He'd always allowed her to caterwaul her way to hell in any way she pleased.

Now she seemed to think that she was going to run his life, since Mama was long dead, and Papa on the ropes. She'd soon be disabused of that notion.

'Take it easy,' he advised her. 'Your love affair, or whatever it is that you've got happening now, is strictly your own lookout. I got nothing against this Jerry character.' He chuckled. 'Hell, I pity him.'

'Thanks a lot. His name's Jerry Mulcahey. *Doctor . . . Gerald . . . Mulcahey.*'

He'd never seen a look like the look on Juanita's face as she recited that name. It was like a cross between a schoolgirl's crush and the ultravampish look of a bad actress on a Mexican soap opera. Whatever it was that had bitten her, it had bitten her really bad. 'That's fine, Janey,' he said cautiously. 'I don't have any grudge

29

against him, or any of your hick weirdo friends. Just as long as they don't try to step on my neck.'

'Well, they *will* step on you, Alex, and I'm asking you to put up with it. Not as a brotherly favor to me or anything – I wouldn't ask for that – but just because it's interesting. *Really interesting*, okay? And if you can manage to stay upright for a while, you'll learn something.'

Alex grunted. He gazed out the window again. Dawn was becoming impressive. The Texas High Plains were bleak country by nature, but nature had packed up and left sometime back. The stuff growing by the side of the road looked very happy about this. They were passing kilometer after kilometer of crotch-high, tough-stemmed, olive-drab weeds with nasty little flower clusters of vivid chemical yellow. Not the kind of hue one wanted in a flower somehow; not inviting or pretty. A color one might expect from toxic waste or mustard gas.

Out beyond the roadside flowers was the collapsed barbed-wire fencing of a dead cattle ranch, the long-deserted pastureland overrun with mesquite. They passed the long dawn shadows of a decapitated oil pump, with a half-dozen rust-streaked storage tanks for West Texas crude, a substance now vanished like the auk. The invisible tonnage of drill pipe was quietly rusting deep in the rocky flesh of the earth, invisible to any human eye, but nonetheless there for the geological ages, a snapped-off rotting proboscis from a swatted greenhouse-effect mosquito.

Here and there along the highway dead windmills loomed, their tapered tin vanes shot to hell, their concrete cisterns cracked and dust empty above an aquifer leached to bare sandstone . . . They'd sucked their landscape dry, and abandoned their mechanical vampire teeth in place, like the torn-off mandibles of a tick . . .

They'd mined the place of everything in it that could be sold on the market; and then they'd given up. But after that, the greenhouse rains had come. You could tell that the plant life here wasn't at all used to the kindness of rain. The plants weren't a bit better than humanity, really – just another ugly, nasty, acquisitive species, born to suffer, and expecting little. . . . But the rain had come anyway. Now the Texas High Plains were glutted with rain, and with rich, warm, carbonated air, all under a blazing greenhouse sun. It was Oz, for a cactus. Arcadia for mesquite. Every kind of evil weed that stank, stabbed, or scratched was strutting its stuff like nouveau riche Texas hicks with an oil strike.

Juanita touched her music box.

'Can you knock it off with that Thai stuff?'

'What do you want me to play?'

'Something a little less incongruous. Some kind of – I dunno – crazed lonesome fiddle music. Cedar flutes and bone whistles. Listening to that tropical stuff out here in the savage boonies makes me feel like I'm losing my mind.'

'Alex, you don't know anything about surviving out here. You need enough imagination to at least *think* you're somewhere else, or the plains can really get to you.' she laughed. 'You'll get the Long Stare, brother. Just *ride off* into that landscape and kill-and-eat jackrabbits till you die . . . Hey, you want to really go run?'

'Huh?'

Juanita raised her voice. 'Charlie?'

'Yes, Juanita?' the car said.

Alex was surprised. 'Hey Janey, how come this car calls you Juanita?'

'Never mind. Long story.' She gripped his shoulder. 'You buckled in tight? You feel up to this, right? Not carsick or anything?'

Alex patted the smart cushions beneath him. 'Not in a reactive seat like this one. I'd have better luck getting carsick on a living-room couch.'

'Yeah, well, you're about to learn why they installed that kind of scat in here.' Juanita reached over, took the paper bag of granola from his lap, saw it was empty, then folded it neatly and stuck it in the waistband of her denim shorts. 'Charlie, do a local map.'

The car extruded a flexible tongue of white screen from the dash. A high-definition map bloomed across the screen, topography at the meter scale. The map flashed briefly into a comparative series of ultradetailed satellite renditions. Juanita picked up the loose end of the map gently, examined the flickering imagery, then tapped the screen with her finger. 'Charlie, see this little hill?'

'Two thousand three hundred twelve meters north,' the car replied, outlining the crest of the hill in orange.

'Charlie, take us there, fast.'

The car slowed and pulled over off the road shoulder, its prow toward the hill.

'Hold tight,' Juanita said. Then the car leaped into the air.

It got up speed in the first dozen meters, bounding, and then began to clear the tops of mesquite trees. The car moved in a wild series of twists and hissing pounces; it was like being blown through the air by jets. Alex felt the seat's support cells repeatedly catching him, rippling like the flesh of a running animal.

'Look at those wheels now!' Juanita shouted gleefully, pointing. 'See, they're not even rolling. Hell, they're not even wheels. The spokes are smart pistons. Feels like a hovercraft, right?'

Alex nodded dumbly.

'We're hovering on computation. The big power drain in this car isn't the engine. It's the sensors and the circuits that keep us from hitting stuff while we jump!' Juanita crowed with laughter. 'Isn't this wild? God bless the military!'

They cleared the last of the thick brush, and then the car slid unerringly up the cracked slope of the hill, its pistons barely raising dust. Alex could tell from the eerie smoothness of the ride that the car never skipped, and never skidded. The intelligent pads at the base of each spoke contacted the earth with a dainty and tentative touch. Then the pistons set themselves firmly and punched up against the diamond hub, lifting the car in repeated, near-silent, precise staccato, faster than any human eye or ear could follow. It was like riding the back of a liquefied cheetah.

At the hill's crest, the car stopped gently, as if settling into tar. 'Time for a stretch,' Juanita announced, her hazel eyes glowing with delight. She put down the fabric top, and a morning breeze swept the now silent car. 'Let's get out.'

'I got no shoes,' Alex realized.

'Hell, I forgot . . . Oh well.' She jammed her sock-clad feet into her unlaced trail boots, opened the door, and stepped out alone. She shook herself cheerfully and stretched through some kind of calisthenic routine, then gazed across the landscape with one hand raised to her eyes, like a minor-league Sacagawea. To Alex, the view from the hilltop was dismally unimpressive; clumps of mesquite and cedar, sparse leathery grasses, and three distant, squalid little hills. The entire plain was ancient seafloor, flat as the bottom of a drained bond. The hills were tired lumps of limestone that, unlike the rest of the landscape, had not quite collapsed yet.

'This car must have cost you plenty,' he said.

'No, it was cheap, considering! Government tries to keep 'em rare, though, because of the security threat.' The vivid glare of dawn was spilling all across the landscape, the orange-yellow sun too bright to look at. 'You can order a car like this to follow a map top speed, to any locale. And they're damn hard to spot, when they jump top speed cross-country, ignoring all the roads. With a big truck bomb aboard, you can structure-hit like nobody's business.' She smiled cheerfully. 'They did that a lot in the Malaysian resettlement wars – this is a Malaysian attack vehicle. War surplus. Of course, they're real popular with border smugglers now.' Juanita turned to face the wind and ran both hands through her hair. 'I think they're still technically illegal for civilians in the U.S. In some states, anyhow.'

Texas?'

'Heck no, anything's legal in Texas now . . . Anyway, Texas Rangers love these cars. Cheap, fast, ignores roads – what's not to like? The only real problem is the batteries. They're superconductives.'

'Superconductives sure aren't cheap.'

'No, and they wear out fast too. But they're getting better. . . . They'll be everywhere someday, cars like this. Just for fun. A car just for fun, isn't that a wild idea?' She strolled around the car, almost on tiptoe in her big but lightweight trail boots. 'It's a megatasty design. Don't you love the look of it?' She patted the jointed rim of the rear wheel. 'It's that truly elegant design that people always use when they make things to kill each other.'

She flipped open a small metal toolbox in back, behind the passenger compartment, and fished out a pair of sunglasses. The reactive lenses went dark the moment she slipped them on. 'Charlie is my flying hell spider . . . A real beauty, isn't he . . . ? I love him, really . . . Except for the *goddamned hopeless military interface!*' Juanita scowled beneth her shades. 'I don't know what morons the Pentagon got to hack interface, but they should have been choked in their bunkers!'

'You own this car, Janey?'

'Sort of,' she said. 'No. Not really. I wouldn't want it registered in my name.'

'Who does own it, then?'

'It's a Troupe car.' She shut and locked the toolbox, then opened the door and slid back into the driver's seat.

Alex hesitated. 'You know, I kind of like this car too. I could go for one of these.'

She smirked. 'Right, I bet you could . . . Charlie, let's go.'

The car picked its way gently down the slope.

Alex examined a big tuft of torn-off yellow grass embedded in the right front wheel hub. 'You'd think you'd get really airsick, considering the acrobatics, but it has a very smooth ride. Hell, I've been in wheelchairs that were worse than this.'

'Yeah? Well, they designed it for very smooth. So you can sight automatic weapons off the bumpers at full throttle. Charlie comes from commando stuff, death-by-darkness tiger teams and military structure hits and all that weird ugly crap. . . . But he sure has some killer apps in civilian life.' Juanita ducked as the edge of a long mesquite branch whipped across the windshield, then she put up the roof again, with a jab of her thumb. 'The Troupe used to chase storms in old dune buggies. But we were punching the core once on an F-4, and the hail *wrapped* real hard, and hailstones just beat 'em to death, dented the hoods and roof all to hell . . . But Charlie just laughs at hailstones.'

'You must be pretty big on hailstones.'

'Hailstones have been pretty big on me, Alex. In Oklahoma last spring I got caught in the open. They leave welts on you as big as your fist.'

'What's that mean, when you say "punch the core"?'

Juanita looked surprised. 'Well, um . . . it means you shoot the vortex when you're running the drones.'

'Oh,' Alex said.

CHAPTER

2

The vertebrae of tall transmission towers stenciled the horizon.
Juanita's people had set up their tent complex a kilometer from the highway, on a low limestone rise where they could keep a wary eye on any passing traffic. Morning sunlight lit a confusion of round puffy circus tents and the spiked cones of white tepees.

Juanita had dozed off in the journey's last two hours, mopping up bits of twitchy, REM-riddled sleep like a starving woman dabbing gravy from plate. Now Alex watched with interest as his sister became a different person. In the last few minutes, as they'd neared the camp, she'd become alert, tight-mouthed, warriorly, nervous.

Juanita found a security cuff beneath the passenger seat, and she carefully strapped it on her left wrist. The cuff had a readout watch and a thick strap of tanned, hand-beaded, hand-stitched leather. Some of the beads were missing, and the leather was worn and stained, and from the look on Juanita's face as she strapped it on, Alex could see that she felt a lot better to have it back on again.

Almost as an afterthought, she gave Alex a flimsy-looking plastic cuff, with a cheap watch sporting an entirely useless array of confusing little orange push buttons. 'You'll wanna keep that on at all times so you can pass in and out of camp,' she told him.

'Right. Great.'

Juanita's car rolled uphill through a last stretch of sparse grass and between a pair of electronic perimeter stakes.

'What's the drill?' Alex asked.

'I have to go talk to Jerry now. About you.'

'Oh good! Let's both go have a nice chat with Dr Jerry.'

Juanita glanced at him in nettled amazement. 'Forget it! I've got to think this through first, how to present the situation to him . . . Look, you see those people over there by the kitchen yurt?'

'By the what?'

'By that big round tent. The people with the tripod and the pulley.'

'Yeah?'

'Go over there and be nice to them. I'll come fetch you later when I've cleared things.' Juanita threw the car door open, jumped out, and half trotted toward the center of camp.

'I got no *shoes!*' Alex yelped after her, but the wind whipped his words away, and Juanita didn't look back.

Alex pondered his situation. 'Hey car,' he said at last. 'Charlie.'

'Yes, sir?' the car replied.

'Can you drive me over to that group of people?'

'I don't understand what you mean by the term *group of people*.'

'I mean, twenty meters, um, northwestish of here. Can you roll across that distance? Slowly?'

'Yes, sir, I could perform that action, but not at your command. I can't follow the orders of any passenger without a security ID.'

'I see,' Alex said. 'She was right about your interface, Jack. You are totally fucked.'

Alex searched through the car, twisting around in his seat. There was no sign of any object remotely shoelike. Then his eyes lit on the cellular phone mounted on the dash. He plucked it up, hesitated over the numeral '1', then speed-dialed '4' instead.

A woman answered. 'Carol here.'

'Hi, Carol. Are you a Storm Trouper?'

'Yeah,' the phone replied. 'What's it to ya?'

'Are you presently in a camp on a hillside somewhere off the side of Highway 208 in West Texas?'

'Yeah. That's right.' She laughed.

'Are you standing in the middle of a bunch of people who are trying to haul some kind of animal carcass up on a tripod?'

'No, man, I'm in the garage yurt working repair on a fucked-up highway maintenance hulk, but I know the people you're talking about, if that's any help.'

'Could you get one of them to bring me a pair of shoes? Size eight?'

'Who the hell are you?'

'My name's Alex Unger, I'm fresh in from Mexico and I need some shoes before I'm gonna leave this car.'

Carol paused. 'Hold on a sec, Alex.' She hung up.

Alex settled back into the seat. After a moment's idleness, he whipped up the phone again and dialed Información in Matamoros. He asked for the current alias of one of his favorite contacts and had no trouble getting through. He hung up hastily, though, in the midst of the ensuing conversation, as a woman approached the car.

The stranger, a black woman, had short black braids cinched with wire, over a broad, windburned, cheerful face. She looked about thirty-five. She wore a paper refugee suit that had been spewed through somebody's full-color printer, with remarkable results.

The woman handed Alex a pair of sandals through the open door. The sandals were flat soles of thick dark green vinyl, with broad straps of white elastic cloth freshly glued across the top of the foot.

'What are these?' Alex said. 'They look like shower mules.'

She laughed. 'You *need* a shower, kid. Put 'em on.'

Alex dropped the impromptu sandals on the ground and stuffed his feet into them. They were two sizes too big, but they were more or less the proper shape of his feet and seemed unlikely to fall off. 'That's not bad for two minutes' work, Carol.'

'Thanks a lot, dude. Since you and your sister are both richer than God, feel free to give me several thousand dollars.' Carol looked him over skeptically. 'Boy, you're all Jane said you were, and much, much more!'

Alex let that one hang for a moment. 'Juanita said I should stay with those people over there, until she came back.'

'Then that's what you'd better do, man. But do 'em a favor and stay downwind of 'em.' Carol stepped back from the car. 'And don't mess with our phones anymore, okay? Peter gets real nervous when amateurs mess with our phones.'

'Nice to meet you,' Alex said. Carol spared him a half wave as she left.

Alex decamped from the car and stepped carefully across the West Texas earth. The narrow-leafed prairie grass looked okay, but the sparse, pebbled ground was scattered about with a scary variety of tiny, wire-stemmed little weeds, all chockablock with burs and hooks and rash-raising venomous bristles.

Alex minced carefully to the group at the tripod. They were busy. They had a velvet-horned buck up by its neck, at a pulley mounted at the junction of three tall tepee poles. There were four of them: two men in long-sleeved hunter's gear, and two hard-bitten women in bloodstained paper and trail boots. One of the men, the one with glasses, had an electric rifle over his back. They were all wearing Trouper cuffs.

'¿Qué pasa?' Alex said.

'We're butchering Bambi,' the second man told him, grunting as he cinched off the end of the pulley rope.

The hunters had already cut the entrails from the animal and dumped them somewhere along the trail. Alex closely examined the animal's lean, swaying, eviscerated carcass.

The taller woman drew a bowie knife of ice-pale ceramic and stepped up to her work. She took each of the buck's dangling rear legs in hand, then slashed out some meaty, ill-smelling gland from within the hocks. She tossed the bloody gland aside, wiped and holstered her bowie knife, and fetched up a smaller knife about the length of her thumb.

The man with the rifle gazed at Alex indifferently. 'Just get in to camp?'

'Yeah. My name's Alex. Juanita's my sister.'

'Who's Juanita?' the rifleman said. The second man silently jerked his thumb toward the camp's central yurt. 'Oh,' the rifleman realized. 'You mean Janey.'

'You'll have to forgive Rick here,' the taller woman said. 'Rick programs.' She circled the deer's neck with a swift shallow cut, then carved straight down its throat to the chest and out at right angles to the end of each foreleg. She was very deft about it. With the help of the second woman, she began methodically shredding the hide down over the sleek naked meat.

Alex shook one of the tripod poles. It seemed very sturdy. The lacquer on the bamboo was one of those modern lacquers. 'Are you planning to eat this thing? I don't think I ever ate a wild animal before.'

'You'll eat the weirdest crap in Texas when Ellen Mae's around,' said the second man.

'Suck it up, Peter,' said Ellen Mae spiritedly. 'If you don't like real food, stick to Purina Disaster Chow.' She glanced at Alex. 'These mighty hunters don't appreciate me. Hand me that bone saw.'

Alex examined Ellen Mae's butcher tools on their bed of rawhide. He recognized the bone saw by its long, glacier-colored, fractal edge. He stooped and picked it up. It had a slight permanent bloodstaining in the ceramic, and a worn checkered grip, but its serrated teeth were every bit as sharp as freshly broken glass. It was a beautiful tool, and one of the objects in the world one would least like to be struck with. Alex made an experimental slash or two at the air and was a bit surprised to see the others leap immediately out of his reach.

'Sorry,' he said. 'Mega-tasty item.' He gripped the back of the blade carefully and offered Ellen the handle.

Ellen took it impatiently and began to saw the buck's legs off at the knee joints. It took her about a minute flat to do all four of them. The second woman neatly stacked the severed limbs aside.

'Y'know, you don't look much like Jane at first, but I'm starting to get the resemblance,' Peter told him.

'Maybe,' Alex told him. 'Are you the Peter who does the phones around here?'

'Yeah, that's right,' Peter said, pleased. 'Peter Vierling. I hack towers. Satellites, cellular coverage, the relays, that's all my lookout.'

'Good. You and me are gonna have to do some business.'

Peter looked at him with such open contempt that Alex was taken aback. 'After lunch or whatever,' Alex amended. 'No big hurry, man.'

'You look like you *need* lunch, kid,' said Rick the programmer. 'You need some real meat on your bones.' He patted his backpack. 'Got you a special treat here. You can have Bambi's liver.'

'Great,' Alex said. 'Bambi's lats and pecs look pretty chewy . . . Any of you guys ever try human meat?'

'*What?*' Peter said.

'I had human meat last time I was in Matamoros,' Alex said. 'It's kind of fashionable now.'

'*Cannibalism?*' Rick said.

Alex hesitated. He hadn't expected them to act so alarmed. 'It wasn't my idea. It just sort of showed up during the meal.'

'I've heard of that stuff,' Ellen Mae said slowly. 'It's a Santeria thing.'

'Well, it's not like they bring you out a big human steak,' Alex demurred. 'It comes out in this little pile of cubes. On a silver platter. Like fondue. It's a bad idea to eat the meat raw because of the, you know, infection risk. So everybody cooks it on these little forks.'

They were silent for a long moment. The two women even stopped their methodical skinning work. 'What's it taste like?' Rick asked.

'Well, not much, by the time you get through cooking it,' Alex said. 'Everybody sort of dipped 'em in the fondue pot, and took 'em out to cool on these little fork rests. And then we ate 'em one after another, and everybody looked really solemn about it.'

'Did anybody say prayers?' said the second woman.

'I wouldn't call 'em prayers exactly . . . It used to be like Santeria, I guess, but now it's mostly kind of a dope-trade custom. A lot of those dope-trade guys got into organ smuggling and stuff after the legalizations, so there's lots of . . . you know . . . '

'Spare parts around?' Peter suggested.

'This guy's bullshitting us,' Rick concluded.

Alex said nothing. His hosts in Matamoros had told him it was human meat, but they hadn't brought in any fresh bones or anything, so it could have just as easily been rabbit. He didn't see much real difference anyway, as long as you *thought* you were eating human meat . . .

'It's just a border thing,' he said at last. '*Una cosa de la frontera.*'

'You really hang out with dope dealers?' Rick said.

'I don't care about dope,' Alex said. 'I'm into medical supplies.'

The four of them burst into laughter. For some reason this central fact of his life seemed to strike them as hilarious. Alex concluded swiftly that he was dealing with mentally damaged hicks and would have to adjust his behavior accordingly.

'Tell our friend Alex about the special tour of the camp,' Rick urged.

'Oh yeah,' Peter said. 'Y'see, Alex, we get a lot of visitors. Especially in the peak storm season, during the spring. And we've discovered that the easiest way to get a good overview of Troupe operations is to fly an ultralight over the camp.'

'An aircraft,' Alex said. He glanced at Ellen and the other shorter woman, whose name he had still not learned. The two women were deliberately paying a lot of attention to severing the animal's left shoulder.

'Yeah. We have two manned ultralights. Plus three powered parafoil chutes, but those are for experts. You interested?'

'Never tried that before,' Alex said.

'The ultralight's got its own navigation,' Peter said. 'Just like a car! Only even safer, 'cause in midair there's no traffic and no tricky road conditions. You don't have to lift a finger.'

'Does it go really fast?' Alex said.

'No, no, not at all.'

'How about high, then? Does it go really high?'

'No, it won't take you very high either.'

'Then it doesn't sound very interesting,' Alex said. He pointed at the carcass. 'What's with that weird discoloration on the shoulder blade? Are they always like that?'

'Well,' Rick broke in, 'It *can* go pretty damned high, but you'd have to take oxygen with you.'

'You people got *oxygen*?' Alex said.

Rick and Peter exchanged glances. 'Sure.'

'Can I skip the tour, and just have some oxygen?'

'Wait till you see the machine,' Peter hedged. 'You're gonna want this bad, after you see the machine.'

Alex followed the pair of them across camp, stepping cautiously on the treacherous earth. His occasional curious glances up from his endangered feet across camp didn't much impress him. There was a monkish air about the place, a kind of military desiccation. Four skeletal towers dominated the camp, with microwave dishes, racks of spiny aerials, wrist-thick wiring and cable guides, and whirling cup-shaped wind gauges. Three large, dirty buses were parked side by side under a flat paper sunshade, along with three robot bikes. A tractor with a dozer blade and a spiraled posthole digger had planted a set of tall water-distillation stacks, which were dripping into a fauceted plastic reservoir.

The three of them stopped by the curtained door of another yurt. Two monster winches flanked the entrance, with thin woven cable on motor-driven drums.

Alex followed the two men inside, past a thick hanging door

curtain. The yurts were quilted paper, stretched over crisscrossed expandable lattices of lacquered wood. The diamond-shaped ends of these lattices were neatly and solidly lashed together, and eight of the lattices, curved into a broad ring, formed the yurt's round wall. Sixteen slender bent poles of lacquered bamboo ran from the tops of the lattices up to a central ring, bracing the white paper top of the dome.

The paper walls flapped a bit in the constant wind, but the interior had a surprisingly rich and pearly glow, and with its carpeted flooring, the yurt seemed remarkably snug and solid and permanent. Alex realized that the place was a minor aircraft hangar, all kites and keels and foamed-metal spars and great bundles of reinforced sailcloth. A Trouper was at work in the place, sitting cross-legged on a cushion amid a confusion of specialized hand tools. He had a gaunt weather-beaten face and an almost bald, freckled dome of skull, with a few lank strands of colorless shoulder-length hair. He wore black cotton leotards and had a blackened lump of metal on a rawhide thong around his neck.

'How's it goin', Buzzard?' Peter said.

Buzzard looked up from his rapt examination of a flexing cabled joint. 'Who's the geek?'

'Alex Unger,' Alex said. He stepped forward across the blissfully carpeted yurt flooring and jammed out his hand.

'Boswell Harvey,' said Buzzard, surprised, dropping his eviscerated bit of machinery as he reached up for Alex's hand. 'I hack, uh . . . I hack ornithopters.'

'Buzz, we need to boot the ultralight,' Rick said.

'Well, Amethyst is down,' Buzzard said.

'Beryl will do,' Peter said.

'Oh,' Buzzard said. 'Oh, okay.' Alex saw dawning comprehension spread across Buzzard's hooded eyes. 'I can boot her from here, off the station.' He stalked across the yurt and dropped into a crouch over a cabled laptop on the floor. He flipped it open, stared at the result on the flat screen, and pecked at the keyboard.

Peter and Rick took Alex outside to a nearby section of anchored sunshade. The paper shelter, up on bamboo poling, had its back to the wind and was firmly pitoned to the limestone earth. The ultralights beneath the shelter, both of them missing their wings, were heavily staked down with cabling. Just in case of sudden wind bursts, presumably.

Rick checked a set of input jacks on the motor housing while Peter industriously began assembling the left wing.

'I know this wing doesn't look too great right now,' Peter assured Alex, 'but when it inflates it gets very aerodynamic.'

'No problem,' Alex muttered.

'And check this out for safety – diamond bolts and nuts on every spar! Man, I can remember when we didn't have *any* construction diamond. I used to tower-monkey around Oklahoma working towers for TV stations, and we had to worry about, like, *mechanical stress*,' Peter laughed. 'Sometimes using diamonds to build everyday stuff seems like some kind of cheat! But hell, here it is, man; if you got a resource like that, you just gotta use it.'

'Yeah,' Rick mused aloud, 'a lot of the basic thrill went out of hardware design when diamond got really cheap.'

'Yeah,' Alex offered, 'I can remember my mom being pretty upset about that development.' He examined the ultralight. The wings seemed absurdly long and thin, but as Peter tightened their struts with a nut driver, they became convincingly tough and rigid. The little aircraft had a big padded bicycle seat with foamed-metal stirrups. There was a foam-padded skeletal back and neck rest, with a sturdy lap belt and shoulder harness. The motor and propeller were rear-mounted in a large plastic housing.

A controlling joystick and a rollerball were set into a plastic ridge between the pilot's knees. 'Where's the instrument panel?' Alex said.

'It's in the virching helmet,' Peter said. 'Do you do virtuality?'

'Sure. Doesn't everybody?'

'Well, it doesn't matter much, because you're not going to be flying this thing anyway. It's all controlled from the ground.' With the ease of long habit, Peter swabbed the interior band of the helmet with rubbing alcohol, then scrubbed the faceplate inside and out. 'But take good care of this virching helmet, because it's worth twice as much as the aircraft.'

'Twice, hell, three times,' Rick said. 'Let me do that, Peter.' He methodically adjusted the virtuality helmet's interior webbing for Alex's narrow skull, then set and wiggled it onto Alex's head. It felt like having one's head firmly inserted into a lightweight plastic bowling ball. 'Now see, if you want a naked-eyeball look, the faceplate just hinges up like this . . . And feel that com antenna back there? Don't snag that antenna on the left-hand spar there, okay?'

'Right,' Alex said. Despite Peter's alcohol scrub, the interior of the helmet still smelled strongly of someone else's old excited sweat. Alex began to settle into the mood. There was a momentum to this situation that appealed to him. He'd always rather enjoyed having his head at the mercy of someone else's media system.

With a resourcefulness that surprised himself, he rolled up the pant legs of his paper suit to the knee and stuffed both his makeshift sandals securely into the big baggy paper cuffs. Then he straddled the seat, barefoot, and tried it on for size. With a bit of stirrup-shifting and linchpin work, the seat was not too bad. 'Where's my oxygen?'

They insisted that he wouldn't really need any oxygen, but Alex counterinsisted with such leaden, pigheaded emphasis that they quickly gave in.

Rick had to confer with Buzzard by belt phone to find the dust-covered oxygen tank. Then its mask had to be sterilized – purely a matter of routine, Peter assured him, they always sterilized any equipment that might carry strep, flu, or TB. . . . Finally the chrome-yellow tank was strapped neatly behind the pilot's seat, its accordion tube draped over Alex's right shoulder, and the mask's elastic firmly snagged at the nape of his neck.

Then they rolled him, snugly socketed within his plane, out of the paper hangar. The plane bumped along easily on its little pipe-stem undercarriage. After rolling the plane eighty meters, the two Troupers faced the ultralight into the west wind.

Rick turned the helmet on, and Alex was rewarded with a meaningless pull-down menu of virtual instrumentation across the upper rim of his faceplate. Alex dinked around a bit with the rollerball and click button. The system seemed to be functional.

Five new Troupers now made their appearance, attracted by the fuss. They were three men, a woman, and, to Alex's surprise, a teenage boy. The boy hauled a hundred meters of winch cable out to the ultralight, and the towline was snapped to the aircraft's nose. Two new guys wedged a ten-meter bamboo bipod against the nose of the aircraft.

Buzzard, lurking distantly at the door of his yurt, drew in the slack on the winches until the launch cable thrummed with tension.

'Ready, Alex?' Rick shouted at the side of the helmet.

'Right.' Alex nodded. 'Let's do it.'

'Just relax, it's gonna be fine! You'll enjoy this!'

Alex flipped up his faceplate and glared at Rick. 'Look, man, *stop persuading me*. I'm here already, okay? You got me strapped down, I got my oxygen. Launch the son of a bitch.'

Rick's face fell, and he stepped back. He strode out the way of the wings, then pulled his belt phone and barked into it.

The cable snapped to, the bipod jammed itself in the limestone earth, and the aircraft was instantly catapulted skyward.

The drum reeled up with vicious, singing efficiency, and the aircraft climbed as steeply as a roller coaster. The cable detached and fell earthward, and the engine kicked in, and Alex was in free flight.

The aircraft veered inside to avoid the guy cable on one of the larger towers. It then methodically began vectoring upward, gaining height in a clockwise spiral.

'How's it going, Alex?' Peter asked over the headphones.

'Okay, I guess,' Alex said. He saw the prairie below, sunblasted straw and patches of poisonous green, the black strap of highway, a lot of stunted cedars clustered at a nearby draw. In the tug of wind his white paper sleeves flapped like cheap toy flags. The metal stirrups bit at his bare soles.

Deliberately, Alex swayed back and forth in his seat. The distant ends of the ultralight's wings dipped in response, like the ends of a seesaw, but they soon righted themselves in a chip-aided loop of feedback. And the ground beneath him dwindled steadily.

He was being gently juggled in midair by the hands of an invisible giant. He was lounging in a folding chair at the parapet of a twelve-story building. If he wanted to, he could pull the harness strap loose, step out on a stirrup, lean out, and drop to earth as sweet and clean as a meteor. Death was near. *Death was near* . . .

Alex flipped up his faceplate and felt the dry wind strip the sweat from his cheeks. 'Go higher, man!'

'You'll notice that we have six major yurts and four vehicle hangars,' Peter told him. 'Three of those towers are telecom, and we have four smaller towers for weather instrumentation. The black gridwork over by the latrine tents is a big patch of solar arrays.'

Alex grunted. 'Yeah, yeah.'

'We're running on solar now, but the wind generators run around the clock.'

'Huh . . .'

'All those big white rods, staked out in a circle around the camp, are our perimeter posts. They're motion detectors, and they've got some security muscle built in; you're gonna want to be a little careful with those. We have a set of 'em staked out by the highway too. Those big yellow panels are mosquito lures. They smell just like skin does, but any mosquito that lands on those lures gets instantly zapped.'

Alex flipped his faceplate back down. He rollerballed to the menu bar, pulled down a section labeled *telecom*, and switched to cellular. Peter vanished into telephonic limbo in the midst of his tour-guide spiel.

A handy phone menu rolled down with fifteen speed-dial numbers. They were thoughtfully accompanied by names.

1 Jerry Mulcahey.

2 Greg Foulks.

3 Joe Brasseur.

4 Carol Cooper.

5 Ed Dunnebecke.

6 Mickey Kiehl.

7 Rudy Martinez.

8 Sam Moncrieff.

9 Martha Madronich.

10 Peter Vierling.

11 Rick Sedletter.

12 Ellen Mae Lankton.

13 Boswell Harvey.

14 Joanne Lessard.

15 Jane Unger.

This looked very much like the Storm Troupe's idea of a digital pecking order. Alex was amazed to see that Juanita had somehow meekly settled for being number fifteen.

He clicked fifteen and got Juanita's voice mail, an I'm-not-in-right-now spiel. He hung up and clicked four.

'Carol here.'

'It's me again. I'm now flying over your camp.'

Carol laughed into his helmeted ears. 'I know, man, word gets around.'

'Carol, am I correct in assuming that this is some kind of hick hazing ritual? And pretty soon they're gonna tell me there's some kind of terrible software malf in this aircraft? And I'm gonna go through a whole bunch of, like, crazy barrel rolls and Immelmanns and such?'

Carol was silent for a moment. 'You don't miss much, for a guy your age.'

'What do you think I should do? Should I act really macho about it? Or should I scream my head off over the radio channel and act completely panicked?'

'Well, personally, I screamed bloody murder and threw up inside the helmet.'

'Macho it is, then. Thanks for the advice. Bye.'

'Alex, don't hang up!'

'Yeah?'

'I think I'd better tell you this . . . If you don't scream, and scream a whole lot, then they might just push the envelope on that little bird until its wings tear off.'

'You sure have some interesting friends,' Alex said. He hung up and switched back to radio channel.

' . . . support the generators. And it's useful for keeping track of goats,' Peter was droning.

'That's really remarkable,' Alex assured him. He switched the catch on the oxygen mask and pressed the mask firmly over his mouth and nose. For a moment he thought he'd been gypped, that he'd get nothing for his effort but the dry stink of plastic hose, but then the oxygen hit him. It spiked deep into his lungs and blossomed there, like a sweet dense mat of cool blue fur.

The paper walls of the camp dwindled beneath him as the aircraft continued its climb, spiraling up with the mathematical precision of a bedspring. As pure oxygen flushed through him to the sharp red marrow of his bones, Alex realized suddenly that he had found the ideal method to experience the Texas High Plains. The horizon had expanded to fantastic, planetary, soul-stretching dimensions. Nothing could touch him.

At this height, the air at ground level showed its true character. Alex could witness the organic filth in the low-lying atmosphere, banding the horizon all around him. It was a sepia-tinted permanent stain, a natural smog of dirts and grits and pollens, of molds and stinks and throat-clogging organic spew . . . By contrast, the high sweet air around him now, cool and thin and irresistible, was a bone-washing galactic ether. He felt as if it were blowing straight through his flesh.

In the distance, half a dozen buzzards corkscrewed down a thermal in pursuit of earthly carrion.

Peter's voice buzzed in his ears.

Alex tugged the mask from his face. 'What?'

'You okay, man? You're not answering.'

'No. I mean, yeah! No problem. It's beautiful up here! Go higher!'

'We seem to be having a little software trouble down here at base, Alex.'

'Really?' Alex said in delight. 'Hold on a sec . . . ' He pressed the mask to his face, huffed hard at it three times. From some lurking tarry mess deep within his tubercles, blue goo suddenly fizzed like a rack of sparklers. 'Go!' he screamed.

'What?'

'Hit it, man, push the envelope!'

Peter fell silent.

The wings wobbled, building up to a convulsion. Suddenly the craft pitched over nose-first and headed straight toward the earth. The descent lasted five heart-stopping, gut-gripping seconds. Blood left his heart, sweat jetted instantly from every pore in his body, and he felt a lethal chill grip his arms and legs.

Then the machine caught itself with a vicious huff of fabric and swooped through the pit of a parabola. Alex's head snapped back against the seat hard enough to see stars, and he felt his hands and feet fill with blood from g-forces. Great gummny bubbles rose in his chest.

The plane soared trembling toward the zenith.

Alex jammed his trembling blood-sausage fingers against the mask and gulped down fresh oxygen.

The plane was now flying upside down, piercing some timeless peak of weightless nothingness. Alex, his head swimming within his helmet, examined the enormous platonic sprawl of blue beneath his naked feet, through eyes that were two watery congested slits. Pulling loose and flinging himself into that limitless wonder would be worth not one, but a dozen lives.

JANE OPENED THE door flap of the command yurt. Inside the big tent, pacing the carpet at the end of his thick fiber-optic leash, was Jerry Mulcahey. Jerry's head was encased in the Troupe's top-of-the-line virching helmet, and both his hands were in stripe-knuckled data gloves. Jerry was wearing paper, a refugee suit that had seen some road wear. His right paper sleeve, and both his paper legs, were covered in his pencil-scrawled mathematical notation.

As Jerry turned and paced back toward her Jane glimpsed his bearded face through the helmet's dark display plate, his abstracted eyes stenciled with gently writhing white contour lines.

Jerry had ten-kilogram training weights strapped to each ankle, which gave him a leaden, swinging tread. Jane had often seen him pace with those weights, in marathon virching sessions, for hours on end. Every other hour or so, Jerry would suddenly stop, deliberately pull the weights from his ankles, and then strap them onto both his hairy wrists.

Jane Velcroed the yurt's doorway shut behind her, against the rising gusts of dusty west wind. Then she waited, her arms folded, for her presence to register on him, and for Jerry to surface from whatever strange sea of cyberspace had tangled his attention.

At length Jerry's pacing slowed, and the karate chops and Balinese hand gestures with the data gloves became a bit more perfunctory, and finally he glided to a stop in front of her. He pulled the blank-screened helmet off and set it on his hip and offered her a big bearded smile.

'We need to talk,' Jane said.

Jerry nodded once, paused, then raised his shaggy blond brows in inquiry.

Jane turned her head toward one of the two attached subyurts. 'Are Sam or Mickey in right now?'

'No. You can talk, Jane.'

'Well, I went down to Mexico and I got Alex. He's here right now.'

'That was quick,' Jerry said. He seemed pleasantly surprised.

'Quick and dirty,' Jane told him.

Jerry set his tethered helmet down on the carpet, crouched, and sat heavily beside it. 'Okay then, tell me. How dirty was it?'

Jane sat down beside him and lowered her voice. 'Well, I structure-hit the power to the clinic, then I broke into the place when it was blacked out, and I found him with a flashlight, and I carried him out on my back.'

Jerry whistled. 'Damn! You did all that? We've created a monster!'

'I know that was a really stupid thing to do, but at least it was over in a hurry, and I didn't get caught, Jerry. I didn't get caught, I got him out, and I aced it!' She shivered, then looked into his eyes. 'Are you proud of me?'

'I guess,' Jerry said. 'Sure I am. I can't help it. Were there witnesses?'

'No. Nobody knows, besides you and me. And Carol and Greg, they know, but they'll never tell. And Leo, of course.'

Jerry frowned. 'You didn't tell Leo about this little escapade, did you?'

'No, no,' Jane assured him. 'I haven't been in contact with Leo since he found Alex for me.' She paused, watching his face carefully. 'But Leo's smart. I know Leo must have figured out what I was up to. I could tell that much, just from the E-mail he wrote me.'

'Well, don't figure out Leo anymore,' Jerry said. 'You don't know Leo. And I don't want you to know Leo. And if you ever do get to know Leo, you'll be very sorry that you did.'

She knew it would annoy Jerry if she pushed, but she had to push anyway. 'I know you don't trust Leo, and neither do I. But you know, he's been very helpful to us. It can't have been easy to track Alex. Leo didn't have to do that for me, just because he's your brother. But he did it anyway, and he never asked you or me for anything in return.'

'My brother is a spook, and spooks are professionally affable,' Jerry said. 'You've got what you needed now. Let Leo alone from now on. Your brother's one thing, but my brother's another. It's bad enough that your no-good brother's shown up in camp, but if *my* brother ever arrives here, then all hell will break loose.'

Jane smiled. 'Y'know, Jerry, it does me a lot of good to hear you say that. In a very sick, paradoxical way, of course.'

Jerry grimaced and ran his hand over his sandy hair. He was losing some of it in front, and the virching helmet had mashed the sides down over his ears, like a little boy's hair. 'Family is a nightmare.'

'I'm with you,' Jane said. She felt very close to him suddenly. Family troubles were one of their great commonalities. It had been good of him to agree to let her brother into the Troupe, when she'd been so frank about Alex's shortcomings. She was sure that Jerry would never have done such a thing for anyone else. She was being stupid and reckless and troublesome, and Jerry was letting her do it, as a kind of gift. Because he loved her.

'We gotta think this through, some,' she told him. 'The Troupe's not gonna like this much. Alex is no star recruit, that's for sure. He has no skills. And not much education. And he's an invalid.'

'How sick is he? Is he badly off?'

'Well, I've always thought Alex was nine tenths malingerer, at heart. Dad's dropped thousands on him, but never pinned down what's wrong with him. But I can guarantee he's not contagious.'

'That's something, at least.'

'But he does get bored, and touchy, and then he gets these spells. They're pretty bad, sometimes. But he's always been like that.'

'No one stays with the Troupe who can't pull weight,' Jerry said.

'I know that, but I don't think he'll stay for long. If he doesn't run off by himself, then the Troupe'll throw him out after a while. They're not patient people. And if there's a way to make trouble here, Alex will probably find it.' Jane paused. 'He's not stupid.'

Jerry silently drummed his fingers on his papered knee.

'I had to do this, because he's my little brother, and he was in really bad trouble, and I felt sure he was going to die.' Jane was surprised at how much it hurt her to say that, at how much real pain and sense of failure she felt at the thought of Alex dead. She'd resented Alex for as long as she could remember, and in rescuing him, she'd thought she was doing something tiresome and familial and obligatory. But at the thought of Alex dead, she felt a slow burn of deep unsuspected emotion, a tidal surge of murky grief and panic. She wasn't being entirely frank with Jerry. Well, it wasn't exactly the first time.

She took a breath and composed herself. 'I've just dragged Alex out of the mess he was in, but I wish I could be responsible for him. But I can't. I believe in the work here. You know I believe in the work, and I do what I can to help. But now I've done something that really doesn't help the Troupe. I just brought you a big load of trouble. I'm sorry, sweetheart.'

Jerry was silent.

'You're not angry with me, Jerry?'

'No, I'm not angry. It is a complication, and it's not helpful. But it's simple, if you can let it be simple. As far as I'm concerned, your brother is just like any other wannabe. He pulls his weight here, or out he goes.'

She said nothing.

'We throw people out of the Troupe every season. It's ugly, but it happens. If it happens to your brother, you'll just have to accept that. Can you do that for me?'

She nodded slowly. 'I think so . . . '

That earned her one of Jerry's looks. 'You'd better tell me that you can do that, Jane. If you can't, then we'd all be better off if I threw him out right now.'

'All right,' she said quickly. 'I can do that, Jerry.'

'Maybe Alex can measure up. We'll give Alex his chance.' Jerry stood and fetched up his helmet left-handed, dangling it by one strap.

Jane stood too. 'I'm not real hopeful, but maybe he can do it, Jerry. If you'll back him a little.'

Jerry nodded. He swung up his helmet at the end of its strap and caught it in his other hand. 'I'm glad you're back. You picked a good time for it. We've got a show for your little brother. Tomorrow it's gonna break loose along the dryline from here to Anadarko.'

'Wonderful! At last!' Jane jumped to her feet. 'Is it mega-heavy?'

'It's not the F-6, but the midlevel stream has serious potential. We're gonna chase spikes.'

'Oh that's great!' She laughed aloud.

A shadow appeared at the door of the yurt. It was Rudy Martinez, from the garage. Rudy stood flatfooted, visibly sorry to interrupt. Jane aimed her brightest smile at him, wanting him to know that life would go on, the Troupe was moving, she'd aced another one.

Jerry nodded. 'What's up, Rudy?'

Rudy cleared his throat. 'Just tuning up for the chase . . . What's with the malf in Charlie's right front hub?'

'Oh hell,' Jane said. 'Hell hell hell . . . Take me there, Rudy, we can fix that, let's go see.'

ALEX WAS SITTING in a flaccid plastic bath with a trickling sponge on his head. He was in the back of the hangar yurt, where Peter and Rick had dragged him, after pulling him, unconscious, from the seat of the ultralight.

Buzzard, severed from all things earthly by his virching helmet, crouched on his cushion in the yurt's center. He was methodically putting his remote-control ornithopters through their paces, in preparation for the chase to come.

Carol Cooper sat on the floor near the tub, methodically stitching a set of carpal tunnel wrist supports out of tanned deerskin.

'You think I could have some more water in here?' Alex said. 'Maybe like a couple hundred cc's?'

Carol snorted. 'Dude, you're damn lucky to draw what you got. Most days we wash in, like, four tablespoons. *When* we wash, that is.'

A Trouper in bright yellow Disaster Relief paramedical gear entered the yurt, circled around the oblivious Buzzard, and handed Carol a plastic squeeze bottle and a paper pack of antiseptic gloves. 'I brought the sheep dip.'

'Thanks, Ed.' Carol paused. 'This is Alex.'

'Yo,' Alex offered, sketching out a half salute.

Ed gave Alex a long gaze of silent medical objectivity, then nodded once and left.

Alex plucked the sponge from his head and began to dab at his armpits. 'I take it you folks aren't real big on bathroom privacy.'

'Ed's a medic,' Carol told him. 'He was checking you out here earlier, when you were flat on your back and covered with barf.' Carol compared her leather cutout to a pattern displayed on her laptop screen, then deftly nicked away another sliver with her pencil knife. 'There's never much privacy in camp life. If we Troupe types want to have sex or something, then we sneak into one of the tepees and move some of the storage crap out of the way. Or if you want, you can drive out way over the horizon and toss a blanket over some cactus.' Carol put her leather stitchwork aside and hefted the squeeze bottle. 'You feel okay, now Alex?'

'Yeah. I guess so.'

'You're not gonna pass out again, or anything?'

'I didn't "pass out,"' Alex said with dignity. 'I just was really getting deeply into the experience, that's all.'

Carol let that ride. 'This stuff is heavy-duty antiseptic. Kind of a delousing procedure. We have to do this to all the wannabes now, ever since a staph carrier showed up at camp once and gave us a bad set of boils.

'I've had staph boils,' Alex nodded.

'Well, you never had staph like that stuff; it was like one of the plagues of Egypt.'

'I've had Guatemalan Staph IVa,' Alex told her. 'Never heard of the Egyptian strains before.'

Carol pondered him for a long moment, then shrugged and let it go. 'I've got to wash you down in this stuff. It's gonna sting a little.'

'Oh good!' Alex said, sitting up straighter. The flaccid camp bath swashed about in its thin metal frame, and the pathetic dribble of water in the bottom did its best to slosh. 'Y'know, Carol, it eally good of you to take so much time for me.'

'That's okay, man. It's not everybody I know who can throw up blue goo.' she paused. 'I did mention that you have to clean out the helmet later, right?'

'No, you didn't mention that. But I'm not real surprised to hear it.'

Carol tore the paper pack open and pulled out the thin plastic gloves. She drew them on. 'This stuff stings some at first, but don't panic. You don't need to panic unless you get it in your eyes. It's pretty tough on mucous membranes.'

'Look, stop making excuses and just pour it in the god-damned sponge,' Alex said, holding it out.

Carol soaked the sponge down with the squeeze bottle and emptied the rest into the tub. Alex began to lather himself up. The slithering soapy concoction wasn't bad at all – kind of a pleasantly revolting medical peppermint.

Then it began to acid-etch its way into his skin.

Alex gritted his teeth, his eyes watering, but deliberately made no sound.

Carol watched him with an interesting mix of compassion and open pleasure in his suffering. 'Blood will tell, huh, Alex? I swear to God I saw your sister get exactly that same expression on her face . . . Close your eyes tight, and I'll do your back and scalp.'

The sharp gnawing edge of the antiseptic faded after a moment, in Carol's steady scrubbing and the blood-colored darkness of his own closed eyelids, and he began to feel merely as if he were being laundered and drastically over-bleached. The antiseptic was doing something very peculiar to the caked sweat, sebum, and skin flakes at the roots of his hair. Great metropolitan swarms of his native bacteria were perishing in microscopic anguish.

Carol allowed him another dribble of clean water then, enough to rinse his hair and free his eyes. He was more than clean now. He was cleaner than he ever wanted to be again. He was scorched and smoking earth.

Juanita chose this moment to storm headlong into the yurt, in boots, shorts, T-shirt, and a pair of big grimy work gloves, her square jaw set with fury and her hair knotted in a kerchief. She had to pause in midrush to skip her way over the fiber-optic trip wires of Buzzard's networked laptops. 'Alex!' she yelled. 'Are you all right?'

He looked up mildly. 'Did you bring a towel?'

'I heard those bastards stunted you until you fainted!' She stopped short at his tub. She glanced at Carol, then back at him. 'Is that true?'

'I like ultralights,' he told her. 'They're interesting. Get out of my bathroom.'

Carol burst into laughter. 'He's okay, Jane.'

'Well, they were wrong to do that! If they'd hurt you, I'd have . . . well, you should have *told* them that you were *never* supposed to– ' Juanita broke off short. 'Hell! Never mind. We've got to chase storms. We've got to calibrate.' She threw the back of one work glove to her sweating forehead. 'Never mind . . . Alex, just for me, please, try and stay out of trouble for ten goddamn minutes, okay?'

'I'm only doing what you *wanted* me to do,' Alex pointed out, exasperated. 'Can't we discuss this while *you're* having a bath?'

'Alex, don't drive me crazy!' Juanita stared at him. 'I guess you're okay after all, huh . . . ? Y'know, you don't look half so bad now!

you're still kinda pale and airsick looking, but you do look a lot better clean.'

Stung, Alex switched to their childhood household Spanish. '*Listen to me, all of the world will be more happy when you get away from me, and stay away from me!*'

Juanita looked startled. 'What? Slow down.' She shook her head. 'Never mind, I get it. Okay, I'm leaving. Have it your way.' She turned to Carol, frowning. 'Peter and Rick! I'm gonna think up something special for Peter and Rick.'

Carol pursed her lips. 'Be nice, Janey.'

'Yeah, right, sure.' Juanita left the yurt.

Alex waited until his sister was well out of earshot. 'She sure hasn't changed much,' he said. 'How do you people put up with that crap?'

'Oh, for us, she's an asset,' Carol assured him. 'I like Jane! I always liked her. I liked her even when she first showed up in the fucking limo! I'm one of your sister's big partisans.'

'Huh,' Alex said. 'Well, that's your lookout, I guess.' He rinsed his arms, then gazed around the yurt. 'How long does it take around here before us lowly wannabes are actually given real clothes?'

'Well, that's *your* lookout, dude. Maybe I could be persuaded to cut-and-paste you a paper suit that would fit you a little better.' Carol shrugged. 'But you'll have to pull some weight for me, in return. What are you good at?'

'What do you mean?'

'I mean what do you hack?'

Alex thought it over. 'Well, I'm pretty good at ordering weird stuff with charge cards. If I can get an encrypted phone line, that is.'

Carol's eyes narrowed. 'Huh.'

THERE WASN'T MUCH wrong with Charlie. He had what was known in the trade as a vegetable jam. A whip-thin length of West Texas briar had managed to work its way into the fullerene grease around the right front axle, and had been liquefied into a burned-caramel goo. Jane fetched and carried for Greg and Rudy for a while, dismounting and remounting Charlie, running diagnostics off the older Pursuit Vehicle Baker, and trying to pamper the dinosaurlike alcohol-burning Dune Buggy Able. As time ticked on, though, and the two experienced mechanics worked their way into the finer tolerances, she could sense their patience with her amateurism beginning to wear.

Jane took some time then to work on the maintenance hulk, one of the dirt-stupid machines that the state of Texas used to keep up its county roads. The Troupe sometimes made a little money working repair on busted state robotry, and it kept them in a better air with sheriff's deputies and the Texas Rangers. Out in West Texas, official repair yards were very few and far between, and worse yet, for some reason, the locals seemed to dote on structure-hitting highway machinery. The hulk in their shop had been put out of its misery by a fusillade of twenty-four shots from a deer rifle.

Jane followed the repair coaching of a state-government on-line expert system for about an hour, extending Carol's weld-and-glue work, till she hit some tangled wiring she didn't feel competent to hack.

She left the garage yurt. The wind was picking up, pulling a tangled pennant of mesquite smoke from the vent hole in the dome of the kitchen. With the approach of evening, the dry wind off the continental uplands had ripped the morning's cumulus to desiccated shreds – the dryline was pushing east.

Jane stepped into the command yurt – no sign of Jerry there – and stepped into its left annex, the telecom office.

She picked up a spare laptop between the silent helmeted heads of Mickey Kiehl, the Troupe's network sysadmin, and Sam Moncrieff, Jerry's meteorological disciple. She logged into the Troupe's own local net, then onto the federal SESAME Net.

First, a quick scan of the satellite view. It loked very tasty. Half of Texas was swamped under a classic springtime gush of suffocating damp stratus from the Gulf of Mexico.

She scrolled north. So far, 2031 did not seem to be shaping up as an El Niño year, which was something of a rarity, lately. The high midcontinental jet stream was more or less behaving itself, doing some mildly odd and tortuous things at the rim of a cold front over Iowa.

Jane kicked out of satellite view and into SESAME's complex of ground-level Doppler Lidars. She saw at once what Jerry had meant about the midlevel local jet. Along the edge of the torpidly encroaching damp there was a great flat ribbon of spew; down around San Antonio it was chopping the advancing stratus into a mass of roller bars.

Mickey's voice emerged from the laptop's speaker. 'What do you think, Jane?'

She glanced over at Mickey. Mickey sat on the carpet, his gloved hands gently pawing the air, his head and face hidden in his personal virching helmet. The side of his helmet was logo'd with the peeling emblem of a mockingbird perched on a lightning bolt. It struck Jane as a little odd that a guy sitting three steps away from her would network a vocal signal over fiber-optic wiring, when he might have just lifted his faceplate and started talking. But that was Mickey all over.

She clicked patiently through three levels of pull-downs into a vocal-chat mode and leaned into the laptop's dorky little inset mike. 'Well, Mickey, I think if that midlevel local jet impacts the dryline, we are gonna have vorticity to burn.'

'Me too,' Mickey offered tinnily. The miked acoustics inside his helmet were exactly like the bottom of a barrel. 'Are you chasing tomorrow?'

'Of course I'm chasing, man, I always do pursuit!'

'Well, SESAME has two dead relays south of Paducah, we're either gonna have to route around 'em or get our own relay up.'

'Hell,' Jane said. 'Stupid structure-hit vandals, I hate those people!' She peered into her laptop screen. 'Well, it looks to me like it'll break well south of Paducah, though. What do you think, Sam?'

Sam Moncrieff lifted his faceplate and gazed at her in total distraction. 'Huh? Did you just say something?'

She paused. 'Yeah, I did. Where's it gonna break?'

Sam circled his gloved hand three times in the air, stabbed out with his forefinger. 'Stonewall County. Boom!'

'Damn near right on top of us,' Jane said.

Sam's freckled face was the picture of satisfaction. 'Jerry doesn't often miss.' He shut his faceplate again with a snap.

A piece of groupware now took it upon itself to hunt Jane down on the local Net and make its presence known. Jane was rather proud about the groupware. It was the only groupware she'd ever installed – ever *seen*, even – that actually worked, in the sense that it genuinely helped a group manage rather than slowly driving its users bughouse. Unfortunately the code was cryptware – it reencrypted itself every goddamn month and demanded a payoff before unfreezing – but she kept up the lease out of her own pocket, even though paying actual money for code was an archaic pain in the ass.

Jane fed the groupware a couple of clicks. It opened up. It was Jerry's assignments.

Calibration Tonight 2100 HQ Yurt

11 Mar 2031
ABLE: Greg Foulkes, Carol Cooper.
BAKER: Rudy Martinez, Sam Moncrieff.
CHARLIE: Rick Sedletter, Jane Unger.
AERODROMETRUCK: Boswell Harvey, Martha Madronich, Alex Unger.
RADARBUS: Peter Vierling, Joanne Lessard.
NAVIGATION, SUPPORTJEEPS: Joe Brasseur.
BACKUPTEAM: Ellen Mae Lankton, Ed Dunnebecke, Jeff Lowe.
NETWORKCOORD: Mickey Kiehl.
NOWCASTER: Jerry Mulcahey.

ABLE team departs 0630 to plant monitors along storm track and cover the north flank. RADAR BUS departs 0700 to deploy kite relays and cover Paducah hole around SESAME Net. BAKER departs 0800 to pursue midmorning towers on left flank. AERODROME crew departs behind dryline 0900 for chaff launch and ornithopter virching. CHARLIE departs approx 1200 to pursue secondary propagation towers.

So she was riding with Rick. How lovely. It looked as though Alex would be crammed into the back of the aerodrome truck. If Alex thought that stunting an ultralight was hairy, he'd learn otherwise if Buzzard virched him in an ornithopter to punch the core . . .

A tinny ringing came from Jane's laptop. In unison, Sam and Mickey both yanked the virching helmets from their heads. 'God*damn* it!' Mickey said, massaging his ears. 'I wish she'd stop doing that!'

Sam looked rueful, climbing to his feet. 'When Ellen Mae wants you to eat, you'd better devirch and go eat, and that's all there is to it.'

'I wish she'd use something else besides a chuckwagon triangle at fifty decibels, man.'

Jane smiled silently. It was good to be able to pull network weight for good old Ellen Mae.

CHAPTER

3

A lex climbed out of five levels of complex nightmare to find someone kicking his ribs. He gazed up for a long, deeply dazed moment into the conical funnel of a tepee, then focused on a tall, bony young woman looming at the side of his sleeping bag.

'Hey, Medicine Boy,' she said. She was sharp-nosed and bright-eyed and wearing a sleeveless multipocketed jacket and jeans.

'Yeah,' Alex croaked. 'Hi.'

'I'm Martha, remember? You're s'posed to be on our chase team. Get up, dud.'

'Right,' he muttered. 'Where's the sauna?'

Martha smiled thinly. She swung out one long arm – her fingertips lacquered black. 'The latrines are over that way.' Her arm swung again from the shoulder, like the needle of a compass. 'The truck's chargin' up by the solar rack. You got ten minutes.' She left the tepee, leaving its flap hanging open to a malignant burst of morning glare.

Alex sat up. He'd slept all night, naked inside a padded cloth bag on a big round floor mat of bubblepak. The bag itself was old and dusty and torn, and he was pretty sure that two people in a doubtful state of cleanliness had spent a lot of time having sex in it. As for the bubblepak, it was clearly a stuff of deep unholy fascination for Storm Troupers. To judge by what he'd seen so far, the Troupe spent half their lives sprawling, sitting, and sleeping on carpet-covered bubblepak, big blisterwards of condom-thin but rawhide-tough translucent inflated film. Bubblepak was one of the basic elements of their nomad's cosmos: Bubblepak, Paper and Sticks; Chips, Wire, &

Data; Wind, Clouds, & Dirt. He'd just spent the night inside a rolled-up tepee cone of polymerized recycled newsprint, a thing of paper and sticks and string, like something a little kid might make with tape and scissors.

Alex clambered slowly to his feet. His knees shook, and his arms and back were sore; the bones of his spine felt like a stack of wooden napkin rings. He had a minor lump on his head that he didn't remember receiving.

But his lungs felt good. His lungs felt very good, amazingly good. He was breathing. And that was all that mattered. For the first time in at least a year, he'd spent the entire night, deeply asleep, without a coughing fit.

Whatever vile substance he'd received in the lung enema, and whatever msiguided quack doctrine had guided the *clínica* staff, the treatment had nonetheless worked. The street rumors that had guided him were true: the sons of bitches in Nuevo Laredo actually had something workable. He wasn't cured – he knew full well that he wasn't cured, he could sense the sullen reservoirs of baffled sickness lurking deep in his bones – but he was much better. They had hacked him back, they had patched him up, they had propped him on his feet. And just in time to have him stolen away.

Alex laughed aloud. He had rallied; he was on a roll again. It was very welcome; but it was very strange.

Alex had had spells of good health before. The longest had been a solid ten months when he was seventeen, when the whole texture of his life had changed for a while, and he had even considered going to school. But that little dream had broken like a bubble of blood, when the blight set its fishhooks into him again and reeled him back gasping into its own world of checkups, injections, biopsies, and the sickbed.

His latest siege of illness had been the worst by far, the worst since his infancy, really. At age eighteen months, he had almost coughed to death. Alex didn't remember this experience, naturally, but his parents had made twenty-four-hour nursery videotapes during the crisis. Alex had later discovered those tapes and studied them at length.

In the harsh unsparing light of Texas morning, Alex stood naked by his battered sleeping bag and examined himself, with a care and clarity that he'd avoided for a while.

He was past thin: he was emaciated, a stick-puppet creature, all tendon and bone. He was close to gone, way too close. He'd been neglectful, and careless.

Careless – because he hadn't expected to emerge from those shadows again. Not really, not this time. The *clínica* had been his last hope, and to pursue it, he had cut all ties to his family, and his family's agents. He'd gone underground with all the determination he could manage – so far underground that he didn't need eyes anymore, the kind of deep dark underground that was the functional equivalent of a grave. The hope was just an obligatory long shot. In reality, he'd been quietly killing off the last few weeks of lease on his worn-out carcass, before the arrival of the final wrecking ball.

But now it appeared he was going to live. Somehow, despite all odds, he'd got another lease extension. That wasn't very much to rely on, but it was all he'd ever had: and if it lasted a while, then he could surely use the time.

The Trouper camp might be good for him. The air of the High Plains was thin and dry, cleaner somehow, and less of a burden to breathe.

Alex felt particularly enthusiastic about the Troupe's oxygen tank. Most of the doctors of his experience had been a little doubtful about his habit of sneaking pure oxygen. But these Troupers weren't doctors; they were a pack of fanatical hicks, with a refreshing lack of any kind of propriety, and the oxygen had been lovely.

Alex climbed quickly into his baggy paper suit and zipped it up to the neck. Let the stick puppet disappear into his big paper puppet costume. It wouldn't do for the Troupers to dwell on his medical condition. He couldn't describe them as bloodthirsty or sadistic people; they lacked that criminal, predatory air he'd so often seen in his determined slumming with black marketeers. But the Troupe did have the stony gaze of people overused to death and killing: hunters, ranchers, butchers. Thrill freaks. Euthanasia enthusiasts.

Alex put on his new shoes – the same makeshift plastic soles as yesterday, but trimmed closer to the shape of his foot, with a seamed-paper glued-on top, and a paper shoe tongue, and a series of reinforced paper lace holes. If you didn't look hard, Carol Cooper's constructions were practically actual clothes.

Alex tottered squinting across the camp and into the peaked latrine tent. The Troupe's lavatory features were simplicity itself: postholes augered about two meters down into the rocky subsoil, with a little framework seatless camp stool to squat on. After a prolonged struggle, Alex rose and zipped his drop seat back in place, and looked for the aerodrome truck.

Buzzard and Martha's telepresence chase truck was a long white wide-bodied hardtop, spined all over with various species of antenna. It had a radar unit clamped to the roof, in a snow-white plastic dome. Buzzard was topping off the batteries with a trickle of current from the solar array; Martha Madronich had the back double doors open and was stowing a collapsed ornithopter into an interior wall-mounted rack.

'Got any water?' Alex said.

Martha stepped out of the truck and handed Alex a plastic canteen and a paper cup. Martha limped a bit, and Alex noticed for the first time that she had an artificial foot, a soft flesh-colored prosthetic with dainty little joints at the ankles and toes, in a black ballet slipper.

Alex poured, careful not to touch the paper cup to Martha's possibly infectious canteen rim, and he gulped thirstily at the flat distilled water. 'Not too much,' she cautioned him.

He gave the canteen back and she handed him a dense wedge of cornmeal-and-venison scrapple. 'Breakfast.' Alex munched the mincemeat wedge of fried deer heart, deer liver, and dough while he slowly circled the truck. The truck had two bucket seats in front, with dangling earphones and eye goggles Velcroed to the fabric roof, and an impressive arsenal of radio, radar, microwave, and telephone equipment bolted across the dash.

'Where do I ride?' he said.

Martha pointed to a cubbyhole she'd cleared on the floor of the truck, a burrowed nook amid a mass of packed equipment: big drawstring bags, a pair of plastic tool chests, three bundles of strapped-down spars.

'Oh yeah,' Alex said, at length. 'Luxury.'

Martha sniffed and ran both bony hands through her black-dyed hair. 'We'll nest you down in some bubblepak, you'll do okay. We don't do any rough cross-country stuff. Us telepresence types always stick close to the highways.'

'You'll have to move when we pull that chaff bag,' Buzzard warned.

Alex grunted. Buzzard unrolled a flattened sheet of bubblepak, fit it to a palm-sized battery air pump, and inflated it with a quick harsh hiss and crackle.

Martha wadded the bubblepak helpfully into the hole, then climbed back out. Alex's cheap cuff emitted a loud hour chime. Martha glanced at her wrist, then back up at Alex again.

'Aren't you calibrated?' she said.

'Sorry, no.' Alex lifted his wrist. 'I couldn't figure out how to set the clock on this thing. Anyhow, it's not a real Trouper cuff like yours, it's just my sister's cheap wannabe Trouper cuff.'

Martha sighed in exasperation. 'Use the clock in the laptop, then. Get in, man, time's a-wastin'.' She and Buzzard went to the front of the vehicle and climbed in.

The truck took off downhill, hit the highway, and headed north. It drove itself and was very quiet. Besides the thrum of tires on pavement, the loudest sound in the truck was the crinkling of Alex's bubblepak and paper suit as he elbowed bags aside and settled in place.

'Hey, Medicine Boy!' Buzzard said suddenly. 'You like that ultralight?'

'Loved it!' Alex assured him. 'My life began when I met you and your machinery, Boswell.'

Buzzard snickered. 'I *knew* you liked it, man.'

Alex spotted a gray laptop under Boswell's driver seat and snagged it out. He opened it up, and placed the clock readout in the corner: *12 May, 2031, 9:11:46 A.M.* Then he started grepping at the hard disk. 'Hey Buzzard, you got the Library of Congress in here,' he said. 'Nice machine!'

'That's the 2015 Library of Congress,' Buzzard said proudly.

'Really?'

'Yeah, the one they released right after the data nationalizations,' Buzzard said. 'The whole on-line works! The complete set, no encryptions, no abridgments! They tried to recopyright a lot of that stuff, after the impeachments, y'know.'

'Yeah, like the government could get it back after doing *that*,' Alex sniffed.

'You'd be surprised how many losers just gave back that data!' Buzzard said darkly. 'Sent federal cops out to raid the universities and stuff . . . Man, you'll get my Library of Congress *when you pry my cold dead fingers off it!*'

'I see you've got the 2029 release of the Library in here, too.'

'Yeah, I've got most of that one . . . there's some pretty good new stuff in that '29 release, but it's not like the classic 2015 set. I dunno, you can say what you want about the State of Emergency, but the Regime had some pretty dang good ideas about public domain.'

Alex opened the 2015 Library, screened up a visualization of its data stacks, zipped down randomly through its cyberspace architecture through three orders of fractal magnitude, and punched at random into a little cream-yellow cube. The thing unfolded like the usual origami trick and he found himself gazing at a full-color digital replica of an illuminated twelfth-century French manuscript.

It was almost always like that when you screwed around with the Library. He'd hammered away in the Library on occasion, when absolutely sick of cable television, but the way he figured it, the big heap of electric text was way overrated. There were derelicts around who could fit all their material possessions in a paper bag, but they'd have a cheap laptop and some big chunk of the Library, and they'd crouch under a culvert with it, and peck around on it and fly around in it and read stuff and annotate it and hypertext it, and then they'd come up with some pathetic, shattered, crank, loony, paranoid theory as to what the hell had happened to them and their planet . . . It almost beat drugs for turning smart people into human wreckage.

Alex looked up from the screen, bored. 'What do you hack, Martha?'

'I hack kites,' she told him. 'Balloons, chaff, ultralights, parafoils . . . Chutes are my favorite, though. I like to structure-jump.'

'You do *structure hits*, Martha?'

She whirled in her seat to glare at him. 'Not structure hits, you moron! Structure *jumps*! I don't blow things up! I just climb up on top of things when the wind is right, and I jump off them with a parachute.'

'Oh. I get it. Sorry.' Alex thought about it. 'What kinda things d'you jump off, Martha?'

'Bridges are pretty good,' she said, relaxing a bit. 'Mountains are great. Urban skyscrapers are mega-cool, but you have to worry about, like, private security guards and stupid city cops and moron straight civilians and stuff . . . The coolest, though, is really big transmission towers.'

'Yeah?'

'Yeah, I like the really big antique ones without any construction diamond in 'em.' She paused. 'That's how I lost my foot.'

'Oh. Right. Okay.' Alex nodded repeatedly. 'How'd someone like you come to join the Storm Troupe?'

Martha shook her head. 'I'll give you some advice, little dude. Don't ever ask people that.'

Fair enough. Alex retreated back into the laptop screen.

They drove on. Every ten minutes Buzzard and Martha would stop to trade laconic updates with the Trouper base camp, or parley with Greg and Carol in the dune buggy Able, or send some side-of-the-mouth remark to Peter and Joanne in the Radar Bus. Their traffic was all acronyms and in-jokes and jargon. Every once in a while Martha would scrawl a quick note in grease pencil on the inside of the windshield. When Alex's cuff chimed again, she took it off his wrist, fixed it brusquely, and handed it back.

After a long hour on the road, Buzzard began methodically gnawing at a long strap of venison jerky. Martha started picking her way daintily through a little drawstring bag of salted sunflower seeds, tongue-flicking her chewed-up seed hulls through the half-open passenger window. Alex had a strong stomach – he could read text off a laptop in a moving vehicle without any trace of headache or motion sickness – but at the sight of this, he shut his laptop and his eyes, and tried to sleep a bit.

He lounged half-awake for a while, then he sank with unexpected speed and impetus into a deep healing doze. A month's worth of narcotic-suppressed REM sleep suddenly rose from his bloodstream's sediments and seized control of his frontal lobes. Vast glittering tinsel sheets of dream whipped and rippled past his inner eye, hyperactive visions of light and air and speed and weightlessness . . .

Alex came to with a start and realized that the truck had stopped.

He sat up slowly in his nest of bubblepak, then climbed out the open back double doors into simmering, eye-hurting, late-morning sunlight. The Troupers had left the highway and worked their way up a scarcely used dirt track to the top of a low flat hill. The hill was one of the limestone rises typical of the region, a bush-spattered bump in the landscape that had tried and failed to become a mesa.

However, the hill had a respectably sized relay tower on it, with its own concrete-embedded solar array and a small windowless cement blockhouse. Buzzard and Martha had parked, and they'd laced a section of blue fabric to the side of the truck's roof. They were stretching the fabric out on a pair of sticks to form a sunshade veranda.

'What's up?' Alex said.

Buzzard had slung a long narrow-billed black cap over his balding noggin, the base of its bill resting on the outsized nose bridge of a pair of insectile mirrorshades. 'Well,' he allowed, 'we'll put up a relay kite on some coax, boot the packet relay, try and tap in on this tower node . . . and then maybe launch a couple ornithopters.'

'You can go back to sleep if you want,' Martha offered.

'No, that's okay,' said Alex, rubbing his eyes. He envied Buzzard the sunglasses. They were a matter of survival out here.

Alex shook the stiffness out of his back and gazed over the landscape, shading his eyes right-handed. This had once been cattle country, of a sort; never thriving, but a place you could squeeze a living from, if you owned enough of it. Alex could trace the still-lingering ligature scars of rusted and collapsed barbed-wire fencing, old scalpel-straight incisions across the greenly flourishing wild expanses of bunchgrass and grama and needle grass and weed. Since the mass evacuations and the livestock die-offs, much of the abandoned pastureland had grown up in mesquite.

Here, however, the mesquite was mysteriously dead: brown and leafless and twisted, the narrow limbs peeling leprous rotten gray bark. Stranger yet, there was a broad path broken through the dead mesquite forest, a series of curved arcs like the stamping of a gigantic horseshoe. The dead forest was scarred with ragged, overlapping capital *C*s, some of them half a kilometer across. It looked as if somebody had tried to set a robot bulldozer on the pasture, to knock the dead wood down, but the dozer had suffered some weird variety of major software malf.

'How come all those mesquite trees are dead down there?' he said.

'Looks like herbicide.'

Martha shook her head. 'No, dude. Drought.'

'What the heck kind of drought can kill a mesquite tree?'

'Look, dude. If it doesn't rain *at all*, for more than a year, then *everything* dies. Mesquite, cactus, everything. Everything around this place died, fifteen years ago.'

'Heavy weather,' Buzzard said somberly.

Martha nodded. 'It looks pretty good right now, but that's because all this grass and stuff came back from seed, and this county has been getting a lot of rain lately. But man, that's why nobody can live out here anymore. There's no water left underground, nothing left in the aquifer, so whenever a drought hits, it hits *bad*. You can't water your stock, so the cattle die of thirst and you go broke, just like that.' Martha snapped her fingers. 'And you sure can't farm, 'cause there's no irrigation. Anyway, those new-style genetic crops with the chlorophyll hack, they need a lot of steady water to keep up those super-production rates.'

'I see,' Alex said. He thought it over. 'But there's plenty of grass growing wild out there now. You could still make some money if you drove cattle back and forth all over the rangeland, and didn't keep 'em all confined in one ranch.'

Martha laughed. 'Sure, dude. You could cattle-drive 'em up the old Chisolm Trail and slaughter 'em in Topeka, just like the old days, if they'd let you. You're not the first to think of that idea. But there's no free range anymore. The white man still owns all this land, okay? The range war is over, and the Comanches lost big time.'

'But the land's not worth anything to anybody now,' Alex said.

'It's still private property. There's still a little bit of money in the mineral rights and oil rights. Sometimes biomass companies come out and reap off the brush, and turn it to gasohol and feedstocks and stuff. It's all in state courts, all absentees and heirs and such, it's a god-awful mess.'

'We're trespassing right now,' Buzzard announced. 'Legally speaking. That's why the Troupe's got its own lawyer.'

'Joe Brasseur's a pretty good guy, for a lawyer,' Martha allowed tolerantly. 'He's got friends in Austin.'

'Okay,' Alex said. 'I get it with the legal angle. So what happened down there with the bulldozer? Somebody trying to clear off the pastureland?'

Martha and Buzzard traded glances, then burst into laughter.

'A bulldozer.' Buzzard chuckled. 'What a geek. A bulldozer. This kid is the tenderfoot dude wannabe geek of all time!' He clutched his shaking ribs below his black cotton midriff.

Martha pounded Buzzard's back with the flat of her hand. 'Sorry,' she said, controlling her smirk. 'Boswell gets like this somtimes . . . Alex, try and imagine a big wind, okay? A really, really, big wind.'

'You're not telling me that's a tornado track, are you?'

'Yeah, it is. About five years old.'

Alex stared at it. 'I thought tornadoes just flattened everything in their path.'

'Yeah, an F–4 or F-5 will do that for sure, but that was a little one, maybe F-2, tops. Those curves in the damage path, those are real typical. They're called suction spots. A little vortex that's inside the big vortex, but those suction spots always pack the most punch.'

Alex stared downhill at the broken path through the dead mesquite. He could understand it now: those overlapping C-shaped marks were the scars of some narrow spike of savage energy, a scythe embedded in the rim of a bigger wheel, slashing through the trees again and again as the funnel cycled forward. The twister had pulled dead trees apart and left their limbs as mangled, dangling debris, but the lethal suction spot had splintereened everything it touched, snapping trunks off at ground level, ripping roots up in dense shattered mats, and spewing branches aside as a wooden salad of chunks and matchsticks.

He licked dry lips. 'I get it. Very tasty . . . did you see this happen? Did you chase this one, back then?'

Martha shook her head. 'We can't chase 'em all, dude. We're after the *big ones*.'

Buzzard lifted his shades, wiped tears of laughter, and adjusted the cap on his sweating scalp. 'The F-6,' he said, sobering. 'We want the F-6, Medicine Boy.'

'Are we gonna find an F-6 today?' Alex said.

'Not today,' Buzzard said. 'But if there's ever one around, Jerry can find it for us.' He stepped into the back of the truck.

Alex stared, meditatively, at the twister's scarred track. Martha edged closer to him and lowered her voice. 'You're not scared now, are you?'

'No, Martha,' he said deliberately. 'I'm not afraid.'

She believed him. 'I could tell that about you, when they were stunting you in the ultralight. You're like your sister, only not so . . . I dunno . . . not so fucking classy and perfect.'

'Not the words I'd have chosen,' Alex told her.

'Well, about the F-6,' Martha confided quickly, glancing over her shoulder. 'The thing is – it's virtual. There's never been any actual F-6 tornado in the real-life atmosphere. The F-6 only lives in Jerry's math simulations. But when the F-6 hits, the Troupe will be there. And we'll document it.'

Buzzard emerged from the truck with a long bundle of spars and cloth and a thick spool of kite cable. He and Martha set to work. The kite was made of a very unusual cloth: like watered blue silk with flat plastic laths half-melted into the fabric. The plastic had an embedded grid of hair-thin ribs of wiring.

The two Troupers took such loving pride in assembling their box kite that Alex felt quite touched. He felt a vague urge to photograph them, as if they were ethnic exotics doing some difficult folk dance.

When they'd popped and snapped and wedged the box kite's various spars and crossbars into place, the kite was two meters wide. Martha had to steady it with both her hands – not because of its weight, which was negligible, but because of its eagerness to catch the wind.

Buzzard unreeled its cable then. The kite string looked very much like old-fashioned cable-television line. Buzzard anchored the kite's double guy wires to a specialized collar on the end of the cable, then carefully screwed the cable's end jack onto a threaded knob on the center of one hollow spar.

The kite suddenly leaped into eerie life and shook itself like a panicked pterodactyl. 'Yo!' Buzzard cried. 'Didn't you check the diagnostics on this sucker?'

'It's a bad boot, man,' Martha yelled, her slippers skidding in the dust as she fought the kite. 'Power-down!'

Buzzard jumped in the back of the truck and hit keys on the kite's laptop. The kite went dead again.

'Smart cloth,' Martha explained, shaking the kite with a mix of fondness and annoyance. 'Smart enough to screw up bad sometimes, but it's got lift potential right off the scale.'

'She's a good machine,' Buzzard hedged, rebooting the kite and patiently watching the start-up progressing on the screen. 'On a good day, you can float her off the thermal from a camp stove.'

The kite came to life again suddenly, thrumming like a drumhead. 'That's more like it,' Martha said. She carried the kite into the light prevailing breeze.

Buzzard clamped the kite's spool to the rear bumper of the truck and watched as Martha drew line out a dozen meters. 'Go!' he yelled, and Martha threw the big kite with an overhand heave, and it leaped silently into the sky.

The kite paid out line on its spool, with deft little self-calculated reelings and unreelings, until it caught a faster wind. It took on height quickly then, with deliberate speed, arcing and rearcing upward, in a neat set of airborne half parabolas.

'Smart cloth,' Alex said, impressed despite himself. 'That is very sweet . . . how many megs does she carry?'

'Oh, just a couple hundred,' Buzzard said modestly. 'It doesn't take much to fly a kite.'

Martha then took it upon herself to hack the ceramic blockhouse of the tower. The tower's stolid, windowless blockhouse looked practically indestructible, an operational necessity in an area practically abandoned. Alex had not seen any wasteland structure vandals yet: word was that the major gangs had been ruthlessly tracked and exterminated by hard-riding posses of Texas Rangers. He'd been assured, though, that there were still a few structure vandals around: looters, scavengers, burglars, hobbyist lunatics from out of the cities. They tended to travel in packs.

Martha established that the relay tower belonged to a bank: it was an electronic-funds-transfer cell. The fact that the cell was out in the middle of nowhere suggested that the funds under transference were not entirely of a state-sanctioned variety. She then began the tedious but largely automated process of figuring out how to use it for free. Almost all networks had some diplomatic recognition of other networks, especially the public-service kinds. If you brought up the proper sequence of requests, in the proper shelter of network identity, you could win a smaller or greater degree of free access.

In the meantime, Buzzard took out his ornithopters. These were hollow-boned winged flying drones with clever foamed-metal joints and a hide of individual black plastic 'feathers.' The three ornithopters could easily pass for actual buzzards at a distance. Provided, that is, that one failed to notice their thin extrudable antennas and their naked, stripped-metal heads, which were binocular videocams spaced at the width of human eyes.

It took a lot of computational power to manage the act of winged flight. Like most buzzards, the ornithopters spent much of their time passively soaring, wings spread to glide, the algorithmic chips in their wired bellies half shut down and merely sipping power. Only when they hit real turbulence would the 'thopters begin to outfly actual birds by an order of magnitude. The machines looked frail and dainty, but they were hatchlings of a military technology.

With the ease of long habit, Buzzard hooked the first ornithopter's breastbone to the notched end of a long throwing stick. He preened the machine's feathered wings back, then ran forward across the hilltop with the long hopping steps of a javelineer and flung the machine skyward with a two-handed over-the-shoulder whip of his arms.

The ornithopter caught itself in midair with a distantly audible whuff of its wings, wheeled aside with dainty computational precision, and began to climb.

Buzzard swaggered back to the rear of the truck, his throwing stick balanced over his shoulders and his long floppy hands draped over it. 'Fetch me out another birdie,' he told Alex.

Alex rose from his seat on the bumper and climbed into the truck. He detached the second ornithopter from its plastic wall clips and carried it out.

'What's that really big bundle next to the wheel well?' Alex said.

'That's the paraglider,' Buzzard said. 'We won't be using it today, but we like to carry it. In case we want to, you know, fly up there in actuality.'

'It's a *manned* paraglider?'

'Yeah.'

'Well, *I* want to fly it.'

Buzzard tucked the bundled ornithopter in the crook of his arm and pulled off his sunglasses. 'Look, kid. You got to know something about flying before you can ride one of those. That thing doesn't even have a motor. It's an actual glider, and we have to tow it off the back of the truck.'

'Well, I'm game. Let's go.'

'That's cute,' Buzzard said, grinning at him with a flash of yellow teeth. 'But your sister would get on my case. Because you would fall right out the sky, and be a bloody heap of roadkill.'

Alex considered this. 'I want you to teach me, then, Boswell.'

Buzzard shrugged. 'That's a big weight for me to pull, Medicine Boy. What's in it for me?'

Alex frowned. 'Well, what the hell do you want? I've got money.'

'Shit,' Buzzard said, glancing uphill at Martha, still hard at work accessing the tower. 'Don't let Martha hear you say that. She hates it when people try to pull money stuff inside the Troupe. Nobody ever offers us money who's not a geek wannabe or a goddamn tourist.' Buzzard stalked away deliberately, hooked his second bird to the throwing stick, and flung it into the sky.

Alex waited for him to return and handed him the third flier from the truck. 'Why does Martha have to know?' he persisted. 'Can't we work this out between us? I want to fly.'

''Cause she'd *find out*, man,' Buzzard said, annoyed. 'She's not stupid! Janey used to throw money around, and you shoulda seen what happened. First month Janey was here, she and Martha had it out in a major mega-scrap.'

Alex's eyes widened. 'What?'

'It was a brawl, man! They went at it tooth and nail. Screamin', punchin', knocking each other in the dirt – man, it was beautiful!' Buzzard grinned, in happy reminiscence. 'I never heard Janey scream like that! Except when she and Jerry are gettin' it on after a chase, that is.'

'Holy cow,' Alex said slowly. He metabolized the information. 'Who won?'

'Call it a draw,' Buzzard judged. 'If Martha had two real feet, she'd have kicked Janey's ass fer sure . . . Martha's skinny but she's *strong*, man, she can do those climber's chin-ups forever. But Janey's big and sturdy. And when she gets real excited, she just goes *nonlinear*. She's a wild woman.'

'Jerry let them fight like that?' Alex said.

'Jerry was out-of-camp at the time. Besides, he wasn't actually fucking Janey back then; she was just hanging around the Troupe, trying to buy popularity. She was being a pain in the ass. Kind of like you're being right now.'

'Oh.'

'I noticed Jerry took Jane a lot more seriously after that fight, though,' Buzzard mused. 'Got her started on the weight training and stuff . . . Kinda shaped Janey up, I guess. She acts better now. I don't think Martha would want to tangle with her nowadays. But Martha's sure not one of Janey's big fans.'

Alex grunted.

Buzzard pointed into the back of the truck. 'See those deck chairs? Set 'em up under the sunshade.'

Alex dragged the two collapsible deck chairs out of the truck. After prolonged study of their slack fabric supports and swinging wooden hinges, he managed to assemble them properly.

Buzzard launched his third ornithopter, then retreated into the cab of the truck. He emerged with a tangle of goggles, headphones, his laptop, and a pair of ribbed data gloves.

Buzzard then collapsed into his reclining chair, slipped on the gloves, the goggles, and the phones. He propped his elbows on the edge of the chair, extended his gloved fingers, wiggled the ends of them, and vanished from human ken into hidden mysteries of aerial telepresence.

Martha returned and collapsed sweating into the second deck chair. 'What a mega-hassle, man, banks are the most paranoid goddamn networks in the universe. I *hate* banks, man.' She shot Alex a narrow glare of squinting anger. 'I even hate *outlaw* banks.'

'Did you get through?' Alex said, standing at her elbow.

'Yeah, I got through – I wouldn't be sitting here if I didn't get through! But I didn't pull much real use out of that tower, so we're gonna have to depend on that relay kite or we'll be droppin' packets all over West Texas.' She frowned. 'Jerry's gonna give us shit when he sees how we ran down the batteries.'

'You'd think they'd at least give you some of their solar power,' Alex said. 'It just goes to waste otherwise.'

'Only a fuckin' bank would want to sell you sunshine,' Martha said bitterly.

Alex nodded, trying to please. 'I can hear those racks humming from here.'

Martha sat up in her chair. 'You hear humming?'

'Sure,' Alex said.

'Real low? Electrical? Kind of a throbbing sound?'

'Well, yeah.'

Martha reached out and poked the virch-blind Buzzard between the ribs. Buzzard jumped as if gun-shot and angrily tore off his goggles and phones.

'Hey, Buzz!' Martha said. 'Medicine Boy hears The Hum!'

'Wow,' Buzzard said. He got up from his chair. 'Here, take over.' He helped Martha out of the chair and into his own. Martha began wiping the phones down with a little attached Velcro pack of antiseptic tissues.

Buzzard fetched up his shades and cap. 'Let's get well away from the truck, dude. C'mon with me.'

Alex followed Buzzard as they picked their way down the western slope of the hill, down the dirt track. Off in the distance, a broken line of squat grayish clouds was lurking on the horizon. The approaching violent storm front, if that was indeed what it was, looked surprisingly unimpressive.

'Still hear the hum?' Buzzard said.

'No.'

'Well, *listen*.'

Alex strained his ears for half a silent minute. Insect chirps, a feeble rustle of wind, a few distant bird cries. 'Maybe. A Little.'

'Well, *I* hear it,' Buzzard said, with satisfaction. 'Most people can't. Martha can't. But that's the Taos Hum.'

'What's that?'

'Real low, kind of a wobbling sound . . . about thirty to eighty hertz. Twenty hertz is about as low as human hearing can go.' He spread his arms. 'Sourceless, like it's all around you, all around the horizon. Like an old-fashioned motor, or a fuel-burning generator. You can only hear it when it's really quiet.'

'I thought it was the solar rack.'

'Solar racks don't hum,' Buzzard told him. 'They hiss a little, sometimes . . . '

'Well, what is it?'

'They call it the Taos Hum, 'cause the first reports came out of

New Mexico about fifty years ago,' Buzzard said. 'That was when the first real greenhouse effects started kicking in. . . . Taos, Santa Fe, Albuquerque . . . then parts of Florida. Y'know, Jerry was born in Los Alamos. That's where Jerry grew up. *He* can hear The Hum.'

'I still don't understand what it *is*, Boswell.'

'Nobody knows,' Buzzard said simply. 'Jerry's got some theories. But The Hum doesn't show up on instruments. You can't pick up The Hum with any microphone.'

Alex scratched his stubbled chin. 'How d'you know it's really real, then?'

Buzzard shrugged. 'What do you mean, "real"? The Hum drives people nuts, sometimes. Is that real enough for ya? Maybe it's not a real sound. Maybe it's some disturbance inside the ear, some kind of resonant power harmonic off the bottom of the ionosphere, or something . . . Some people can hear the northern lights, they say; they hear 'em sort of hiss and sparkle when the curtains move. There's no explanation for that, either. There's a lot we don't understand about weather.' Buzzard clutched the lump of blackened metal on the leather thong around his neck. 'A *lot*, man.'

They stared silently at the western horizon for a long moment. 'I'm sending the 'thopters out to scan those towers,' Buzzard said. 'They're gonna break the cap by noontime.'

'You don't happen to have a spare pair of those shades, do you?' Alex said. 'This glare is killing me.'

'Naw,' Buzzard said, turning back toward the truck. 'But I got some spare virching goggles. I can put you under 'em and patch you in to the 'thopters. Let's go.'

They returned to the truck, where Martha was remotely wrapped in flight. Buzzard rummaged in a tool kit, then produced a pair of calipers. He measured the distance between the pupils of Alex's eyeballs, then loaded the parameters into a laptop. He pulled spare goggles and phones from their dustproof plastic wrap and sterilized them with a swab. 'Can't be too careful with virching equipment,' he remarked. 'People get pinkeye, swimmer's ear . . . in the city arcades, you can get head lice!'

'I got no chair,' Alex pointed out.

'Sit on some bubblepak.'

Alex fetched his bubblepak mat and sat on it, sweating. There was a faint hot wind from the southeast, and he couldn't call it damp, exactly, but something about it was suffocating him.

A lanky mosquito had landed unnoticed on Martha's virch-blinded arm and was filling its belly with blood. Alex thought of reaching over to swat it, then changed his mind. Martha probably wouldn't take a swat on the arm all that well.

'Here ya go,' Buzzard said, handing him the goggles. 'Telepresence is kind of special, okay? You can get real some somatic disturbance, 'cause there's no body sensation to go with the movement. Especially since you won't be controlling the flight. You'll just be riding shotgun with me and Martha, kinda looking over our wings, right?'

'Right, I get it.'

'If you start getting virch-sick, just close your eyes tight till you feel better. And for Christ's sake, don't puke on the equipment.'

'Right, I get it, no problem!' Alex said. He hadn't actually thrown up during his ultralight experience. On the contrary: he'd coughed up about a pint of blue goo from the pit of his lungs, then passed out from oxygen hyperventilation. He thought it was wiser not to mention this. If they thought it was merely vomit, so much the better.

Alex slipped the goggles on and stared at two tiny television screens, a thumb's width from the surface of his eyes. They were input-free and cybernetic blue, and the display had seen some hard use; the left one had a light pepper sprinkling of dead black pixels. He felt sweat beading on his goggle-smothered eyelids.

'Ready?' came Buzzard's voice from the distant limbo of the real world. 'I'm gonna leave the earphones off awhile so we can talk easier.'

'Yeah, okay.'

'Remember, this is going to be a little disorientating.'

'Would you just *shut up and do it*, man? You people kill me!'

White light snapped onto his face. He was halfway up the sky, and flying.

Alex immediately lost his balance, pitched over backward, and thunked the back of his head onto the hard plastic of the truck's rear tire.

Eyes wide, he squirmed on his back with his shoulders and heels and flung out both his arms to embrace the drifting sky. He felt both his arms fall to the bubblepak with distant thuds, like severed butcher's meat.

He was now soaring gut-first through space. The ground felt beautifuly solid beneath his back, as if the whole weight of the planet was behind him and shoving. The outline of distant clouds shimmered slightly, a hallucinatory perceptual crawl. Computational effects; when he looked very closely, he could see tiny dandruff flakes of pixel sweeping in swift little avalanches over the variants in color and light intensity.

'Wow,' he muttered. 'This is *it*. Mega, mega heavy . . .'

Instinctively, he tried to move his head and gaze around himself. There was no tracking inside the goggles. The scene before him stayed rock steady, welded to his face. He was nothing but eyeball, a numbed carcass of amputated everything. He was body-free . . .

He heard the squeak of the lawn chair as Buzzard settled into his own rig. 'You're on Jesse now,' Buzzard said. 'I'll switch you onto Kelly.'

The scene blinked off and on again, flinging him electronically from machine to machine, like a soundless hammer blow between the eyes.

'We're gonna climb now,' Buzzard announced. The machine began flapping soundlessly, with slow wrenching dips in the imagery.

'We want to get up to the cap,' Buzzard said. 'That's where the action is right now.'

'Gimme those headphones,' Alex demanded, stretching out one arm. 'I'll put 'em over just one ear.'

Buzzard handed him the headphone rig and Alex adjusted it by feel. The earphones had a little attached mouth mike, a foam blob on a bent plastic stick. Under his fumbling blind fingers, Alex's head felt unexpectedly huge and ungainly. His head felt like somebody else's head, like a big throw pillow upholstered in scalp.

With his ears secured beneath the pads of the earphones, Alex suddenly felt The Hum again, buzzing and tickling at the edge of his perception. The Hum was flowing right through him, some creepy rumbling transaction between the rim of outer space and planetary magma currents deep below. He strained his ears – but the harder he tried to hear The Hum, the less there was to perceive. Alex decided that it was safer not to believe in The Hum. He pulled the pad off his left ear. No more Hum. Good.

Then he began to hear the keening wind of the heights.

'We got ourselves a storm situation,' Buzzard announced, with satisfaction. 'What we got, is two air masses in a scrap. You listening, Alex?'

'Yeah.'

'That line of cloud dead ahead, that's the cutting edge of some damp hot air off the Gulf. It's wedging up a front of hot dry air coming off New Mexico. That dry air aloft – we're coming into that right now – that's the cap. Right now it's suckin' steam off the tops of those cumulus towers and strippin' 'em off flat.'

Alex understood this. He was gazing down across the tops of clouds, approaching them unsteadily on flapping digital wings. The climbing, bubbling sides of the heap were the normal cauliflower lumps, but the flattened tops of the towers looked truly extraordinary: great rippling plazas of turbulent vapor that were being simultaneously boiled and beaten.

The drone fought for more height for a while, then veered in a long panorama across the growing squall line. 'See how ripped up it looks, way up here?'

'Yeah.'

'That cap is working hard. It'll push all that wet air back today, west to east. But to work like that is costing it energy, and it's cooling it off some. When it cools, it gets patchy and breaks up. See that downdraft there? That big clear hole?'

'I see the hole, man.'

'You learn to stay away from big clear holes. You can lose a lot of height in a hurry that way . . . ' The drone skirted the cavernous blue downdraft, at a respectful distance. 'When these towers underneath us build up enough to erode through the cap and soar up right past us, then it's gonna get loud around here.'

The drone scudded suddenly into a cloud bank. The goggles swathing Alex's eyes went as white and blank as a hospital bandage. 'Gotta do some hygrometer readings inside this tower,' Buzzard said. 'We'll put Kelly on automatic and switch over to Lena . . . whoops!'

'The flying I like,' Alex told him. 'It's that switching that bugs me.'

'Get used to it.' Buzzard chuckled. 'We're not really up there anyhow, dud.'

The machine called Lena had already worked its way past the line of cloud, into the hotter, drier air behind the advancing squalls. Seen from the rear, the cloud front seemed much darker, more tormented, sullen. Alex suddenly saw a darting needle of aerial lighting pierce through four great mounds of vapor, dying instantly with the muffled glow of a distant bomb burst.

Thunder hammered at his right ear, under the earphone.

Martha's voice suddenly sounded, out of the same ear. 'Are you on Lena?'

'Yeah!' Alex and Buzzard answered simultaneously.

'Your packets are getting patchy, man, I'm gonna have to step you down a level.'

'Okay,' Buzzard said. The screens clamped to Alex's face suddenly went perceptibly grainier, the cascading pixels slowing and congealing into little blocks of jagginess. 'Ugh,' Alex said.

'Laws of physics, man,' Buzzard told him. 'The bandwidth can only handle so much.'

Now, belatedly, Alex's clear left ear – the one outside the headphones – heard a sudden muffled rumble of faraway thunder. He was hearing in stereo. His ears were ten kilometers apart. At the thought of this, Alex felt the first rippling, existential spasm of virch-sickness.

'We're running instruments off these 'thopters, too, so we gotta cut back on screen clarity sometimes,' said Buzzard. 'Anyway, most of the best cloud data is the stuff a human eye can't see.'

'Can you see *us* from up here?' Alex asked. 'Can you see where our bodies are, can you see where we're parked?'

'We're way ahead of the squall line,' Buzzard told him, bored. 'Now, over there south, lost in the heat haze – that's where the base camp is. I could see the camp right now, if I had good telescopics on Lena. I did, too, once – but that 'thopter caught a stroke of lightning, and fried every chip it had . . . a goddamn shame.'

'Where do you get that kind of equipment?' Alex said.

'Military surplus, mostly . . . depends on who you know.'

Alex suddenly felt his brain becoming radically overstuffed. He tore his goggles off. Exposed to the world's sudden air and glare, his pupils and retinas shrank in pain, as if ice-picked.

Alex sat up on his bubblepak and wiped tears and puddled sweat from the hollows of his eyes. He looked at the two Troupers, a-sprawl on their lounge chairs and indescribably busy. Buzzard was gently flapping his fingertips. Martha was groping at empty air like a demented conjurer.

They were completely helpless. With a rock or a stick, he could have easily beaten them both to death. A sudden surge of deep unease touched Alex: not fear, not nausea either, but a queer, primitive, transgressive feeling, like a superstition.

'I'm . . . I'm gonna stay out for a while,' Alex said.

'Good, make us some lunch,' said Buzzard.

ALEX MANAGED THE lunch and ate his share of the rations, too, but then he discovered that Buzzard and Martha wouldn't give him enough water. There simply wasn't water to spare. It took a while for this to fully register on Alex – that there just *wasn't water*, that water was a basic constraint for the Troupe, something not subject to negotiation.

The Troupe had an electric condenser back in camp that would pull water vapor from the air onto a set of chilled coils. And they had plastic distillery tarps too; you could chop up vegetation and strew it in a pit under the tarp, and the transparent tarp would get hot in the sun and bake the sap out of the chopped-up grass and cactus, and the tarp's underside would drip distilled water into a pot. But the tarps were clumsy and slow. And the condenser required a lot of electrical energy. And there just wasn't much energy to spare.

The Troupe carried all the solar racks that they could manage, but even the finest solar power was weak and feeble stuff. Even at high noon, their modest patches of captured sunshine didn't generate much electricity. And sometimes the sun simply didn't shine.

The Troupe also had wind generators – but sometimes the wind simply didn't blow. The Troupe was starving for energy, thirsty for it, and watchful of it. They were burdened by their arsenal of batteries. Cars. Trucks. Buses. Ornithopters. Computers. Radios. Instrumentation. Everything guzzling energy with the implacable greed of machines. The Troupe was always running in the red on energy. They were always creeping humbly back to civilization to recharge a truckload of their batteries off some municipal grid.

Energy you could beg or buy. But you couldn't hack your way around the absolute need for water. You couldn't replace or compress water, or live on virtual water or simulated water. Water was very real and very heavy, and a lot of trouble to make. Sometimes the Troupe captured free rainwater, but even a rainy year in West Texas never brought very much rain. And even when they did catch rainwater, they couldn't ship much water with them when they moved the camp, and the Troupe was always moving the camp, chasing the fronts.

It was simple: the more you wanted to accomplish, the less you had to drink.

Now Alex understood why Buzzard and Martha lay half-collapsed in their sling chairs beneath their sunshade, the two of them torpid as lizards while their eyes and ears flew for them. Sweat was water too. Civilization had been killed in West Texas, killed as dead as Arizona's Anasazi cliff-dweller Indians, because there just wasn't enough water here, and no easy way to get water anymore.

Alex stopped arguing and followed the lead of Buzzard and Martha by steadily tucking scraps of venison jerky into his mouth. It kept his saliva flowing. Sometimes he could forget the thirst for as long as ten minutes. They'd promised him a few refreshing mouthfuls every half hour or so.

The wind from the east had died. The smart kite's wiring, once taut and angular, now hung in the sky in a listless swaying curve. The wind had been smothered in a tense, gelatinous stillness, a deadly calm that was baking greased sweat from his flesh. The rumbles of distant western thunder were louder and more insistent, as if something just over the horizon were being clumsily demolished, but the unnatural calm around the aerodrome truck seemed as still and solid as the smothering air in a bank vault.

Alex squatted cross-legged on his bubblepak, mechanically chewing the cud of his venison jerky and wiping sweat back through his hair. As the heat and thirst and tension mounted, his paper suit was becoming unbearable.

The suit's white, plasticized, bakery-bag sheen did help with the heat some. It was a clever suit, and it worked. But in the final analysis, it didn't really work very well. His spine was puddled with sweat, and his bare buttocks were adhering nastily to the drop seat. His shoulder blades were caught up short whenever he leaned forward. And the suit was by far the loudest garment he had ever worn. In the tense stillness, his every movement rustled, as if he were digging elbow-deep through a paper-recycling bin.

Alex stood up, peeled the suit's front zip down, pulled it down to his waist, and crudely belted it around his midriff with its dangling white paper arms. He looked truly awful now, pallid, skeletal, heat-prickled, and sweaty, but the others wouldn't notice; they were virch-blind and muttering steadily into their mikes.

Alex left the sunshade and walked around the truck, sweat running in little rills down the backs of his knees.

He found himself confronting an amazing western sky.

Alex had seen violent weather before. He'd grown up in the soupy Gulf weather of Houston and had seen dozens of thunderstorms and Texas blue northers. At twelve, he'd even weathered the fringes of a fairly severe hurricane, from the family's Houston penthouse.

But the monster he was witnessing now was a weather event of another order. It was a thunderhead like a mountain range. It was piercing white, and dusky blue, and streaked here and there with half-hidden masses of evil greenish curds. It was endless and rambling and columnar and tall and growing explosively and visibly.

And it was rolling toward him.

A tower had broken the cap. It had broken it suddenly and totally, the way a firecracker might rupture a cheap tin can. Great rounded torrents of vengeful superheated steam were thrusting themselves into the upper air, like vast slow-motion fists. The dozens of rising cauliflower bubbles looked as hard and dense as white lumps of marble. And up at the top of their ascent – Alex had to crane his neck to see it – vapour was splashing at the bottom of the stratosphere.

Alex stood flat-footed in his plastic-and-paper shoes, watching the thunderstorm swell before his eyes. The uprushing tower had a rounded dome at its very top, a swelling blister of vapor as big as a town, and it was visibly trying to break its way through that second barrier, into the high upper atmosphere. It was heaving hard at the barrier, and amazingly, it was being hammered back. The tower was being crushed flat and smashed aside, squashed into long flattened feathers of ice. As the storm's top thickened and spread to block the sunlight, the great curdled uprushing walls of the tower, far beneath it, fell into a dreadful gloom.

It was a thunderstorm anvil. An anvil was floating in the middle of the blue Texas sky, black and top-heavy and terrible. Mere air had no business trying to support such a behemoth.

Lightning raced up the nimbus, bottom to top. First a thin, nervous sizzle of crazy brightness, and then, in the space of a heartbeat, one, two, three rapid massive channeled strokes of electrical hell, throwing fiery light into the greenish depths of the storm.

Alex ducked back around the truck. The thunder came very hard.

Buzzard tugged his goggles and earphones down, into an elastic mess around his neck. 'Gettin' loud!' he said cheerfully.

'It's getting *big*,' Alex said.

Buzzard stood up, grinning. 'There's a gust front comin' our way. Gonna kick up some bad dust around here. Gotta get the masks.'

Buzzard fetched three quilted mouth-and-nose masks from a stack of them in a carton in the truck. The paper masks were ribbed and pored and had plastic nose guards and elastic bands. Martha put her mask on and methodically wrapped her hair in a knotted kerchief. Buzzard shut the doors and windows of the truck securely, checked the supports of the sunshade, and tightened the strap of his billed cap. Then he put all his gear on again, and lay in the chair, and twitched his fingers.

All around the hill, little birds began fluttering westward, popping up and down out of the brush in a search for cover.

The searing light of early afternoon suddenly lost its strength. The spreading edge of the anvil had touched the sun. All the hot brilliance leached out of the sky, and the world faded into eerie amber.

Alex felt the cramp of a long squint easing from his eyelids. He put his mask on, tightly. It was cheap paper, but it was a good mask – the malleable plastic brace shaped itself nicely to the bridge of his nose. Breathing felt cleaner and easier already. If he'd known breathing masks were so easy to get, Alex would have demanded one a long time ago. He would keep the mask handy from now on.

Alex put his masked face around the corner of the truck. The storm was transmuting itself into a squall line, tower after tower

85

springing up on the mountainous flanks of the first thunderhead. Worse yet, this whole vast curdled mass of storms was lurching into motion, the mountainous prow of some unthinkably vast and powerful body of hot transparent wind. There was nothing on earth that could stop it, nothing to interfere in the slightest. It would steam across the grassy plains of Tornado Alley like a planetary juggernaut.

But it would miss them. The aerodrome truck was parked out of range of the squall line, just past the southern rim of it. The Troupers had chosen their stand with skill.

Alex walked into the open, for a better look. Off to the northwest, a patch of the squall's base had ruptured open. A dark skein of rainfall was slowly drifting out of it. Distant shattered strokes of lightning pierced the sloping clouds.

Alex watched the lightning display for a while, timing the thunderclaps and pausing periodically to swat mosquitoes. He'd never had such a fine naked-eye view of lightning before. Lightning was really interesting stuff: flickering, multibranched, very supple, and elaborately curved. Real lightning had almost nothing to do with the standard two-dimensional cartoon image of a jagged lightning bolt. Real lightning looked a lot more like some kind of nicely sophisticated video effect.

Out on the western horizon, the grass and brush suddenly went crazy. It bent flat in a big spreading wave. Then, it whipped and wriggled frantically in place. The grass seemed to be crushed and trampled under some huge invisible stampede.

A flying wall of dirt leaped up from the beaten earth, like the spew from a beaten carpet.

Alex had never seen the like. He gaped in astonishment as the wall of dirty wind rushed forward. It was moving across the landscape with unbelievable speed, the speed of a highway truck.

It rocketed up the slope of the hill and slammed into him.

It blew him right off his feet. Alex landed hard on his ass and tumbled through the spiky grass, in a freezing, flying torrent of airborne trash and filth. A shotgun blast of grit spattered into both his eyes, and he was blinded. The wind roared.

The gust front did its level best to strip his clothes off. It had his paper suit around his knees in an instant and was tearing hard at his shoes, all the while scourging him with little broken whips of airborne pebble and weed. Alex yelled in pain and scrambled on hands and knees for the shelter of the truck.

The truck was heaving back and forth on its axles. The fabric veranda flapped crazily, its vicious popping barely audible in the gusting howl.

Alex fought his way back inside the writhing, flapping paper suit, and he tunneled his grimy arms into its empty sleeves. His eyes gushed painful tears, and his bare ankles stung in the gust of dirt beneath the truck. The wind was very cold, thin, and keening and alpine. Alex's fingers were white and trembling, and his teeth chattered behind the mask.

More filth was gusting steadily beneath the truck. The dirty wind skirled harmlessly under the bottoms of the Troupers' sling chairs. Though Alex couldn't hear what they were saying, he could see their jaws moving steadily below their paper masks. They were still talking, into the little bent sticks of their microphones.

Alex trawled up his windswept virching gear as it danced and dangled violently at the end of its wiring. He jammed his back against the lurching truck and clamped the earphones on.

'Feels nice and cool now, doesn't it?' Buzzard commented, into Alex's sheltered ears. Buzzard's voice was mask-muffled and cut with microphone wind shrieks.

'Are you crazy?' Alex shouted. 'That coulda killed us!'

'Only if it caught us in the open,' Buzzard told him. 'Hey, now we're cool.'

'Carol's got circulation!' Martha said.

'Already?' Buzzard said, alarmed. 'It's gonna be a long day . . . Bring Jesse in for a chaff run, then.'

The violence of the gust front faded quickly, in a series of windy spasms. It was followed by a slow chill breeze, with a heavy reek of rain and ozone. Alex shivered, bunching his numbed fists into his paper armpits.

The insides of his virching goggles were full of windblown grit. Alex took his mask off, spat onto the screens, and tried to wash them clean with his thumbs.

Buzzard pulled his own goggles off and stood up. Something landed heavily on the stretched fabric of the veranda. Buzzard hopped to the edge of the veranda, jumped up, and snagged it: a landed ornithopter.

Buzzard brushed dust from his leotards and looked at Alex with ungoggled eyes. 'What the hell! Did you get caught in that gust front?'

'How do I clean these?' Alex said evasively, holding up the goggles.

Buzzard handed him an antiseptic wipe. Then he opened the back of the truck and ducked in.

He reemerged with a duffel bag and slammed the doors. The bag was full of reels of iridescent tape. Buzzard picked a patch of yellow stickum from the end of one reel and pulled at the tape. A section of shining ribbon tore lose in his fingers and fluttered in the breeze.

He handed it to Alex. 'Smart chaff.'

The chaff looked like old-fashioned videotape. Both ends of the tape were neatly perforated. The strip of chaff was as wide as two fingers and as long as Alex's forearm. It was almost weightless, but its edges were stiff enough to deal a nasty paper cut, if you weren't careful.

It had a lump embossed in one end: a chip and a tiny flat battery.

Buzzard screwed the axle of the chaff reel snug against the ornithopter's breastbone. Then he fetched his throwing stick again, walked out into the wind, and launched the machine. It rocketed upward in the stiff breeze, wings spread. 'We got a hundred strips per reel,' Buzzard said, returning. 'We deploy 'em through the spike.'

'What good are they?' Alex said.

'Whaddya mean?' Buzzard said, wounded. 'They measure temperature, humidity . . . and wind speed, 'cause you can track that chaff on radar in real time.'

'Oh.'

'Any little updraft can carry chaff.' Buzzard fetched up his virching rig. 'So chaff will stay with a spike till it ropes out. C'mon, virch up, dude, Greg 'n Carol have got circulation!'

Alex sat on his bubblepak. He pulled the back of the mat up and over his shoulders, like a blanket. The plastic bubbles of trapped air cut the chill wind nicely. He might have been almost comfortable, if not for the windblown filth clinging greasily to his sweat-stained face, neck, and chest. He put on his goggles.

In an instant Alex was miles away, on the wings of Lena, confronting a long white plateau of roiling cloud. Above the plateau, the great curling mountain of the thunderhead was shot through with aerial lightning.

Martha's ornithopter dived below the base of the cloud. The bottom of the thunderhead was steadily venting great ragged patches of rain. But the southern edge of the cloud base was a long, trailing dark shelf, slightly curved and free of any rain. Seen from below, the storm was charcoal black veined with evil murky green, leaden, and palpably ominous.

'How'd you get in place so fast?' Buzzard asked Martha.

Martha's voice dropped crackling into the channel. 'I caught the midlevel jet, man! It's like a goddamn escalator! Did you see that *lenticular* shit up there? The jet's peeling the front of that tower like a fuckin' onion!' Martha paused. 'It's *weird*.'

'There aren't any normal ones anymore, Martha,' Buzzard said patiently. 'I keep tryin' to tell you that.'

'Well, we might get an F-3 out of it, tops,' Martha diagnosed. 'That's no supercell. But man, it's plenty strange.'

Buzzard suddenly yelped in surprise. 'Hell!' I see what you mean about that midlevel jet . . . Damn, I just lost two strips of chaff.'

'Get your 'thopter's ass up here, man, that wall cloud is movin'.' Martha's Okie drawl thickened as her excitement grew.

'What exactly are we looking at?' Alex asked her.

'See that big drawdown at the base?' Martha told him. 'Between the flankin' line and all that rain? Look close and you can see it just now startin' to turn.'

Alex stared into his goggles. As far as he could tell, the entire cloud was a mass of indistinguishable lumps. Then he realized that a whole area of the base – a couple dozen lumps, a cloudy sprawl the size of four, maybe five football fields – was beginning a slow waltz. The lumps were being tugged down – powerfully wrenched and heaved down – into a broad bulging round ridge, well below the natural level of the cloud base. The lumps were black and ugly and sullen and looked very unhappy about being forced to move. They kept struggling hard to rise into the parent cloud again, and to maintain their shape, but they were failing, and falling apart. Some pitiless unseen force was stretching them into long circular striations, like gaseous taffy.

Suddenly a new voice broke in, acid-etched with a distant crackling of lightning static. 'Carol in Alpha here! We got dust whirl, over!'

'Nowcaster here,' came Jerry Mulcahey's calm voice. 'Give me location fix, over.' Good old Jerry, Alex realized, had the advantage of the Storm Troupe's best antennas. He seemed to be hovering over the battlefield like God's recording angel.

'Greg in Alpha here,' came Greg Foulks. 'How's the data channel holdin' up, Jerry, over?'

'Clear enough for now, over.'

'Here's your coords, then.' Greg sent them, in a digital screech. 'We gotta move, Jerry. That wall cloud's gonna wrap hard, and the truck's getting radar off a sheet of big-ass hail to northwest, over.'

'Then move behind the hook and get the array booted,' Jerry commanded. 'Report in, Aerodrome. Where's the chaff, over?'

'Boswell in Aerodrome,' Buzzard said, and though he was speaking from an arm's length away, his rerouted voice signal was unexpectedly thin and crispy. 'I got Jesse loaded and moving in hard on the jet stream, and Kelly coming out to Aerodrome to load a second reel, over.'

'Lena is right in position, now, Jerry, should I strafe that dust whirl for you, over?' said Martha.

'Beautiful, Martha,' Jerry told her, his deep voice rich with praise and satisfaction. 'Let me bring you up on monitor. . . . Okay, Martha, go! Nowcaster out.'

Martha's voice lost its static and settled again at the very edge of Alex's ear. 'You with me, little dude?'

'Yeah.'

'This is where it gets hairy.'

The ornithopter fell out of the sky, in a long slow dive. The wall cloud above them was much thicker now, though it didn't seem to be moving any faster. The 'thopter tilted, and Alex suddenly noticed a messy puff of filth, way down at ground level. The cloud of dust didn't seem to be spinning much. Instead, the dust cloud was spewing. It was clumsily yanking up thin dry gouts of ochre-tinted soil and trying to fling them aside.

Martha scanned the dust cloud, circling. Alex had never seen dirt behave in such an odd and frantic fashion. The dirt kept trying hard to fall, or spin loose, or escape just any old way back to the natural inertness of dirt, but it just couldn't manage the trick. Instead, whole smoky masses of the stuff would suddenly buckle and vanish utterly, as if they were being inhaled.

Then water vapor began to condense, in the very midst of the dry churning filth, and for the first time Alex fully realized the real shape, and the terrible speed, of the whirlwind. The air was being thrashed into visibility through sheer shock.

The infant tornado had a strange ochre-amber tint, like a gush of magician's stage smoke running backward in an antique movie reel. Some weird phase change, somber and slow and deeply redolent of mystery, was moving up the structure. Translucent bands of amber damp, and ochre filth, reeled slowly up the spike, silhouetting it against the sky and earth. It was very narrow at the bottom, growing broader and thicker with height . . .

Martha swooped in hard beside the tornado, in a complex banking figure eight, and she gained a lot of very sudden altitude. Alex winced with disorientation. Then he saw the top of the twister, dead ahead – the spinning wall cloud shoving thick vaporous roots slowly downward toward the earth.

The 'thopter dodged and leveled out, circling back. The twister's middle looked treacherously empty: a core of utter nothingness with a great black wall melting down from above, and a bottleneck of tortured dirt rising up. But then the wall's funnel moved down very suddenly, in four thick, churning, separate runnels of octopus ink, and it seized the little dust whirl and ate it, and the world was filled with a terrible sound.

The twister's howling had crept up on Alex almost without his notice. But now, as the twister reached its full dark fury, it began to emit a grotesque earthshaking drone. Even over the ornithopter's limited microphones, it seemed a very rich and complex noise, grinding and rattling and keening, over a dreadful organ-pipe bass note, a noise that crammed the ears, mechanical and organic and orchestral.

The funnel began to migrate. It grew steadily fatter, and it spun steadily faster, and it rolled forward fitfully, across the earth. There was nothing much for it to hurt here, nothing but grass and bushes.

Every bush it touched either disappeared or was knocked into tattered knots, but the tornado didn't seem to be damaging the grass much. It was casually tearing at the grass a bit, and leaving it flour-blanched with filth, but it wasn't drilling its way down through topsoil into the bedrock. It was just bellowing and screeching and humming to itself, in a meditative, utterly demonic way, deliberately rubbing the narrow tip of itself through the grass, like a migrating mastodon hunting for stray peanuts.

Martha was wheeling around the structure counterclockwise, keeping a respectful distance. On one pass, Alex caught a sudden glimpse of Pursuit Vehicle Alpha, sitting still behind the twister, shockingly close, shockingly tiny. It was only in glimpsing the Troupe's little pursuit machine that Alex realized the scale of what he was witnessing: the bottom of the twister had grown as wide as a parking lot.

As it reached full speed and size the twister grew livelier. It marched confidently up the gentle slope of a hill, in a brisk, alert fashion, with its posture straight and its shoulders squared. As it marched down the slope it put its whirling foot through the rusting wreckage of a barbed-wire fence. A dozen rotten cedar posts were instantly snapped off clean at the surface of the earth, tumbling thirty meters into the air in a final exultation of tangled rusty wiring.

The fence fell to earth again in a mangled yarn ball. The twister crossed a road in a frantic blast of dust.

Everything around Alex went silent and black. He thought that Martha's drone had been smashed, that he'd lost contact; but then he remembered that the natural color of a dead virching screen was blue, not black. He was seeing blackness: black air. And he could hear Buzzard breathing hard over audio.

'You're gonna want to see this, dude,' Buzzard told him. 'I don't do this every day. I'm gonna punch the core.'

'Where are we?'

'We're on Jesse, and we're right above the spike. We're up in the wall cloud.'

'We can't fly around in here,' Alex said. 'It's pitch-dark!'

'Sure, man. But Greg and Carol have their array up, and the Radar Bus is on-line. I just put ninety-seven chips of straff – hell! I mean *strips of chaff* – down this spike! Jerry's running the camp monitors flat out! We're gonna punch the core, dude! We're gonna go right down this funnel, live, real time, flyin' on instruments! Ready?'

Alex's heartbeat changed gears. 'Yeah! Do it!'

'There's no light inside the core, either. It's almost always pitch-black inside a twister. But Jesse has a little night-light – red and infrared. I dunno what we'll see, dude, but we'll see something.'

'Shut up and go!' Alex pressed the goggles against both eyes with the flats of his hands.

His head flooded with maxed-out roaring. Eerie red light bloomed against his eyeballs. He was shearing down the monster's tightened, spinning throat. The 'thopter trembled violently, a dozen times a second. Inside the twister's core, the wind was moving so fast that its terrible speed was oddly unfelt and unseen, like the spin of the earth.

Hell had a stucture. It had a texture. The spinning inner walls were a blurry streaky gas, and a liquid rippling sheen, and a hard black wobbling solid, all at once. Great bulging rhythmical waves and hollows of peristalsis were creeping up the funnel core, slow and dignified, like great black smoke rings in the throat of a deep thinker.

The 'thopter jerked hard once, harder again, then lost all control and punched the wall. All sound ceased at once.

The image froze, then disintegrated before Alex's eyes into a colored tangle of blocky video trails.

Then the image reintegrated and slammed back into realtime motion. They were outside the twister, flung free of it, tumbling through air with all the grace of a flung brick.

The 'thopter spread its wings and banked. Buzzard crowed aloud in the sudden silence. 'We just blew both mikes,' he said. 'Pressure drop!'

Alex stared into the screens pasted to his face. There was something very wrong with what he was seeing. He felt his eyes beginning to cross, with a complex headachy pang behind the bridge of his nose. 'What's wrong?' he croaked.

'A little alignment problem,' Buzzard admitted grudgingly. 'Not half-bad for a core punch, though.'

'I can't look at this,' Alex realized. 'I'm seeing double, it hurts.'

'Shut one eye.'

'No, I can't stand this!' Alex tore off the goggles.

The veranda was sitting in full sunlight again. The thunderstorm anvil had moved on to the northwest, leaving a trail of thin high cirrus clouds behind it, like a snail's slime track.

Alex stood up, walked past Buzzard and Martha's inert legs, and looked to the north. The entire squall line was receding rapidly, speeding off toward Oklahoma. Alex couldn't even see the tornado whose guts he'd just witnessed. It was either blocked from line of sight by nearer towers, or it was already over the horizon.

Behind the storm line, the air was cool and blue and sweet. The sky looked balmy and clear and full of gentle naïveté, as if tornadoes were all someone else's fault.

Alex walked back under the veranda, plucked up an antiseptic tissue, and started smearing filthy grease from his face and neck. His chest and neck and arms were reddened with little clotted nicks and wind whips, as if he'd tried to stuff a house cat inside his paper suit.

His eyes ached with dust and trapped sweat from the goggles. He was tired and dizzy and very thirsty, and his mouth tasted like gunmetal.

But nothing was bleeding. The scratches weren't serious. He was breathing beautifully. And he was having a really good time.

He sat down again and put on his virching rig.

Martha was circling the twister, with difficulty. The twister's spine had bent way off the vertical; its top was firmly embedded in the moving cloud base, but its tip was stubbornly dragging the earth, far to the rear. The forced stretching was visibly distressing it. The tip was badly kinked inside its corona of flying filth, and the wobbling midsection was flinging off long petulant tatters of dirt.

'You had to punch the goddamn core, didn't you,' Martha said.

'Yeah!' said Buzzard. 'I taped almost four seconds right down the throat!'

'You blew both mikes and you screwed the optics on Jesse, man.'

Buzzard was pained. 'Yeah, but there's no debris in that spike. A little dust, a little grass, it was real clean!'

'You pulled that dumb macho stunt just because you were late with the chaff!'

'Don't fuckin' start with me, Madronich,' Buzzard warned. 'I punched the core and the 'thopter still flies, okay? I'm not asking you to fly Jesse now. You can start flappin' your lips when *you* punch a core and come out in one piece.'

'Jerk,' Martha muttered.

Something very odd had happened to the earth in front of the twister. A huge patch of the ground was snow-white and visibly steaming. It looked volcanic. 'What the hell is that?' Alex said.

'That's hail,' Martha said.

'Cold hail with ground fog off it,' Buzzard said. 'Watch this baby suck it up!'

As the twister approached, streamers of icy fog buckled and writhed, caught up in torrents of suddenly visible ground flow. The tornado lurched headlong through the swath, sucking up torrents of chilly air from all directions, in a giant ragged overhead rosette of tormented fog.

The swatch of fallen hail was only a few dozen meters across. After half a minute the twister had cleared it. But wading knee-deep through the chilly air had visibly upset it. Its violent spew of filth at ground level dropped off drastically. Then it shivered top to bottom. The dry bands of filth around its midsection thinned and dimmed out. As the air grew clearer a pair of dense dirty runnels suddenly appeared within the spike, for all the world like a pair of stumbling, whirling legs.

'See that, dude?' Martha said triumphantly. 'Suction spots!'

The 'thopter nose-dived suddenly and was almost swept into the vortex. Martha careened free, yelping.

'Careful,' Buzzard said calmly. 'It's wrapped that downdraft real hard.'

The twister slowed, hesitated. Down at ground level, its overstretched tip elongated, kinked hard, and reluctantly broke off. The abandoned tip of the whirl vanished in a collapsing puff of liberated dust.

The amputated twister, stranded in midair, took a great pogo hop forward, centering itself under the cloud again. Then it tried to touch down again, to stretch out and rip the earth, but it was visibly losing steam.

The two suction spots, rotating about one another, stumbled and collided. The bigger leg messily devoured the smaller leg. There was a fresh burst of vitality then, and the twister stretched out and touched down, and a torrent of dirt rocketed up the shaft. But now the funnel was much narrower, thin and quick and kinky.

'It's ropin' out,' Martha said. 'I like this part. This is when they start actin' really insane.'

The twister had changed its character. It had once been a wedge, a vast blunt-nosed drill. Now it looked like a sloppy corkscrew made of smoke and string.

Big oblate whirling lumps were travelling up and down the corkscrew, great dirty onions of trapped vorticity that almost choked the life out of it.

Every few seconds one of the trapped lumps would blow out in spectacular fashion, spewing great ribbons of filth that tried to crawl up the cloud base. Sometimes they made it. More often they wriggled and spasmed and swam out into midair and vaporized.

The roped twister grew narrower still, so pinched at points along its length that it looked like a collapsing hose. The clear air around it was still in very violent motion, but no longer violent enough to be seen. The currents of air seemed to be losing cohesion.

The roping twister finally snaked its way into a sloppy, wriggling helix – it seemed to be trying to blend into some larger invisible vortex, to wrap itself around a bigger core and give up its fierce little life in exchange for large-scale wrath again.

But it failed. After that, it lost heart. It surrendered all its strength, in a ripple of disintegration up and down the shaft, a literal last gasp.

Martha methodically scanned the cloud base. The rotating wall cloud had broken. A great clear notch had appeared just behind it, a downdraft channeling cold air from somewhere near the stratosphere, chewing through the source of the vortex and breaking its rotation. The twister was dead and gone.

A light, filthy curtain of rain appeared, conjured up and sucked down by the twister's death spasm.

Martha headed out from under the cloud base into clear sunlit air. 'Seventeen minutes,' she said. 'Pretty good for an F-2.'

'That was an F-3 at maturity,' Buzzard objected.

'You wanna bet? Let Jerry check the numbers on that chaff.'

'Okay, F-2,' Buzzard backed down. 'It's still a little early in the day for a big one. How's Lena's battery?'

'Not good. Let's pull out, charge up the 'thopters, pull up stakes here, and head the hell after the dryline.'

'Good move,' Buzzard said. 'Okay, you and Medicine Boy break camp, and I'll fly the 'thopters in.'

'Have it your way,' Martha said.

Alex pulled off his gear. He watched Martha carefully divest herself of her equipment. She got up off the sling chair, stretched, grinned, shook herself, and looked at him. Her eyes widened.

'What the hell! Did you get caught in that gust front?'

'A little.'

Martha laughed, 'You're a real prize. Well, get up! We gotta pursue.'

'Wait a minute,' Alex said. 'You don't mean to tell me there's gonna be *another* one of those?'

'Maybe,' Martha said, deftly wrapping her gear. 'You've been lucky, for a first chase. Jerry's a good nowcaster, the best around, but he only hits a spike one chase out of two. Okay, maybe three out of five, lately . . . But' – Martha stood up straight, waving her black-nailed hand overhead with a lasso-tossing gesture – 'with this kind of midlevel vorticity? Man, we could log half a dozen spikes out of a front like this one.'

'Oh, man,' Alex said.

'Gotta get movin'. These spring squalls always move like a bat out of hell, they're doing fifty klicks an hour . . . We'll be lucky if we don't end up in Anadarko, by midnight.' She gazed down at Buzzard's inert carcass, seeming to resist a sudden urge to kick him out of his chair.

'Midnight?' Alex said.

'Hell yeah! 'Bout two hours after sundown, that's when nocturnal convection gives everything a fresh dose of the juice.' Martha grinned. 'Dude, you haven't really chased spikes till you've chased 'em in the dark.'

'Don't you people ever relax?' Alex said.

'Kid, we got all goddamn winter to relax. This is storm season.'

Alex thought it over. 'You got any salt tablets?'

CHAPTER

4

Normally, Jane didn't really mind Rick Sedletter. Normally, she got along with Rick Sedletter as well as any interface designer ever got along with any creep-ass techie code grinder. But this was not a normal day. The two of them had been on the road for hours, and she had Rick writhing on the hook of the patented Jane Unger Silent Treatment.

Both of them knew what the struggle was about: Alex. Jane was sure that Rick was already regretting his rashness in harassing her brother. But as the hours and kilometers wore on, Jane had plenty of time to dwell on her own recklessness in bringing Alex to the Troupe in the first place. He was already causing trouble, and that was nothing compared with what he might do. She had dire, recurrent visions of Alex hemorrhaging a spew of Mexican lung narcotics over the unsuspecting Martha and Buzzard.

She'd taken a big, stupid risk to rescue Alex, and his chances of success were so small. Suppose that Alex did make it through his first long hard day of road pursuit. Suppose that Alex got along in the Troupe, and somehow learned how to pull weight for the first time in his life without folding up and falling into little pieces. It would still do her very little good. She might very well have saved his life, but Alex would never be grateful about it, not in a hundred years.

Jane wondered if Alex had spared her even one thought all day – if it had even occurred to Alex to wonder how his sister was getting along. She very much doubted it.

Charlie emitted a not-entirely-necessary bell-and-whistle alert and extruded a map screen from the dash. It held Jerry's latest nowcast.

Rick stopped pecking at his laptop and pretended a lot of deep professional interest in the map's colored contours of upper-air velocity fields.

Rick was doing this just to get back at her. Both of them could see at a glance that nothing was tearing loose at the moment.

Outside, up to the north, lurked the trailing tower of the squall line, rippling in hot midafternoon sunlight and sucking hard for the adiabatic juice. Jerry had been sending them the full spectrum of regular updates: satellite overviews, the progress of the squall's pseudo-cold front, SESAME's wind-shear estimates, big bulging downpours of rain off the Dopplers. The front was gushing precip, dropping hail in big lemon-sized chunks, and blowing some impressive gust fronts. But there were no spikes.

The Troupe had scared up an F-2 early in the day. The spike had come very suddenly, and rather unexpectedly, and out in the middle of nowhere. And that was all to the good, because the Troupe had had the spike all to themselves. Greg and Carol had taped the entire development sequence, from wall cloud to rope-out, at close range from the ground. Buzzard and Martha had nailed it with chaff, so Peter and Joanne in the Radar Bus had got some very good internal data. That one had to be counted a success.

Now the afternoon's solar heat loading was reaching its peak, and the chances had improved for a major F-4 or F-5. The squall line was headed for the Texas-Oklahoma border, moving fast and dragging the midlevel jet with it. The chase situation would be a lot different now. As the Troupe pursued they'd be leaving the abandoned lands, reaching places where the aquifers were still patchily existent, and where a lot of people still actually lived.

Once they had come off the arid plains of King and Stonewall counties and into the great flat floodplain of the Red River, any spikes would be swarming with storm-chase spotters. There would be environmental feds from the national storm centers, and heavy network brass from SESAME. Local cops and firemen, maybe Rangers or Oklahoma National Guard. Television news crews. And amateur chaser wannabes, out on their own, with Christ only knew what kind of homemade equipment. Plus the usual ugly scattering of lurking creeps: wreck freaks, structure hitters, and professional looters.

Plus, of course, the people who were there because they couldn't help it: the everyday, poor damned civilians, trying to mind their own business until a spike tore their town apart.

The help would be the last to show up: choppers food-bombing the disaster area, ground convoys of federal rescue paramedics, bureaucrat refugee managers with their hard-ass official charity of soup-kitchen tents and paper clothes. Eventually, help would arrive, all right. You couldn't keep the government help away. After so many years of heavy weather, the help didn't have a lot of genuine compassion left, but they sure as hell had had a lot of practice.

'For Christ's sake, Janey, lighten up', Rick blurted suddenly. 'It's not like we killed the kid.'

Jane said nothing.

'He took that a lot better than you think!'

Before joining Jerry and the Troupe, Jane had never been much good at saying nothing. But Jane was plenty good at saying nothing now.

She'd had a lot of practice. She'd learned how to say nothing in her second month of Troupe life, after her ugly scream fest and punch-out with Martha Madronich. Jerry hadn't scolded her about the fight. He hadn't taken sides, or made judgments, or criticized. But he had asked Jane to take a formal vow of silence for a week.

Jerry's style as a leader never ran to the standard sicko cult practices of public chew-outs and group humiliations. Jerry rarely raised his voice to anyone, and even in the Troupe's formal powwows, he rarely said anything beyond short summaries and a few measured words of praise. However, Jerry truly excelled at mysterious private conferences. Before the fight, he'd never called Jane in for one of his heavy private head-to-head sessions. But she had seen him quietly take people aside – even the Troupe's hard-bitten core people, like Carol or Greg or Ellen Mae – and she'd seen them emerge an hour or so later, looking shaken and serious and kind of square-shouldered and glowing-eyed.

A vow of silence was a very weird request. But she had never seen Jerry more serious. It was crystal clear that he was giving her a deliberate challenge, setting her an act of ritual discipline. Worst of all, she could tell that Jerry really doubted that she had the necessary strength of charcter to go through with it.

So Jane had quickly made the promise to him, without any complaints or debate. She'd left the tent without a word, and for seven endless days she had said nothing to anybody. No talking, and no phone calls, and no radio links. She hadn't even typed commentary onto a network.

It had been unbelievably hard, far harder than she'd ever imagined. After several reflexive near blunders, she'd secretly kept her upper and lower teeth locked together with a little piece of bent metal pin. The bent pin was a stupid thing, and kind of a cheat, but it sure helped a lot whenever Martha limped by, grinning at her and trying to strike up conversations.

Silence had been truly painful and difficult for Jane. It had been like sweating off a drug addiction. Like fasting. Like running a marathon. It had changed her a lot, inside.

It was no secret to anyone in the Troupe that she deeply fancied Jerry, and she could tell that he knew, and that he was tempted. He'd let her join the Troupe. He'd trusted her with assignments. He'd always politely listened to her advice and opinions. But he'd been painfully scrupulous about keeping his hands to himself.

Jerry was tempted, but he wasn't quite tempted enough. That was the real reason he had set her the challenge. Like everything that really interested Jerry Mulcahey, the challenge was subtle and difficult and for big stakes. The rest of the Troupe might construe it as a punishment, but Jane knew better: it was a very personal trial, make or break. Jerry wanted her to make him a solemn promise and break it. So that he'd have the excuse he needed to politely usher her out of his life. And so she'd have no excuse not to go.

But Jane hadn't broken her promise. She'd kept it. Naturally, she had said nothing at all to anyone in the Troupe about her promise to Jerry. She'd simply walked out of the tent with her mouth shut. In the too close atmosphere of Troupe life, though, they had all very quickly caught on. Her vow had been a painful burden to her, but its effect on the other Troupers was profound and startling. She'd had their grudging respect before, but she'd never had their open sympathy. They knew she was going through hell, and they were pulling for her. By the end of her week of silence, all the Troupers were treating her, for the first time, as if she really belonged.

And after that happened, things between her and Jerry had

quickly turned very mega-different.

'Okay, so he passed out,' Rick whined. 'So he's not exactly the brawny outdoor type. Did you know he's a cannibal?'

'*What?*' Jane blurted.

'Yeah, he was bragging to us about eating human meat! Not that I myself got anything against cannibalism personally . . . ' Rick paused, hunting words. 'Y'know, there's something to that kid. He's kind of an ugly, weedy, crazy little guy, but I think he's got something going there. Actually, I kinda like him!'

'Look, he can't possibly be eating human meat,' Alex said. 'He's only twenty. Well, twenty-one.'

'Hell, we all knew he was bullshitting us! But that's why me and Peter had to stunt him. We're not gonna put up with that! Are we? So what if he's your brother? Come on, Janey!'

'Well, he *is* my brother, Rick, damn it.'

Rick slapped his laptop shut. 'Well, hell, you can't protect him from anything! The Troupe's not your day-care center! We're chasing tornadoes out here! Why'd you even bring your brother out here?'

'Well,' Jane said slowly, 'can you keep a secret?'

Rick's face fell. He looked at her guardedly. 'What is it?'

'I'm broke, Rick. And Alex isn't.'

Rick grimaced. She'd brought up the subject of money; the Troupe's ultimate taboo. From the look on Rick's round, stubbled face, he seemed to be in genuine spiritual pain. She knew he'd be too embarrassed to complain anymore.

Jane gazed thoughtfully at the twenty-thousand-meter thunderhead rising on the horizon ahead of her and wondered if there'd ever been a time when it was a whole lot of good clean fun to have money. Maybe back before heavy weather hit, back when the world was quiet and orderly. Back before the 'information economy' blew up and fell down in the faces of its eager zealot creators, just like communism. Back when there were stable and workable national currencies. And stock markets that didn't fluctuate insanely. And banks that belonged to countries and obeyed laws, instead of global pirate banks that existed nowhere in particular and made up their own laws out of chickenwire dishes, encryption, and spit.

Juanita Unger happened to be an heiress. If she'd been born a hundred years earlier, Jane thought, she might have been some very nice old-fashioned twentieth-century heiress. With family money from something quaint and old-fashioned and industrial and lady-like, like laundry soap or chewing gum. And if she'd happened to get a raging case of the hots for some scientist, then she could have set him up, like, a discreet foundation grant. And she could have driven out to his research site three times a week in her goddamned three-ton internal-combustion fossil-fueled car and fucked his brains out on a backseat the size of a living-room couch.

Maybe somewhere, somehow, sometime, some twentieth-century woman had actually done all that. If so, Jane bore her no real grudge. In fact, Jane kind of hoped that the twentieth-century heiress had really enjoyed herself as she thoughtlessly squandered the planet's resources and lived like a fattened barnyard animal. Jane hoped that it had all turned out okay for the woman in the end, and that she'd been nice and dead and buried before she realized what her way of life had done to her planet. It might have been a really sweet and tasty life, under the circumstances. But it sure as hell didn't bear any resemblance to life as Jane Unger had ever experienced it.

Jane was a Storm Trouper. A Trouper who happened to have money, and she'd never met anyone as resolutely antimoney as the Storm Troupe. They genuinely thought that they could survive on wreckage, scrap, grunge computers, fellow feeling, free software, cheap thrills, and Jerry's charisma. And given that their ideas of self-sufficiency were hopelessly impractical, they'd actually done surprisingly well. There was their repair work, and the occasional bit of salvage. Most of them held city day jobs during the winter, and some of them, herself included, even had the wreckage of once-promising careers. They scraped up some cash that way. And given that they were almost all city-bred urbanites, the Troupe did pretty well at eating things that they killed and/or pulled out of the ground.

But they weren't doing genuine, first-class research, because there wasn't enough capital around for real science, until Jane Unger had shown up.

Jane had first found Dr Gerald Mulcahey's work tucked in an obscure niche of a Santa Fe science network, very strange, very arcane, and elaborately smothered under nonlinear atmospheric mathematics that maybe five guys on the planet could understand.

Jane wasn't quite the first designer to discover Mulcahey's work. The word was just getting out about it in her network circles. The word was still very street level – but Jane had a good ear for the word.

The raw power of those graphics had amazed her. It was virtuoso spectacle, and the guy wasn't even trying. He'd created a hypnotic virtuality of writhing and twisting hallucinatory fluids while seriously attempting to scientifically describe the behavior of the real world. With the proper interface and editing, and a much better choice of color, angle, and detail, the work had definite commercial potential.

So Jane, with a bit of deft network voodoo, had successfuly tracked down Dr Gerald Mulcahey. She'd gone to his research camp out in the desolate ass end of nowhere, met him, talked to him, and cut a deal with him. She'd redesigned the graphics herself and released them with a new front end over an arts distribution network. And although the whole modern structure of copyright and intellectual property was a complete joke – it had been shattered utterly during the State of Emergency and never successfully reassembled or stabilized, by anybody, anywhere, ever – Jane had actually made some money from doing this. And she'd given Mulcahey royalties.

Of course Mulcahey had immediately spent all his royalties on new hardware. And then he'd spent her share of the money too. And then the two of them had gone on, in sweet, collegial fashion, to spend a lot more of her money.

And now all of her money was pretty much gone. Though they sure had a hell of a chase team assembled. She might even get all her money back, someday.

If they found the F-6.

Jane wasn't foolish enough to think that the Troupe would have the F-6 all to themselves. She'd seen Jerry's simulations, and if Jerry was even half-right about the nature of that beast, then the F-6 would be very damned obvious, a spectacular calamity impossible to miss. But if the Troupe found the F-6, they would have a major advantage over any other media competition. Because the Troupe would be the only people in the world who actually understood the full power and horror of what they were witnessing. Because nobody else in the world understood or believed that an F-6 was even possible.

'Rick,' she said.

'What?'

'I've decided to forgive you, man.'

'Oh.'

'On the condition you don't harass Alex ever again.'

'Okay, okay,' Rick said sourly. 'He can stay for all of me. You never see *me* throw anybody out of the Troupe! Jerry throws people out, Greg throws people out, Carol throws people out. Me, I'm just a lowly code geek, I can put up with anybody. I don't even care if he gives me money – hell, I'm not proud. Go ahead, give me money, you *and* your brother! I don't care.'

'Did you know Jerry has a brother?'

'Yeah, I knew that,' Rick said. Rick didn't seem much surprised by the change of subject. 'I never met his brother or anything . . . I think he's in government, state department, military, something like that. He and Jerry don't get along.

'Did Jerry ever talk about his brother, before I showed up?'

'Well, you know Jerry,' Rick said. 'He doesn't exactly broadcast that kind of stuff . . . I did hear the subject come up, though, back when he was breaking up with Valerie. That was Valerie the seismographer, y'know.'

'I know about Valerie,' Jane said tightly.

'Yeah,' Rick said, with an oblivious nod, 'Val was into, like, aquifer collapses and subsidence and stuff, she used to hang with the Troupe and do echo blasts . . . Not much to look at, but a really bright girl, really sharp. It got pretty ugly toward the end before Jerry threw her out. She kept carryin' on about his family.'

'Oh really,' said Jane, with her best pretense of tepid disinterest.

'Yeah!' The long hours of silence had bottled Rick up. 'It's funny what men and women argue about . . . I mean, I've never been married, but from what I see it's like three basic things – sex, money, and commitment. Right?'

Jane said nothing.

'So with Valerie it was commitment. Like, what do you care about more – me or your work, me or your friends, me or your family, me or your brain? I can't figure out why a woman would ever want to ask Jerry that. The guy's obviously a fanatic! He's never gonna rest till he finds what he's looking for! A guy like that, either you pitch in and help him, or you get the hell out of his way! Otherwise, you're just gonna get stepped on. It's like a law of nature.'

Jane said nothing.

Rick adjusted his glasses, and spread his hands expansively. He was wearing a pair of deerskin carpal tunnel wraps on his sunburned forearms. 'I can understand,' he said, 'intellectually speaking of course – why a woman would find Jerry attractive. I mean, he's big and strong, and he's a good-looking guy in his way, and he's *really* smart. And he's not mean, or dishonest. *Ruthless*, sure, but he's not cruel. And he's got, like, pretty serious outlaw sex appeal, because he's the stud duck of this gang of weirdos who follow him around. Women tend to go for that kind of guy. So I can see why some woman would want to ride on the back of Jerry's motorcycle and share his sleeping bag. But hell! Marry him? Have his kids? Try and put him behind a picket fence? What possible good could that do you? I mean, why even try?'

Jane laughed.

'You can laugh, Janey,' Rick said, 'but that's what Valerie was up to. I don't think she ever realized it. I mean, consciously. It was pure genetic imperative, that's what. Some kind of female chromosome thing.'

Jane sighed. 'Rick – you are the prize asshole of all time.'

'Oh,' Rick said, shocked. 'Okay. Sorry.'

'I don't want him to marry me. I don't have a picket fence. I don't want to take him away from the Troupe. I *like* living with the Troupe. It really suits me. It's my Troupe.'

'Sure, okay,' Rick said nodding hastily. 'I never meant you, Janey. You should know that by now.'

'I want the F-6 for my own reasons. And even if Jerry drops down dead, then *I'm* gonna find it. And I'm gonna chase it down and document it and blow the data over every network on this planet. Okay?'

'Okay, Janey.' Rick grinned. 'Have it your way.'

'You never talked to this brother of his, right?'

'No. I don't even know where he is. But if I wanted to find out' – he looked at her – 'I guess I'd start by asking Jerry's mom.'

THEY GOT SPIKES just east of the Foard County line, off State Highway 70. Both sides of the highway were lined with parked spotter vehicles: cops, meandering amateurs with cheap binoculars and hand cams, a monster SESAME lidar bus with tuned lasers and a rack of parabolic arrays.

SESAME and the Troupe's own Radar Bus had both been showing a major circulation hook for almost an hour, and the word was out on the police bands and the public weather alerts. So far, though, there was no visible wall cloud, and the rain-free shelf looked surprisingly cramped and unpromising.

Then, at 17:30, two spikes made a simultaneous appearance; not in the front pocket inside the hook, where they might have been expected, but wriggling off the back of the storm.

Rick picked up the first alert by nicking it off the air traffic of a surprised and excited TV crew. He immediately spread the word to the Troupe and booted the binocular cameras on Charlie's front weapons mount.

Given the chance, Troupers in ground pursuit would anticipate the path of moving spike, getting ahead of it and to the right, so as to silhouette the approaching spike against brighter air. The ideal was to set up a series of target grids of intense, networked instrumentation and have the spike wander through the grids. This was the standard research strategy for the clearest, full-capacity data collection, and the SESAME people with their computational heavy iron probably had much the same idea.

That wouldn't be possible with these new twin spikes, though. Their position off the back of the storm put them right behind a moving wall of hail.

Jane gleefully showed the amateurs what they were up against by ordering Charlie into unconventional mode and leaving the highway entirely in a hot, fence-jumping, cross-country pursuit. The car bounded across a drenched pasture full of young sunflowers and knee-high johnsongrass. The binocular cameras, mounted on their own reactive pedestal, moved along with a rock-solid technological smoothness originally invented for modern fifty-caliber machine guns. Jane's nerves sang with anticipation. She was going where she loved to be: into the thick of it. Alert, alive, and in danger.

Spikes were very dangerous. They carried extremely high winds and often flung large, lethal chunks of debris. But the funnel wasn't the greatest danger in a pursuit. A modern pursuit vehicle could amost always dodge a visible funnel that was already on the ground. The greatest real dangers to the Troupe were big hail, lightning, and collisions.

Hail swaths were hard to predict, and they covered a lot more ground than the tip of a spike. Most hail was only nuisance hail, sleety or mushy or pebbly, but Jane had personally chased storms that dumped rock-solid hail the size of citrus fruit into heaps that were shin-deep.

Big hail didn't fall the way rain or snow or little graupel hail would fall. Big hail fell like jagged-edged lumps of solid ice dropped from the height of a three-thousand-story building. In the Oklahoma Panhandle, in the spring of 2030, Jane had been hit in the ribs by a hailstone that had put her in unguent and elastic wrap for a solid week. That same storm had caught two of the Troupe's early dune buggies and left them measled with hundreds of fist-sized dents.

Hail could be dodged, though, if you stayed out from under the mass of the storm and kept a wary eye on the radar. Lightning was different. There was no dodging lightning; lightning was roll-of-the-dice. In her pre-Troupe days, Jane had heard the usual pious civil-defense nonsense about staying away from exposed heights and throwing yourself flat if you felt your hair start to crackle, but she had seen plenty of no-kidding lightning since, and she had a firm grasp of its essential nature. Lightning was a highly nonlinear phenomenon. Most lightning sizzled along pretending to obey the standard laws of physics, but Jane had often seen even quite minor storms suddenly whip out a great crackling lick of eccentric fury that blasted the hell out of some little remote patch of ground that had absolutely nothing to do with anything. Lightning was crazy stuff, basically, and if it happened to hit you, there was damn-all you could do about it.

As for collisions, well, Charlie was a mega-sweet machine, but he ran on eight hundred and seventy-five million lines of code. Good code, solid, well-tested code, spewed through distributed parallel processors far swifter and more accurate than the nervous system of any human driver. But code was still code, and code could crash. If the code crashed when Charlie was number-crunching high-speed all-terrain pursuit, then crashing Charlie would be the same as crashing any precybernetic car: fast hard stupid metal versus soft wet human flesh.

They rounded a heavily knuckled wall of back shear and saw two spikes curling out of the back of the nimbus shelf like a gigantic pair of curved antelope horns. The twin spikes were fantastically beautiful, and they filled Jane with a deep sweet sense of gratitude and awe, but they looked like F-2s, tops. It was rare to get a really heavy spike off an unorthodox part of the storm.

With the target in sight, Charlie put his code to serious work and got a lot closer in a very short time. Suddenly the chill damp air around them was full of the Train. Only a tornado could do the Train. Once you'd heard the Train you would never forget or mistake it.

Jane loved the Train. That elemental torrent of noise hit something inside her that was as deep and primal and tender as the pulp of her teeth. It did something to her that was richer than sex. A rush of pure aesthetic battle joy rocketed up her spine and she felt as if she could jump out of her skin and spread wings of fire.

'Which one do you want?' she shouted at Rick.

Rick pulled up the rubber-rimmed lenses of the binocular videocam's goggle link. Without his glasses, his eyes looked crazed and dilated and shiny. 'Go for the first to touch down!'

The horn on the right looked like the dominant one of the pair. To judge by the complex curdling of the shelf behind them, the two spikes were trying hard to go into slow orbit around one another. Rick's advice was sound: the first spike to touch down would likely get a better supply of updraft. Over the next few minutes the twin with more juice would probably starve out and eat up the other one.

But you could never tell. Spikes lived on the far side of turbulent instability and sometimes the least little extra puff of energy would push them off trajectory into a monster phase space . . . Jane was coming hard to the point of decision. She slowed the car and stared upward.

'Damn!' she yelled. 'That left one's backward!'

'What?'

'It's anticyclonic! Look at that damn thing spin!'

Rick swung his head, moving the slaved cameras out on the bumper. 'Good Christ!' he said. The spikes were rotating in opposite directions.

It was hard to judge the vortex rotation against the curdled black background of shelf, but once she'd recognized the movement, there was no mistaking it. Jane was flabbergasted. There hadn't been an anticyclonic spike documented since the late nineties. Finding a storm spinning clockwise in the northern hemisphere was freakish, like seeing a guy running down the street who happened to have two left feet.

'We're following that crazy one!' Jane announced. She reached beneath the seat and yanked up a pair of cordless headphones and mike.

'Good choice!' Rick said, his voice high with disbelief.

Jane yelled orders to Charlie, got tired of the verbal interface, and pulled down the steering wheel. She got into a manual-assist mode, where a tug on Charlie's steering wheel was the software equivalent of a tug on a horse's reins. This was an excellent way to pursue a storm, if your horse was a smart machine a thousand times stronger and faster than you were. Excellent, that is, if your horse didn't get its code hung between mode changes. And if you didn't forget that you weren't really driving a car at all, but instead, vaguely chairing a committee on the direction, speed, and tactics of the vehicle. It was certainly vastly safer than driving manually in the wake of a pair of tornadoes. But it was still a really good way to get killed.

Rick yelled a site report at the Troupe while bracketing the anticyclone with the camera's binocular photogrammetry. Jane thought anxiously about the chaff bazooka in the back. The bazooka's chaff rounds cost so damned much that she had never had enough practice to get good with it. Rick, unfortunately, considered himself an excellent marksman, as if it were a real feat to kill deer with a silent, high-velocity, laser-sighted electric rifle. Rick was lousy with the bazooka and overconfident, while she was lousy with the bazooka but at least properly cautious about it.

She punched Rick's shoulder. 'Where's the 'thopters?'

'They're coming. It'll take a while.'

'I gotta chaff-shoot that anticyclonic from the ground then,' she said.

'No use, Janey! Radar Bus just pulled up stakes, nobody'll get the data but SESAME!'

'Let SESAME get it then, we gotta nail it now, the goddamned thing is left-handed! It's for Science!' She stopped Charlie in the middle of the field, opened the door, and leaped out into wet knee-high grass.

Out from under the shelter of Charlie's roof, the sound of the Train was enormous, ground-shaking, cosmic. Jane ran around the car, burrowed into the back, and unstrapped the bazooka from its Velcro mounting. No use looking up at the spikes just yet. No use getting rattled.

She found the chaff rocket, unstrapped it. Removed its yellow safety tape. Twisted the rocket to arm it. Put up the bazooka's flip-up sight. Powered up the bazooka. Booted the bazooka's trajectory calc. Charlie was vibrating in place with the sheer noise of the Train, and violent gusts of entrained updraft were ripping at the grass all around her.

Loading the chaff bazooka was a very complex business. There was a very sweet and twisted intellectual thrill about doing it exactly right in conditions of intense emotional excitement. It was like paying a lot of slow, deliberate, very focused attention to giving somebody else an orgasm.

Jane stepped out into the open, carefully braced her legs, raised the muzzle, and squinted into the bazooka's readout. She pressed the first trigger. A red light came on. She bracketed the twister in the target screen. The red light went out and a green light flicked on. Jane pulled the second trigger.

The rocket took off with a calf-scorching backwash of heat and soared directly toward the spike. It made a couple of wasplike dips as it fought turbulence and it disappeared right into the spinning murk, not quite dead on, but good. Jane stared happily into the readout, waiting for the detonation signal from the chaff's explosive canister.

Nothing. She waited.

Nothing. Another goddamned dud.

Jane lowered the smoking bazooka with a grinding disappointment and suddenly noticed movement and color over to her right. A spindle-wheeled TV camera truck had pulled just to the right of them, maybe ten meters away. A woman correspondent with a head mike and a darling little brass-toggled yellow raincoat had jumped out. She was doing a stand-up.

Not in front of the tornadoes, though. In front of Jane.

Jane was on live television. The realization gave Jane a sudden rush of deep irrational fury. It was all she could do to avoid swinging the muzzle around and threatening to blow the journos away, just to watch the sons of bitches run. The bazooka was empty, though, and she had no more chaff rounds, which was just as well, because otherwise they and their human-interest spot would have been structure-hit to blazing hell-and-gone. Jane flinched away from their cameras and gritted her teeth, and set the bazooka back in place with meticulous professionalism, and ran around the car and got back in and slammed the door.

'That was great!' Rick shouted. 'Damn, Janey, you're good with that thing!'

'It was a dud round,' Jane shouted back.

'Oh! Shit.'

Jane turned on the noise cancellation in her headphones. The Train vanished suddenly, its every sonic wavelength neatly canceled by a sound chip inside the earphones. The echoing roar was replaced by an eerie, artificial, oddly wet-sounding silence, as if she'd thrust her head into a big hollowed-out pumpkin.

When Rick shouted at her once again, his voice was a flat filtered drone. 'We just got dust whirl on that right one! We're gonna lose the anticyclonic.'

'I figured,' Jane murmured, her voice loud in her own ears. Rick lifted his goggles, realized she had her noise-cancellation headphones on, nodded in appreciation, fetched up his own headphones from beneath the passenger seat, and clamped them over his ears.

'Can't tag 'em all,' Rick uttered wetly through the phones. 'I'm gettin' some real good photogrammetry, though. Move up closer on that left one.'

The right-hand spike was on the ground now, trying to stabilize. It was tearing through a patch of high grass a kilometer away, slewing a blur of dirt and straw. No major debris yet, but that straw was no joke; tornado straws were flying high-speed needles that could pierce boards and tree trunks.

She urged Charlie into pursuit again, avoiding the right-hand spike and drawing nearer to the anticyclonic twister. It had not touched down yet, and didn't seem likely to. The backward twister was being dragged off behind the front, in the shadow of its bigger brother, kicking and wriggling in distress.

Twisters were not living things. Twisters had no will or volition, they felt no joy or pain. Truly, really, genuinely, tornadoes were just big storms. Just atmospheric vortices, natural organizations of rapidly moving air that blindly obeyed the laws of physics. Some of those laws were odd and complex and nonlinear, so their behavior was sometimes volatile, but twisters were not magic or mystical, they obeyed laws of nature, and Jerry understood those laws. He had patiently demonstrated their workings to her, in hours and hours of computer simulation. Jane knew all that with complete intellectual certainty.

And yet Jane *still* couldn't help feeling sorry for the anticyclonic. That mutant left-handed runt of the litter . . . the poor damned giant evil beautiful thing . . .

The right-hand twister left the ground, bunched itself, and suddenly made a major and definite maneuver. It ripped loose from its original moorings at the back of the storm and surged forward, root and branch. The whole structure of the cloud base collapsed before it like a shattered ceiling and was torn into foggy chaos. The trailing bent tail that was the anticyclonic buckled, and dwindled, and was sucked away.

A blinding torrent of almost horizontal rain blasted across the landscape. The spike vanished behind it.

Jane immediately wheeled and started to skirt the right-hand edge of the storm. Working her way around it took her twelve long minutes of high-speed pursuit and a painful drain of battery power. On the way they passed a charging land rush of three TV camera crews, five groups of amateur spotters in their rusty ham-hacker trucks, and two sheriff's deputies.

The sky was low and overcast ahead of the twister, an endless prairie of damp unstable Gulf air, tinder before a brushfire. When Jane caught sight of the spike again, it was a squat, massive, roaring wedge, lodged right in the pocket of the circulation hook and smashing northeast like a juggernaut. She turned off her monitor to the ongoing SESAME traffic and opened her mike and headphones to the general Troupe channel. 'Jane in Charlie here. We have the spike in sight again! It's a mega F-4 on the ground and in the hook! This one could go all the way, over!'

'This is Joe Brasseur at Navigation. Copy, Jane. Your spike has habitation ahead – Quanah, Texas. Chasers, watch for fleeing vehicles! Watch for civilians! Watch for debris in the air or on the ground! Remember, people, a spike is a passing thing, but a lawsuit you always have with you. Over.'

It was really nice, what the people of Quanah had done. You met all kinds out on the edge of the wasteland, most of them pretty unsavory kinds, but the citizens of Quanah were a special breed. There were just over three thousand of them. Most of them had settled here since the aftermath of heavy weather. They were hard and clever and enduring people, and they had a kind of rough-hewn civic virtue that, in all sincerity, you could only call pioneer spirit.

They didn't irrigate open fields anymore, because with their aquifer declining that was illegal as well as useless. But they had genetic crops with the chlorophyll hack, and they'd done a great deal with greenhouses. Enormous greenhouses, beautiful ones, huge curved foam-metal spars and vast ribbed expanses of dew-beaded transparent membrane, greenhouses as big as cornfields, greenhouses that *were* their cornfields, basically. Vast expanses of well-designed, modern, moisture-tight greenhouses, pegged down tight and neat across the landscape just like a big sheet of giant bubblepak.

The F-4 walked into the midst of the greenhouse bubbles and methodically wreaked utter havoc. It simply stomped the big pockets of bubblepak and catastrophically ruptured them, with sharp balloon-pop bangs that you could feel in your bones from a mile away. The acres of damp air inside the ruptured bubbles geysered instantly upward in fat twisting rushes of condensation fog, and before Jane's amazed, observant eyes, the F-4 literally drank up those big sweet pockets of hot wet air, just like a thug at a bar doing tequila slammers.

It ripped every greenhouse in its path into flat deflated tatters, and it entirely destroyed all the crops inside them.

The citizens of Quanah were not just farmers. They were modern bioagriculturists. They had set up a silage refinery: stacks, towers, fermentation chambers. They were taking the worst harvest in the world: raw weed, brush, mesquite, cactus, anything – and cracking it into useful products: sugars, starches, fuel, cellulose. Silage refining was such an elaborate, laborious process that it was barely profitable. But it made a lot of honest work for people. And it made some honest use out of the vast expanse of West Texas's abandoned wasteland. Silage refining came very close to making something useful and workable out of nothing at all.

The F-4 waded into the silage refinery and tore it apart. It picked up the pipelines, snapped them off clean at the joints, and wielded them like supersonic bludgeons. It twisted the refinery towers until they cracked off and tumbled and fell, and it threw a hot spew of gene-twisted yeast and fungi into a contaminating acres-wide slop. It blew out windows, and ripped off roofs, and cracked cement foundations, and shorted out generators. It swiftly killed three refinery workers who had been too stubborn and dedicated to leave. After the twister had shattered half the refinery and broken the rest open, its ally the rain arrived, and thoroughly drenched everything that had been exposed.

The twister then chewed its way through Quanah's flat checkerboard of streets, smashing homes and shops, destroying the ancient trees around the courthouse, and annihilating a dance hall.

When it had finished with the town of Quanah, Texas, the twister headed, undiminished, toward the Red River, and the people of the great state of Oklahoma.

WHEN JANE GOT back to the camp, it was five in the morning. She'd managed to sleep a little in the driver's seat during the long haul back, but she was far too full of adrenaline for anything like real rest.

She drove the car under one of the camp's garage tents and prodded Rick awake. Rick got up groggily without a word and staggered off for his tepee.

Jane walked stiff-legged and trembling into the command yurt. There was no sign of Jerry, and all his machines were shut down.

She went to their favorite tepee, the one they usually used for assignations.

Jerry was on the bubblepak floor in a bag, asleep.

Jane threw her sweaty clothes off and fought her way into the bag next to him.

'You've got the shakes,' he told her.

'Yeah,' Jane said, trembling harder to hear him say it. 'I always get the shakes whenever they kill people.'

'Nothing we can do about that,' he said gently. 'We just bear witness.'

Jane stared up at the tepee's dark conical recess. She could see stars through the smoke flap. She was stiff all over and trembling with stress and she smelled really bad.

'My life sure has changed since I met you . . .' she said, 'you crazy son of a bitch.'

Jerry laughed and put his hand on her right breast. 'Yeah?'

'That's right. I've seen people get killed . . . I've raced down highways at two hundred klicks an hour. I've jumped out of airplanes. I climbed up a radio tower and I jumped off it, and I beat up the woman who taught me how to do it.'

'You didn't beat her up very hard,' Jerry said. He slid his bearded face into the hollow of her neck.

Jane started trembling much harder. 'Just once,' she told him, 'I'd like to fuck you in a bed. With a mattress, and clean sheets. When we've both showered. And me wearing something slinky and maybe some perfume. Don't you like that, Jerry? Perfume?'

'What I like is remembering where the condoms are. Where are they?'

'They ought to be tucked over there under that ditty bag, unless somebody used 'em all.'

Jerry climbed out of the bag, naked, found a condom after prolonged search, and crawled back into the bag again. His skin had gone cold in the night air. Jane shivered violently.

Jerry turned her onto her stomach and set his solid hands to work on her shoulders. 'You've got it bad tonight,' he said.

She nodded. 'That's good. Keep doing that. Maybe I'll live.'

Silently, deftly, Jerry worked his way off her shoulders, down her spine and rib cage, going after knotted nerves that were like snarled fishline. It felt so good to have the strong human touch of someone she trusted. Someone who wouldn't stop or hesitate, who knew what he was doing and who had never hurt her. He was pulling the jitters out of her, and it was like he was chasing little devils out of her skin. Jane stretched out on her stomach and went languorous and heavy-lidded.

She turned over and stretched her arms out in welcome. He kissed her briefly, put the condom on, climbed over her, braced himself on his elbows. He slid into her all at once on an oiled film of latex.

She put her feet in the backs of his knees. 'Short and sweet, okay,' she whispered. 'I'm really tired, baby. I'm going right to sleep after this, I promise.'

'Good,' he said, hitting his favorite rhythm.

'Do me, but don't do the daylights out of me.'

He said nothing.

He wasn't violent, and he wasn't ever careless, but he was a big man, a head and a half taller than she was, and he was really strong. He had ropes of muscle in his back where people shouldn't even have muscle. He wasn't acrobatic or elaborately erotic, but he never got winded easily. And when he got up to speed, he tended to hit the groove and to stay there.

She gritted her teeth, rolled her head back in the soft darkness, and had an orgasm. She came out of the far side of it gasping and limp all over, with all the tension gone from her jaw and temples and her arms hanging slack.

He stopped, and hung there over her, and let her breathe awhile. There was a big lumpy rock under her neck, beneath the bag and the bubblepak, and she squirmed on her back to miss it. She'd been very tired before, but now she was fully wrapped in the hot life-giving power of her own libido, and all the weariness and horror of the day was like something that had happened to another woman somewhere far away. When she spoke again it was rough and low.

'I changed my mind about that daylights business.'

He laughed. 'You always say that.'

'Unless you let me get on top, I'm gonna have to scream a little bit.'

'Go ahead and scream,' he told her, moving hard. 'You never scream all *that* much.'

CHAPTER

5

Chasing tornadoes until two in the morning had been pretty bad, but not half so bad as Alex had feared. They'd spent most of those hours humming down darkened roads, with Alex curled in his nest of bubblepak, dozing.

They'd stopped three times to fling machinery into the sky, a fever of virtual activity in the midst of distance and darkness and thunder. They were ardently chasing storms by remote control. And yet there was little sense of real danger.

The storms didn't frighten Alex. He found them impressive and interesting. His only true fear was that the Troupers would discover the real and humiliating extent of his weakness. He could think straight, he could talk, he could eat, and he could breathe beautifully. But he was still bone feeble, with an edge of endurance that was razor thin. He was lucky that Martha and Buzzard hadn't asked him to do anything truly strenuous. It wasn't because they were sparing him, of course. They simply didn't trust him to do anything important.

The day after the chase, Alex was up with the dawn, his lungs still clear, his eyes bright, with no sign of sore throat or fever. He felt better than he'd felt in at least a year. Meanwhile, the road-burned Troupers lay around in their smelly bags and their stick-and-paper cones, in the grip of prolonged siestas. The after-chase day was a busy day for the support crews, but they were busy with *information*, a fourteen-hour-day of annotating, editing, collating, cutting, and copying. The Troupe's road pursuers were physically worn-out, and the rest of them were crouching over their keyboards. Nobody paid

Alex much mind.

Around noon, Carol Cooper made Alex a big paper sombrero, gave him a bag of granola and a small canteen, and sent him out to watch the Troupe's goats. The Troupers had this teenage kid, Jeff, who usually did the goat watching and the firewood fetching and other little gopher chores around camp, but with Alex's arrival, Jeff had been bumped up the pecking order.

Alex didn't mind watching the goats. It was clearly the stupidest and lowest-status job in Troupe life, but at least there was very little to it. All the goats had smart collars, and you could set the herd's parameters on a laptop to give them minor shocks and buzzes when they wandered out of range. They were gene-spliced pharmaceutical goats, 'pharm animals,' and despite their yellow, devillike, reptilian eyeballs, the goats were remarkably docile and stupid. Most of the time the goats seemed to grasp the nature of the collar business, and they stayed where the machine wanted them. They industriously nibbled anything remotely edible and then lay in the shade belching gas from their gene-spliced guts.

Alex spent most of the day up in a mesquite tree at the edge of a brush-filled gully, wearing his paper breathing mask, grepping around with the laptop, and swatting mosquitoes and deer flies. He wasn't too happy about the mosquitoes, but his bite-proof paper hat, mask, and jumpsuit kept them at bay, except on his bare neck and ankles. The deerflies were big, buzzing, aggressive, head-circling pests, and it wasn't too surprising that there were a lot of them around – the brush was crawling with deer. The damned deer were as common as mice.

Alex, a consummate urbanite, had always imagined deer as timid, fragile, endangered creatures, quailing somewhere in the darkened depths of their crumbling ecosystems. This sure as hell wasn't the case with these West Texas deer, who were thriving in an ecosystem that was already about as screwed up as mankind could manage. The deer were snorty and flop-eared and skittish, but they were as bold as rats in a junkyard.

By the time Alex and his entourage of goats returned to camp that evening, he was a lot less impressed about the local diet of venison. There wasn't much to obtaining venison – it was about as hard as finding dog meat at a pound. He and Jeff milked the goats, which produced a variety of odd cheesy fluids, some with U.N.-mandated dietary vitamin requirements, and some with commercial potential in drugstore retail. Milking goats was kind of interesting work on a weird level of interspecies intimacy, but it was also hard manual labor, and he was glad to leave most of it to Jeff.

Greg Foulks had pulled Jeff out of the wreckage of an F-5 a couple years back, from the jackstraw rubble where Jeff had lost both his parents. Jeff had worked his way into the Troupe by simply running away and returning to them, whenever the Troupe tried to place him into better care. Jeff was a cheerful, talkative, sunburned Texas Anglo kid, openly worshipful of Jerry and Greg, and full of what he thought was good advice about Troupe life. Jeff was only sixteen, but he had that drawn, tight-around-the-eyelids look that Alex had seen on the faces of displaced people, of the world's heavy-weather refugees. A haunted, wry look, like the solid earth beneath their feet had become thin ice, never to be trusted again.

Everyone in the Troupe had that look, really. Except maybe Jerry Mulcahey. Examined closely, Mulcahey looked as if he'd never set foot on Earth in the first place.

Next day they put Alex on kitchen duty – KP.

'YOUR SISTER,' SAID Ellen Mae Lankton, 'is a real hairpin.'

'I couldn't agree with you more,' said Alex. He was sitting cross-legged on the bubblepak floor of the kitchen yurt, peeling a root. It was the root of some local weed known as a 'poppymallow.' It looked like a very dirty and distorted carrot, and when peeled, it had some of the less appetizing aspects of a yam.

Ellen Mae had been up at dawn to grub up poppymallows. She was up at every dawn, methodically wandering the fields, snapping miles of old barbed wire with her personal diamond-edged cable cutters and digging up weeds with her sharpshooter shovel. So now Alex had a dozen filthy roots at his elbow, in Ellen Mae's canvas sling bag. Peeling roots, it seemed, was not a popular task among Storm Troupers. Alex, however, didn't mind it much.

Alex rarely minded any kind of work that allowed him to sit very still and breathe shallowly. What he minded about kitchen work was the mesquite smoke. Whenever Ellen Mae turned her back to manage the stewpot, Alex would whip his paper mask up quickly and steal a few quiet huffs of properly filtered air.

As Ellen Mae bustled about, doing her endless round of mysterious kitchen rituals, Alex sat nearby, in the yurt's only draft of clear air. As the morning had worn on, several Troupers had wandered in hunting snacks or water, and they'd seen Alex sitting near Ellen Mae's feet in a humble, attentive, apprentice's posture. And they'd given Ellen Mae a kind of surprised, eyebrow-raised, respectful look. After a while Ellen Mae had warmed up to Alex considerably, and now this strange, witchy-looking, middle-aged woman wouldn't shut up to save her life.

'For one thing, she's got a really strange way o' talkin',' said Ellen Mae.

'You mean her accent?' Alex said.

'Well, that's part of it . . .'

'That's simple,' Alex said. 'We Ungers are German Mexicans.'

'What?'

'Yeah, we're descended from this German guy named Heinrich Unger, who emigrated to Mexico in 1914. He was a German spy. He tried to get the Mexicans to invade the U.S. during the First World War.'

'Huh,' said Ellen Mae, stirring stew.

'He didn't have much luck at it, though.'

'I reckon he didn't.'

'Another German spy named Hans Ewers wrote a couple of books about their mission. They're supposed to be pretty good books. I wouldn't know, myself. I don't read German.'

'German Mexicans,' Ellen Mae mused.

'There's lots of German Mexicans. Thousands of 'em, really. It's a pretty big ethnic group.' Alex shrugged. 'My dad moved over the border and took out U.S. citizenship after he made some money in business.

'When did that happen, exactly?'

'Around 2010. Just before I was born.'

'Must have been one of those free-trade things. When the U.S. sent all the workin' jobs down to Mexico, and the Mexicans sent the USA all their rich people.'

Alex shrugged. His family's entanglement with history meant little to him. He was vaguely interested in the distant and romantic

1914 aspect, but his dad's postindustrial business career was the very essence of tedium.

'Janey doesn't sound German, though. Or Mexican either, for that matter. You don't sound German or Mexican either, kid.'

'I do sound pretty German when I speak Spanish,' Alex offered. 'Can I have some more of that tea?'

'Sure, have all you want,' said Ellen Mae, surprising him. 'We're gonna break camp tomorrow. Can't carry much water on the road.' She poured him a generous paper-cup-ful of some acrid herbal soak she'd made from glossy green bush leaves. It sure as hell wasn't tea, but it wasn't as bad as certain Mexican soft drinks he'd sampled. 'So we'll use up the spare water now. Tonight we can all have a bath!'

'Wow!' Alex enthused, sipping the evil brew.

Ellen Mae frowned thoughtfully. 'What is it you *do*, exactly, Alex?'

'Me?' Alex said. He considered the question. He hadn't often been asked it. 'I'm a play-testing consultant.'

'What's that?'

'Well, network computer games . . . ' Alex said vaguely, 'network dungeons . . . There's not much money in computer games anymore, because of the copyright property screwups and stuff, but there's still, I dunno, cryptware and shareware and the subscription services, right? Some guys who are really into dungeons can still make good money. Sometimes I help with the work.'

Ellen Mae looked doubtful, even though it was almost the truth. Alex had spent most of his teenage years ardently playing dungeons, and since he was generous with his upgrade payments and his shareware registrations, he'd eventually ended up in the fringes of game marketing. Not that he designed games or anything – he didn't have the maniacal attention to detail necessary for that – but he did like to be among the first to play the new games, and he didn't mind being polled for his consumer reactions. On occasion, Alex had even been given a little money for this – all told, maybe five percent of the money that he'd poured into the hobby.

At eighteen, though, Alex had given up dungeon gaming. It had dawned on him that his numerous dungeon identities were stealing what little vitality remained in his own daily life. The dungeons weren't that much of an improvement, really, over the twisted, dungeonlike reality of a series of sickrooms. Since that realization, Alex had given up gaming, and devoted his time and money to exploring the twisted depths of his own medical destiny and the wonders of the pharmaceutical demimonde.

'I also collect comics,' he offered.

'Why?' Ellen Mae said.

'Well, I thought it was really interesting that there was this, like, weird pop-culture thing that's still published on paper instead of on networks.' This remark cut no apparent ice with Ellen Mae. Alex plowed on. 'I own lots of old American paper comics – y'see, nobody does paper comics in the U.S. anymore, but some of the antique ones, the undergrounds and stuff, never got copied and scanned, so they're not on network access anywhere. So if you're a serious collector, quite often you can buy some art that's just not publicly available . . . Some art that nobody else can see . . . A piece of art that nobody's accessed or viewed in years!'

Ellen Mae only looked puzzled; she clearly didn't grasp the basic thrill involved in this hobby. Alex continued: 'My real specialty is modern Mexican paper comics. The *fotonovelas*, and the true-crime manga-rags, and the UFOzines and stuff. They're an antique medium in a modern context, and they're this kind of cool nightmare folk art, really . . . I like them, and they're kinda hard to get. I own lots, though.' He smiled.

'What do you do with them?' Ellen Mae said.

'I dunno,' Alex admitted. 'Catalog 'em, put 'em in airproof bags . . . They're all stored in Houston. I thought maybe that I would pirate-scan them all, and post them on networks, so that a lot more people could see how cool they were. And see how much great stuff I'd collected. But I dunno, that kind of spoils the whole thing, really.'

Ellen Mae looked at him so strangely then that Alex realized he was wading in too deep. He gave her his best smile, humbly offered up a couple of well-peeled roots, and asked, 'What do *you* hack, Ellen Mae?'

'I hack Comanche,' Ellen Mae said.

'What's that mean?'

'I was born out here in West Texas,' she told him. 'I'm a native.'

'Really.' She didn't look like any Comanche Indian. She looked like a big Anglo woman with middle-aged spread in a bloodstained paper suit.

'I grew up out here on a ranch, back when everything was dying out . . . There never were a lot of people in this part of Texas. Most of the people just packed up and left, after the aquifers went. And then during the State of Emergency, when the really big drought hit? Well, everything and everybody out here just blew away, like so much dust.'

Alex nodded helpfully and started on another root with his ceramic peeler.

'Everybody who stayed behind – well, they pretty much stopped farming and ranching, and went into scavenging. Wrecking work, in the ghost towns.' She shrugged. 'They didn't call it structure hitting back then, because we didn't blow up anything that wasn't already abandoned. I mean, we had *reasons* to blow stuff up. We wanted to make some *money*. We didn't blow stuff up just because we liked to watch stuff fall down – all that bullshit came later.'

'Okay,' Alex said, sipping his brew.

'I started to think it through back then, you know . . . See, Alex, the truth is, nobody should have ever done any farming out here. Ever. This land just wasn't cut out for farming. And ranching – running cattle on this land just took way too much out of the soil. It wasn't any *accident* that all this happened. We brought it on ourselves.'

Alex nodded.

'This was nomad land. The High Plains – they were *black* with buffalo from here straight to Canada! The biggest migrating herds of animals ever seen in history. They killed the buffalo off with repeating rifles, in twenty years. It took another hundred fifty years to drain off all the water underground, and of course by then the atmosphere was wrecked too . . . But see, it was all a really bad mistake. The people who settled out here – we destroyed this place. And we were destroyed for doing it.'

Alex said nothing.

'At the time, you know – people just couldn't *believe* it. They couldn't believe that this huge area of the good old USA would just end up abandoned by everybody, that the people who settled the land and tamed it – they used to say that a lot, 'taming the land' – that those people would just be driven right out of existence. I mean, at the time it was unprecedented. Seemed really unlikely and abnormal. Of course, it's a pretty damn common business now . . . But at the time there was a lot of government talk about how it was all just temporary, that they were gonna resettle West Texas as soon as they learned how to pipe water down from Minnesota, or melt icebergs, or some other such damn nonsense . . . Hell Alex, they're never gonna move the *water*. It's a hundred times cheaper just to move the people. They were all living in a dreamland.'

'Dreamlands, yeah,' Alex said, 'I've been in a few of those.'

'And the strangest thing was, that it had all happened before, but nobody learned the lesson. Because it happened to the Comanches. The Comanches lived out here two hundred years – off the land, off the buffalo. But when those buffalo went, well, they were just wiped out. Starved right out of existence. Had to move up to Oklahoma, and live in reservation camps eating food that the government gave 'em, just like us low-down modern weather tramps. No fight left in 'em.' She sighed. 'See, Alex, if you got the basics of life, then you can fight for your place in the world. But if you got no food and water, then you got no place at all. You just leave. Go away, or die.'

'Right,' Alex said. 'I get it.' It was clearly doing Ellen Mae some good to get this matter off her chest. It was obvious that she'd discussed all this before. Probably this was a standard lecture she gave all the Troupe wannabes.

Normally, in a discussion of this sort, Alex would have pitched right in with a few devil's-advocate arguments, just to mess everything up and kinda make it more interesting. Under the circumstances, though, he thought it was wisest to let Ellen Mae talk it out. A good idea, for instance, not to mention the many other places in the world where relocations had been a hundred times worse than in West Texas. After all, the people in West Texas had had the giant, well-developed United States to help them. So that they didn't starve on the spot. They didn't break out in eye-gouging, street-to-street, structure-hitting, down-and-dirty little ethnic wars. And they weren't wiped out by massive septic plagues, all the little predatory bugs that jumped out of the woodwork whenever people got seriously disorganized: dysentery, cholera, typhus, malaria, hantavirus.

It had been pretty damned stupid to dry up the aquifers in West Texas, but it didn't really compare in scale with the planet's truly monumental ecoblunders. Slowly poisoning the finest cropland in China, Egypt, and India with too much salt from irrigation, for instance. Clear-cutting the jungles in Indonesia and Brazil. The spread of the Sahara.

But why bring all that up? It wouldn't make Ellen Mae feel any better. If you lost everything, it didn't really ease your pain much to know that other people, somewhere else, might be hurting even worse. People who wanted to judge your pain by your privileges were mean-spirited people – the kind of people who thought it must be big fun to be an invalid, as long as you were rich. Alex knew better. Sure, if he'd been poor, he'd have been dead long ago – he knew that. He wasn't poor. He was a rich kid, and if he had any say about it, he was going to stay that way. But that didn't make his life a picnic. Let her talk.

'When I figured that much out,' Ellen Mae said, 'I decided I was gonna learn all about Comanches.'

'How come?'

She paused. 'Alex, there are two kinds of people in this world. The people who don't wanna know, even if they *oughta* know. And the people who just *have to* know, even if it's not gonna help 'em.' She smiled at him. 'Troupe people – we're all that second kind. People who just *have to know*, even though we can't do a damn thing about any of it.'

Alex grunted. He was of a different kind, personally. He was the kind who didn't mind knowing, but didn't feel up to devoting much energy to finding out.

'So I read a lot about Comanches. I mean, with the towns empty and the cattle gone, it was a lot easier to understand that kind of nomad life . . . That's one good thing about living nowadays. You can read about anything, for nothing, anywhere where there's a laptop screen. So, I read all these on-line books about Comanches, and how they lived, while I was living off the backs of trucks, hunting, and gathering scrap metal.

'And that's when I started to really understand this land. For instance, why us wreckers got so much heat from the Texas Rangers. Why the Rangers used to just show up out here, and chase down our convoys, and *shoot us*. They had databases and cell phones and all, but there wasn't anything cute and modern about the goddamned Texas Rangers – the Rangers in the 2020s were *exactly the same* as the goddamned Texas Rangers in the 1880s! And if you were some nomad, living out of a tent in West Texas, then the Rangers just weren't gonna be able to stand havin' you around! Simple as that!' She was shaking her soup ladle. 'They just couldn't stand it, that we were out here wreckin' stuff, and that we hadn't cleared out for good and gone exactly where the government said we should, when we should. That we didn't pay taxes, or get vaccinations, or have any rule books.' She stirred her stew, and tasted it, and started crumbling a dried ancho pepper.

'Sure, every once in a while a few wrecker boys would get all liquored up and smash up some stuff in towns where there were still people livin'. That happened, and I'm not denyin' it. We weren't all perfect. But the Rangers used that as their excuse for everything. They came right after the wreckin' gangs, the Rangers did. They just wouldn't let us live. They broke us up, and they shot us and arrested us, and they put us away in camps.'

'What did you do then?'

'Well, I didn't get arrested myself, so I went up to Oklahoma to meet some real Comanches.'

'Really?'

'Hell yes! There's more Comanches up in Oklahoma *right now*, after *everything*, than there were when the tribe was out riding the free range. That's the weirdest part of it. The Comanches didn't die out or anything. They just got changed and moved. They been up there multiplying, just like every other human being in the world. There's *thousands* of Comanches. They're farmers, and they got little stores and stuff . . . they're big on churches, y'know, big churchgoing people. None of that weirdo cult stuff, but good old-fashioned Christians. I wouldn't call 'em prosperous, they're pretty damned poor people for Americans, but you see a lot worse on TV.'

'I see. So what did you learn from that?'

Ellen Mae laughed. 'Well, I married one . . . But they know about as much about living off the buffalo as you know about being a German spy, kid. I dunno . . . the oldest folks still use the language a little, the smell of the old life is still around, just a little bit. I wanted to learn about herbal lore, about living off the land. I ended up learning a lot about botany. But mostly I learned it off text files and databases. Hell, Alex, it's been a hundred and fifty years.'

She sighed. 'That's a long time. I mean, I grew up in West Texas. I was a nice girl from a decent ranchin' family, went to high school, went to church, watched TV, bought dresses and shoes and went to dances . . . We thought we owned this land. How much of that life do you think is gonna be left in a hundred and fifty years? Fuck-all, Alex. Nothin'.'

'Well, I wouldn't say that,' Alex said. 'After all, there's government records. The government's real good about that. Databases and statistics. Stuff on platinum disks that they keep in salt mines.'

'Sure, and in Anadarko there's American Indian museums where everything has got a nice tag on it, but it's gone, kid! The Comanches got smashed and blown away! We got smashed and blown away! First we did it to them. And then we did it to the land. And then we did it to ourselves. And after we're gone for good, I don't know why the hell anybody is gonna want to know about us.'

Alex was impressed. He'd seen old people talking openly about the declining state-of-the-world on old people's television talk shows, the crustier, more old-fashioned talk shows, without many video effects, where people never did very much. But old people usually seemed pretty embarrassed to bring up such matters right in front of young people. Probably because of the inherent implication that the world's old people were ecological criminals. Who probably ought to be hauled into court by a transgenerational tribunal and tried for atrocities against the biosphere.

Not that old people would ever allow this to happen, though. There were shitloads of old people still running everything all over the world, and they were in no hurry to give up their power, despite the grotesquely stupid things they'd done with it. Sometimes they would allude to all the awful consequences of heavy weather, but always in very mealy-mouthed, very abstract ways, as if the disasters surrounding them had nothing to do with anything they'd ever done themselves.

Alex kinda figured that there might be some kind of formal reckoning someday. When everybody who might be found guilty was safely dead and buried. It would probably be like it had been, back when the communist government finally fell in China. Lots of tribunals of guys in suits issuing severe public reprimands to lots of elderly dead people.

'Well, I can tell that you learned something useful,' Alex said. ''Cause I never saw anybody eat like this Troupe eats.'

'Off the land,' Ellen Mae said, nodding. 'It ain't easy, that's for sure. The old species balance, the original ecology, is completely shot out here. Believe me, it's nothing like the High Plains used to be, and it never will be again. There's all these foreign weeds, invader species, depleted soils, and the climate's crazy. But the West Texas flora was always pretty well adapted to severe weather. So there's still Comanche food around. Stuff like pigweed. Hell, pigweed's an amaranth, it's a really nutritious grain, but it'll grow in a crack in a sidewalk. Of course, you'd never think to eat pigweed if you didn't already know what it was.'

'Right,' Alex said. He'd never seen pigweed – or, at least, he'd never recognized it. He felt a dreadful certainty that he was going to have to eat some of it pretty soon.

'It's been a long time since anybody was out here, gathering the wild forage. But now the grazing pressure is off the native plants. And there's no more plowing, or crops, or herbicides, or fertilizers. So even though the weather's bad, some of those native plants are coming back pretty strongly. Stuff like poppymallow, and devil's claw, and prairie turnip. There's nowhere near enough food for a cityful of civilized people. But for a little tribe of wandering nomads, who can cover a lot of ground, well, actually, there's quite a lot of food out here, especially in spring and summer.'

'I guess the Troupe was pretty lucky that you ended up joining them,' Alex said.

'No,' said Ellen Mae, 'there wasn't anything like luck to that.'

AFTER JERRY AND Sam had pored over the forecast, and Joe Brasseur had run through a legal database of likely areas to squat, they picked a destination and announced a route. The Troupe broke camp.

Joe Brasseur, the oldest member of the Troupe, had once referred to breaking camp as 'labor-intensive.' Jane found that a hilariously old-fashioned term, but she understood what it meant, all right –

there was no way to shrug the work off onto machines, so everybody involved just plain had to sweat.

The Troupe pulled up all the carpets, beat a hundred kilos of dust out of them, and rolled them up neatly. They deflated the bubblepak, and rolled that up too. Peter, Martha, and Rick deftly unstacked the towers – a nerve-racking business to watch – while Greg and Carol and Mickey went after the instrumentation and the wind generator.

Then there were the tepees and the yurts to strip, collapse, and pack, and the systems to shut down and uncable and stow away. And then there would be the bonfire, and the last big meal in camp, and the ritual bath . . . Jane pitched in headlong. She felt good after a day off, she felt alert and strong. There was a lot to do, but she knew how to do it. She was ready to work, and she would do it in one daylong blur of harnessed nervous energy, and when it was over, she would sleep in the Troupe bus in the moving dark, and she would feel very satisfied.

She was hauling a bundled stack of tepee poles to one of the trucks when she saw Alex slouching past her.

She scarcely recognized her brother at first: a strange, hunched, gnomelike figure, less like a Troupe wannabe than some kind of prisoner of war. He was wearing a dirty paper jumpsuit, a big cardboard-and-paper sombrero, with a big white mask elastic-strapped over his nose and mouth.

He was carrying a large double-headed digging pick. She'd never seen anyone carry a pick with less enthusiasm – Alex was lugging it clumsily, thigh-high, at the end of his outstretched arms, as if it were some kind of barbell.

He trudged slowly out of the camp. Jane called out to him, waved, then jogged over and caught up to him just past one of the camp's perimeter posts.

'What's on your mind?' he muttered.

'Just wanted to see how you're doing,' she said. She looked into his pale, squinting eyes. 'You mind taking off that mask for a second?'

Alex pulled his mask down, with bad grace. The mask's thin elastic straps had left four little stripes of pale skin across his sunburned cheeks. 'Ellen Mae wants me to dig up a root.'

'Oh.' Jane thought that Alex looked shaky, and she was pretty sure he'd never touched a pickax in his life. 'Are you up to that kind of labor? You just got out of a hospital.'

'I'm not gonna work very hard,' he told her patiently. 'It's just makework bullshit. Ellen Mae's just getting me out of the way so one of those big radio towers won't fall on my head.'

'You got along all right with Ellen Mae?'

'I can get along.' Alex sighed. 'These people of yours are really something. They remind me of some Santeria people I used to know, in a rancho outside Matamoros. Kind of survivalist compound thing? They had the bunkers, y'know, and the security systems and stuff . . . Of course, those dope vaqueros were a much heavier outfit than these jokers.' Alex thumped the broadside of the pick against the base of one of the perimeter posts. 'This thing can't listen to us talking, can it?'

'Well, yeah, it can,' Jane admitted, 'but we never record any speech with it. It's just an intruder alarm, with some tasers and pellets and stuff. We can talk.'

'No problem,' Alex muttered, watching a pack of Troupers strip the paper walls from the hangar yurt. 'Well, you don't have to worry about me. Run along and go do something useful.'

'Is anybody bugging you, Alex? Rick or Peter or anybody?'

Alex shrugged. '*You're* bugging me.'

'Don't be that way. I just want to help you fit in.'

Alex laughed. 'Look! You kidnapped me here, I didn't ask to come. I'm sunburned and covered with mosquito bites, and I'm really dirty. The food stinks here. There's not enough water. There's no privacy. It's dangerous! I'm wearing clothes made of paper. Your friends are a pack of hicks and loons, except for your boyfriend, who's a big cigar-store Indian. Under the circumstances, I'm being a really good sport about this.'

Jane said nothing.

He looked her in the eye. 'Stop worrying so much. I'm not gonna do anything stupid. If I were a bigger guy, and a stronger guy, and a nicer guy, I'd go have it out with your boyfriend about that way you've been groaning at night.' He shook his head, under the big paper hat. 'I won't, though. I think I know what kind of guy Mulcahey is, and I think you're crazy to hook up with a guy like that. But hey, I'm not one to judge. That's your life, that's all your decision.'

'Thanks a lot,' she grated.

He smiled at her. 'You're really *happy* here, aren't you?'

She was surprised.

'I've seen you act really crazy sometimes, Janey, and I still think you're acting pretty strange. But I've never seen you act so happy before.' He smiled again. 'You're chasing tornadoes in a wasteland! But you're waltzin' around here with a smile on your lips, and a song in your heart, and your little bouquet of fresh wildflowers . . . It's kind of sweet, actually.'

Jane straightened to her full height and looked down at him. 'Yes, Alex, I'm happy here. About everything but you, basically.'

'You really belong with these people. You really *like* them.'

'That's right. They're my people.'

Alex narrowed his eyes. 'And this guy you're with. He treats you all right? He wasn't beating you or anything really sick and twisted, was he?'

Jane looked around for eavesdroppers, smoldering with rage, then centered her eyes on him. 'No. He doesn't beat me. I was fucking him. I *like* to fuck him. Hard! Loud! A lot! I'm not ashamed about it, and you can't *make me* ashamed!' There was a hot flush in her cheeks and ears. 'Get this through your head! That is the man in my life! He is my grand passion.' She stared hard at Alex, until he dropped his gaze.

'I never thought I was gonna have a grand passion,' she told him. 'I didn't ever believe in that. I thought it was Hollywood fantasy, or something from a hundred years ago. But I have a grand passion now, and he's the one. There'll never be another man like him for me. Ever!'

Alex took a step back. 'Okay, okay.'

'It's him and me till the sky falls in!'

Alex nodded quickly, his eyes wide. 'Okay, I get it, Janey. Calm down.'

'I *am* calm, you little creep. And it's no joke. You can't ever make it a joke, because you don't know one thing about it. I love him, and I'm happy with him, and we do what we do, and we are what we are, and you just better live with that! And you better never forget what I just told you.'

Alex nodded. She could tell from the way he bit his lip that her words had sunk in – for better or worse, she'd connected. 'It's okay, Janey. I'm not complaining. I'm glad I had a chance to see you acting like this, I really am. It's real weird, but it's refreshing.' He shrugged, uneasily. 'The only thing is – you shouldn't have brought *me* out here. That just wasn't a good idea. I don't belong in any place like this. I'm not like these people. You should have just left me alone.' He lifted the pick carefully and placed it on his narrow shoulder.'

'You're gonna stay with the Troupe awhile, Alex?'

'I oughta make you take me home right away.' He balanced the pick handle on his collarbone, clumsy and restless. 'But I got no home to go to at the moment. Mexico is out, for obvious reasons. I'm sure not going back home to Papa in Houston. Papa acts even stranger than you do, and those clinic people might be lookin' for me there . . . And anyway, there are possibilities in a setup like this. It's stupid for me to stay here, but I think I might do okay for a while, if I can get everybody to mostly ignore me. Especially you.' He turned away.

'Alex,' she said.

He looked over his shoulder. 'What?'

'Learn to hack something. Like everybody else does. Just so you can get along better.'

He nodded. 'Okay, Juanita. Have it your way.'

ALEX FOLLOWED ELLEN MAE's precise but extremely confusing directions, got turned around several times, and finally found the paper-tagged stick she had driven into the earth to mark the spot. The fluttering paper tag marked a low trailing vine on the ground. The vine was about two meters long, with hairy, pointed, conical leaves, and it smelled rank and fetid. It harbored a large population of small black-and-orange beetles. It was called a buffalo gourd.

Alex scraped the vine aside with the flat blade of the pick, got a two-handed choke-up grip on the shaft, and started to chop at the yellow earth. He was impressed with the pick. The tool was well-balanced, sharp, and in good condition. Unfortunately he was nowhere near strong enough to use it properly.

Alex chipped, gnawed, and scraped his way several centimeters down into the miserable, unforgiving soil, until the sweat stood out all over his ribs and his pipe-stem arms trembled.

When he spotted the buried root of a buffalo gourd, he stared at it in amazement for some time, then left the pick beside the hole and walked slowly back to camp.

Carol Cooper had pulled a pair of lattices from the wall of the garage yurt. The highway maintenance hulk rolled out through the big new gap.

Carol watched the machine lumber downhill while she folded and tied the wooden lattices. Alex joined her, tugging down his mask.

The machine hit the highway, hesitated, and began creeping along south at ten klicks an hour.

'Well, let's hope the poor damn thing gets to paint a few road stripes before they shoot it to hell and gone again,' Carol said, stacking the lattices in the back of a truck. 'What's the deal, dude? I'm busy.'

'Carol, what's the weirdest thing you've got around here?'

'What in hell are you talking about?'

'What have you got that's really strange, only nobody else ever hacks with it?'

'Oh,' Carol said. 'I get your drift.' She grinned. 'There's a touch of that in every Trouper. Old-fashioned hacker gadget jones. Toy hunger, right?' Carol looked around the garage, at the scattered tools, the bench mounts, the table vise, an industrial glue sprayer. 'You wanna help me pack all this crap? Rudy and Greg are coming later.'

'I'd like to,' Alex lied, 'but I got another assignment.'

'Well, I'm gonna be glad to have *this* thing off my hands, anyhow. You want to play with something, you can play with this bastard.' Carol walked to the welding bench and pulled off a long, dusty coil of black cable. It looked like a pneumatic feedline for the welding torch, a big coil of thin black plastic gas pipe. As she caught it up and brought it to him, though, Alex saw that the apparent pipe was actually sleek black braided cord.

One end of the cord ended in a flat battery unit, with a belt attachment, a small readout screen, and a control glove.

'Ever seen one of these before?'

'Well, I've certainly seen a battery and a control glove,' Alex said.

She handed him the works. 'Yeah, that's a damn good battery! Superconductive. You could drive a motorbike with that battery. And here I am, keeping that sucker charged up to no good end – nobody ever uses this damn thing!' She frowned. 'Of course, if you work that battery down, kid, you're gonna have to pull some weight to make up for that.'

'I'm pulling, I'm pulling,' Alex told her. 'My people in Matamoros have got that shipment ready, they're just waiting for us to give them the coordinates.'

'Standard satellite global-position coordinates?'

'That's what they use, all right,' he said. 'Just like the Troupe, like the army, just like everybody.'

'I can give you those anytime, it's no big secret where we're pitching camp.'

'That's good. I'll try and phone 'em in, if I can still get that encrypted line.'

No problema,' Carol said, bored. She watched as Alex hefted the cable, then slid the whole coil of it over his right shoulder. It rested there easily. The cable weighed only a couple of kilos, but it felt bizarrely serpentine and supple, somehow dry and greasy at the same time. It was as thick as his little finger, and maybe twenty meters long. 'What is this thing exactly?'

'Smart rope.'

'What's smart about it?'

'Well, there's this chip in the battery box that understands knot topology. You know what topology is?'

'No.'

'It's a kind of math about deforming the geometry of space.'

'Great.'

'Anyhow, that rope is braided from a lot of different cabling. Got sensor cable, power cable, and this is the tricky part, electric reactive fiber. Okay? It'll stretch, it'll contract – hard and fast – it can bend and wiggle anywhere along the length. The damn thing can tie itself in knots.'

'Like the smart cloth in kites,' Alex said, 'except it's a line, not a sheet.'

'That's right.'

'Why'd you try to spook me with that topology crap, then? You just use the damned glove, right?'

'Right,' she said. 'Except technically, you won't understand what you're actually doing.'

'So what? Who cares?'

Carol sighed. 'Look, just take the damn thing out of here, and try not to hurt yourself. I don't wanna see that rope again, okay? I thought it was really cool hardware when I first heard about it, and I spent a lot of Janey's money to buy it. I was sure there'd be a million uses for smart rope around a camp, and hell, there *are* a million uses – so *many* goddamn uses that nobody ever uses it! Nobody ever remembers that it's around! Nobody's ever liked it! It gives everybody the creeps.'

'Okay!' said Alex cheerfully. This last little speech had sent his morale soaring. He liked the smart rope already. He was glad to have it. He was kinda sorry he didn't have two of them. 'I'll take real good care of it. Don't forget about the phone. *Hasta la vista.*'

Alex left the tent and shuffled out of camp again, back to the root from hell. He scraped and chipped and dug at the root for a while, until he was out of breath again. Then he stretched the rope out to its full twenty-pace length across the weedy earth. He turned the power switch on.

The rope lay there, totally inert. The little readout screen suggested: INPUT PARAMETERS FOR HYPERBOLIC CURVATURE.

He tried on the power glove. It had the usual knuckle sensors along the back and a thousand little beaded pressure cells across the palms and the fingers. It was a right-hand glove, and the fit was pretty good. The fingertips were free, and the glove slid very nicely along the rope, a nice mix of grip and slickness.

Alex punched a few numbers at random into the readout box, then flopped the rope around with the glove. Nothing much happened. He put the rope aside and wore the glove to dig with the pick. The glove had a good grip and helped quite a bit with the incipient blisters.

Along about sundown, Peter and Rick showed up. They were wearing paper gear fresh off the roll, and they'd been bathed and their hair was combed.

'You'd better come on in, Medicine Boy,' said Peter. 'They're washin' the clothes, everybody's takin' a bath, we're all gonna eat pretty soon.'

'I'm still busy,' Alex said.

Rick laughed. 'Busy with what?'

'Pretty big job,' Alex said. 'A buffalo gourd. Ellen Mae said the root weighs thirty kilos.'

'You can't have a root that weighs thirty kilos, man,' said Rick. 'Look, *trees* don't have roots that weigh thirty kilos.'

'Where's the plant?' Peter said.

Alex pointed to the severed gourd vine, which he had cast aside. The vine had shriveled badly in the sunlight.

'Hell,' said Rick, contemptuous. 'Look, it's a matter of simple physics. It takes a lot of energy to grow a root – starches and cellulose and stuff. Look at the photosynthetic area on those vine leaves. You can't grow something that weighs thirty kilos off a plant with no more solar-collecting area than that!'

Peter stared into the shallow hole and laughed. 'Ellen Mae sent you on a snipe hunt, dude. She's had you diggin' all day for nothin'. Man, that's cold.'

'Well, he hasn't been digging very hard,' Rick judged, kicking the small heap of calichelike soil with the toe of his boot. 'I've seen a prairie dog turn more earth than this.'

'What's with the rope?' Peter said.

'I thought it might help me haul the root out,' Alex lied glibly. 'I can't even lift thirty kilos.'

Peter laughed again. 'This is pathetic! Look, we're outta here, right after sundown. You better get back to camp and figure out how you're gonna hitch a ride.'

'How are *you* riding?' Alex asked.

'Me?' Peter said. 'I'm riding the ultralight! I'm ridin' escort duty.'

'Me too,' Rick said. 'With a rifle. There are bandits out on these highways, sometimes. Structure-hit people, bush-whackers. Most folks in a convoy like ours, with all this fine equipment, they might run a pretty big risk. But not the Troupe. The Troupe's got air support.'

'You're not gonna find any structure-hit creeps with any air support,' Peter said.

'Exactly,' Rick said. 'You're flying up there in the dark, no lights, silent, with the infrared helmet and a laser-sighted silent rifle – if it should ever come to that, you are *death from above*.'

'One shot, one kill, no exceptions,' said Peter.

'Panoptic battlefield surveillance,' said Rick.

'Float like a butterfly, sting like a bee.'

'Aerial counterinsurgency – the only way to travel.'

Alex blinked. 'I wanna do that.'

'Sure,' said Peter.

'Trade you my root for it, Peter.'

Peter laughed. 'There's no such thing, man.'

'Wanna bet? C'mon, bet me.'

Peter glanced into the hole. 'Bet what? There's nothing in there, man. Nothing but that big shelf of rock.'

'That shelf of rock *is* the root,' Alex said. 'Not thirty kilos, either. I figure it's gotta weigh at least eighty . . . That sorry little vine has gotta be two hundred years old.'

Rick stared into the hole, then spat on his hands and hefted the pick. 'He's gotcha there, Pete. He's right, you're wrong, he's flyin' escort, and you're dog meat and you're riding the bus with Janey.' He barked with laughter and swung the pick down with a crunch.

JANE'S EYES STILL stung from the antiseptic. The baths always hurt. She had refused to take antiseptic baths at first, until she'd glimpsed the cratered scars on Joanne Lessard's shoulders. Joanne was fair-skinned and dainty, and the staph boils that had hit the Troupe had come close to killing her. Bombay Staph IIb was wicked as hell; it just laughed aloud at broad-spectrum antibiotics. Modern strains of staphylococcus were splendidly adapted for survival on the earth's broadest, widest, richest modern environment. The world's vast acreage of living human skin.

Jane's eyes stung, and her crotch itched, but at least her hair was clean, and she smelled good. She'd even come to enjoy the sensation of fresh clean paper over damp nakedness, the closest one came in Troupe life to padding around in terry cloth with your hair in a towel. Outside the command yurt, the camp rang with bestial howls as Ed Dunnebecke poured another big kettleful of scalding water into the fabric tub. Hot water felt so lovely – at least till the pores opened and Ed's sheep dip started to bite.

Shutting down the Troupe's systems was delicate work. Even the minor systems, for instance, the little telephone switches, had a million or more lines of antique corporate freeware. The software been created by vast teams of twentieth-century software engineers, hired labor for extinct telephone empires like AT&T and SPRINT. It was freeware because it was old, and because everybody who'd ever made it was either dead now or in other work. Those armies of telephone engineers were now as scattered and extinct as the Soviet Red Army.

Those armies of engineers had basically been automated out of existence, replaced by higher-and-higher-level expert systems, that did error checks, bug hunts, resets, fault recoveries. Now a single individual could use the technology – any individual with a power plug and a desk. The sweat and talent of tens of thousands of clever people had vanished into a box you could hold in your hand and buy in a flea market.

The Troupe's switching stations were cheap-ass little Malaysian-made boxes of recycled barf-colored plastic. They cost about as much as a pair of good shoes.

There wasn't a single human being left in the world who fully understood what was going on inside those little boxes. Actually, no single human being in the world had *ever* understood an intellectual structure of that complexity. Any box running a million lines of code was far beyond the direct comprehension of any human brain. And it was simply impossible to watch those modern screamer-chips grind that old code, on any intimate linc-by-line basis. It was like trying to listen in on every conversation in a cocktail party bigger than Manhattan.

As a single human individual, you could only interface with that code on a very remote and abstract level – you had to negotiate with the code, gently, politely, and patiently, the way you might have dealt with a twentieth-century phone company. You *owned* a twentieth-century phone company – it was all inside the box now.

As you climbed higher and higher up the stacks of interface, away from the slippery bedrock of the hardware grinding the ones and zeros, it was like walking on stilts. And then, stilts for your stilts, and stilts for your stilts for your stilts. You could plug a jack in the back of the box and run like the wind of the wind. Until something crashed somewhere, that the system's system's system couldn't diagnose and figure out and override. Then you threw the little box away and plugged in another one.

The Troupe's system was temperamental. To say the least. For instance, the order in which you detached the subsystems mattered a lot. There was no easy or direct explanation as to *why* that should matter, but it mattered plenty.

Jane kept careful professional track of the system's incongruities, its wealth of senseless high-level knots and kinks and cramps. She kept her notes with pencil and paper, in a little looseleaf leather notebook she'd had since college. Mickey the sysadmin and Rick the code grinder had given Jane wary, weary looks when she'd first started working seriously on the Troupe's system, but she'd more than proved her worth since then. She'd resolved screwups, seizures, and blockages that had had Mickey cursing wildly and Rick so mired in code that he staggered around camp like a blacked-out drunk.

The difference between hacking code and hacking interface was like the difference between a soldier and a diplomat. Certain crises would only yield to a political solution.

Jane kept her notebook inside a plastic case, glued to the underside of Jerry's connectionist simulator. This was the safest storage place in camp, because Jerry's simulator was the Troupe's most valued machine. The simulator was the only box in the crowd of them that actually impressed Jane. The U.S. government had gone nuts over climate simulators during the State of Emergency, pouring money into global climate modeling at a frantic rate that impressed even the Pentagon. Boxes like Jerry's were Brobdingnagian – Jerry's lone system had more raw computational power than the entire planet had possessed in 1995.

Officially, Jerry's system was 'on loan' from the SESAME Collaboratory, a research net in which Jerry had fairly good standing, but nobody was going to come and repossess it. Nobody but the Troupe gave a damn about Jerry's box, really. It was stone obvious now that the problems of climate modeling simply weren't going to yield to raw computational power. Power wasn't the bottleneck at all; the real bottleneck was in the approaches, the approximations, the concepts, and the code.

Jane opened her favorite laptop, dragged the system monitor onto it off Mickey's sysadmin machine, and checked to see that all the instrumentation was safely down. Peter, Greg, and Martha had been on the job: all the towers were off-line and down now, except for the telecom tower. They always left the telecom for last. It made more sense, really, to take down the security system last, but the perimeter posts were pig stupid and paranoid little entities that reacted to any sudden loss of packets as prima facie evidence of enemy sabotage. Unless they were petted to sleep first, the posts would whoop like crazy.

An icon appeared on Jane's screen. An incoming phone call – to her own number. Surprised, she took the call.

A postcard-sized video inclusion appeared in the upper right-hand corner of her laptop. It was a stranger: clean shaven, sandy-haired, distinguished looking, close to forty maybe. Ruggedly handsome, in a funny, well-groomed sort of way. Oddly familiar looking. He wore a shirt, jacket, and tie.

'Hello?' the stranger said. 'Is this Juanita?'

'Yes?'

'Good,' the stranger said, smiling and glancing down at his desk. 'I didn't think this would quite work.' He seemed to be in a hotel lobby somewhere, or maybe a very nicely furnished office. Jane could see a lithograph behind his head and a spray of leaves from an exotic potted plant.

The stranger looked up from his console. 'I'm not getting any video off my side, should I shut down my video feed?'

'Sorry,' Jane said, leaning forward to speak into the laptop's little inset mike. 'I'm getting this off a laptop, I've got no camera here.'

'Sorry to hear that,' the stranger said, adjusting his tie. 'Y'know, Juanita, I've never actually seen you. I was quite looking forward to it.'

The stranger had Jerry's ears on the sides of his head. Jane could scarcely have been more surprised if he'd had Jerry's ears on a string around his neck. But then the bump of shock passed, and Jane felt a little cold thrill of recognition. She smiled shyly at the laptop, even though he couldn't see her. 'This is Leo, isn't it?'

'Right,' Leo Mulcahey said, with a gentle smile and a wink. 'Can we talk?'

Jane glanced around the command yurt. Mickey and Rick were both in the bath line. They usually gave her a while to work alone before they'd show up to run diagnostics and start lugging machines to the trucks.

'Yeah,' she said. 'I guess so. For a little while.' It was the first time she had seen Jerry's brother. Leo looked older than Jerry, his cheeks thinner and a little lined, and she was shocked at how good-looking he was. His head had just the shape of Jerry's head, but his haircut was lovely. Jane had been cutting Jerry's hair herself, but she could see now that as a hair designer, she was dog meat.

'I understand you've been talking with Mom,' Leo said.

Jane nodded silently, but Leo of course couldn't see her. 'Yes I have,' she blurted.

'I happen to be in the States again, at the moment. Mom's been filling me in on Jerry's activities.'

'I didn't mean any harm by it,' Jane said. 'Jerry hardly ever calls your mother, but he doesn't mind if I do it . . . Sorry if that seemed intrusive on my part.'

'Oh, Mom thinks the world of you, Juanita,' said Leo, smiling. 'Y'know, Mom and I have never seen Jerry carry on in quite this way before. I'm convinced you must be someone very special.'

'Well . . .' Jane said. 'Leo, I just thought of something – I have some photos on disk here, let me see if I can pull them up and feed them to you.'

'That would be good.' Leo nodded. 'Always feels a little odd to speak to a blank screen.'

Jane punched up the digital scrapbook. 'I wanted to thank you for helping me find my brother . . . Alejandro.'

Leo shrugged. '*De nada*. I pulled a string for you. Okay, two strings. That's Mexico for you . . . walls within walls, wheels within wheels . . . An interesting place, a fine culture.' He looked down again. 'Oh yes. That's coming across very well. Nice photo.'

'I'm the one in the hat,' Jane said. 'The other woman's our camp cook.'

'I could have guessed that,' Leo said, sitting up intently. He seemed genuinely intrigued. 'Oh, this one of you and Jerry is very good. I didn't know about the beard. The beard looks good, though.'

'He's had the beard ever since I met him,' Jane said. 'I'm sorry that, um . . . well, that it's been so long. And that you and he don't get along better.'

'A misunderstanding,' Leo offered, weighing his words. 'You know how Jerry can be . . . very single-minded, am I right? If you're addressing some issue, and it doesn't quite chime with Jerry's current train of thought . . . He's a very bright man of course, but he's a mathematician, not very tolerant of ambiguity.' Leo smiled sadly. He has his dignity, Jane thought. That magnetism Jerry has, and that ruthlessness too.

She found him extremely attractive. Alarmingly so. She could easily imagine fucking him. She could hotly imagine fucking both of them. At once.

And when they went for each other's throats she'd be smashed between them like a mouse between two bricks.

She cleared her throat. 'Well . . . is there something I can do for you in particular, Leo?'

'Actually, yes,' Leo said. 'By the way, you don't mind if I hard-copy these photos, do you?'

'Oh, go ahead.'

'It's about this strange business with the F-6,' said Leo as his printer emitted a well-bred hum. 'I wonder if you could explain that to me a little more thoroughly.'

'Well,' Jane said, 'the F-6 is a theory Jerry has.'

'It sounds a bit *alarming*, doesn't it? A tornado an order of magnitude larger than any seen before?'

'Well, strictly speaking it wouldn't be a tornado per se – more of a large-scale vortex. Something smaller than a hurricane, but with a different origin and different structure. Different behavior.'

'Was I right in hearing that this thing is supposed to be a *permanent feature of the atmosphere*?'

'No,' Jane said. 'No. I mean, yes, there is some indication in the models – if you set the parameters just right, there are some, um, indicators that an F-6 might become a stable configuration under certain circumstances . . . Look Leo, we don't emphasize that aspect, okay? The woods are full of nutty amateurs running homemade climate models and declaring all kinds of crazy doomsday crap. It would look really bad if the press started telling everybody that Jerry's forecasting some kind of giant permanent storm over Oklahoma. That's just not responsible behavior from a scientist. Jerry's got problems enough already with the labcoat crowd, without that kind of damage to his credibility,'

'Jerry does think, seriously, that an F-6 will actually occur, though.'

'Well, yes. We do think that. The mesoscale convection is shaping up, the Bermuda High, the jet stream . . . Yeah, we think that if it's gonna happen at all, then this is the season. Probably within the next six weeks.'

'A giant, unprecedently large, and violent atmospheric storm. Over the heartland of the United States.'

'Yes, that's right. That's it exactly.'

Leo was silent, and looked grave and thoughtful.

'Leo, you don't double the amount of carbon dioxide in the atmosphere without some odd things happening.'

'I'm used to odd things,' Leo said. 'I don't believe I'm quite used to *this* however.'

'Jerry's not alone in this line of thought, you know. He's out on a limb, but he's not *way* out. There are paleoclimatologists in Europe who think that giant storms were real common during the Eemian Interglacial. There's physical evidence in the fossil record.'

'Really.'

'There was also a paper out this year saying that the so-called Akkadian volcanism wasn't volcanic at all, that the dust layers, and their three-hundred-year drought, were entirely atmospheric. That was the Akkadian culture in the Tigris and Euphrates.'

'I beg your pardon?'

'The Akkadians were the first civilization – 2200 BC., in Mesopotamia? They were the first culture ever, and also the first culture ever destroyed by a sudden climate change.'

'Right,' Leo said, 'I'm certain these matters have been covered by our gifted and crusading popular press. Exhaustively. And to the full satisfaction of the scientific community.' He shrugged, elegantly. 'I understand that the weather is crazy now, and the weather will be crazy the rest of our lives. What I don't understand is why Jerry is taking *you* into this.'

'Me?' Jane said. 'Oh! Well, I hack interface. For the Troupe. And I kinda have to get back to work right now, actually.'

'Juanita, you're not taking my point. Suppose this is a really big storm. Suppose that it is a permanent vortex in the atmosphere – as

Jerry has said, something like Earth's own version of the Great Red Spot of Jupiter. A permanent planetary sinkhole for excess greenhouse heat, centered somewhere near North Texas. I know that seems like a bizarre supposition, but suppose it's really the truth.'

'Yeah? Well, then I'll be there watching it.'

'You'll be killed.'

'Maybe. Probably. But I'll be there anyway. We'll document it.'

'Why?'

'Why? Because we can! Because we know! It's what we do! We'll do it for the sake of the survivors, I suppose.' Jane ran her hands through her hair, her face stiff. 'Anyway, if the F-6 is really a worst-case F-6, then the survivors are gonna be the unlucky ones.'

Leo said nothing. Jane heard an odd rumbling, then realized he was rapidly drumming his fingers on the desktop.

'I have to go now, Leo. There's a lot of work.'

'Thank you for being so frank with me, Juanita. I appreciate that.'

'My friends call me Janey.'

'Oh. Of course. *Hasta la vista*, Janey.' Leo hung up.

Jane shivered, looked around herself once more.

Rick entered the yurt.

'I've got Med – I mean, I've got Alex riding shotgun in the ultralight tonight,' he said. 'He said he *wanted* to go.'

Jane stared at him blankly.

Rick smiled at her. 'I told you that kid really liked all of this.'

ALEX WAS NIGHT-FLYING over Texas with his head in a helmet and his face wrapped in oxygen. A tiny amber light glowed between his knees, lighting the joystick and rollerball. More light leaked from the translucent face shield of the virching helmet, the phantom watery glow of the menu bar falling off his own brow onto the pitch-black wings of the aircraft.

The hot spark of a global surveillance satellite showed at the horizon. Overhead were a million stars, a sliver of moon, a galactic river fog of Milky Way, a curl of high feathery cirrus. The fan behind his back pushed almost silently, merely sipping power, as it kept slow pace with the Troupe's land convoy, far below.

If there was anything more pleasant than this, Alex hadn't yet discovered it.

This time they were letting him actually fly the machine by hand. Buzzard had booted Ultralight Beryl with an obligatory big-dummy's control setting. Any ham-handed lurch at the joystick was instantly dumbed down into a gentle, nonlethal veer or dip.

Flying under these conditions strongly reminded Alex of riding a motorized wheelchair. Those same dainty fingertip controls, that same almost silent buzz of engine, and that same sense of sitting, wrapped with cloying security, in the care of a smart machine. Alex direly wanted to try something stupid, but he wasn't about to try anything stupid under these circumstances. He'd wait till he'd won their confidence, till they gave him a lot more initiative and leeway. *Then* he'd try something stupid.

Rick was in Ultralight Amber, casing the landscape behind the Troupe. Rick had his rifle. Just before their launches, Rick had given Alex a hair-raising lecture about the cunning and cruelty of backwoods bandits and the dire necessity for constant alertness while 'riding point.'

Alex found this pretty hard to swallow – at least as hard as the night's rations had been, a gruesome chop suey of jack-rabbit, parched corn, and buffalo-gourd root. It had been a hell of a root, though. It took two men to carry it, and it tasted like a cross between celery and pencil shavings. It was the biggest root the Troupe had ever unearthed.

Alex couldn't help but feel rather proud of this. And riding point for the Troupe beat the hell out of riding one of the crammed, overloaded buses. But Alex couldn't imagine that riding point was really all that dangerous. After all, the Troupe chase teams drove on the backroads all over West Texas, and they'd never been stopped and robbed.

Granted, most bandits, assuming there were any bandits around, wouldn't want to hassle with Juanita and her combat-retrofitted jumping hell spider. Juanita's pursuit car didn't have any guns, but it sure looked as if it ought to, and it moved like a bat out of hell. But the Aerodrome Truck and the Radar Bus were pretty fat and easy targets, chock-full of valuable equipment, yet nobody had bothered them.

Alex reasoned that if bandits were too timid and out of it to bushwhack a lone bus, there was no way they'd tackle the entire

Troupe convoy. The convoy was behind him now, slowly winding its way along the pitch-black road. Two pursuit vehicles, two robot buses hauling trailers, the Radar Bus, the Aerodrome Truck, an old dune buggy, two robot supply jeeps with trailers, three robot pedicab bikes with sidecars, and a small tractor.

Not a headlight in the lot. All moving in darkness, supposedly for greater security. The smart pursuit cars were leading the way, sniffing out the road with microwave radar. Every once in a while Alex would catch a faint glimpse of light through a bus or truck window – somebody's flipped-up laptop screen, where some Trouper was catching up on work or killing time grepping a disk.

The convoy looked rather more interesting when Alex clicked the virching helmet into infrared. Then there were vivid putt-putts of grainy pixeled heat out of the alcohol-fueled buses and the ancient dune buggy. The tractor, too. Everything else ran on batteries. There was a faint foggy glow of human body heat out the windows of the buses. It was cold at night in a High Plains spring, and the buses were crowded.

Alex had no gun. He was kind of glad the Troupe hadn't handed out a lot of guns. In his experience, unusual minority social groups with lots of guns tended to get mashed rapidly underfoot by nervous, trigger-happy government SWAT teams. So he had no weapon. He had six dusty, dead-looking emergency flares and a big flashlight.

Rick had also surreptitiously passed him some ibogaine chewing gum for maximum combat alertness. Alex hadn't tried chewing the gum yet. He wasn't sleepy yet. And besides, he didn't much like ibogaine.

His earphones crackled. 'Rick here. How ya doin'? Over.'

'Fine. Comfy. I reset the seat, over.'

'How'd you do that?'

'I got out and stood in the stirrups and pulled the pin.'

'You're not supposed to do that.'

'Rick, listen. It's just you and me up here. Nobody's listening, nobody cares. I'm not gonna fall out of this thing. I'd have better luck falling out of a grocery cart.'

Rick was silent a moment. 'Don't be stupid, okay?' He clicked off.

Alex rode on, most of another long hour. It was all right. An hour with oxygen was never boring. He was trying to make the oxygen last, sipping at the tank bit by bit, but he knew the tank would be empty by the time he landed. After that, he was going to have to buy more oxygen somehow.

He was going to have to start buying stuff for the Troupe.

For all their rhetoric, Alex could see that this was the crux of the deal, as far as he was concerned. The same unspoken bargain went for Juanita, too, mostly. These people weren't hanging out with Juanita just because they really liked big chunky-hipped ciber-art-school grads. They liked Juanita because she bought them stuff, and looked after their numerous assorted needs. She was their patroness. And he, Alex, was on track to be the next car in the gravy train.

For all that, though, there was the puzzling matter of Jerry Mulcahey. Troupe life all boiled down to Mulcahey in the end, because any Trouper who didn't fear, love, and worship the guy would obviously get their walking papers in short order. Alex still wasn't too sure about Mulcahey's real motives. Mulcahey was a genuinely twisted individual. Alex had been watching Mulcahey closely, and he was pretty sure of two things: (A) Mulcahey was genuinely possessed of some kind of genius, and (B) Mulcahey didn't have much idea what the hell money was. When he and Juanita were face-to-face in public, Mulcahey would treat her with an odd archaic courtliness: he let her sit down first at the campfire, he'd help her to her feet after, he wouldn't eat until she'd started eating, that sort of thing. Neither of them ever made a big deal of these silent little courtesies, but Mulcahey rarely missed a chance to do them.

And quite often, if some minor Troupe hassle came up, Mulcahey would let Juanita do all the talking for him. She'd get really animated and deeply into the topic, and he'd get really stone-faced and abstract and reserved. It was just as if he was letting her have his emotions for him. And the two of them clearly thrived on this arrangement. Every once in a while he would suddenly finish one of her sentences, and everyone else would flinch.

Mulcahey's weirdest symptoms happened when Juanita wasn't watching him at all. She'd be doing her version of some comely girl-thing, like maybe a big stretch-and-bend-over in her thin paper jumpsuit, Mulcahey would all of a sudden get this very highly flammable expression. Like he was a starving man and she was an expensive cordon bleu dinner and he was really trying to be careful, but it was all he could do not to rip the tablecloth right off her and eat from the broken china on his hands and knees. The look would pass in a hurry, and Mulcahey would get his usual overcontrolled cigar-store-Indian face, but the look was definitely there all right, and it was not the kind of look that a man could fake.

Alex wasn't sure how all this was going to turn out for Juanita. She'd known this guy for at least a year now, and it was pretty damned odd for a man and woman who'd been lovers that long not to calm down some. Maybe they *were* calm now. In which case, the beginning must have been something pretty seriously strange.

Alex looked down across the landscape. No sign of the convoy. He'd left the convoy far behind as he mulled things over. Time to turn around and head back a bit.

As he wheeled the ultralight around, with sluggish machine-assisted caution, he passed the shoulder of a hill. In the infrared, the highway – it happened to be a paved one – smoldered a bit with trapped day heat, but there was a lot of vivid heat on the far slope of that hill.

Alex stopped his maneuver and decided to check it out.

At first, he thought there was an entire army standing there in the road. At least a hundred people. Then he realized that most of the glowing patches of heat were standing on all fours. They were deer. No, goats.

Somebody had a herd of goats out on the highway.

Alex clicked open the radio channel. 'Alex here,' he said. 'Rick, the road is full of goats, man, over.'

'Copy, Alex. You see anybody?'

'Yeah – I think so. Kinda hard to tell from this height. Rick, why would anybody have a herd of goats out on the road in the middle of the night, over?'

'You got me beat, dude.'

'Maybe they travel at night for better security, like we do.'

'Are they moving?'

'No, man. Just sitting there.'

'Those could be pharm goats, and they could be goat rustlers, just about to rendezvous with one of those meat-packing trucks out of the city.'

'People do that? Rustle goats?'

'Some people do anything for money, dude.' Alex heard Rick loudly smacking his wide-awake gum into the microphone. 'Or maybe they're blockin' the road with goats on purpose, and they got an ambush set up in the brush, over.'

Alex lifted his faceplate and looked out bare-eyed. Pretty hard to tell in the dark, but it looked like there was some pretty thick mesquite on both sides of the road. Good-sized mesquite, too, a couple of stories tall. You could have hidden a big tribe of Comanches in it.

'Maybe you better come up here, Rick.'

'No way, man, you don't want to desert the rear of the convoy in a possible ambush situation.'

'But you've got the gun, man.'

'I'm not gonna shoot anybody, are you kidding? If these are real *bandidos*, we're gonna pull the hell back and call the Texas Rangers!'

'Right,' Alex said. '"Death from above." I kinda figured.' He laughed.

'Look, Medicine Boy, I'll shoot if I have to. But if we just start blowing people away, out in the middle of nowhere without askin' any questions, then *we're* the ones who are gonna get stomped by the Rangers.'

'Oh.'

'Cut your motor and buzz 'em, get a good quiet look.'

'Right,' Alex said. 'I get it.'

He took several deep huffs of oxygen. It felt lovely. Then he discovered that the motor would not shut down. He couldn't override the controls. Oh well. It wasn't a loud motor, anyway.

He dropped down a dozen meters over the treetops and crossed the road at an angle, right to left. The goats didn't seem to notice, or care. He did, however, spot the intense infrared glow of some kind of smokeless electric heater at the edge of the mesquite trees. There were people there too – at least half a dozen. Standing up.

He opened the channel. 'Alex here. I count about eighty goats and at least six guys standing by the brush. They're awake. I think they're cooking something, over.'

'I don't like this, over.'

'Me either. Man, you gotta be some kind of hard-ass to steal goats from people who'd raise goats in an awful goddamn place like this.'

Alex felt surprised at the sudden depth of his own anger. But hell – he himself herded goats. He'd developed a genuine class feeling for goat ranchers.

'Okay.' Rick sighed. 'Lemme see who's awake in the convoy.'

Alex circled the herd, slowly. More glowing bipedal figures appeared, this time at the other side of the road.

'Greg says drop a flare and check it out,' Rick reported.

'Right,' Alex said.

He plucked one of the flares from its plastic clip-on mount on the right-hand strut. The flares were old and dusty and covered with military issue stenciling in Cyrillic. He hadn't imagined them working too well, but at least they were simplicity itself to use.

He yanked the top off. The flare popped and smoldered and then burst into welding-torch brilliance. Surprised despite himself, Alex dropped it.

The flare tumbled in a neat parabola and landed bouncing on the highway, at the edge of the goat herd, which immediately panicked. The goats didn't get far, though; they were all hobbled.

Sharp bangs came from the edge of the road. Alex blinked, saw several men in big hats and shaggy, fringed clothing.

'Rick,' he said, 'they're shooting at me.'

'What?'

'They've got rifles, man, they're trying to shoot me.'

'Get out of there!'

'Right,' Alex muttered. He put some effort into gaining height. The ultralight responded with the trace and speed of a sofa lugged up a flight of stairs. Blinded by the flare down on ground level, they couldn't seem to see him very well. Their shooting was ragged and they were using old-fashioned, loud, banging, chemically propelled bullets. That wouldn't matter, though, if they kept shooting.

Alex had a sudden deep conviction that he was about to be shot. *Death was near*. He had a rush of terror so intense that he actually felt the bullet strike him. It was going to hit him just above the hipbone and pass through his guts like a red-hot burning catheter and leave him dying in his harness dripping blood and spew. He would bleed to death in midair in the grip of a smart machine. The Troupe would call the machine in to land, and they would find him still strapped in his seat, cold and gray and bloody and dead.

Knowing with irrational conviction that his life was over, Alex felt a dizzy spasm of terrible satisfaction. *Shot dead by men with rifles.* It was so much better than the way he'd always known he would die. He was gonna die like a normal person, as if his life had meant something and there had been some real alternative to dying. He was going to die like a Trouper, and anybody who learned about his death would surely think he'd died that way on purpose. Like he'd died for their Work.

For an insane moment Alex actually did believe in the Work, with his whole heart. Everything in his life had led up to this moment. Now he was going to be killed, and it was all fated, and had all been meant this way from the beginning.

But the men with guns kept missing him. And after a while the firing stopped. And then a crouching man in the shaggy clothes ran out rapidly to the burning flare in the road, and he stomped it into embers.

Alex realized that Rick had been shouting scratchily in his ears for some time.

'I'm okay!' Alex said. 'Sorry.'

'Where are you?'

'Ummmm . . . between them and the convoy. Up pretty high. I think they're herding the goats off the road now. Hard to tell . . . '

'You're not hurt? How about the aircraft?'

Alex looked around himself. The ultralight was entirely invisible. He pulled the flashlight from its holster and waved it over the wings, the bow, the propeller housing.

'Nothing,' he said, putting the light away. 'No damage, they missed me by ten kilometers, they never even knew where I was.' Alex laughed shrilly, coughed, cleared his throat. 'Goddamn, that was great!'

'We're gonna pull back now, man. There's another route . . . come back to the convoy now.'

'You don't want me to throw another flare at 'em?'

'Fuck no, man! Just stay away from the bastards.'

Alex felt a sudden burst of fury. 'There's nothing to these people, man! They're crazy, they're nothing! We should go kick their asses!'

'Alex, calm down, man. That's the Rangers' job. We chase storms, we don't chase crooks.'

'We could wipe 'em all out right now!'

'Alex, talk sense. I'm tellin' you there are other routes. We just back up a few klicks and we take a different road. It'll take us half an hour. What do you wanna do – lose half an hour, or walk into a firefight and lose some of your friends?'

Alex grunted.

'That's why we put people flying point in the first place, man,' Rick said, smacking his gum. 'You did a fine job there. Now just relax.'

'Okay,' Alex said. 'Sure, I get it. If that's the way you want it, sure. Have it your way.' He was still alive. Alive and breathing. Alive, alive, alive . . .

CHAPTER

'The profession of design,' sniffed April Logan, 'having once lost its aspiration to construct a better world, must by necessity decay into a work-for-hire varnish for barbarism.' April Logan's noble, aquiline head, with its single careful forelock of white hair, began, subtly at first and then with greater insistence, to stretch. Rather like taffy. 'The density of information embodied in the modern technological object creates deep conceptual stress that *implodes* the human-object interface . . . Small wonder that a violent reactive Luddism has become the definitive vogue of the period, as primates, outsmarted by their own environment, lash out in frenzy at a postnatural world.'

The critic's head was morphing like a barber pole on the slender pillar of her tanned and elegant neck. 'The same technology that makes our design tools more complex, vastly increases the number of options in determining how any designed object may appear and function. If there are no working parts visible to the naked eye, then techne itself becomes liquid and amorphous. It required the near collapse of the American republic to finally end the long, poisonous vogue for channel switching and ironic juxtaposition . . . ' April Logan's head was gently turning inside out, in full fine-grain pixelated color. Even her voice was changing, some kind of acoustic sampling that mimicked a female larynx evolving into a helix, or a Klein bottle.

Jane's belt phone buzzed. At the same instant a classic twentieth-century telephone appeared in midair, to Jane's right. A phone designed by one Henry Dreyfuss, Jane recalled. Professor

Logan often spoke of Henry Dreyfuss.

Jane paused the critic's lecture with a twitch of her glove, then pulled off her virching helmet. She plucked the flimsy little phone from her belt and answered it. 'Jane here.'

'Janey, it's Alex. I'm out with the goats.'

'Yes?'

'Can you tell me something? I got a laptop here and I'm trying to pull up a fine-grain of the local landscape, and I got some great satellite shots, but I can't find any global-positioning grids.'

'Oh,' Jane said. Alex sounded so earnest and interested that she felt quite pleased with him. She couldn't remember the last time Alex had openly asked a favor of her, that he'd simply asked her for her help. 'What longitude and latitude are you looking for, exactly?'

'Longitude 100° 22′39″, latitude 34° 07′25″.'

'That's real close to camp.'

'Yeah, I thought so.'

'Should be about three hundred meters due east of the command yurt.' Jerry always set the yurt right on a gridline if he could manage it. It helped a little with radiolocation and Doppler triangulation and such.

'Yeah, that's where pretty much where me and the goats are now, but I was just checking. Thanks. Bye.' He hung up.

Jane thought this over for a moment, sighed, and put her helmet away.

She passed Rick and Mickey, beavering away on the system, and the helmeted Jerry, back at his usual weighted pacing. Jerry was starting to seriously wear the carpet. Jane put on her sunglasses and left camp.

Lovely spring sky. Sweet fluffy altocumulus. You'd think a sky like that could never do a moment's harm.

She found Alex sitting cross-legged under the shade of a mesquite tree. Getting shade from the tiny pinnate leaves of a mesquite was like trying to fetch water in a sieve, but Alex wore his much-glued sombrero as well. And he was wearing his breathing mask.

He was messing languidly with the flaccid black smart rope. Jane was surprised, and not at all happy, to see the smart rope again. The thing's primitive user-hostile interface was a total joke. The first time she'd used it, the vicious rope had whipped back like a snapping strand of barbed wire and left a big welt on her shin.

She walked up closer, boots crunching the spiky grass. Alex suddenly turned.

'Hi,' she said.

'*Hola, hermana.*'

'Y'know, if I'd been a coyote, I coulda just walked off with one of these goats.'

'Be my guest.' Alex took off the mask and yawned. 'Walk off with one of these tracking collars, and Rick will come out with his rifle and exterminate you.'

'What's going on out here?'

'Just basking in my glory as hero of the day,' Alex drawled. 'See my throng of enthusiastic admirers?' The smart rope twitched uneasily as he tried, without success, to fling it at the goats. 'I wish you hadn't called the Texas Rangers. I really don't wanna talk to those guys.'

'The Rangers never stay for long. What are you up to?'

Alex said nothing. He opened his laptop, checked the clock on the screen, then stood up theatrically and looked to the south.

She turned to match his gaze. An endless vista of odd hump-shaped caprocks dotted with juniper and mesquite, here and there the blobby green lobes of distant prickly pear, a yellow sparkling of tall waving coneflowers. Far to the south a passenger jet left a ragged contrail.

'Whoa,' he said. 'There it is. Here it comes. I'll be damned.' He laughed. 'Right on time too! Man, it's amazing what a kind word and a credit card can do.'

Jane's heart sank. She didn't know what was about to happen, but already she didn't like it. Alex was watching the horizon with his worst and most evil grin.

She stepped behind his shoulder and looked across the landscape.

Then she saw it too. A bouncing machine. Something very much like a camouflage-painted kangaroo.

It was crossing the hills with vast, unerring, twenty-meter leaps. A squat metal sphere, painted in ragged patches of dun and olive drab. It had a single thick, pistoning, metal leg.

The bounding robot whipped that single metal leg around with dreadful unerring precision, like some nightmare one-legged pirate.

It whacked its complex metal foot against the earth like a hustler's cue whacking a pool ball, and it bounded off instantly, hard. The thing spent most of its time airborne, a splotchy cannonball spinning on its axis and kicking like a flea against the Texan earth. It was doing a good eighty klicks an hour. As it got closer she saw that its underside was studded with grilled sensors.

It gave a final leap and, God help her, a deft little somersault, and it landed on the earth with a brief hiss of sucked-up impact. Instantly, a skinny little gunmetal tripod flicked out from beneath it, like a triple set of hinged switchblades.

And there it sat, instantly gone as quiet as a coffee table, not ten meters away from them.

'All right,' she said. 'What is that thing?'

'It's a dope mule. From my friends in Matamoros.'

'Oh, Jesus.'

'Look,' he said, 'relax. It's just a cheaper street version of Charlie, your car! Charlie's a smuggler's vehicle, and this is a smuggler's vehicle. It's just that instead of having two hundred smart spokes and driver's seats and roll bars like that big kick-ass car does, it's only got one spoke. One spoke, and a gyroscope inside, and a global positioning system.' He shrugged. 'And some mega chip inside so it never runs into anything and no cop ever sees it.'

'Oh,' she groaned. 'Yeah, this is great, Alex.'

'It'll carry, I dunno, maybe forty kilos merchandise. No big deal. Dope people have hundreds of these things now. They don't cost much to make, so it's like a toy for 'em.'

'Why didn't you tell me about this?'

'Are you kidding? Since when do I ask your permission to do anything?' He walked up to the mule.

She hurried after him. 'You'd better not.'

'Get away from there!' he yelped. 'They're hot-wired.' Jane jumped back warily, flinching, and Alex chuckled with pleasure. 'Tamperproof! Put in the wrong password, and the sucker explodes on the spot and destroys all the evidence! And what's more – if you're not, like, their friend? Or they're tired of dealing with you? Then sometimes they just booby-trap it, and blow you away the second you touch the keypad.'

He laughed. 'Don't look so glum. That's all just legend, really.

Doper brag talk. The dope vaqueros hardly ever blow anyone up. You and me both know the border doesn't mean anything anymore. There are no more borders. Just free and open markets!' He chuckled merrily. 'They can send me whatever the hell they want. Dope, explosives, frozen human hearts, who cares? They're just another delivery service.'

Alex punched a long string of numbers, with exaggerated care, into a telephone keypad welded into the top of the mule. The robot mulled the matter over, then hissed open on a stainless-steel hinge, showing a big rubber O-ring around its midsection.

Alex started pulling out the goods. Lots of plastic-wrapped cloth. A pair of cowboy boots. A yellow cylinder tank. A plastic jug. Designer sunglasses in a shockproof case. A handgun.

Alex tried the sunglasses on immediately, clearly delighted with them. 'Here, you can have this,' he said, tossing her the handgun. 'I'm not interested.'

Jane caught it with a gasp. The handgun was all injection-molded ceramic and plastic, a short-barreled six-shot revolver. It felt hard as a rock and utterly lethal. It weighed about as much as a teacup. It would pass any metal detector in the world and had probably cost all of two dollars to make.

'You're full of shit!' she said. 'If the Rangers found out about this, they'd go ape.'

'Yeah, and the Houston cops wouldn't like it either, if the vaqueros were dumb enough to send a mule bouncin' right down the streets of Houston, but they're not gonna do that, are they? Nobody's that stupid. Nobody knows about this but you and me. And Carol, that is.' Alex pulled out a gleaming metal bracelet. 'I got Carol this barometer watch! She doesn't know that I bought it for her, but I think she'll like it, don't you? It'll match her Trouper cuff.' He tipped his floppy paper sombrero back on his head. 'Carol's the only one around here who's been really decent to me.'

'Carol isn't going to approve of this – '

'Oh, get off it!' Alex snapped. 'Carol is bent! Carol loves this!' He grinned beneath his new gold-framed shades. 'Carol is old-time structure-hit people, for Christ's sake! And she's fucking Greg, and Greg is some kinda ex-Special Forces demolition spook, a scary, heavy guy. I'm real glad they chase storms now instead of knocking bridges down, but Carol and Greg are very bent people. They're not from milk-and-cookie land.'

'I've never seen Carol or Greg commit any act of vandalism,' Jane said with dignity.

'Yeah,' he scoffed. 'Besides helping you break into Mexican hospitals.' He shook his head. 'You're just pissed off because I didn't get *you* anything, aren't you? Well, there's a nice handgun for ya! If boyfriend gets wandering eyes, blow him away!' He laughed.

Jane stared at him. 'You think this is *funny*, don't you?'

'Janey, it *is* funny.' He pulled the plasticwrap from a hand-stitched denim shirt. Then he peeled off his paper suit. He stood there naked in his big paper hat and shades, the paper suit pooled around his ankles, tugging the fine blue shirt onto his skinny arms. 'You can get all hot and bothered about the implications and the morality and all that shit, if you really want to. Or else, you can just try and live in the modern world! It doesn't make a damn bit of difference either way!'

He kicked the paper suit off his feet, then stood on top of the paper and pulled off his right shoe. 'The border is fucked, and the government is fucked!' He pulled off the left shoe and flung it aside. 'And society is fucked, and the climate is *really* fucked. And the media are fucked, and the economy is fucked, and the smartest people in the world live like refugees and criminals!' He ripped the plasticwrap off a pair of patterned silk boxer shorts and stepped into them. 'And nobody has *any idea* how to make things any better, and there *isn't* any way to make things better, and there isn't gonna *be* any way, and we don't control *anything important* about our lives! And that's just how it is today, and yes, it's funny!' He laughed shrilly. 'It's hilarious! And if you don't get the joke, you don't deserve to be alive in the 2030s.'

Alex climbed into a satiny pair of brown jeans, carefully tucking in the denim shirttails. 'And what's more, right now I've got myself a really nice shirt. And real nice pants too. And boots, too, look, these boots are hand-tooled in Mexican leather, they're really beautiful.' He unrolled a pair of thick cotton boot socks.

'The Troupe aren't gonna appreciate this. They're not really into, y'know, play-cowboy gear.'

'Janey, I don't give a rat's ass what your friends think about my goddamn clothes.' He stepped into the socks, jammed his feet in the boots, then walked over to the robot mule, looked into its empty cavity one last time, and slammed its top.

After a three-second pause, the mule suddenly whipped its tripod shut and fired itself into the air. 'If it were up to you and our friends,' Alex said, watching it bounce madly away, 'I'd be wearing plastic toilet paper the rest of my life. I'm not a weather refugee, and I'm not gonna pretend to be one. And if they don't like what I'm wearing, they can make me ride point again, if they're too goddamned timid to do it themselves.' He watched the machine bounding off southward, as he carefuly buttoned his shirt cuffs. 'I am what I am. If you want to stop me, then shoot me.'

THE RANGER POSSE showed up at three that afternoon. Jane was unhappy to see them. She was never happy to see Rangers, and worse yet, she had a yeast infection and was running a low-grade fever.

It wasn't the first time she'd had yeast. Yeast was common. The pollution from overuse of broad-scale antibiotics had made candida fiercer and scarier, the same way it had super-charged staph and flu and TB and all the rest. Candida hadn't bootstrapped its way up to the utter lethality of, say, Bengali cholera, but it had gotten a lot more contagious, and nowadays it actually *was* a genital infection that you could catch off a toilet seat.

A few discreet inquiries around camp established that none of the other Troupe women had yeast, so it had to be a repeated flare-up of her old curse, the yeast she'd caught back in 2027. That one had flared up in sullen little bouts of nastiness for almost six months, until her immune system had finally got on top of it. She'd hoped she had the yeast knocked down for good, but yeast was a lot like staph or herpes, it was always there lurking low-level, and it went crazy when it got a good excuse.

And she had to admit that it had a pretty good excuse now. She'd been having sex until it hurt. It wasn't very sensible to do that, but sex wasn't very much use to her when it was sensible. Jane hadn't truly appreciated sex, really, until she'd got into headlong sex at full tilt. Hard, clawing, yelling sex that didn't stop until you were sweaty and chafed and sore. Sex on a nice comfy bed of rock-hard Texas dirt, with a guy in top physical condition who was a lot taller than you were and outweighed you by twenty kilos. It was like discovering a taste for really hot food. Like a taste for whiskey. Except that whiskey was a poison, and you regretted whiskey in the morning, but a really passionately physical affair had been a tonic for her, and she'd never regretted it for a moment.

It had changed her. In a surprising number of ways. Physically, even. It was kind of weird and didn't sound real plausible, but she could swear that her pelvis had actually changed shape in the past year. That her hipbones fit at a different angle and she actually walked differently now. Differently and *better*, with her back straight and her head up. But she was only flesh and blood. The spirit was willing and the flesh was more than willing, but the body could only take so much. She'd asked too much of the body. And now she had the crud.

And then there was that even more harassing annoyance, the cops. The Rangers. There were six of them, and they rode boldly into camp in three hand-me-down U.S. Army pursuit vehicles. They rolled in a cloud of yellow dust right through the camp's perimeter posts, which immediately went into panic mode, whooping and flashing lights and arcing electricity in big harmless crackling gouts. One of them fired a taser dart on a leash, which missed.

Greg rushed into the command yurt and quickly shut off the alarms while the Rangers slowly climbed out of their slab-sided carbon-armored prowl cars and stood there in the settling dust, in their hats and sunglasses and guns.

Once upon a time the Texas Rangers had basically been packs of frontier vigilantes violently enforcing the peace on pretty much anything that moved. A hundred years later Texas was settled and civilized, and the Texas Rangers were paragons of professional law enforcement. And then a century later yet, everything had pretty much gone to hell. So now the Texas Rangers were pretty much what they'd been two hundred years ago.

One Ranger tradition always rang true, though. Texas Rangers always carried an absolute shitload of weaponry. If a bad guy had a six-gun, then a Ranger had two six-guns, plus a rifle and a bowie knife. If bad guys had rifles, then Rangers had tommy guns, shotguns, and gas grenades. Now bad guys had crazy stuff like plastic explosive and smart land mines and electric rifles, so Rangers had toxic fléchette pistols and truck-mounted machine guns and rocket-slug sniper rifles and heat-seeking aerial drones. Plus satellite backup and their own cellular bands.

The leader of the Rangers was a Captain Gault, down from what was left of Amarillo. Captain Gault had a white cowboy hat, a neat gray-streaked ponytail in a silver band, smart sunglasses, and a drooping black mustache. Captain Gault was in creased khaki trousers and a bellows-pocketed, long-sleeved khaki shirt with a silver-star badge at the breast. He wore a neatly knotted black tie and two broad, silver-buckled, black-leather belts, one belt for the khaki trousers, the other for his twin, pearl-handled pistols. They were beautifully polished fléchette pistols in elaborate black leather holsters. The captain's shining guns were so radiant of somber police authority that there was something almost papal about them.

The four Ranger privates were in chocolate-chip U.S. desert camou fatigues. They had brown cowboy hats with the Lone Star on the crown, and brown leather holsters with the Lone Star inset in the leather, and trail boots with the Lone Star on the uppers, and one of them even had a little silver Lone Star inset in his front tooth. They were bearded and hairy and slit-mouthed and dusty, and they bristled with guns and cell phones, and they looked extremely tough.

And then there was the last guy. He was wearing a khaki T-shirt and cutoff fatigue pants and running shoes, and he had a beat-up cloth fatigue cap and a nasty-looking, well-worn rifle across his back.

This last guy was black. He had a mess of kinky buffalo-soldier locks. Jane never put much emphasis on skin color. People who made fine ethnic distinctions always smacked of weird ethnic race-war craziness to her, and considering her own ethnic background, Jane figured she had a right to be a little nervous about that kind of hairsplitting attitude. Carol was black, and nobody much noticed or cared. Rudy Martinez looked kinda like some grandparent of his might have been black. But this Ranger guy was *really* black, like inhumanly satin black. Sometimes people did odd chemical things to their skin nowadays. Especially if they spent a lot of time out in the open sun, and thought a lot about ozone damage.

Jerry came out of the command yurt to greet the Rangers, flanked by Greg and Joe Brasseur, trailed by a reluctant, shuffling Alex. Jerry had thrown off his usual ratty paper suit and was wearing clean slacks and a decent buttoned shirt and a white coat. Joe Brasseur had a shirt and a tie and glasses, and was carrying a clipboard and looking very lawyerly. Greg looked pretty much like Greg always did: jeans, army shirt, shades, muscle. Alex was in his new shirt and brown jeans and looked like he wished he was on some other continent.

The men gathered around the Ranger prowl cars and started muttering deep in their chests. This was another thing Jane didn't like about Rangers. They were unbelievably chauvinist. Jane knew that a few Texas policewomen had joined the Rangers decades back, but when the Rangers had started routinely shooting people in large numbers again, the whole sex-integration thing had suddenly evaporated. It was as dead as drug-law enforcement and racial integration and universal health care and other perished niceties of the period. There were no women in combat positions in the Texas Rangers, or the state National Guard units, or the U.S. Army for that matter. And the men in these little all-male enclaves of violence were more than a little obnoxious about it.

Alex submitted to Captain Gault's brief interrogation and then left in a hurry, with relief all over his face.

The extremely black guy noticed Jane watching from the sidelines. He dogtrotted over to her, grinning. 'Got any water? Got any salt?'

'Sure, Officer.' Jane called Ellen Mae on the phone.

The black Ranger nodded peaceably, dipped into the baggy pockets of his cutoffs, and began to hand-roll a marijuana cigarette. The guy's shins and forearms were chicken-scratched with fine scars. He had a big scarred crater in the side of his neck that Jane could have put the end of her thumb into.

'I'm not sure a law enforcement officer on duty ought to be smoking marijuana,' Jane said.

The Ranger flicked a wooden match with his callused thumbnail, lit the joint, and inhaled sharply. 'Get a life,' he suggested.

Young Jeff Lowe appeared on the trot from the kitchen yurt, with a canteen and an antiseptic paper cup, two salt tablets, and a couple strips of jerky. He handed them shyly to the Ranger.

'Are you smoking dope?' Jeff said, wide-eyed.

'I got glaucoma,' the Ranger offered. He bolted the salt pills, knocked back three cups of water, took a last long huff off his joint, then stomped it out and began hungrily gnawing the jerky.

'Good jerky,' he said, mouth full. 'You don't meet many folks these days who can really cure a deer.' He began sidling back toward his vehicle.

'Wait a sec,' Jane said. 'Please.'

The Ranger raised his brows.

'What's it all about?'

'Livestock smugglers,' the Ranger told her. 'They got those pharm goats hot-wired to do all kinds of weird shit nowadays . . . Run 'em up backroads by night, mix 'em up with meat goats, and you can't tell no difference without a DNA scan . . . That was a pretty tough outfit you met, we been watchin' out for 'em awhile, y'all was lucky.'

'What kind of "weird shit" do you get from illegal goats?' Jeff asked.

'Plastic explosive, for one thing. Strain it out of the milk, make cheese out of it, put a fuse in it, and structure-hit the hell right out of anything.'

'Explosive goat's milk,' Jane said slowly.

'You're kidding, right?' Jeff said.

The Ranger smiled broadly. 'Yeah, folks, I'm kidding, sorry.'

Jane stared at him. The Ranger stared back. There was no expression in his reflective shades. 'What are you gonna do now?' Jane said.

'Find the contact point, I'll track 'em through the brush. . . . We'll catch 'em by morning. Maybe noon. Cap'n Gault likes to go by the book, he'll give 'em a chance to throw down their guns and come quiet. Thanks for the water, ma'am. Y'all take care now.' The Ranger trotted off.

Jeff waited until the Ranger was out of earshot. Then he spoke with hushed amazement and respect. 'Janey, they're gonna kill them all.'

'Yeah,' Jane said. 'I know.'

VIOLENT, DEADLY STORMS broke out in profusion in the last two weeks of May 2031. Unfortunately they were in Kansas, Iowa, Missouri, Nebraska, and Arkansas. A minor front swept Tornado Alley on May 27, ardently pursued by the Troupe, but it yielded no spikes.

Statistically, this was not unusual. However, the statistics themselves had become pretty damned unusual as the century had progressed. Before heavy weather, there had been about nine hundred tornadoes every year in the United States. Nowadays, there were about four thousand. Before heavy weather, a year's worth of tornadoes killed about a hundred people and caused about $200 million (constant 1975 dollars) in damage. Now, despite vastly better warning systems, tornadoes killed about a thousand people a year, and the damage was impossible to estimate accurately because the basic economic nature of both 'value' and 'currency' had gone nonlinear.

Tornadoes were, for obvious reasons, easier to find nowadays. But most storms, even violent storms with good indicators, never spawned tornadoes. Many hunts were simply bound to turn up dry, even with excellent weather monitoring and rapid all-terrain deployment. And even the much-ravaged Texas-Oklahoma Tornado Alley, the planet's premier spawning ground for twisters, had to get some peace and quiet sometimes.

The dry spell visibly affected the Troupe's morale. Alex saw that they were still on their best behavior around Mulcahey, but Mulcahey himself became withdrawn, wrapping himself in marathon simulation sessions. The Troupe got bored, then petulant. Carol and Greg, whose relationship seemed unstable at the best of times, starting openly sniping at one another. Peter and Rick took a motorcycle and sidecar into Amarillo 'to get laid,' and came back hung over and beaten up. Rudy Martinez went to San Antonio for a week to visit his ex-wife and his kids. Martha and Buzzard, who found one another physically repulsive but couldn't seem to let one another alone, got into a mean, extensive quararel over minor damage to one of the ultralights. And Juanita spent a lot of her time tearing around uselessly in the dune buggy, ostensibly to give its new, improved interface a shakedown, but more, Alex suspected, for the sake of her own nerves than anything to do with the car.

The High Plains down around Big Spring and Odessa had got generous rains this year, but the Troupe had since moved far north, near Palo Duro Canyon. Up here, the grasslands had got a good start for spring and then stalled. The unnatural lushness of greenhouse rain had faded to the windy dryness once more natural to the Texas Panhandle, and the supercharged vegetation started to hesitate and shut down. It didn't wither exactly – stuff like hairy grama, elbowbush, and buffalo grass was way too tough and mean-spirited to do anything as sissy as 'withering' – but it got yellow and tight and sere and spiky. And up in the Oklahoma Panhandle, it hadn't rained since late March.

Alex had a high tolerance for boredom. True restlessness required a level of animal energy that he simply didn't possess. Unlike the Troupers, he didn't fidget or complain. Given working lungs, a screen to look at, and a place to sleep, Alex felt basically content. He hadn't asked to join a group of touchy thrill freaks as their unpaid amateur goatherd, and he recognized the true absurdity of his situation, but he didn't actually mind it much. The weather was lovely, the air was clear, his health was good, and he was being left alone all day with some goats and the Library of Congress and a smart rope.

This suited him. The goats were an appreciative audience for his growing repertoire of rope tricks, and they made excellent targets for the new wicked noose he had installed at the rope's end. As a bonus, now that he had his big leather boots from Matamoros, Alex no longer fretted much about thorns, spines, stinging nettles, and big slithering venomous rattlesnakes. The main inconvenience of his existence was the three meals a day, when he had to deal face-to-face with the Troupers. Besides, the food was awful.

Being shot at for the cause had very much helped Alex's social position in camp. Not many of the Troupers had actually been shot at under any circumstances. Except for Ellen Mae several times, and Peter once, and Rudy on a couple of occasions in civilian life, and Greg 'lots of times.' Surviving gunfire was an experience the Troupers valued highly, and being shot at in the actual service of the Troupe itself brought Alex a certain cachet. He'd got a few grudging, snotty remarks about his new clothes, but the clothes didn't stay new for long. Alex never changed them, rarely washed, and had stopped shaving. His jeans and embroidered shirt were soon filthy, and the paper sombrero, which never left his head, grew steadily more wadded and hideous. Plus, he grew a patchy blond beard. After that, nobody paid him much attention. He'd got his wish, and become a cipher.

As tension mounted in the camp, though, Alex decided that his situation had become solid enough for him to take a few useful steps. He quietly approached Joe Brasseur about his legal and financial situation.

Alex was used to lawyers. He'd grown up in the company of his father's numerous hired attorneys. Brasseur was a bent attorney – that odd and highly exceptional kind of lawyer who wasn't personally well-to-do. Alex strongly suspected that Brasseur had been on the wrong side of politics during the State of Emergency.

Most people had got over that period of history and managed to forget the peculiar way they'd been behaving at the time, but Joe Brasseur, like other Troupers, was pretty clearly not most people.

Alex knew that it was useless talking to lawyers unless you were willing to tell them a lot of embarrassing things. He felt pretty sure that Brasseur was not a narc or some cop's little finger, so he told Brasseur in detail about his financial arrangements with the *clínica* in Nuevo Laredo.

Most people went through life without ever using a private currency. Most people were, of course, poor. They didn't have enough wealth to buy into the private-money system, or enough contacts or market smarts to use private currencies effectively. Except, of course, during the State of Emergency, when every American, rich and poor alike, had been forced to use a private currency because the Regime had privatized the U.S. dollar.

Alex wasn't exactly sure how 'currency privatization' had been accomplished, back at the time. He was similarly vague about the Regime's massive 'data nationalizations.' Joe Brasseur, however, seemed to have an excellent grasp of these principles. Brasseur was in charge of the Troupe's financial books, and they were a rat nest of private currencies.

Alex was well-to-do, and he had some unlikely friends, so he had the basics down pretty well. It all had to do with unbreakable encryption, digital authentication, anonymous remailing, and network untraceability. These were all computer networking techniques that had once been considered very odd and naughty. They were also so elementary to do, that once they were in place, they couldn't be stopped without tearing the whole Net down.

Of course, once these techniques were in place, they conclusively destroyed the ability of governments to control the flow of electronic funds, anywhere, anytime, for any purpose. As it happened, this process had pretty much destroyed any human control at all over the modern electronic economy. By the time people figured out that raging nonlinear anarchy was not exactly to the advantage of anyone concerned, the process was simply too far gone to stop. All workable standards of wealth had vaporized, digitized, and vanished into a nonstop hurricane of electronic thin air. Even physically tearing up the fiber optics couldn't stop it; governments that tried to just found that the whole encryption mess oozed swiftly into voice mail and even fax machines.

One major upshot of the Regime's privatization of the currency was that large amounts of black-market wealth had suddenly surfaced. This had been part of the plan, apparently – that even though the government was sabotaging its own ability to successfully impose any income tax, the government would catch up on the other end, by imposing punitive taxes on previously hidden black-market transactions.

They'd swiftly discovered, however, that the scale of black money was titanic. The black-market wealth in tax evasion, kickbacks, official corruption, theft, embezzlement, arms, drugs, prostitution, barter, and off-the-books moonlighting was far huger than any conventional economist had ever imagined. The global ocean of black money was so vast in scope that it was instantly, crushingly obvious that the standard doctrines of conventional finance had no workable contact with reality. Economists who'd thought they understood the basic nature of modern finance had been living in a dogmatic dreamland as irrelevant as Marxism. After that terrible revelation, there'd been savage runs on most national currencies and the stock markets had collapsed.

As the Emergency had deepened, the panicking Regime had rammed its data nationalizations through Congress, and with that convulsive effort, the very nature of money and information had both mutated beyond any repair.

The resultant swirling chaos had become the bedrock of Alex's everyday notions of modern normality.

Alex did not find it surprising that people like the Chinese Triads and the Corsican Black Hand were electronically minting their own cash. He simply accepted it: electronic, private cash, unbacked by any government, untraceable, completely anonymous, global in reach, lightninglike in speed, ubiquitous, fungible, and usually highly volatile. Of course, such funds didn't boldly say 'Sicilian Mafia' right on the transaction screen; they usually had some stuffy official-sounding alias such as 'Banco Ambrosiano ATM Euro-DigiLira,' but the private currency speculators would usually have a pretty good guess as to the solvency of the issuers.

Quite often these private currencies would collapse, through sheer greed, mismanagement, or just bad luck in the market. But the usual carnivorous free-enterprise market forces had jolted some kind of rough order into the mess. Nowadays, for a lot of people, private currencies were just the way money was.

When you used private, digital cash, even the people who sold you their money didn't know who you were. Quite likely you had no real idea who they were, either, other than their rates, their market recognition, and their performance history. You had no identity other than your unbreakably encrypted public key word. You could still use government currencies if you really wanted to, and most people did, for the sake of simplicity or through lack of alternatives. Most people had no choice in the matter, because most people in the world were poor.

Unfortunately, thanks to their catastrophic loss of control over basic economics, so were most governments. Government-issued currencies were scarcely more stable than the private kind. Government, even the governments of powerful advanced countries, had already lost control of their currencies to the roiling floodwaters of currency trading as early as the 1990s. That was the main reason why the Regime had given up backing U.S. dollars in the first place.

Joe Brasseur's private-currency node in the Troupe's system was not untypical in the trade: it was the digital equivalent of an entire twentieth-century banking conglomerate, boiled down to a few sectors on a hard disk.

In order to gain admittance to the *clínica* in Nuevo Laredo, Alex had left a hefty wad of private currency under a secured lien by a third party. He hadn't got the money back, had no real idea how to get his money back, but he thought that maybe Brasseur would be the logical choice to find that money and fetch it out somehow. If so, then the Troupe was welcome to use it.

Brasseur took in Alex's confession with a calm, priestlike air, gazing solemnly at him over the rims of his glasses, and then Brasseur had nodded and set to work, and Alex had never heard another word about the subject. Except that things perked up markedly for the Troupe after a week and a half. A bunch of former Troupers, Fred and José and Maureen and Palaniappan and Kenny, showed up in a convoy with a lot of canned food and a beer keg. The command yurt got a new carpet. A new improved air condenser arrived that weighed less than the old one, used less energy, and supplied more water. There was a party, and everyone's mood improved for a few days.

Nobody thanked Alex for this. Just as well, Alex thought, that there was no public fuss made about himself or his role. Those who needed to know were going to know. Alex had already concluded that almost everything that really mattered in Troupe life took place way under the surface. It was a lot like life in a barracks, or a dorm, or a TB ward.

Some Troupers, such as Mulcahey, Brasseur, and Carol and Greg, knew pretty much everything, pretty much immediately. The second rank were those who were gonna catch on pretty fast on their own, like Ellen Mae and Rudy Martinez and Mickey Kiehl. Then there were those who were gonna get told the official version by somebody else, like Peter and Rick and Martha and Sam. And certain beloved characters were gonna be gently protected from the full awful truth for their own good, like Buzzard and Joanne and Jeff and, in her own unique way, Juanita.

The very last and lowest rank were the passing wannabes, and city boy/girlfriends, and ex-husbands/ex-wives, and hangers-on and netfriends and himself, Alex Unger, and the various other non-Troupe subhumans. And that was the way it was always gonna be with the Storm Troupe, until they all turned on each other, or they were all shot by bandits or hit by lightning, or until they found the F-6.

Alex didn't know if he believed in the F-6. But he believed that the Troupe believed. With every day that passed, they were getting more keyed up to plunge headlong into something truly dreadful. And the bottom line was that he didn't want to leave – not until he knew what they would find and what it would do to them.

On May 31, as if to change their luck, Mulcahey deliberately moved camp twenty kilometers northwest, into Hall County. The burst of action seemed to help morale some.

On June 2, heavy weather hit again. The luck of the assignment – as if there were any 'luck' involved where Mulcahey's orders were concerned – had Alex confined to the camp as 'support crew.' Alex figured this was just as well. Let the others have a chance to blow off steam.

And then there was another, and far more serious, matter: his cough was back. It had started really small at first, just a little throat-clearing rasp, but Alex had known for some time that the dosage of blue goo was losing its charm. His lungs no longer felt like sweet slick paper dipped in oil. Slowly but with terrible sureness, they were starting to feel a hell of a lot more like his own lungs. He'd worn the breathing mask faithfully, until his tanned face had a white triangular muzzle of untanned skin just like a raccoon's, but that wasn't enough. He was going to have to take steps.

The June 2 pursuit was all-out. They were up before dawn, and Mulcahey himself went into the field. The only people left in camp were Joe Brasseur doing navigation, Buzzard as network coord, and Sam Moncrieff as nowcaster. And, of course, Alex, nominally in charge of the support jeeps.

This was not a very taxing job. The support jeeps were unmanned, and were supposed to carry supplies into the field through global positioning. If called upon, Alex was supposed to instantly load the jeeps with spare whatchamacallits and then route them long-distance to a rendezvous.

Alex assumed that this assignment was a subtle reference on Mulcahey's part to Alex's covert use of a dope mule. Kind of a deliberate shoulder tap there on the part of the Troupe jefe. To Alex's deep relief, Mulcahey almost never took any notice of Alex, favorable or unfavorable. He'd never called Alex in for one of those head-to-head encounter sessions that seemed to leave the other Troupers so bent out of shape. But every once in a while there would be these ambiguous little jabs. Intended, Alex figured, to intimidate him, to assure him that Mulcahey did have an eye on him, so he wouldn't try anything really stupid. When you came right down to it, this tactic worked pretty well.

In reality, Alex's support job consisted mostly of fetching venison chili for Sam, Joe, and Buzzard, since the men were leashed to their machinery. The goats were taken care of: the Troupe had stretched a line of wire around the perimeter posts and had corralled the goats inside the camp. The goats were cropping all the grass in camp, and crapping all over the ground as well, but they'd be breaking camp tomorrow and leaving, so it didn't matter much.

Sam Moncrieff was thrilled with his nowcaster status. He'd been Mulcahey's star grad student before Mulcahey had left academia (in a shambles), and Sam took the exalted central role of Troupe nowcaster with complete and utter seriousness. He was stomping around blindly in the command yurt with his head in a virching helmet, burrowing through scientific visualizations like some kind of data-gloved gopher.

Joe Brasseur had his own navigation setup in the command yurt's left-hand annex.

So Alex found himself alone in the right-hand annex, the sysadmin station, with Buzzard.

Buzzard was in a peculiar mood.

'I hate what Janey has done to this system, dude,' Buzzard opined, clumsily rolling a marijuana cigarette. 'It don't crash as much now, and Christ knows it *looks* a lot prettier, but it's a real mud bath to run.'

Alex examined the gridwork of the display for his support jeeps. It always amazed him how many forgotten little ghost towns there were, out in West Texas. 'I guess you'd rather be out virching your 'thopters.'

'Aw, you can't chase 'em all,' Buzzard said tolerantly. 'Let Kiehl get his chance out in the field, this candy-ass sysadmin desk work would drive anybody nuts.' He lit his joint with a Mexican cigarette lighter and inhaled. 'Want some?' he squeaked.

'No thanks.'

'When the cat's away, dude.' Buzzard shrugged. 'Jerry would get on my case about this, but I tell ya, you spend fourteen straight hours shuffling icons, and it downright *helps* to be ripped to the tits.'

Alex watched as Buzzard plunged into his thicket of screens and menus. Alex guessed that he was tweaking the flow of data from distant Troupe weather instruments, but as far as Alex knew, Buzzard might as well have been bobbing for digital apples.

Buzzard worked a long time, in a glassy-eyed trance of efficiency, stopping twice to decant some dire herbal concoction into a paper cup.

Alex, testing his ingenuity to its limits, managed to pry open one of the Troupe's communication channels on a spare laptop. Rudy and Rick, in the Baker pursuit vehicle somewhere in Cimarron County, Oklahoma, were getting very excited about hail. Not so much the size of it, as the color. The hail was black.

'Black hail,' Alex remarked.

'That's nothing,' Buzzard said, tugging on the metal lump he wore on a thong around his neck. 'Just means there's a little dust in it. It's gettin' real dry up in Colorado. Lotta dust, lotta haze up top . . . black hail. It can happen.'

'Well, I've never seen black hail before,' Alex said. 'And it sounds like they haven't either.'

'I saw a stone fall out of the sky once,' Buzzard said. 'It hit my fuckin' house.'

'Really?'

'Yeah. And this is the one.' Buzzard tugged the metal lump, sharply. 'The biggest piece of it, anyhow. Came right through the roof of my bedroom. I was ten.'

'Your house was hit by a meteor?'

'Gotta happen to somebody,' Buzzard said. 'Statistics prove that.' He paused, stared into the screen in deep abstraction, then looked up. 'That's nothin' either. Once I saw a rain of meat.'

'What?'

'Meat fell out of the sky,' he said simply. 'I saw it with my own two eyes.' He sighed. 'You don't believe me, do ya, kid? Well, go back in the anomaly records sometimes and have a look at the stuff people have seen in the past, falling out of the sky. Amazing stuff! Black hail. Black rain. Red rain. Big rocks. Frogs, Rains of fishes. Snails. Jelly. Red snow, black snow. Chunks of ice have fallen out of the sky as big as fuckin' elephants. Dude, I saw *meat* fall out of the sky.'

'What kind of meat?' Alex asked.

'*Shaved* meat. No hair on it, or anything. Looked kinda like, I dunno, sliced mushrooms or sliced potatoes or something, except it was red and bloody wet and it had little veins in it. It just kinda fell out of a dark cloudy sky one summer, fallin' kinda slow, like somebody throwing potato chips. A little shower of sliced-up meat. About as wide as, I dunno, a good-sized highway, and about eighty meters long. Enough to fill up a couple of big lawn bags, if you raked it up.'

'Did you rake it up?'

'Fuck no, man. We were scared to death.'

'There were *other* people seeing this?' Alex said, surprised. 'Witnesses?'

'Hell yes! Me, my dad, my cousin Elvin, and my cousin Elvin's probation officer. We were all scared to death.' Buzzard's eyes were dilated and shiny. 'That was during the State of Emergency . . . Most of middle America was one big dust bowl. I was a teenage kid in a suburb in Kentucky, and the sky would get black at noon, and you'd get a layer of airborne Iowa or Nebraska or some shit, onto your doors and windows, dry brown dirt in layers as thick as your fingers. Heavy weather, man. People thought it was the end of the world.'

'I've heard of big dust storms. I've never heard of any shaved meat.'

'I dunno, man. I saw it happen. I never forgot it, either. I think my Dad and Elvin managed to forget about it after a couple years, kinda block the memory out, but *I* sure as hell never did. Sometimes I get the feeling that people must see shit happen like that all the time. But they're always too scared to report it to anyone else. People don't like to look like they're crazy . . . And you *sure* didn't want to do it during the State of Emergency, they were doing that "demographic relocation" shit at the time, and people were really scared they were gonna end up in weather camps. It was mega-heavy, mega-bad . . .'

Buzzard glanced down at his screen. 'What the hell is this?' He dug down in the maze of screens and came up with a flashing security alert. 'Hell, we got some kind of ground car outside the camp! Dude, run outside and see!'

Alex didn't run, but he left the yurt at a brisk walk and looked. There was an almost silent, spanking-new civilian truck outside the camp, a big cream-colored four-wheeler with tinted windows and an air-conditioned camper. The truck stopped well outside the perimeter in a spew of dust, exciting the goats, who bounded off timidly among the tepees.

Alex ducked back inside the command yurt. 'Somebody's here, man! Some kind of fancy truck with a big aerial.'

'Hell!' Buzzard looked annoyed. 'Storm spotters, wannabes. You go tell 'em to get lost, man, tell 'em there's nothing going on here. If you need any help, yell, and me and Joe amd Sam will back you up.'

'Okay,' Alex said. 'I get it. No problem.'

He walked deliberately into the open outside the yurt, waved his paper hat at the truck, and waited for them to open fire on him.

The strangers didn't shoot. Two men climbed peaceably out of their nice truck and stood there. His heart rate slowed. Life would go on.

Alex began to feel almost fond of the two men. It seemed very decent of them to be so obligingly normal, to just be a couple of guys in a truck, instead of nightmarish maniac structure-hit bandits randomly shooting up the camp while everyone else was in Oklahoma. Alex put his hat back on and strolled toward the strangers, slowly and with his hands in plain sight. He deliberately hopped the wire around the perimeter posts.

As he walked slowly closer he recognized one of the men. It was the black Ranger bush tracker, one member of the Ranger posse who'd visited camp a couple of weeks earlier. The Ranger was in civilian gear, ragged jean cutoffs and a beat-to-shit yellow T-shirt with the legend NAVAJO NATION RODEO on it. No rifle this time, apparently.

To Alex's considerable surprise, he recognized the other man as well.

The circumstances came back at him with a sharp chemical rush.

He'd been in a backroom of the Gato Negro in Monterrey, with four of his dope-vaquero acquaintances. They were on a field trip from Matamoros, where Alex had been undergoing treatment at the time. The vaqueros were killing time waiting for their man from Monterrey to show with some of the medically necessary. So they were doing lines of cocaine off the marble café table, cocaine cut with one of Don Aldo's home-brewed memory stimulants, one of those blazingly effective smart-drug concoctions that had so thoroughly fucked the ability of government and business leaders to function in the longer term.

Being dope vaqueros, their idea of a good time was to get really wired on this shit and then play a big-stakes tournament of the Spanish-language version of Trivial Pursuit. Cocaine gave Alex heart fibrillations, and he didn't drink, either, and thanks to enormous gaps in his education and his general life experience, he was dog meat at any kind of Trivial Pursuit, much less a Mexican version. But Don Aldo had favored him with a thumbnail's worth of the smart drug, and Alex hadn't quite dared to spurn the good Don's hospitality. He snorted it up and began placing little side bets on the progress of the game. Alex was a very good loser. It was the key to his popularity in these circles.

After about twenty minutes, everything in the Gato Negro had started to take on that false but radiant sense of deep meaning that always accompanied chemical memory enhancement, and then these *other* guys had come in. Three of them, very well dressed. They breezed past the muscle guy at the door, without being patted down for weapons. And this caused Don Aldo, and Juan, and Paco, and Snoopy immediate concern, for Monterrey was not their turf, and their own ceramic Saturday-night specials were in the possession of the house.

The three strangers had regally ignored the vaqueros and had sat down at the room's far corner, and had ordered café con leche and immediately plunged into low, intense conversation.

Don Aldo had beckoned a waiter over with a brisk gesture of somebody else's hot-wired platinum debit card, and had a few words with the waiter, in a border Spanish so twisted with criminal argot that even Alex, something of a connoisseur in these matters, couldn't follow it. And then Don Aldo smiled broadly, and he tipped the waiter. Because one of the three strangers was the police commissioner for the state of Sinaloa. And it was none of their business who El General's two good friends were.

Except that one of El General's friends was the very gentleman who had just stepped out of the truck. He'd been of no special relevance to Alex at the time, but thanks to that snort of mnemonics, the guy's face and mannerisms had been irrevocably punch-pressed on the surface of Alex's brain. At the very sight of him, that haircut, the sunglasses, the neatly cut safari jacket, Alex had flashbacked with such intensity that he could actually taste the memory dust on the back of his throat.

'*¿Qué pasa?*' he said.

'How do you do?' said the stranger politely. 'I'm Leo Mulcahey, and this is my traveling companion, Mr Smithers.'

'How do you do, Mr Smithers?' said Alex, sliding instinctively into parody. 'How pleasant to see you again.'

'Yo,' grunted Smithers.

'And you are?' said Mulcahey.

Alex looked up at the thin rose-quartz lenses of Mulcahey's shades, and felt instantly, with deep and total conviction, that this encounter was not in the best interests of himself or his friends. The tall, charming, and distinguished Leo Mulcahey was exuding a bone-chilling reek of narc atmosphere. Rangers were bad, bad enough anyway, but the well-groomed spook friend of El General was not the sort of person who should ever be in the camp of the Storm Troupe, for any reason, under any circumstances.

'Mr Leo Mulcahey,' Alex said. 'Any relation?'

'I'm Jerry's big brother,' said Leo Mulcahey, with a gentle smile.

'Must feel pretty special to have a little brother who could break your back like a twig.'

Mulcahey twitched. Not a big reaction, but a definite startled twitched. 'Is Jerry here? May I speak to Jerry?'

'Sorry to tell you that Jerry's out of camp, he's off doing storm pursuit.'

'It was my understanding that Jerry always *coordinated* the pursuits. That he stayed in camp as the group's . . . I forget the term.'

'Nowcaster. Yeah, that's the usual, all right, but right now Jerry's off chasing spikes somewhere in Oklahoma, so under the circumstances I'm afraid I can't allow you into the camp.'

'I see,' said Leo.

'What the fuck you talkin' about?' said Smithers suddenly. 'Kid, we were just in your camp three weeks ago and I been lookin' forward to more o' that jerky.'

'*No problema,*' Alex said. 'Give me some positioning coords and I'll route you all the jerky you want. Today. No charge.'

'Is there someone *else* we can talk to?' Leo said.

'No,' Alex said. Brasseur would temporize. Buzzard would knuckle under. Sam Moncrieff would do whatever seemed best. 'No, there isn't.'

'Kid, don't be this way,' said Smithers. 'I'm the heat!'

'You're the heat when you're running with Rangers. You're not the heat when you're running with this guy. If you're cops, show me some ID and a warrant.'

'I'm not a police officer, for heaven's sake,' Leo said, chidingly. 'I happen to be a developmental economist.'

Smithers, surprised, looked at Leo in frank disbelief, then back at Alex again. 'Kid, you got some cojones pullin' that city-boy crap out here. Where's *your* goddamn ID?'

Alex began to sweat. The fear only made him angry. 'Look, Smithers, or whatever the hell your real name is, I thought you were a heavier guy than this. How come you're shaking me down for this fucking narc? This guy's not even a cop! How much is he *paying* you?'

'That's my name!' objected Smithers, wounded. 'Nathan R. Smithers.'

'I don't understand why this has become so unpleasant,' said Leo, reasonably.

'Maybe you ought to give some thought to the way you treated your good friend the *general de policía*, back in Sinaloa.' It was a shot in the dark, a blindly launched harpoon, but it landed hard. Leo reacted with such a start that even Smithers seemed alarmed.

'Sinaloa,' Leo mused, recovering himself. He stared down hard at Alex. He was very tall, and though he didn't have the weightlifter beef of his brother Jerry, he looked, in his own smooth way, like a bad man to cross. 'Of course,' he concluded suddenly. 'You must be Alex. Little Alejandro Unger. My goodness.'

'I think you'd better leave,' said Alex. 'You and your kind aren't wanted here.'

'You've been here less than a month, Alejandro! And already you're carrying on like Jerry's guard dog! It's amazing the loyalty that man inspires.'

'Have it your way, Leo,' Alex said. 'I'll let you in the camp when *Jerry says* you can come in, how about that?' He suddenly sensed weakness, and pounced. 'How about you wait here while I call Jerry up? I can contact Jerry out in the field, easy enough. Let's see what Jerry says about you.'

'I have a counterproposal,' Leo said. 'Why don't I assume that you have no authority whatever? That you're simply inventing all this on the fly, through some silly grudge all your own. That you're an unbalanced, sick, spoiled little rich-boy punk, who's in way over his head, and that we can simply walk right past you.'

'You'll have to knock me down first.'

'That doesn't look difficult, Alex. You're still emaciated from that black-market shooting parlor in Nuevo Laredo. You look quite ill.'

'You're gonna look quite dead, Leo, when the guy who put that laser dot on your forehead pulls the trigger and your brains fly out.'

Leo turned slowly to Smithers. 'Mr Smithers. Do tell. Do I in fact have a laser rifle sighted on my person?'

Smithers shook his head. 'Not that I can see. Kid, it is *really* fuckin' stupid to say something like that to a guy like me.'

Alex took his sunglasses off, and then his hat. 'Look at me,' he told Smithers. 'Do I look afraid of you? You think I'm *impressed*?' He turned to Leo. 'How about you, Leo? Do I look like I *care* whether we get in a fistfight right now, and you end up shot? You really wanna hit me, and risk catching a very real bullet, just so you can swan around in some empty paper tents and pull a fast one on your brother when he comes back – probably with all his friends?'

'No,' said Leo, decisively. 'There's no need at all for any of this foolishness. We don't want Juanita upset, do we? Jancy?'

'You stay the hell away from Jane,' Alex said, in throttled fury. 'Letting that one slip was a real blunder! Get away from me and my sister, and stay away from us, you spook narc son of a bitch. Get out of here now, before you lose it and try something even stupider than showing up here in the first place.'

'This is completely pointless,' Leo said. 'I don't see what you think you've accomplished with this ridiculous junkie's bravado. We can simply return at some later time, when there are some sane people here.'

Alex nodded and crossed his arms. 'Okay. Yeah. It's pointless. Come back next Christmas, big brother. In the meantime, go away. Now.'

Leo and Smithers exchanged glances. Leo shrugged eloquently, his shoulders rising beneath the padding of his spanking-new safari jacket.

Without haste, the two men climbed into the truck. Smithers started the machine, and it turned and left. As it vanished Alex saw Leo lifting a videocam to his face, methodically scanning the camp.

Alex walked slowly back to the command yurt. Buzzard was waiting at the door flap. Sam was still in his nowcaster helmet. There was no sign at all of Joe Brasseur.

'Who were those guys?' Buzzard said.

Alex shrugged. 'No problem. I took care of 'em. A coupla wannabes.'

CHAPTER

7

An unbroken malignant high had been sitting, for six long weeks, over Colorado. It seemed to be anchored there. The high hadn't moved, but it had expanded steadily. A great dome of dry, superheated air had spread from Colorado to northeastern New Mexico and the Panhandles of Oklahoma and Texas. Beneath it was the evil reign of drought.

Jane was rather fond of Oklahoma. The roads were generally in worse condition than Texas, but the state was more thoroughly settled. There was good civil order, and the people were friendly, and even way outside the giant modern megalopolis of Oklahoma City, there were living little rural towns where you could still get real breakfast and a decent cup of coffee. The sky was a subtler blue in Oklahoma, and the wildflowers were of a gentler palette than the harshly vivid flowers of a Texas spring. The soil was richer, and deeper, and iron red, and quite a lot of it was cultivated. The sun never climbed quite as punishingly high in the zenith, and it rained more often.

But there was no rain now. Not under the slow swell of the continental monster. Rushing storm fronts had scourged Missouri and Iowa and Kansas and Illinois, but the high at the foot of the Rockies had passed from a feature, to a nuisance, to a regional affliction.

SESAME's Climate Analysis Center liked to netcast a standard graphics map, 'Departure of Average Temperature from Normal (C),' a meteorological document that SESAME had inherited from some precybernetic federal-government office. The map's format was rather delightfully antiquated, both in its old-fashioned distinction of 'Centigrade' (the old Fahrenheit scale had been extinct for years) and in its wistful pretense that there was still such a thing in American weather as 'Normal.' The map's colored shadings of temperature were crudely vivid, with the crass aesthetic limits of early computer graphics, but for the sake of archival continuity, the maps had never been redesigned. In her Troupe career, Jane had examined dozens of these average-temperature maps. But she'd never before seen so much of that vividly anomalous shade of hot pink.

It was only June, and people were already dying under those pixelated hot-pink pools. Not dying in large numbers; it wasn't yet the kind of heavy weather where the feds would start sending in the iron-barred evacuation trucks. It was still only early June, when heat could be very anomalous without becoming actually lethal. But it was the kind of heat that kicked up the stress several notches. So the old folks' pacemakers failed, and there'd be gunfire in the evening and a riot at the mall.

The temperature map dissolved on Charlie's dashboard readout, then blushed again into a blotchy new depiction: ground-level SESAME Lidar.

'I've never seen it like this before,' Jerry commented, from Charlie's passenger seat. 'Look at the way it's breaking, way outside the rim of that high. That's not supposed to happen.'

'I don't see how *anything* can happen until that air mass moves,' Jane said. 'It doesn't make any sense.'

'The core's not moving for hell, but it's still ripping loose today, all along that secondary dryline,' Jerry said. 'We're gonna see some F-2s, F-3s drop out of this, and they're going to be' – he thought it over – 'a minor feature.'

Jane looked up at the northern horizon: the storm line that was their destination. Beyond a line of wilting Oklahoma cottonwoods, there were towers rising – sheetlike in parts, half-concave, starved for moisture. They didn't look powerful, but they didn't look minor; they looked convulsive. 'Well,' she said, 'maybe we're finally seeing it, then. Maybe this is what it looks like when it starts.'

'The F-6 isn't supposed to shape up like this. The mesosphere's all wrong and the jet stream is hanging north like it was nailed there.'

'Well, this is where the F-6 ought to be. And the time is right. So what else could it be?'

Jerry shook his head. 'Ask me when it starts moving.'

Jane sighed, and munched a handful of government granola from her paper bag, and pulled her booted legs up in the driver's seat. 'I can't believe that you gave up nowcasting, and came out to hammer some spikes with me, and now you're telling me they're a *minor feature*.'

Jerry laughed. 'Spikes. They're like sex. Just 'cause you've nailed 'em once before, doesn't mean you lose all interest the next time.'

'It's good to have you out here with me.' She paused. 'You're being real sweet to me lately, under the circumstances.'

'Babe,' he said, 'you were in camp two months before all willpower shattered, remember? If we can't make love, we won't. Simple.' He hesitated. 'It's *hell*, true, but it's simple.'

Jane knew better than to take this male bravado at face value. All was not well in camp. Her infection, the drought. Nerves, restlessness. Missed connections.

One of the things Jane loved best about chasing spikes was that liberating way that gigantic storms smashed flat and rendered irrelevant all the kinks in her personal life. You couldn't sweat your own angst in the face of a monster spike; it was stupid and vulgar and deeply beside the point, like trying to make the Grand Canyon your spittoon.

She did love Jerry; she loved him as a person, very dearly, and she often thought she might have loved him almost as much, even if he'd never given her any tornadoes. She could have loved Jerry even if he'd been something everyday and nonexotic and dull, like, say, some kind of economist. Jerry was skilful and accomplished and dedicated and, when you got used to him, rather intensely attractive. Sometimes Jerry was even funny. She often thought that even under other circumstances, she might easily have become his lover, or even his wife.

It would have been much more like her other affairs, though; the ones with the vase throwing and the screaming fits and the shaking sense of absolute black desperation in the back of a limo at three in the morning.

Jerry made her do crazy things. But Jerry's crazy things had always made her better and stronger, and with Jerry around, for the first time in her life she no longer felt miserably troubled about being her own worst enemy. She'd always been wrapped too tight, and wired too high, and with a devil inside; in retrospect, she could see that clearly now. Jerry was the first and only man in her life who had really appreciated her devil, who had accepted her devil and been sweet to it, and had given her devil some proper down-and-dirty devil-things to do. Her devil no longer had idle hands. Her devil was working its ass off, all the time.

So now she and her devil were quite all right, really.

It was as if acting crazy, and taking crazy risks, had completely freed her of any obligation to actually become crazy. It might sound rather sappy, but really and truly, Jerry had made her a free woman. She was dirty and she was broke and she smelled bad most of the time, but she was free and in love. She'd spent most of her life in a fierce, determined, losing battle to make herself behave and make sense and be good and be happy; and then she'd met Jerry Mulcahey and had given up the war. And when all that old barbed wire snapped loose inside of her, she'd discovered surprising reservoirs of simple decency and goodwill in herself. She wasn't even half as bad as she'd thought she was. She wasn't crazy, she wasn't wicked, she wasn't even particularly dangerous. She was a mature adult woman who wasn't afraid of herself, and could even be a source of real strength to other people. She could give and sacrifice for other people, and love and be loved, without any fear or any mean calculation. And she acknowledged all this, and was grateful for it.

It was just that she really, really hated to talk about it.

Jerry wasn't any better at discussing it than she was. Jerry Mulcahey wasn't like other men. Not that that was entirely to Jerry's credit; Jerry wasn't much like any kind of human being. Jane was a bright person, and Jane knew what it was like to be brighter than other people; bright enough to be disliked for it, sometimes. But she knew she wasn't bright like Jerry was. In particular areas of his comprehension, Jerry was so bright as to be quite alien. There were large expanses of his mental activity that were as blank and hot and shiny as someone on drugs.

Jane had no gift for mathematics; math was something that she had to crawl through on her belly, like mud. It had taken her quite some time to fully comprehend that this strange man in the wastelands of West Texas with his cobbled-up crew of eccentrics was, really and truly, one of the brightest mathematicians in the world.

Jerry's parents had both been computer-science researchers in Los Alamos. They'd both been good at their work too; but their son Jerry had been doing cutting-edge magnetohydrodynamics when he was twelve. Jerry had pioneered in fields like multidimensional minimal-surface manifolds and higher-order invarient polynomials, things that made your brain explode just to look at them. Jerry was good enough at math to frighten people. His colleagues couldn't make up their minds whether to envy him for his gifts, or resent him for not publishing more often. Every once in a while Jane would have some net-idiot give her a hard time about Jerry's 'professional qualifica-tions,' and she would E-mail the skeptic the paper that Jerry'd done back in 2023 that established the Mulcahey Conjecture, and the skeptic would try to read it and his brain would explode, and he would quietly slink away and never be heard from again.

Unless he turned out to be one of the math wannabes. The Troupe attracted all kinds of wannabes, most of them rather nutty, but every once in a while some anxious weedy-looking guy would show up at camp who didn't give a shit about tornadoes and really, really wanted Jerry to forget all about it and get back to proving how many soap bubbles could fit inside a collapsing torus in hyperspace. Jerry was always terribly kind to these people.

The weight lifting was another prominent aspect of Jerry's oddity. He hadn't always been that way. She'd seen pictures of Jerry as a teenager – his mother had sent them – and Jerry had been lithe and slender, with a tall kid's wary stoop. Lots of Troupers were into weights; Jane lifted weights herself, enough to get strong, enough to get the point of doing it. But Jerry was doing weights *just because it saved him time*. It saved him time and effort to be as big as a house so he could briefly surface out of his abyss of distraction, and snap out something, and have people just jump up and run do it for him. Because he radiated raw physical authority, Jerry didn't have to slow down to explain very much. Plus, the weights gave Jerry something to do while he was thinking seriously and Jerry liked to think seriously for about five hours straight, every day. The fact that he was lugging thirty kilos of steel on his legs at the time never seemed to register on him much.

There was no question that the great trial of Jerry's life was relating to other human beings. Jerry had really worked terribly hard at this problem, with such painstaking patience and suffering and dedication, that her heart truly melted for him.

Jerry didn't readily empathize with people, because Jerry just wasn't a very peoplelike being. But he could model people. He could dryly comprehend the whole structure of their personalities, and recreate them as a kind of dry run in his own head. He had built his relationships with the other Troupers like a one-armed man building model cathedrals out of toothpicks.

And when he had it all figured, then he would sit you down. And start telling you exactly what you were really thinking, and what it was that really motivated you, and how you could get what you wanted and how that would, by the way, help him and the others too. It would be laid out with such amazing clarity and detail that your own self-image would crumble by comparison. Jerry would have *invented* this thing, just by watching you closely and speculating, but it was so much more like you than you were that it felt more real than your own identity. It was like confronting your ideal self, your better nature: smoother, more sensible, wiser, a lot better managed. All you had to do was let the scales fall from your eyes and reach out for it.

Jane had gone through this proces exactly once. Well, half of once, actually. It was hard to seduce someone while in a paper jumpsuit. You could zip it down to the waist and coyly peel it open, and it felt like you were offering a guy a couple of bran muffins out of a bakery bag. But once he'd started in on her with the toothpick analysis, she'd known that the only way to break him out of it was to knock him down and straddle him.

It had worked brilliantly too. It had shut Jerry up to the great satisfaction of all concerned. Now she and Jerry could freely and openly discuss all kinds of things: spies, interfaces, tools, camp, feds, Rangers, other Troupers, even money. But they didn't discuss The Relationship. The Relationship didn't even have a name. The Relationship had its own shape and its own life and it was not made of toothpicks.

But Jerry had assigned himself to her car. He never did this without reason. Sooner or later the shoe would drop. The big hot core was gone from The Relationship, and both of them were hurting, and some rational analysis was going to come out of Jerry. She was hoping for the best.

'For the first time I'm really getting afraid of this,' he said.

Jane set her granola bag on the floorboard. 'What is it you're afraid of, darling?'

'I think we may be shaping up toward the bad scenario.'

'What's bad about it?'

'I've never told you fully what I thought this would be like if it became a permanent fixture.'

'All right,' she said, bracing herself. 'If that's on your mind, tell me, then.'

'The winds are not the half of it. It could strip the earth's surface right down to bedrock. It could vent more dust into the troposphere than a major volcanic eruption.'

'Oh,' she said. 'You mean the F-6.'

He gave her the oddest look he'd ever given her. 'Are you okay, Janey?'

'Yeah, sure. I'm as okay as anybody with a yeast infection ever is. Sorry, I thought you were discussing something else. What about the F-6, sweetheart?'

'Oh, nothing really,' Jerry said, staring straight ahead. 'Just that it might kill everyone within hundreds of kilometers. Including us, of course. All in the first few hours. And after that – a giant, permanent vortex on the planet's surface. That could happen! It could actually take place in the real world.'

'I know that,' Jane said. 'But for some reason, I just don't worry about it much.'

'Maybe you should worry a lot more, Jane. It could mean the end of civilization.'

'I just can't believe in it enough to worry,' she told him. 'I mean, I do believe something really awesome is going to break loose this season, but I can't believe it means the end of anything. It's like – somehow – I just can't believe that civilization is going to *get off the hook that easy*. "The end of civilization" – *what* end? What civilization, for that matter? There isn't any end. We're in way too deep to have any end. The kind of troubles we got, they aren't *allowed* to have any end.'

'The troposphere could saturate with dust. There could be a nuclear winter.' He paused. 'Of course a major drop in temperature would starve out the vortex.'

'That's just it! It's always something like that! Things can get totally awful, but then something else comes up that's so amazingly screwy that it makes it all irrelevant. There never was any nuclear war or nuclear winter. There's never gonna be one. That was all just stupid hype, so they could go on ruining the environment, so we'd end up living just like we're living now, living with the consequences.'

She sighed. 'Look, I saw the sky turn black when I was a kid – I saw it turn black as the ace of spades! It didn't last, though. It was just a big dust bowl. Even if the F-6 is really awful, somebody somewhere would survive. Millions of people, billions maybe. They'd just march into some fucking salt mine, with the chlorophyll hack and some gene-splicing and some superconductives, and as long as they had their virching and cable TV, most of 'em would never even notice!'

'People talked like that before heavy weather,' Jerry said. 'It wasn't the end of the world, but they noticed, all right. If they lived long enough.'

'Okay,' Jane said. 'Have it your way. Let's assume for the sake of argument that the F-6 *is* the end of the world. What do you wanna do about it?'

He said nothing.

'You wanna go down to Costa Rica? I know this cute little hotel there, they've got frozen margaritas and hot showers.'

'No.'

'You're gonna go and hack the F-6 no matter what, aren't you? Of course you are. And good ol' Janey's gonna go with you to do it. Of course I am. End of story.'

'It bothers me when you talk like this, Jane. You're not that cynical.'

Jane stopped. It was rare of Jerry to confess so openly that he was upset. She lowered her voice. 'Darling, listen to me. Don't be so anxious about us. Everybody in the Troupe knows that this is very dangerous. You haven't been hiding that from us, that's not any

surprise to us. You can't protect us, we know that. We're all adults –
well, almost all adults – and we know what we're doing.' She
shrugged. 'Pretty much, anyhow. A lot more than those dumb feds
at SESAME. And a hell of a lot more than the poor damned
civilians.'

'I think we'd better have a Troupe powwow after this chase, and
make all of this very clear and straightforward to everyone.'

'Good. Fine. If that'll make you feel better. But I can already tell
you what's gonna happen. Nobody's gonna jump up and say, "Oh
wait, Jerry! A really big tornado? Nope, no, sorry, I'm too scared to
go watch." That'll never happen in eight million years!' She laughed.
'You couldn't keep 'em away with a cattle prod.'

'The F-6 is not just a spike. I'm thinking more and more . . .
along the lines of a different order of storm, something unprecedented. We'll be going up against something I don't understand.
The Troupe are good people. They trust my judgment, and they
might be killed because of that. It wouldn't be right.'

'Jerry, we Troupers are like soldiers, we don't need any rights.
Anyway, we'd all be chasing spikes even if you weren't around. If
you think I'm doing all this just to please you, you can think
otherwise. The F-6 is the big one, it's the payoff. It's what I want.'
She fetched up her granola bag. 'I can get April Logan to come down
here.'

'Your design professor? Why?'

'April's way out of academia now, she's mega-big in net-critique!
She has real influence! She's the heaviest netfriend I have. If April
Logan puts the word out that we have a hot presentation coming up,
we can pull some mega postproduction people. People who can take
our data, and do it up really right for once. We'll pull a major
audience.'

'Money, you mean.'

'That's right, Jerry. Money. Pots of it.' She shrugged. 'Well, the
net-equivalent. Attention, access. Fame. I can turn that into money.
It ain't easy, but there are ways.'

'I see.'

'Good. So you can forget all that gallant stuff about protecting
little me from the big bad storm.'

'All right,' he said. 'That's good, Jane. You've done well and I've come to expect that from you. But what about after the storm?'

'What do you mean?'

'That's the other eventuality, the one that really stuns me. Suppose that we survive the F-6. That we ace this. That we nail it and make pots of money and fame, and we put it all behind us. What'll we do then? What will become of us? You and me?'

She was surprised, and more than a little alarmed, to hear Jerry bring this up. 'Well, nothing has to change, darling! It's not like I never had money before! I can deal with money, you know I can! That's not a problem for us! We'll kick back on the off-season, like the Troupe always does. And we'll upgrade our hardware, really decently this time. You can write a paper, and I'll have plenty of network on my hands . . . Then we'll wait for next season.'

'There's not gonna be an F-6 next season. And with the global CO_2 finally dropping, there may not ever be another F-6.'

'So what? There will always be other spikes. Even if the CO_2 drops, that doesn't mean the weather's gonna get any calmer. There was less CO_2 in the air during the State of Emergency! Besides, CO_2's just one part of the climatic disruption. There's still tropical deforestation and delayed ocean warming.'

Jerry said nothing.

'There's thermal pollution from cities. And changes in the North Atlantic currents. Glacier retreats in Antarctica, and higher albedos in Africa, and CFCs in the ozone, and that permanent hitch in the ENSO cycle, and the solar variation . . . Christ, I can't even *count* them all. Jerry, the weather's never gonna calm down and be normal. Not in our lifetime. Probably not in three hundred years. We'll have all the spikes we ever want! You and me, we're disaster experts with an endless supply of disaster! And if you nail the F-6 while the feds are sitting on their hands saying an F-6 isn't even possible, then you'll be famous forever.'

'Jane, I've been forecasting the F-6 for ten years. I don't just chase spikes, anyone can chase spikes. Spikes aren't enough. There are thousands of spikes, and thousands of weather people, but I'm different, and the F-6 is why. I'm been so obsessed by it, so consumed and fascinated and intent on this terrible thing, that I have no real idea how I'll live when it's gone. Everything has been honed for this crisis, and we're in top condition to do it, we're all united to do this, to go through hell to nail this thing. But after that, what's to become of us?'

'Jerry . . . ' She bit her lip. 'Jerry, I promise you, as long as I'm in your life, you're never gonna lack things to do, and a reason to live. All right?'

'That's sweet of you, but it's just not like that,' he said, sadly. 'It's hard to explain, but . . . I have to have the Work. And it has to be big, bigger than myself, because the way I do my Work is with something that's too big. It's me all right, it's very much part of me, but it's not something I'm in command of, and I don't control it. It's like a force, a compulsion, that tears at things, and shreds them, and chops them up, and comprehends them, and I don't control it, and I never have. I can't. You understand?'

'Yes. I do understand. It's like a spike, inside.'

'Yes.'

'I have one of those, too, you know. It's just very different from yours. And being with you, Jerry, it's helped me with it, and I'm better! What we have together, what we give to each other, it's not hurtful or doomed or destructive, it's really good and strong! We do see a lot of hurt. And I don't know, the world around us might be doomed. And we study destruction all the time, every day. But what you and I have, together, in the middle of all of that, it's really good and strong! There's nothing weak or frail about it. I'll never love anyone else, the way I've learned to love you.'

'But when this monster has smashed everything, what if we're part of the wreckage?'

'I'll still want you and love you.'

'I might become something very different, after the F-6. I know I won't be able to stand still. I'll have to change, there's no avoiding that. Who knows? I might become something like Leo.'

She sat up very straight. 'What do you mean by that? Tell me.'

'I mean that I just bear witness, Jane. The Troupe, we all just bear witness. Half of Oklahoma could be smashed into rubble, and we'll just bear witness. But there are those who talk about the weather – as I do and you do – and those who do something about it. Leo, and his friends, his people, they all do things. He's a man of the world, my older brother, he's a man of competence, a man of influence. And it's a dreadful world, and my brother does some very dreadful things. I watch destruction, but Leo abets it. I'm nothing but eyes, but Leo has hands.'

Jerry shook his head. 'I don't know exactly what Leo's done, or how he's done it or who helped him – he doesn't tell me, for good and ample operational reasons, and I don't want to learn. But I know why. I know why Leo does what he does, and I know why the prospect of action fascinates him. You see, it's not just one spasmodic passing horror in a small locality, like a spike is. The modern world of global strategic politics and economics, that's Leo's world, and it's eight billion people who've lost all control over their destiny, and are gnawing the planet down to the bone. It's our civilization, turned into an endless world-eating horror, just like the F-6 itself may well turn out to be. And Leo, he lives inside that, and feeds it energy, and tries to bend it to his will. He'd very much like me to join him in there, you know. To help him maneuver the chaos, by whatever means necessary. And I can understand my brother. I can sympathize. My brother and I, we have a similar affliction. We understand one another, as few people ever do.'

'All right,' Jane said. She put her hand on his. 'Jerry when this is over, then that's what we're going to do. When the F-6 is over, and it's all behind us, and we've shown the whole world what we know and what we witnessed, then we're going to go after your brother. You and me, together, and we're going to rescue him from whatever trouble he's in, and we'll set him all straight.'

'That's a major challenge, darling.'

'Jerry, you said you wanted a big problem. Well, you've got a big problem, I see that now. I don't care how many political friends your brother has, he's a big problem but he's just a human being, and he's not as big as a storm that can smash Oklahoma. I'm not afraid of your storm, and I'm not afraid of you, and I'm not afraid of your brother. You can't scare me away from you with any of this talk, I love you and I'm staying with you, and nothing will take you from me, nothing but death. We can do this thing. We're not helpless watchers, we are doers too, in our own way. In our own way, you and I, we are both very practical people.'

'Darling,' he said, and meant it, 'you are very good to me.'

The speaker erupted. 'This is Rick in Baker! We got circulation!'

*

ENDLESS RAIN COULD depress you, and there was no disaster like a flood, but there was something uniquely mean and pinched and harsh about a drought. Drought was a trial to the soul.

They'd followed the spike along the rim of the great high. It was a long, ropy, eccentric F-2, and it had moved, with particular oddity, from the north toward the southwest, a very unusual storm track for Tornado Alley. The F-2 had been exceptionally long-lived, never achieving true earthshaking power, but sipping some thread of persistent energy from the edge of the high. And there had been hail with it, nasty, black, dust-choked hail; but scarcely a drop of rain.

Now the F-2 had roped out and Jane and Jerry were in the canyonlands west of Amarillo, the part of the Texas Panhandle people called the Breaks. They'd been running cross-country in a flat plain, and then the earth opened up in front of them. The Canadian River of the Panhandle was not a major river now, but it had been a very major river during the last ice age, and it had done some dreadful things to the landscape here. Real mesas, not the slumped hills of the south High Plains. Mesas weren't mountains. They were not vigorous upthrustings in the landscape. Mesas were remnants, mesas were all that was left, after ages of stubborn resistance to rainsplash and sheetwash and channel cutting. The mesas had a layer of hard sandstone, a caprock, up on top, but below that caprock layer was a soft, reddish, weak, and treacherous rock that was scarcely petrified mud. That rock was so weak you could tear off clods of it and crumble it to dust with your fingers. The mesas were toothless and terribly patient and all wrinkled down the sides, eaten away with vertical gullies, their slopes scattered with the cracked remains of undereaten sandstone slabs.

It was very old and very wild country. It had few roads, and those in poor repair. Around local creekbeds and water holes, people sometimes found twelve-thousand-year-old flint spearheads, mixed with the blackened, broken bones of extinct giant bison. Jane always wondered what the reaction of those flint-wielding Folsom Point people had been when they realized they had exterminated their giant bison, wiped them into extinction with their dreadful high-tech atl-atls, and their cutting-edge flint industry, and the all-consuming giant wildfires they'd used to chase whole assembly lines of bison pell-mell off the canyon cliffs. Maybe some had condemned the wildfires and atl-atls, and tried to destroy the flints. While others had been sick at heart forever, to find themselves party to such a dreadful crime. And the vast majority, of course, simply hadn't noticed.

The canyon walls of the Breaks played hell with communications. They cast a major radio shadow, and if you got really close to them they could even block satellite relay. That posed no challenge for Pursuit Vehicle Charlie, though, who put his superconductive to work and scuttled up the slope to the top of the largest mesa in the neighborhood. That mesa was helpfully festooned with big towers and microwave horns.

Jane and Jerry weren't the first to come here for their own purposes. Most of the horns were lavishly stenciled with bullet holes, some old, some new. A structure-hit gang had tagged the tower blockhouses with much-faded graffiti. Old-fashioned psycho-radical slogans like SMASH THE BALLOT MARKET and LET THEM EAT DATA and SCREAMING WOLF SURVIVES, done with that kinky urban folk intensity that urban graffiti had once had, before the spirit had suddenly and inexplicably leached out of it and the whole practice of tagging had dried up and gone away.

There was a fire pit with some ancient burned mesquite stubs, and a mess of scattered beer cans, the old aluminium kind of beer container that didn't melt in the rain. It was easy to imagine the vanished Luddite marauders, up here with their dirt bikes and guns and howling, chanting boom boxes.

Jane found this intensely sad, somehow more lonely than if there had never been anyone here in the first place. She wondered who the gang had been, and what in hell they had thought they were doing way out here, and what had become of them. Maybe they were just plain dead, as dead as the Folsom flint people. The state of Texas had always been remarkably generous with the noose, the chair, and the needle, and in the early days of parole cuffs there'd been little complaint about tamperproofing them with contact nerve poison. And that was just the formal way – the polite and legitimate way of erasing people. If the gang had been jumped by Rangers they'd be unmarked graves by the roadside now, green lumps in some overgrown pasture. Maybe they had blown themselves up, trying to cook demolition bombs out of simple household chemicals. Had they snapped out of the madness and achieved a foothold in what passed for real life? Did they have jobs now?

She'd once asked Carol, tactfully, about the Underground, and Carol had said bluntly: 'There is no more alternative society. Just people who will probably survive, and people who probably won't.' And Jane could pretty much go with that assessment. Because from her own experience with structure-hit activity, the people who were into that radical bullshit were just like Rangers, only stupider and not as good at it.

The sun was setting. Off in the western distance beneath the dissolving clouds, Jane could see, with intense and lovely clarity, the skeletal silhouetting of very distant trees. The trees were whole kilometers away and no bigger than a fingernail paring, and yet she could see the shape of their every branch in the clear still air, stenciled against the colors around the sun, great bands of subtle, gradated, desert color, umber to amber to translucent pearly white.

The chase was over now. It was time to call camp.

Jerry got the spider antenna out of its bag and kicked its tripod open and started cranking it into full extension.

And then the wind stopped. And it grew terribly still.

And then it began to get hot.

Jane looked at the barometer readout. It was soaring – moving visibly even as she looked.

'What's going on?' she said.

'It's a solitary wave,' Jerry said. 'It must have peeled off the high somehow.' Not a wind, not something you could feel as moving air, but a kind of silent compression wave in the atmosphere, a silent rippling bulge of pressure and heat. Jane's ears popped loudly. The hot air felt very dry, and it smelled. It smelled of drought and ozone.

She leaned against the car and the edge of the door stung her hand with a sharp pop of static electricity.

Jerry looked up at the tallest of the microwave horns. 'Jane,' he said in a tight voice, 'get back in the car, get the cameras running. Something's happening.'

'All right.' She got in.

It grew darker, and then she began to hear it. A thin, flowing hiss. Not a crackle, but a sound like escaping gas. The tall tower had begun to vent something, to ooze something, something very ood, something like wind, something like fur, something like flame.

White, striated, gaseous spikiness, a flickering, rippling presence, at the corners of the old tower's braced galvanized-iron uprights and crossbars. All on one side, growing up and down one metal corner of the tower, like glowing ball moss. It hissed and it flickered and it moved a little, fitfully, like the spitting breath of ghosts. She watched it steadily through the binocular cameras, rock steadily, and she called out, very unsteadily, 'Jerry! What is it?'

'It's Saint Elmo's fire.'

Jane suddenly felt the hair rise all over her head. She didn't stop recording, but the electric fire had fallen on her now, it had seeped down and come inside the car with her. The corona lifted her hair like a pincushion. Deep natural electricity was discharging off the top of her head. Her whole scalp, from nape to forehead, felt like an eyelid felt when an eyelid was gently peeled back.

'I've seen this at Pike's Peak,' Jerry said, 'I've never seen it at this low an elevation.'

'Will it hurt us?'

'No. It should pass us when this wave passes.'

'All right. I'm not afraid.'

'Keep recording.'

'Don't worry, I've got it.'

And in less than a minute the wave passed. And the fire was gone away from them, the strange deep fire was gone completely. Just as if there had never been anything.

IT WAS VERY hard to sleep together when you weren't allowed to sleep together. Jane had always had trouble sleeping, always ready to prowl around red-eyed and pull an all-nighter. Jerry had no such problems. Jerry was good at catnaps; he could turn off his virching helmet, lie down on the carpet with his head inside the casket of blackness, sleep twenty minutes, and then get right up and resume his calculations.

But tonight, although Jerry was silent and sitll, Jerry wasn't sleeping. Jane had her head in the hollow of his left shoulder, a place that fit her as if it had been designed for her, the place where she had passed the most sweetly restful nights of her life. They would come away from the chase and have a furious encounter, and then she would fling one naked possessive leg over him and put her head on his shoulder, and she'd close her eyes and hear his heart beating, and she would tumble headlong into a dark sated slumber so deep and healing that it would have set Lady Macbeth to rights.

But not tonight. Her nerves felt as tight and high-pitched as a mariachi violin, and she found no comfort in Jerry. Somehow he didn't smell right. And she didn't smell right either: she smelled of topical vaginal ointment, possibly the least erotic scent known to humankind. But unless at least one of them got some real rest, something awful was going to happen.

'Jerry?' she said. In the still of camp – the ticking of insects, the distant whoosh of the wind generator – even a tender whisper sounded loud as a gunshot.

'Mmmph.'

'Jerry, I'm getting better now, I really am. Maybe we should try something.'

'I don't think that's a good idea.'

'Okay, maybe you're right, but that's no reason why you should have to lie there stiff as a board. Let me try something, darling, let me see if I can make you feel better.' Before he could say anything, she slipped her hand down and gripped his cock.

His penis felt so odd and hot in her fingers that for one shocked instant she thought something had gone terribly wrong with him. Then she realized that he didn't have a condom on. She'd touched it before, and even stroked it and kissed it, but never without the condom.

Well, no harm done. Not just with fingers.

'All right?' she said.

'All right.'

He didn't seem to lack enthusiasm. And if she stopped and got out in the pitch darkness and made him put a condom on, it would be a mega drag. Forget it: so far, so good. She stroked him patiently and persistently, until she got a bad cramp in her forearm. Then she burrowed down into the sleeping bag and tried kissing for a while, and although he didn't come, he at least began to make the right noises.

Then she came out of the bag for some much-needed air and tried rubbing some more.

It was taking a very long time. At first she felt intensely

embarrassed; and then she got used to it, and began to feel better, thinking that even if this was a very ungainly and unsatisfactory substitute for sex, at least she was doing something practical. At least she was taking charge of their troubles. Then she thought that he was never going to come, that she wasn't skilled or sweet enough to make him do it, and that brought the threat of a cavernous sense of failure.

But he was stroking her neck and shoulder in an encouraging way, and finally he started breathing seriously hard. Then he groaned in the dark, and she held it carefully, and she felt it pulsing.

The wetness on her fingers felt viscous and drippy. It felt rather like motor oil. She had seen semen before, and she even knew that odd and particular smell that it had, but never in her life had it actually touched her skin. It was an intimate bodily fluid. Intimate bodily fluids were very dangerous.

'I'm twenty-six years old,' she said, 'and this is the first time I've ever touched this stuff.'

He put his arm around her shoulders and hugged her to him. 'My sweet darling,' he said, quietly, 'it won't hurt you.'

'I know that. You don't have any viruses. You're not sick! You're the healthiest person I know!'

'You have no real way to really know that, though.'

'Have you ever had sex with anybody, without using a condom?'

'No, never, of course not.'

'Me either. So then how could you possibly have any STD?'

'Blood transfusion, maybe? IV drugs? Anyway, I might be lying about the condom use.'

'Oh, for heaven's sake! You're not a liar, I've never known you to lie. You never lie to me!' Her voice trembled. 'I can't believe that I've known you all this time, that you're the man I love more than anyone else in the world, and yet I never really knew about this simple thing that you do, this simple thing that comes out of your body.' She burst into tears.

'Don't cry, sweetheart.'

'Jerry, why is our life this way?' she said. 'What did we ever do to deserve this? We don't hurt each other! We love each other! Why can't we be like men and women used to be? Why is everything always so *difficult* for us?'

'It's for protection.'

'I don't need any protection from you! I don't *want* any protection from you! I'm not afraid about this! Christ, Jerry, this is the part of being with you that I'm *never* afraid about! This is the part that's really wonderful with us, it's the part that we're really good at.' She held on to him and sobbed.

He held her close and tight for a long time as she shook and wept. Finally he began to deliberately kiss the tears away from her inflamed and aching face. When their mouths met, she felt a rush of passion so intense that her soul seemed to flow from her lips. She slid on top of him in a patch of cooling stickiness and jammed his cock into her aching, needful body.

And it really hurt. She wasn't at all well, she was sick, she had yeast. It stung and burned, but nowhere near enough to make her want to stop. She put her arms out straight to support herself and started rocking on him in the darkness.

'*Juanita, yo te quiero.*'

It was such a perfect, intoxicating thing for him to say at that moment that she lost all sense of herself. She went way past the hurt and into frenzy. Maybe forty seconds of it, something like forty aeons in the hottest Tantric circle of Nirvana. Her yell of exultation was still ringing in her ears when he grabbed her hips hard enough to bruise and rammed into her from underneath and he came, he pulsed, deep inside of her.

She slid off him, exhausted and drenched with sweat. 'My God.'

'I didn't know it was going to feel like that.' He seemed stunned.

'Yes,' she said thoughtfully, 'it was sort of . . . quick.'

'I couldn't help it,' he said. 'I didn't know it was going to feel so intense. It's like a completely different experience.'

'Is it really, sweetheart? It's nice for you that way?'

'Yes. Very.' He kissed her.

She felt perfectly calm now. Everything was becoming very clear. That mean-tempered tight-stretched whine in her nerves was completely gone, turned to something like the mellow vibratory afterglow of gently plucked angelic harp strings, and everything was suddenly making a lot of solid good sense.

'Y'know, Jerry, I think maybe it's the *latex* that's at fault.'

'What?'

'I think the *condom* is my health problem. That I'm allergic to the latex, or whatever they make condoms out of these days, and that's why I got all messed up in the first place.'

'How could you suddenly develop an allergy like that, after a whole year?'

'Well,' she said, 'from repeated exposure.'

He laughed.

'I do have allergies, you know. I mean, not like Alex does, but I have a couple of them. I think we should always have sex this way, from now on. It's sweet, it's good, it's perfect. Except that . . . well, everything's all wet. But that's okay.'

'Jane, if we always have sex like this, you're going to get pregnant.'

'Holy mackerel! I never thought of that.' The concept amazed her. She might get pregnant. She could conceive a child. Yes, that astounding event could actually take place; there was nothing left to stop it from happening. She felt like a fool for not considering pregnancy, but she simply hadn't; the long shadows of disease and disaster had overwhelmed that whole idea.

'Just like men and women used to be. Before birth control.' Jerry laughed. 'Maybe we should count our blessings. If these were the 1930s instead of the 2030s, you'd be a down-trodden faculty wife with five kids.'

'Five kids in less than a year, Professor? You're some kinda guy.' Jane yawned, sweetly and uncontrollably. Sleep was near, and sleep was going to be so good. 'They've got those pills for taking care of that, though. Those month-after pills.'

'Contragestives.'

'Yeah, you just eat one pill and your period comes right back. No problem! Government-subsidized and everything.' She hugged him. 'I think we've got this beat, darling. We're going to be all right now. Everything will be all right. I feel so happy.'

MOST OF THE Troupers were hard at work shuffling data. They were assembling some fairly major net-presentation, to impress some bigwig netfriend of Juanita's, who was due for a visit to camp.

None of the Troupers struck Alex as showing a particular dramatic flair for net-presentation work, with the possible exception of Juanita herself. But net-presentation was the kind of labor that could be distributed to a million little cut-rate mouse-potato desktoppers all over the planet, and knowing Juanita, it probably would be.

Carol Cooper, however, wasn't having any of that. Carol Cooper was doing some welding in the garage. 'I don't like systems,' she told Alex. 'I'm very analog.'

'Yes,' said Alex, clearing his throat, 'I recognized that about you the moment we met.'

'So what's in that big plastic jug there?'

'You're very direct, I noticed that also.'

Carol put a final searing touch to a length of bent chromed pipe and set it aside to cool. 'You sure are a sneaky little fucker, for a guy your age. Not everybody would have thought to spot-weld a noose on the end of that smart rope.' She took off her welding goggles and put on safety glasses.

'It's a smart lariat now. Lariats are useful. Comanches used to catch coyotes with lariats. From horseback, of course.'

'Of course,' Carol scoffed. 'Did you know that Janey threw that gun you bought her right down the latrine?'

'Just as well, it was probably pretty dumb to trust her with a firearm in the first place.'

'You oughta go more easy on Janey,' Charol chided. She picked up a dented length of bumper from the dune buggy, and fitted it methodically into a big bench vise. She was wearing her barometer watch, under her slashed-paper sleeve. On her right wrist, the opposite wrist from the Troupe cuff.

'She sure was noisy last night,' Carol remarked, meditatively, as she tightened the vise. 'Y'know, the first time I ever heard Janey cut loose like that, I thought we were under attack. And then I thought, Christ, she's doing some kind of sick-and-twisted status thing, like she wants everybody to know that Jerry's finally doin' her. But then after a couple weeks, I figured out that's just the way Janey is. Janey just plain needs to yell. She's not *okay* unless she yells.'

Carol picked up a big lead-headed mallet and gave the bumper a pair of hard corrective wallops. 'But the weirdest part is that we all got so *used to it*. For months we all thought it was mega-hilarious, but now we don't even make jokes about Janey's yelling. And then when she *stopped* yelling for a couple weeks there, we all started to get really *worried*. But last night, y'know, off she goes. And today, I feel okay again. I feel like maybe we're gonna ace this thing after all.'

'People can get used to anything,' Alex said.

'No, they don't, dude,' Carol said sharply. 'You only think that 'cause you're young.' She shook her head. 'How old do you think I am?'

'Thirty-five?' Alex said. He knew she was forty-two.

'No way, I'm almost forty. I had a kid once who could almost be your age now. Kid died, though.'

'I'm sorry to hear that.'

She swung the hammer. *Bang. Wham. Clank clank clank.* 'Yeah, they say having a kid can keep your marriage alive, and it's really kinda true, because a kid gives you something to pay attention to, besides each other. But they never tell you that losing your kid can kill your marriage.' *Whack. Crunch.* 'Y'know, I was young and kind of stupid back then, and I used to fight with that guy a lot, but hell, I married him on purpose. We got along. And then our kid died. And we never got used to that. Not ever. It just murdered us. We couldn't stand the sight of each other, after that.'

'What did your child die of?'

'Encephalitis.'

'Really? My mom died of encephalitis.'

'You're kidding. Which wave?'

'The epidemic of '25 was pretty bad in Houston.'

'Oh, that was a late one, my little boy died in 2014. It was a State of Emergency thing.'

Alex said nothing.

'Can you fetch me that big-ass vise grip over there?'

Alex pulled the coil of smart rope from his shoulder, put his gloved hand on it. The thin black rope slid out instantly across the bubblepak flooring, reared like a cobra, seized the end of the vise grip in its metal-collared noose, and lifted the tool into the air. It then swayed across the floor, the vise grip dangling gently from the noose, and hung the tool in midair, within her easy reach.

'Christ, you're getting good with that thing.' Carol took the vise grip, with gingerly care. The rope whipped back to coil around Alex's shoulder.

'I've got something I need to tell you,' Alex said.

She clamped the vise grip onto the bumper and put her back into twisting it. 'I know that,' she grunted. 'And I'm waiting.'

'Do you know Leo Mulcahey?'

Her hands froze on the vise grip and she looked up with eyes like a deer in headlights. 'Oh hell.'

'You *do* know him.'

'Yeah. What about Leo?'

'Leo was here at camp yesterday. He came in a truck. He wanted to see Jerry, he said.'

She stared at him. 'What happened?'

'I sent him off with a flea in his ear, I wouldn't let him come in the camp. I said I would punch him out, and that there was a Trouper in the tents who would shoot him. He had a Ranger with him, that tracker guy who was here earlier. But I wouldn't let him in camp, either.'

'Christ! Why?'

'Because Leo is evil. Leo's a spook, that's why.'

'How do you know that bullshit?'

'Look, I just know he's a spook, okay?' Alex coughed, then lowered his voice. 'Spook biz has this atmosphere, you get to where you can smell it.' It had been a bad mistake to get excited. It felt as if something had peeled loose inside his chest.

'How did he look? Leo?'

'Very smooth. Very spooky.'

'That's him all right. Very charming.' Carol picked up her mallet, looked at it blankly, sat it back down. 'Y'know,' she said slowly, 'I like Greg. I like Greg a lot. But on the off-season, I don't hear word one from that guy. Not a phone call. Not even E-mail. He'll be off mountain climbing or shooting rapids or some fucking thing, and he never calls me, never.' She was scowling. 'That's why you need to be nicer to Janey. It's not like other Troupe romances, if you can call them romances, whatever the hell they are, when tornado freaks get together. But Jane really loves Jerry. She's loyal to him, she's good to him, she'd go through hell for Jerry. If I had a sister like that, and I was her brother, I'd try to look after my poor sister some, I'd try to help her be all right.'

Alex digested this strange speech, and reached the only possible conclusion. His throat was really starting to hurt. 'Are you telling me you've been *fucking* Leo?'

Carol stared at him, guilt written all over her face. 'I hope I never hit you, Alex. Because you're not the kinda guy that I could hit just once.'

'It's okay,' he said hoarsely. 'I figured Leo must have some plant inside the camp. That's why I didn't tell anybody yet. I'm still trying to figure how to break the news to His Highness.'

'You want *me* to tell Jerry about it?'

'Yeah. If you want to. That might be good.' He drew a breath. 'Tell Jerry that I wouldn't let Leo in camp, unless Jerry said it was okay first.'

'You know what Leo is?' Carol said, slowly. 'Leo is what Jerry would be, if Jerry wanted to fuck with people's heads, instead of fucking with the whole universe.'

'I don't know what Jerry is,' Alex said. 'I never saw anything like Jerry before. But Leo – you can ask any dope vaquero in Latin America about a guy like Leo, they all know what he is, and what he's doing. They may not know up here in Estados Unidos, but down in El Salvador they know, in Nicaragua they know, they all fuckin' know, it's not any secret to anybody.' He broke into a fit of coughing.

'What the hell is with you, Alex? You look awful.'

'That's the other part I have to tell you,' Alex said. He began, haltingly, to explain.

By the time he finished, Carol had become quite pale.

'They call it a *lung enema*?' she said.

'Yeah. But it doesn't matter what they call it. The point is that it works, that it really helps me.'

'Lemme see that jug.'

With an effort, Alex hefted the plastic medical jug onto the workbench. Carol squinted at the red-on-white adhesive label.

'Palmitic acid,' she read aloud, slowly. 'Anionic lipids. Silicone surfactant. Phosphatidylglycerol . . . Jesus Christ, this is a witches' brew! And what's all this *other* shit down here, all this stuff in Spanish?'

'Isotherm of a PA/SP-B1-25m on a $NaHCO_3$-buffered saline subphase,' Alex translated swiftly. 'It's just a Spanish-language repetition of the basic ingredients.'

'And I'm supposed to put a tube down your throat and decant this stuff into you? And then *hang you upside down*?'

'That's pretty much the story, yeah.'

'Sorry, no way.'

'Carol, listen. I'm sick. I'm a lot sicker than anyone here realizes. I've got a major syndrome, and it's coming down on me hard right now. And unless you help me, or *somebody* helps me, I could die here, in real short order.'

'Why don't you go back home?'

'They can't help me at home,' Alex said simply. 'All their money can't help me, nobody can fix what's wrong with me. Not that they didn't try. But it's not just encephalitis, or cholera, or one of those things that kill you quickly. I'm not that lucky. What I've got, it's one of those *complicated* things. Environmental. Genetic. Whatever. They've been patching me up since I was six days old. If I'd been born in any other time but now, I'd have died in my crib.'

'Can't you get somebody else to do this fucking thing for you? Janey? Ed? Ellen Mae?'

'Yeah. Maybe. And I'll ask 'em, if I have to. But I don't want anybody else to know.'

'Oh,' Carol said. 'Yeah, and I can see why not . . . Y'know, Alex, I've been wondering why you've been hangin' out here with us. Anyone can tell that you and Janey don't get along for hell. And it ain't because you like to play games with rope. It's because you're hiding. You're hiding something.'

'Yeah, that's right,' Alex told her. 'I was hiding. I mean, not so much from those contrabandista medicos that I burned down in Nuevo Laredo - they're a tough outfit in their way, but hell, they don't really give a shit about me, they've got a line of no-hope suckers outside that *clínica* that's longer than the Rio Grande. I was hiding here from my own goddamn life. Not my life, but that thing that I do, that other people call living. I am real close to dead, Carol. It's not all in my head, I'm not making this up. I can't prove to you what's wrong with me, but I know it's the truth, because I've lived in this body all my life, and I can feel it. There's not much left of me. No matter what anybody does, no matter how much money anybody spends, or how many drugs they pump into me, I don't think I'm gonna make twenty-two.'

'Christ, Alex.'

'I'm just hiding up here because it's like - a different life. A realer life. I never do very much for the Troupe, because I just can't do much, I'm just too sick and too weak. But when I'm here with you people, I'm just some kid, I'm not just some dying kid.' He stopped a moment, thinking hard. 'But Carol, that's not all of it, either. I mean, that's what it was like at first, and it's all still true, but it's not the way I really feel anymore. You know what? I'm *interested*.'

'Interested?'

'Yeah. Interested in the F-6. This big thing that's been hanging over us. I really believe in it now. I really know it's there! I know it's gonna really happen! *And I really want to see it.*'

Carol sat down, heavily, on a folding camp stool. She put her head in her hands. Strong, wrinkled hands. When she looked up again, her face was wet with tears.

'You had to come pick on me, didn't you? You had to come tell *me* that you're dying.'

'I'm sorry, Carol, but you're the only one here that I really trust.'

'Because I've got a big soft heart, you little fucker. Because you know you can pick on me! Christ, this is just what I went through with Leo. No wonder you scoped him out so fast. Because there's not a dime's worth of difference between you and him.'

'Yeah, except that he kills people, and I'm fucking dying! C'mon, Carol.'

'We didn't kill anybody,' Carol said bitterly. 'All that structure-hit stuff – it's just killing *things*, is what it is. Leo knew. Hell, Leo was the best we ever had. You never saw us just mow people down, even though we could have done that real easily. We were just trying to *kill the machinery*. Get rid of it. All that junk that had killed our world, y'know, the bulldozers and the coal plants and the logging machines and the smoke-stacks, the Goliath, the Monster, Behemoth, the Beast. *It!*' She shook herself, and wiped at her cheeks with the backs of her hands. ''Cause it was too late to stop it any other way, and we all knew damn well what was happening to the world . . . And if you think the Underground is all gone now, well, you got it wrong! They're not gone at all. Hell no, they're just real different now. They've got power now, a lot of 'em. They're actually in the government, what passes for the government these days. Now they've got real power, not that hopeless pissant rebel shit with the Molotovs and the monkey wrenches and the bullshit manifestos, I mean real power, real plans, terrible power, terrible plans. They're all people like him.'

'Sorry . . . '

'Guys like *you*, though . . . you new kids, you hopeless little chickenshits . . . People will get used to anything, yeah, if they're young enough! People used to *scream their heads off* at the thought of dying of stupid shit like TB or cholera, now you don't even raise your voice, you just make it your own little secret, and you keep watching TV until you drop dead discreetly on the couch. People just put up with living in hell! They just ignore it all, and they're sure the world is always, always gonna get worse, and they don't ever wanna hear about it, and they're just grateful they're not in the relocation camp.'

'I'm not giving up, Carol. I'm asking you to help me. Please help me.'

'Look, I'm not a medic. I can't do anything like that. It's too awful, it's too much like it was in the camps.'

'Carol,' he grated, 'I don't care about the weather camps. I don't care about your crazy Luddite friends. I know it was heavy then, and I know it was horrible then, but I was only five years old then, and it's all history to me, it's dead history. I'm living in a camp right now, *this* camp right now, and if I die in a camp I'll think that I'm *lucky*! I'm not gonna *have* any history. I'm not even gonna make it through another year! I just want to see this thing that's coming, that's all that I'm asking of you!' He leaned against the table, heavily. 'Frankly, I kinda hope that the F-6 is gonna kill me. I kinda like that idea, it's worthwhile and it saves a lot of trouble all around. So now, if you'll just help me out here, I think I'm gonna be able to see it while I'm standing up on my own feet, that maybe I can pass for a human being while I'm busy getting killed. Will you help me please, Carol? Please!'

'All right. Stop crying.'

'You started it.'

'Yeah, I'm stupid.' She stood up. 'I cry. I have a big mouth, I have no operational discretion at all, and that's why I hang out here in the ass end of nowhere, instead of with a real life in some real city, where some good-looking male cop can wheedle it all out of me, and yank a bunch of my former friends out of their condos and bust them all on a terror-and-sabotage rap. I'm a born sucker, I'm a real moron.' She sighed. 'Look, if we're gonna do this at all, let's get it over with quick before anybody sees us, because it's a really sick and twisted thing for me to do to you, and Greg has got a big jealous bone.'

'Okay. Right. I get it. Thanks a lot.' Alex wiped his eyes on his sleeve.

'And I want you to promise me something, Medicine Boy. I want you to promise to stop picking on your sister. She doesn't need any trouble out of a damned fool like you, she's a good person, she's an innocent person, she means well.'

'Maybe,' Alex said. 'But she used to beat the shit out of me when we were kids. I have tapes of her trying to smother me to death with a pillow.'

'*What?*'

'I was three, she was eight. I'd been coughing a lot, at the time. I think it got on her nerves.'

Carol stared at him a long time, then rubbed her reddened eyes with her thumbs. 'Well, you're just going to have to forgive her that.'

'I forgive her, Carol. Sure. For your sake.' Alex climbed up onto the workbench and lay down flat on his back. He pulled a narrow translucent hose from his jeans pocket and a flat packet of anesthetic paste. 'Here, take this and screw it on that threading on the end of the jug.'

'Wow, this jug is hot.'

'Yeah, I kept it out in direct sun today, it's pretty damn close to blood heat.'

'I can't believe we're actually doing this.'

'My whole life is just like this.' Alex tilted his head back and practised relaxing his throat. 'Do you have any idea how deep Jerry is into her? I mean, financially?'

'I think he's pretty much wiped her out, Alex. Not that he wants to do that, but he just doesn't care about anything except hacking storms.'

'Well, don't tell anybody. But I've made Juanita my sole heir. I think that'll probably help the Troupe some. A lot, really.'

Carol hesitated. 'That was a pretty dumb thing to tell me. I'm a Trouper, too, y'know.'

'It's all right. I want you to know.'

'You really *do* trust me, don't you?'

'Carol, I think you're the only actually good person here. One of the few truly good people I've ever met. Thank you for helping me. Thank you for looking after me. You deserve to know what's going on, so I told you, that's all. I'm probably gonna pass out during this. Try not to worry too much.'

He opened the packet of anesthetic paste, smeared it with his smart-gloved fingers over the nozzle of the tubing, and then, with a single gesture that took all the courage he had, deliberately shoved it down his own throat. He successfully avoided the back of his tongue, felt it flicker down his sore and swollen larynx, down through the beating center of his chest. He'd nerved himself to do this, maybe even to talk, but as the anesthetic kicked in, all the strength flew out of him like an exploding covey of quail, and left him empty and cold and sick.

Then the fluid came. *Are you a good swimmer, Alex* ?It was cold. It was too cold, it was cold as death, cold as the red Laredo clay. A great rippling belch burst out of his lungs. He heaved for air, eyes bulging in panic, and felt a great interior tide of the stuff slide through his tubercles, a deadly, crazy, cold amoeba. His teeth clamped on the hose, he panicked, he sat upright. Liquid shifted inside him like a strong kick to a half-empty beer keg, and he began coughing convulsively.

Carol stood there with the jug still clutched in her arms, the picture of disgust and terror. Alex pulled the hose, pulled the hose, pulled the hose, like a hateful battle with some deadly tapeworm, and finally it came free, in a frothy spew. Carol jumped back as the jug kept siphoning, the hose trailing and spewing, and Alex kept coughing. His lungs felt like bloody foam rubber.

He stood up. He was extremely weak. But he was still conscious. He was half-full of lung-enema fluid, and he was still conscious. He was carrying the weight of it around inside him like some kind of obscene gestation.

He tried to talk, then. He faced Carol and moved his mouth and a sound came out of him like a drowning raccoon and his mouth filled with great crackling sour bubbles.

Something inside him broke, then, and it really started to hurt. He fell to his knees, doubled over, and started venting the stuff across the bubblepak floor. Great deadly vomitous gouts of it, a huge insupportable fizzing bolus. His ears rang. His hands were spattered with it. It was all over his clothes. And he still wouldn't, couldn't pass out.

It was starting to feel good.

Carol stared at him in disbelief. All the fluid was draining from the jug, trickling relentlessly from the hose. *Shut it off, shut it off,* he gestured, making a drowned gobbling noise, and then another fit of the coughing seized him, and he made another long, blackening, agonized swoop toward collapse.

Some moments later he felt Carol's arms locked around him. She sat him up, propping him against the leg of the table. She looked into his face, checked his eyelid with her thumb, her broad-cheeked face pale and grim. 'Alex, can you hear me?'

He nodded.

'Alex, that's arterial blood. I've seen it before. You're hemorrhaging.'

He shook his head.

'Alex, listen to me. I'm gonna get Ed Dunnebecke, and we're going to take you to a hospital somewhere in the city.'

Alex swallowed hard. 'No,' he whispered. 'I won't go, you can't make me. Don't tell. Don't tell. I'm getting better.'

CHAPTER

8

By June 15 it was obvious to the veriest wannabe weather tyro that an outbreak from the dimension of hell was about to descend upon Oklahoma. As a direct consequence, the state was having its largest tourist boom in ten years.

Everyone with the least trace of common sense had battened down, packed up, and/or evacuated. But the sensible evacuees did not begin to match the raw demographic numbers of people without any common sense, who had come swarming in an endless procession of trailers, chartered buses, and motorized bicycles. Oklahoma had become an instant mecca for heavy-weather freaks. And there were far more of these people than Jane had ever imagined.

After some hesitation, many of the people with sense had shamefacedly returned to ground zero, to make sure that the freaks were not stealing everything. Which, in fact, the freaks were doing, in their jolly distracted sort of way. Anadarko, Chickashaw, Weatherford and Elk City, their cheaper hotels packed and their city parks full of squatters' tents, had turned into slobbering, good-natured beer busts, punctuated with occasional nocturnal shootings and smash-and-grab raids. The National Guard had been called out to maintain order, but in Oklahoma the National Guard was pretty much always out. The National Guard was one of the largest employers in the state, right up there with crops, livestock, timber, and Portland cement. The paramilitary Guard sold the marauders souvenir T-shirts and Sno-Kones by day, then put on their uniforms and beat the shit out of them by night.

To judge by the franctically enthusiastic local TV coverage, not everybody involved was perversely and frankly enjoying the hysterical, unbearable edge of weather tension. The sky was canary yellow and full of dust, and great fearsome sheets of dry heat lightning crackled all evening, and everything smelled of filth and sweat and ozone, and the people were actively savoring this situation. The drought had simply gone on too long. The people of Tornado Alley had suffered far too much already. They had gone far past fear. They had even gone past grim resignation. By now, the poor bastards were deep into convulsively ironical black humor.

The people trickling in from all over America – including, of course, Mexico and Canada – were a far different crowd of wannabes than the standard tornado chasers. The standard tornado freak tended to be, at heart, a rather bookish, owlish sort, carefully reading the latest netcasts and polishing his digital binoculars so he could jump out the door and frantically pursue a brief, elusive phenomenon that usually lasted bare minutes.

But the current heavy-weather crowd was a different scene entirely, not the weather people Jane was used to, not the ones she had expected. Even though they were in the heart of the continent and long kilometers from any shore, they were much more like your basic modern hurricane crowd.

Heavy-weather freaks came in a lot of sociological varieties. First, there were a certain number of people who genuinely didn't give a damn about living. People in despair, people actively hunting their own destruction. The overtly suicidal, though a real factor and kind of the heart-and-soul of the phenomenon, were a very small minority. Most of these mournful black-clad Hamlets would suddenly rediscover a strong taste for survival once the wind outside hit a solid, throbbing roar.

Second, and far more numerous, were the rank thrill freaks, the overtanned jocks and precancerous muscular surfer-dude types. It was amazing how few of these reckless idiots would be killed or maimed, by even the worst storms. They usually sported aqualungs and windsurfing smart boards, with which to hunt the Big Wave, the Really Big Wave, the Insanely Big Wave. No surf in Oklahoma, though, so, with the grotesque ingenuity of a leisure industry far gone into deep psychosis, they had brought dozens of mean-ass little diamond-hubbed 'wind schooners,' sail-powered vehicles so inher-

ently unpredictable that even their onboard computer navigation
acted crazy. And yet the sons of bitches who rode the things seemed
to bear a charmed life. They were as hard to kill as cockroaches.

Then there were the largest group, the variant people who simply
admired and doted on storms. Most of them didn't hack storms.
Sometimes they took photos or videos, but they had no intellectual or
professional interest. They were simply storm devotees. Some of
them were deeply religious. Some wrote really bad net-poetry. Some
few of them were very private people, with tattoos and chains and
scab art, who would take hallucinogens and/or held deliberate orgies
in bunkers at the height of the troubles. They all tended to have a
trademark look of vacant sincerity, and odd fixations in dress and
diet.

Fourth, thieves. People on the lookout for the main chance.
Looters, black marketeers, rip-off people. Structure-hit people, too.
Not tremendous numbers, not whole marauding armies of them, but
plenty to worry about. They tended to leave mysterious chalk-mark
symbols wherever they went, and to share mulligatawny stew in
vacant buildings.

And last – the group rising up the charts, and the group that Jane
found, basically, by far the least explicable, the creepiest, and the
most portentous – evacuation freaks. People who flourished *just after*
storms. People who liked to dwell in evacuation camps. Perhaps
they'd grown up in such a camp during the State of Emergency, and
always perversely missed the experience afterward. Or maybe they
just enjoyed that feeling of intense, slightly hallucinatory human
community that always sprang up in the aftermath of a major natural
diaster. Or maybe they just needed disaster to really live, because
having grown up under the crushing weight of heavy weather, they
had never possessed any real life.

If you had no strong identity of your own, then you could become
anyone and everyone, inside an evacuation camp. The annihilation
of a town or suburb broke down all barriers of class, status, and
experience, and put everyone into the same paper suit. Some people
– and growing numbers of them, apparently – actively fed on that
situation. They were a new class of human being, something past
charlatan, something past fraudster or hustler, something without
real precedent, something past history, something past identity.

Sometimes – a lot of times – the evacuation freak would be the heart and soul of the local recovery effort, a manic, pink-cheeked person always cheerful, with a smile for everybody, always ready to console the bereaved, bathe the wounded, play endless games of cot-side charades with the grateful crippled child. Often they passed themselves off as pastors or medical workers or social counselors or minor-league feds of some kind, and they would get away with it, too, because no one was checking papers in the horror and pain and confusion.

They would stay as long as they dared, and eat the government chow and wear the paper suits and claim vaguely to be from 'somewhere around.' Oddly, evacuation freaks were almost always harmless, at least in a physical sense. They didn't steal, they didn't rob, they didn't kill or structure-hit. Some of them were too dazed and confused to do much of anything but sit and eat and smile, but quite often they would work with literally selfless dedication, and inspire the people around them, and the people would look up to them, and admire them, and trust them implicitly, and depend on these hollow people as a community pillar of strength. Evacuation freaks were both men and women. What they were doing was not exactly criminal, and even when caught and scolded or punished for it, they never seemed able to stop. They would just drift to some fresh hell in another state, and rend their garments and cover themselves with mud, and then stagger into camp, faking distress.

But the very weirdest part was that evacuation freaks always seemed to travel entirely alone.

'Juanita,' said April Logan, 'I always sensed you might prove to be one of my star students.'

'Thank you, April.'

'How do you count yourself, in this little social analysis of yours?'

'Me?' Jane said. 'Scientist.'

'Oh yes' – April nodded slowly – 'that's very good.'

Jane laughed. 'Well, you're here, *too*, you know.'

'Of course,' April Logan said. Her styled hair lifted a little in the dry, sour breeze, and she gave a long, meditative stare around the Troupe camp, sucking in everything with her flat, yellowish, all-comprehending gaze.

If not for the drought, it would have been a very pretty area. The

Troupe was camped west of El Reno on Interstate 40, an area of red
cliffs of crumbling sandstone, red soil, creek bottoms full of pecans
and aspens and festooned with honeysuckle, a place of goldenrod and
winecup and coneflowers and trailing purple legume. Spring hadn't
given up yet. It was parched and covered with dust, but spring
hadn't given up.

April Logan was wearing a tailored paper jumpsuit printed in gold
leaf: a perfectly body-morphed adaptation of one of the more lysergic
ornaments from the Book of Kells. It was just like April to wear
something like that: costume as oxymoron. Gilded paper. Preindust-
rial handicraft warped by postindustrial machine, a consumer
conundrum from the warring no-man's-land of Cost versus Value
versus Worth. And it was, coincidentally, quite beautiful. 'I'm still
riding the back of the Project,' April Logan said. 'The Project
wanted me to come here, you know.'

'You're kidding.'

'Oh no,' said April. 'The Project is sometimes crazy, but it never
kids.'

Jane had helped to build the Project, as an undergraduate. It was
something Professor Logan had been patiently assembling and
refining for years – an eldritch chimera of monster clipping service,
genetic algorithm, and neural net. A postliterate, neoacademic
Correlation Machine, a megachipped Synchronicity Generator.
There were a lot of lumps in April's vast analytical stew: demograph-
ics, employment records, consumption trends. Geographical distribution of network data trafficking. Mortality rates, flows of
private currency. And various arcane indices of graphic design – like
April herself, the Project was very big on graphic-design trends.

When discussing her Project, April liked to dwell on the eldritch
twentieth-century correlation between women's hemlines and the
stock market. The market would go up, hemlines would go up. The
market would drop, hemlines would drop. Nobody knew why, or
ever learned why, but the correlation held quite steady for decades.
Eventually, of course, the stock market lost all contact with reality,
and women no longer gave a damn about their hemlines even if they
bothered to wear skirts, but, as April said, the crux of her Project was
to discover and seize similar modern correlations while they were still
fresh, and before the endless chaos of society necessarily rendered

them extinct. Given that chaos, the 'why' of the correlation was indeterminate. And given those genetic algorithms, causation wasn't even logically traceable within the circuits of the machine. In any case, reason and causation were not the point of April's effort. The crux of the matter was whether April's massive simulation would parallel reality closely enough to be a useful design tool.

The Project wasn't that much different, in its basic digital operation, from Jerry's weather modeling – except that Jerry's simulations were firmly based on openly testable, fully established laws of physics, while April Logan was not a scentist but an artist and design critic. As far as Jane could figure, April's analytical armature wasn't much of a genuine intellectual advance over a tarot deck. And yet, like a tarot deck, no matter what nonsense the damn thing threw out, it always seemed to work somehow, to make a certain deep and tantalizing sense.

It wasn't science, and didn't pretend to be, but it had made April Logan into a very wealthy and influential woman. She had left academia – where she had been doing quite well – and now commanded enormous fees as a private consultant. People – sensible, practical people – paid April Logan huge sums to predict things like 'the color of the season.' And whether there might be a mass market for disposable fastfood plasticware that you could chew up and eat. And why hotels were suffering a plague of teen suicides inside glass elevators, and why installing bright pink carpeting might help. April had become a genuine Design Guru.

The years hadn't been kind to April. Seeing her teacher in person again, outside the hard controlled gleam of April's precisely calculated public image, Jane noticed tremor and flakiness there, a touch of madness, even. April Logan was not a happy woman. But success hadn't changed her much. April had always had that innate jitter and tang, and it was slowly and visibly eating her heart out – but April Logan had a lot of heart. She had her muse in a hammerlock, and she was possessed by the Work. Just to be around April was to feel a radioactive glow from a capable, perceptive, brilliant woman, someone paying a focused and terrible attention to things most human beings couldn't even see. April was a real artist, the truest artist Jane had ever met. The genuine article. Even the worst and most dismal commercial bullshit in a hell-bound planet couldn't kill them all off.

'True innovation tends to afflict the eccentric . . . ' April mused. 'A minority of the eccentric, one in a hundred, maybe.' She paused. 'Of course, that leaves society with the burden of ninety-nine pretentious, ill-behaved basket cases.'

'Same old Professor Logan.'

'I might have known I'd see you end up in the heart of an event like this, Juanita. There's no question that it's an event of some pivotal importance. I've watched it work its way from speculation, to fad, to near mania . . . If it's a natural disaster that matches its advance billings, this could become a long-term societal landmark.'

'And we're documenting it.'

'It's very dangerous, isn't it? Not only physically, but it is clearly attracting a large nexus of unstable social elements.'

'Fortune rewards the brave,' Jane said cheerfully. 'We'll be fine. We know what we're doing. And so will everyone else, if you will help us.'

'Interesting,' April said. From her, that was high praise. 'I did a comprehensive category search through the Project for neural weightings for your friend, Dr Mulcahey. It's rare for the Project to single out any individual, especially one as publicly little known as he is, and yet Dr Mulcahey registers in no less than fourteen different categories.'

'Really.'

'That's quite extraordinary. And yet he has an even lesser-known brother who showed up in no less than seventeen!'

'Do you ever look *yourself* up in the Project?'

'Every day. I've got as high as five, sometimes. Six once, briefly.' She frowned. 'Of course, you could argue that a lower number of categories deepens the basic societal influence.'

'Right. Have you looked *me* up, lately?'

April gazed tactfully across the camp. 'What is that device they're launching?'

'Weather balloon,' Jane said, standing up. No use taking offense. It was just a big damn fortune-telling machine. 'Would you like to watch?'

JERRY STOOD BEFORE the firelight, his head bare, his hands behind his back. 'Tomorrow we are going to track the most violent storm in recorded history,' he said. 'It will break tomorrow, probably by noon, and it will kill thousands, probably tens of thousands of people. If it's stable and it persists beyond a few hours, it may kill millions. If we had time, and energy, and opportunity, I would try to save lives. But we don't, and we can't. We don't have time, and we don't have authority, so we can't save anyone. We can't even save ourselves. Our own lives are not our top priority tomorrow.'

The people in the powwow circle were very silent.

'In the terrible scale of tomorrow's event, our lives just don't matter much. Knowledge of the F-6 is more important than any of us. I wish this weren't the case, but it's the truth. I want you to understand that truth and accept it, I want you to take it into your hearts and feel it, and resolve to act on it. People, you've all seen the simulations, you know what I mean when I say F-6. But people, the damned thing is finally upon us. It is here, it's real, no playback this time, no simulacrum. It is with us in stark reality. We have to know all that we can about the real F-6, at all costs. It is a terrible event that must be documented – at all costs. Tomorrow, we must seize as much of the truth as we can possibly steal from this dreadful thing. Even if we all die doing this, but some survivor learns the truth about it because of our efforts, then that will be an excellent price for our lives.'

Jerry began to pace back and forth. 'I don't want any recklessness tomorrow. I don't want any amateurism, I don't want any nonsense. What I want from you is complete resolve, and complete understanding of the necessity and the consequences. We have only one chance. This is the greatest heavy-weather challenge that our Troupe will ever face, and I hope and believe it will be the single most violent weather event we will see in our natural lifetimes. If you believe that your life is more important than hacking this storm, I can understand that belief. It's wise. Most people would call it sensible. You are all here with me now because you're definitely not most people, but what I'm asking from you now is a terrible thing to ask of anyone. This isn't just another storm pursuit. It's not just another front, and another spike. This thing is Death, people. It's a destroyer of worlds. It's the worst thing human action has brought into this world since Los Alamos. If your life is your first priority, you should leave this camp immediately, now. I am forecasting a weather event that is more swift, more volatile, more massive, and more violent than the strongest F5 maxitornado, by a full order of magnitude. If you want to escape the disaster, you should flee right now, due east, and not stop until you are on the far side of the Mississippi. If you stay, stay in the full knowledge that we are going after this catastrophe head-on.'

Nobody moved. Nobody said anything.

Suddenly the air was split with a bloodcurdling bestial yell, a warbling, yodeling, exultant screech like a madwoman gloating over a freshly severed scalp.

It was Joanne Lessard. They all stared at Joanne in complete astonishment. Joanne was sitting cross-legged on a patch of bubblepak near the campfire. She had just washed her thin blonde hair and was combing it. She said nothing, but only smiled sunnily in the flickering fireleight, and shrugged her shoulders once, and kept combing.

Even Jerry seemed stunned.

'I've said enough,' Jerry realized, and deliberately sat down.

Rudy Martinez stood up. 'Jerry, are you nowcasting tomorrow?'

'Yeah.'

'I'll go anywhere as long as Jerry is nowcasting. I've said enough.' Rudy sat down.

Joe Brasseur stood up. 'I'm available for consultation by anyone who hasn't made their will. Dying intestate, that's no joke for your heirs. We got enough time tonight to record a will, put on a digital signature, and pipe it to an off-site backup. This means you, Dunnebecke. I've said enough.' He sat down.

Nobody said anything for a long time.

Finally Jane felt she had to stand up. 'I just want to say that I feel really proud of everybody. And I have a good feeling about this. Good hunting tomorrow, people. I've said enough.' She sat down.

April Logan stood up. 'Forgive me for interrupting your deliberations, but if it's all right with the group, I'd like to ask all of you something.'

April Logan looked at Jerry. Jerry lifted his brows.

'Actually, it's something of a poll query.'

'Go ahead, just ask,' Jane hissed at her.

'My question is: When do you think the human race conclusively lost control over its own destiny? I'd like everyone here to answer, if you don't mind.' April produced a handheld notepad. 'Please just start anywhere in the circle – here at my left, will do.'

Martha Madronich stood up, reluctantly. 'Well, I hate to go first, but in answer to your question, um, Professor, I always figured we lost it for good sometime during the State of Emergency.' She sat down.

Ed Dunnebecke stood up. 'I'd have to say 1968. Maybe 1967. If you look at the CO_2 statistics, they had a good chance to choke it all back right there, and they knew full well they were screwing the environment. There was definitely revolutionary potential in the period, and even some political will, but they squandered the opportunity in the drugs and the Marxism and the mystical crap, and they never regained the momentum. Nineteen sixty-eight, definitely. I've said enough.'

Greg Foulks stood up. 'I'm with Ed on that one, except there was one last chance in 1989 too. Maybe even as late as '91, after the First Gulf War. Well, that one was actually the Second Gulf War, strictly speaking. But after they blew their big chance at genuine New World Order in '89 and '91, they were definitely trashed. I've said enough.' He sat down.

Carol Cooper stood up. 'Well, you hear this question quite a bit, of course . . . Call me romantic, but I always figured 1914. The First World War. I mean, you look at that long peace in Europe before the slaughter, and it looks like mediation might have had a chance to stick. And if we hadn't blown most of the twentieth century on fascism and communism and the rest of the ism bullshit, maybe we could have built something decent, and besides, no matter what Janey says, Art Nouveau was the last really truly decent-looking graphic-art movement. I've said enough.'

Sam Moncrieff took his turn. 'Late 1980s . . . there were some congressional hearings on global warming that everybody ignored . . . Also the Montreal Accords on chlorofluorocarbons; they should have passed those with some serious teeth about CO_2 and methane, and things would be a lot better today. Still heavy weather, probably, but not insanely heavy. Late eighties. Definitely. I've said enough.'

Rick Sedletter rose. 'What Greg said.' He sat down.

Peter Vierling stood up. 'Maybe it's just me, but I always felt like if personal computers had come along in the 1950s instead of the 1970s, everybody would have saved a lot of time. Well . . . never mind.' He sat down.

Buzzard stood up. 'I think they blew it with the League of Nations in the twenties. That was a pretty good idea, and it was strictly pig-stupid isolationism on the part of the USA that scragged that whole thing. Also the early days of aviation should have worked a lot better. Kind of a real wings-over-the-world opportunity. A big shame that Charles Lindbergh liked fascists so much. I've said enough.'

Joanne stood up. 'Nineteen-forty-five. United Nations could have rebuilt everything. They tried too. Some pretty good declarations, but no good follow-through, though. Too bad. I've said enough.'

Joe Brasseur stood. 'I'm with Joanne on the 1940s thing. I don't think humanity ever really recovered from the death camps. And Hiroshima too. After the camps and the Bomb, any horror was possible, and nothing was certain anymore . . . People never straightened up again after that, they always walked around bent and shivering and scared. Sometimes I think I'd rather be scared of the sky than that scared about other human beings. Maybe it was even worth heavy weather to miss nuclear Armageddon and genocide . . . I wouldn't mind discussing this matter with you later, Professor Logan. But for the meantime, I've said enough.'

Ellen Mae Lankton spoke. 'Me? If I gotta blame somebody, I blame Columbus. Five hundred thirty-nine years of oppression and genocide. I blame Columbus, and that bastard who designed the repeating rifle. You'd never find an F-6 on any plain that was still covered with buffalo . . . But I've said this before, and I've said it enough.' She sat down.

Ed Dunnebecke stood up again. 'Funny thing, but I think the French Revolution had a very good chance and blew it. Europe wasted the next two centuries trying to do what the Revolution had right in its grasp in 1789. But once you stumble into that public-execution nonsense . . . Hell, that was when I knew the Regime had lost it during the State of Emergency, when they started cablecasting their goddamn executions. Give 'em to Madame Guillotine, and the Revolution will eat its young, just as sure as hell . . . Yeah, put me down for 1789. I've said enough.'

Jeff Lowe rose to his feet. 'I don't know very much about history. Sorry.'

Mickey Kiehl stood up. 'I think we lost it when we didn't go for nuclear power. They coulda designed much better plants than they did, and a hell of a lot better disposal system, but they didn't because of that moral taint from the Bomb. People were scared to death of any kind of 'radiation' even when a few extra curies aren't really dangerous. I'd say 1950s. When the atomic-energy people hid behind the military-security bullshit instead of really trying to make fission work safely for real people in real life. So we got all-natural CO_2 instead. And the CO_2 ruined everything. I've said enough.'

Jerry stood up. 'I think it's fruitless to look for first causes or to try to assign blame. The atmosphere is a chaotic system; humanity might have avoided all those mistakes and still found itself in this conjunction. That begs the question of when we lost control of our destiny. We have none now; I doubt we ever had any.'

'I'm with Jerry on this one,' Jane said cheerfully. 'Only more so. I mean, if you look back at the glacial records for the Eemian Period, the one before the last set of ice ages, there were no people around to speak of, and yet the weather was completely crazy. Global temps used to soar and dip eight, nine, ten degrees within a single century! The climate was highly unstable, but that was a completely natural state. And then right after that, most of Europe, Asia, and America were covered with giant cliffs of ice that smashed and froze everything in their path. Even worse than agriculture and urbanization! And a lot worse than heavy weather is now. I'm real sorry that we did this to ourselves and that we're in the fix we are in now, but so-called Mother Earth herself has done worse things to the planet. And believe it or not, the human race has actually had things worse.'

'Very good,' said April Logan. 'Thanks very much for that spectrum of opinion by people who ought to know. Since I have no intention of being here when Dr Mulcahey's forecast is tested, I'll be taking his advice and leaving Oklahoma immediately. I wish you all the very best of luck.' She turned to Jane. 'If I can do anything for you, leave E-mail.'

'Thanks, April.'

'Wait a moment,' Carol said aloud. 'You don't want to miss the night's entertainment.'

'I beg your pardon?'

'Alex is doing something for us, right after the powwow.'

Alex. Where was Alex? Jane realized with a guilt-stricken start that she hadn't even missed him.

'Yeah,' Rick blurted. 'Where is ol' Alex?'

Carol smiled. 'Ladies and gentlemen, Alex Unger and his Magic Lariat!'

Alex wandered into the circle of firelight. He was wearing leather chaps and pearl-buttoned shirt and a ten-gallon hat. He'd polished his Mexican boots and put clown white and lipstick on his face.

'Yippee-ti-yi-yo,' Peter suggested warily.

Alex whipped the smart rope off his shoulder. He had done something to it, greased it or oiled it somehow; it looked very shiny tonight.

He whipped a little energy into it with a pop of his skinny arm, then sent a big loop of it rotating over his head. His face was stony, perfectly solemn.

The loop hung over him like a halo for a moment, humming with speed. Then he somehow bent the loop sideways and began to jump through it. Not much of a jump really; a feeble hop, so that his bootheels barely cleared the earth; but the loop of smart rope went whizzing past him with impressive buzzing speed, kicking up brief gouts of dirt.

Alex threw the thing a full twenty meters into the air, then sent the loop at its end ricocheting back and forth, over the heads of the crowd. It went hissing through every point of the circle, darting among them like the head of a snake. People whooped and flinched, some of them whacking out at it with their hands.

The lariat loop at the end of the rope suddenly went square: a raggedly revolving square of spinning rope. Then it turned triangular. Then, amazingly, a five-pointed Texas star. It was more than a little odd to see a cowboy's rope behaving in that fashion; it was, Jane thought dizzily, downright outré.

Alex tugged the star inward; toward himself, then bounced it around the circle, stenciling the star across the earth, bouncing it on its points. Alex turned slowly on his heels. The rope passed unharmed through the flames of the campfire.

People began laughing.

Alex waved with his free hand, in acknowledgment, and then began catching and tossing pieces of flaming wood. He lassoed a burning length of cedar from the fire, tossed it high in the air, and caught it with the end of the loop. He flipped the flaming branch end over end, lassoing it repeatedly with unerring, supernatural accuracy. After a moment Jane realized that the trick wasn't that hard; he wasn't actually casting the rope, he was holding the loop up in waiting, then snapping it shut as the stick fell through it. But the effect was so unnaturally fluid and swift that it actually did look magical. It was just as if her little brother had hog-tied the laws of physics. Jane broke into a gale of laughter. It was the funniest thing she had seen in ages, and by far the funniest thing she had ever seen Alex do.

Now, amazingly, Alex somehow hog-tied his own waist and lifted himself up, hanging in midair. He seemed to lift himself by his own bootstraps. He hung there in space, magically hoist by his own Hindu rope trick, while the wide loops of smart rope spun around on the earth beneath him, like the rim of a wobbling corkscrew.

First he rolled awhile, slowly spinning himself around, like some lost fancy sock in a laundry. Then he began, clumsily, to hop. He'd mutated the smart rope into a spiraled, wiry pogo stick. The Troupers were falling all over themselves with hilarity. Carol was clinging onto Greg's shoulder, so convulsed with laughter that she was hardly able to look. Even Jerry was laughing aloud.

'My word,' April Logan commented. 'Why, he's rather good!'

'That's Alex!' Jane told her. 'He's my – ' She stopped. 'He's one of our Troupe.'

Jane felt a hand on her shoulder. It was Ed Dunnebecke. Ed bent low, beside her right ear. 'I didn't know he was this funny, did you?'

'No, I didn't.

'I gotta leave, Jane, I got business tonight, but your little brother can really hack that thing.'

'Yeah, Ed, he can, can't he?'

'It's not a real useful hack, I guess, but hell, this is real entertainment! He's got imagination!'

'Thanks, Ed.'

'I'm glad you brought him here. Bye, Janey.' He patted her shoulder and left.

Alex was holding on to the rope with both hands, with extra loops sneaked around his ankles, and he was rolling around the edge of the circle of Troupers, doing a giant cartwheel. Alex went head over heels, head over heels, head over heels, his clown-white face scything along, while the night rang out with whoops and applause.

Then he lost it suddenly, and wobbled, and fell. He fell headlong, and he fell pretty hard. Dust whumped the earth where his booted legs flopped down.

Everyone was silent. Jane heard the fire crackle.

Alex got up again, quickly but shakily. He slapped dust from his fancy shirt, trying gamely to smile. He'd been to town, somehow, into some neowestern clothing store. Probably snaked off on a bike to Oklahoma City while nobody was paying attention to him.

He said his first words of the evening. 'Spinnin' a rope is fun,' he shouted raggedly, 'if yore neck ain't in it!'

The Troupe broke into howls of laughter.

'Now for my goldurn *pièce de résistance*,' Alex shouted. He began whipping energy into the rope, his dust-smeared pale face set grimly. The rope rose, began to spin, then to spiral inward. Narrow at the bottom. Broader at the top. It spun so fast that the lines of rope became a glimmering blur.

And faster yet. The fire billowed in the wind of its passage. It was sucking up dust from the ground.

A little toy spike.

The whipping rope was blowing hard enough to feel. As the vortex wandered past her at the end of the rope, Jane felt the rush of wind tugging the hair. Then, up at the very top, the end of the smart rope whipped loose, lashing out above their heads with a nasty whip crack of toy thunder. It cracked again, then a third time. The spike spun faster, with a mean dynamo hum. Alex was putting everything into it that the battery could hold. Jane saw him crouching there, flinching away below, wary, at the edge of control, frightened of his own creation.

Then he turned it off. It sagged in midair, and fell over in a heap of loops. A dead thing, dead rope.

The Troupe applauded wildly.

Alex stooped and gathered the dead rope up in both his arms.

'That's all I've got for y'all,' he said, bowing. 'Thanks a lot for your kindly attention.'

CHAPTER

The day dawned bilious yellow and veined with blue, like a bad cheese. The jet stream had shifted, and at last, the high was on the move.

Jane and Alex took Charlie west down Highway 40 in pursuit of ground zero. Jane didn't know why Jerry had assigned her Alex as a chase companion, on this criticial day of all days. Maybe to teach her some subtle lesson about the inevitable repercussions from an arrogant good deed.

She had anticipated a mean-spirited battle of wills between herself and her brother, but Alex was unusually subdued. He looked genuinely ill – or more likely doped. It would have been only too much like Alex, to sneak into Oklahoma City and score some hellish concoction.

But he did as he was told. He took orders, he tried running the cameras, he kept up with the chase reports from camp, he downloaded maps and took notes. She couldn't call him enthusiastic, but he was watchful and careful, and he wasn't making many mistakes. Actually, Alex wasn't any worse as a traveling companion than any other Trouper. Somehow, despite everything, he'd actually done it. Her brother had become just another Trouper.

He had his rope with him. He always carried the rope now, looped around his bony shoulder like a broken puppet string. But he'd put away his play-cowboy finery and was wearing a simple paper refugee suit, fresh off the roll. And he'd sponge-washed, shaved, and he'd even combed his hair.

For once, Alex wasn't wearing the breathing mask. She almost wished that he was. With his pale muzzle and striped cheeks, and the waxy skin and too neat hair, he looked like some half-finished project off an undertaker's slab.

Long kilometers of western Oklahoma went by in silence, broken by reports from the Aerodrome Truck and the Radar Bus.

'What's with the paper suit, Alex?'

'I dunno. The other clothes just didn't fit anymore.'

'I know what you mean.'

A lot more long silence.

'Put the top back,' Alex said.

'It's really dusty out there.'

'Put it back anyway.'

Jane put it back. The car began to fill with fine whirling grit. There was a nasty hot breeze down at ground level, a breeze from the far west with a bad smell of ashes and mummification.

Alex craned his narrow head back and gazed straight up at the zenith. 'Do you see that stuff up there, Janey?'

'What?'

'It looks like the sky is breaking into pieces.'

There was a low-level yellowish haze everywhere, a dust haze like the film on an animal's teeth, but far up above the dust, it was dry and clearer. Clear enough so that somewhere at the stratosphere, Jane could see a little cirrus. More than a little cirrus, when she got used to looking for it. A very strange, spiderwebby cirrus. Long, thin, filaments of feathery cloud that stretched far across the sky, not in parallel waves either, as might be expected from cirrus, but crossing at odd angles. A broken grid of high, razor-thin ice cloud, like a dust-filthy mirror cracking into hexagons.

'What is that stuff, Janey?'

'Looks like some kind of Bénard convection,' Jane said. It was amazing how much better heavy weather felt when you had a catchprase for it. If you had a catchprase, then you could really talk successfully about the weather and it almost felt as if you could do something about it. 'That's the kind of stratus you get from a very slow, gentle, general uplift. Probably some thermal action way up off the top of the high.'

'Why aren't there towers?'

'Too low in relative humidity.'

On 283 North, just east of the Antelope Hills, they encountered a rabbit horde.

Although she had eaten far more than her share of gamy, rank, jackrabbit tamales over the past year, Jane had never paid much sustained attention to jackrabbits. Out in West Texas, jackrabbits were common as dirt. Jackrabbits could run like the wind and jump clean over a parked car, but in her own experience, they rarely bothered to do anything so dramatic. There just weren't many natural predators around to chase and kill jackrabbits, anymore. So the rabbits – they were hares, if you wanted to be exact about it – just ate and reproduced and died in their millions of various nasty parasites and plagues, just like the other unquestioned masters of the earth.

Jackrabbits had gray-brown speckled fur, and absurdly long, veiny, black-tipped ears, and the long, gracile limbs of a desert animal. Glimpsed loping around through the brush, eating most anything – cactus, sagebrush, beer cans, used tires, old barbed wire maybe – jackrabbits were lopsided, picturesque animals, though their bulging yellow rodent eyes rivaled a lizard's for blank stupidity. Until now, Jane had never seen a jackrabbit that looked really upset.

But now, loping across the road like some boiling swarm of gangling, dirt-colored vermin, came dozens of jackrabbits. Then, hundreds. Then thousands of them, endless swarming ragged loping rat packs of them. Charlie slowed to a crawl, utterly confused by a road transmuted into a boiling, leaping tide of fur.

The rabbits were anything but picturesque. They were brown and gaunt with hunger, and trembling and desperate, and ragged and nasty, like junked, threadbare stuffed animals that had been crammed through a knothole. Jane was pretty sure that she could actually smell the jackrabbits. A hot panicky smell rising off them, like burning manure.

The car pulled over and stopped.

'Well, that tears it,' said Alex, meditatively. 'Even these harebrained things have more common sense than we do. If we had any smarts, we'd turn off the road right now and head wherever they're heading.'

'Oh, for heaven's sake, Alex. It's just a migration. It's because of the drought. The poor things are all starving.'

'Maybe they are, but that's sure not why they're running. You seen any birds around here lately? Red-tailed hawks? Turkey vultures? Scissortails? Me neither.'

'What are you getting at?'

'Janey, every wild creature that can get away from this place is running as fast as it can run. Get it? That's not any accident.' He coughed a bit, cleared his throat. 'And I've been doing some research,' he announced. 'There are certain towns in this area that have a lot of available shelter. Really good, solid storm shelter. Like, say, Woodward. That town got wiped flat by an F-4 about ten years ago, so they got themselves a bunch of diamond drills and they dug out underground in a mega way. Big-city shelters, whole malls down there, lots of private shelters too. And it's only twenty minutes from here.'

'You don't say. It's nice of you to take so much initiative.'

'I want to make you a deal,' Alex said. 'When this thing really rips the lid off, I want you to get to a shelter.'

'Me, Alex? Me, and not you?'

'Exactly. You won't lose anything by doing that. I can get you all the data you want. I'll punch the core on the thing for you, I swear to God I will. I will do that. But you need to live through this so you can put it all together later, and understand it. And sell it too. Right? If I don't make it through this experience, it's no big loss to anybody. But Janey, if you don't survive this, it's gonna put a pretty serious long-term crimp in your career.'

'Alex, this *is* my career.'

'You've got nothing, unless you stay alive. That makes good sense, so think about it.'

'Do I look afraid to you? You think I want to run for cover? You think I like this stupid idea of yours?'

'I know you're real brave, Janey. That doesn't impress me. I'm not afraid, either. Do I look afraid to you?' He didn't. 'Do I look like I'm kidding about this?' He wasn't. 'All I'm telling you is that it's a bad idea for both of us to get killed today. Both the Unger kids killed at once? What about our dad?'

'What about him?'

'Well, he's no prize, our *querido papá*, but he cares! I mean, he cares some. At least, he wouldn't send his daughter into a death trap, just to gratify his own curiosity!' Alex started talking really quickly. 'I think Mulcahey does care about you some, when he can be bothered to notice you instead of his mathematics, and in fact that's why Jerry stuck me in here with you today, so you would slow down some, and not do anything really crazy. Right? Right! That's him all over!'

Jane stared at him, speechless.

'So maybe Jerry cares about you, I grant you that, *but he doesn't care about you enough!* I don't care what charming bullshit he gave you, or how he convinced you to live his life for him, but if he loved you the way somebody ought to love you, he would never have sent you out here, never! This is a suicide mission! You're a young woman with a lot going for you, and you shouldn't end up as some kind of broken, stomped, bloody doll out in this goddamned wasteland!' He broke into a fit of coughing. 'Look at those clouds, Jane!' he croaked. 'Clouds are never supposed to look like that! We're gonna get ridden down and stomped flat out here, just like two of those rabbits!'

'Take it easy! You're losing it.'

'Don't talk down to me, just look up at the sky!'

Jane, against her own will, looked up. The dust had thinned, and the sun was higher, and the cirrus looked utterly bizarre. There were hundreds of little growing patches of it now. Shapes just like frost on a windowpane like patchy mutant snowflakes. The clouds looked like a down feather might look if you shot ten thousand volts through it.

But that wasn't the half of it. The crazy thing was that all the little feather clouds were all exactly the same shape. They weren't the same size. Some were huge, some were tiny. They were pointed in different directions. Not *all* directions, mind you – exactly six different directions. And yet hellishly, creepily, the clouds were all identical. A little comma drip on one end, a curved spine with a hook at the other, and hundreds of fine little electrified streamers branching off from both sides.

It looked like a tiling pattern. Like ceramic tiling. The Oklahoma sky was tiled with a bathroom floor.

'Bénard convection does that sometimes,' Jane babbled. 'The cells have six different axes of rotation and that self-similarity has gotta mean that the cell updraft vectors are all, well . . . ' Words failed her. Words failed her quite suddenly, and really badly. A kind of software crash for language. Words – yeah, even scientific words – there were times and contingencies when reality ripped loose from verbal symbolism and just went its own goddamned way. And this was one of those times.

'What's that big sea growing up the middle?' Alex said.

'I dunno. Get the cameras on it.'

'Good idea.' Alex put his face into the camera goggles and tilted them upward on the weapons mounts. 'Wow.'

'That's gotta be the jet stream,' Jane said. 'The major, polar jet stream that's been hanging north all this time. It's finally moved.'

'Janey, I don't know much about the jet stream, but I know the jet stream doesn't bend at that kind of angle.'

'Well, it's probably not really bending; it just looks that way from this angle of observation.'

'The hell it is. The hell it does. Janey, I can see it through these cameras a hell of a lot better than you can, and whatever that thing is, it's coming down. It's coming down right at us, it's gonna hit the earth.'

'Great! Keep recording!'

His voice cracked. 'I think we'd better leave this place.'

'Hell no! That's it! Of course! Of course, that's what Jerry's been looking for – a permanent source of power for the F-6, and the jet stream is permanent power! It wraps the whole planet, and it's seven kilometers thick and it's fifty degrees below zero and it does two hundred klicks an hour. God, the jet stream, if the jet stream spikes down out of the stratosphere, then it's all gonna add up!' She grabbed for her headset.

'Janey, that thing's going to kill us. We're gonna die here.'

'Shut up and keep recording.' A remarkably stupid robot truck raced suddenly past them, mangling and crippling dozens of bloodied flopping jackrabbits. The rest of the rabbits exploded off in all directions, like fleas on a hot plate.

'Jane in Charlie here!' she shouted. 'We got a massive outbreak! These are the coords . . . '

She began reading them off, her voice rising.

An avalanche of freezing air fell out of the sky. The stratosphere was ten kilometers up. Even at two hundred klicks an hour, it took the jet stream a good four minutes to fall to earth.

First, the sky cracked open, on a long, furred, spiky seam. Then, maybe ninety seconds down, the vast, thick surge of air hit a warm layer in the upper atmosphere. There was a massive, soundless explosion. Freezing gouts of ice-white cloud blew out in all directions. The clouds touched the sun, and in instants, everything began to darken.

The stream plowed through the spewing clouds like a bullet through an apple, and hit a second thermopause. There was another fantastically powerful explosion. There was still no trace of wind at ground level, but the sound from that first overhead explosion reached the earth then, a cataclysmic roll of thunder that did not vary and did not stop. A cottonwood tree at the side of the road trembled violently, for no visible reason, so violently that it shed all its leaves.

From the second explosion, actual vortices blasted out in every corner of the compass, literal swirls of splitting, freezing, curling air, whirlpool swirls of air as big as towns.

She had one last glimpse up the central core of the falling jet stream. It was clear and cold and vast and lethal. She could see stars through it.

Then the jet stream hit the living earth, maybe three kilometers away. The earth erupted in torment and dozens of vast clotted cobras of filth leaped skyward instantly. Jane jammed her sound-cancellation earphones over her head then so she did not go deaf, but the sound of the F-6 was something far beyond the Train. It was a sonic weapon pressing through her body and crushing her inside. It was more than sound, it was raw shock, terrible, unendurable, deadly.

She fought with the car then, trying to get Charlie to turn and run. Nothing happened; the machine sat as if stunned. Lightning like no lightning she had ever seen came out of the erupting columns of dirt. It was dirt lightning, rock lightning. It was thick and crooked and horizontal, and it looked like flying, spinning swastikas. A great flying complex of crooked lightning flew right over their heads, and it broke apart in front of her eyes into gigantic, glowing, sparking chunks.

The car moved. She turned and ran. The day was gone. They were in black hell, instant Gehenna. A hurricane of dirt had spread all over the sky. They were buried alive under a giant spreading plateau of screaming, crackling filth. The air was half-dirt. The maddened earth had forgotten the difference between air and dirt. Dirt and air were going to be the same thing from now on. The black slurry of wind was hanging over them, it was all around them.

And out at the far edge of it – at the very far, spreading edge, where there was still a little squashed and sickly light at the horizon: there were spikes dropping. Spikes, all around them. Dozens of spikes. A corona of spikes, a halo of spikes. F-1s, F-2s, F-3s. Kinky spikes. Fat spikes. Spikes as squat as footballs. Spikes that whipped like venom-spitting mambas. Spikes that the F-6 had flung out all around itself in a single gesture, spikes it had conjured up and flung to earth in a moment, a chorus line of devils at the skirts of its Dance of Destruction.

Charlie flew as it had never flown before. They ran east over a darkened road, and the pursuit vehicle's complex wheels scarcely touched the ground. Jane glanced at Alex. He was still looking through the cameras. He was still recording – everything that he could. He had the cameras turned backward and he was looking behind the car.

Then suddenly Alex flung the cameras off his face and he doubled over hard, and he wrapped both arms around his head. Jane wondered for a passing instant what he had seen, and then in the next instant, the car simply became airborne. Charlie was actually flying. No illusion. No simulation. No hallucination. A very simple matter.

They were flying through the air. Maybe ten meters off the road. They were up in the air in an arctic, polar, stratospheric gust of wind that had simply caught the car and plucked it from the earth like a paper cup, and it was bearing them along inside it, like a supersonic torrent of black ice.

Jane felt a chill existential horror as they remained airborne, remained flying, and things began to drift gently and visibly past them. Things? Yes, all kinds of things. Road signs. Bushes. Big crooked pieces of tree. Half-naked chickens. A cow. The cow was alive, that was the strangest thing. The cow was alive and unharmed, and it was a flying cow. She was watching a flying cow. A Holstein. A big, plump, well-looked-after barnyard Holstein, with a smart collar around its neck. The cow looked like it was trying to swim. The cow would thrash its great clumsy legs in the chilly air and then it would stop for a second, and look puzzled.

And then the cow hit a tree and the cow was smashed and dead, and was instantly far behind them.

And then Charlie hit another, different tree. And the air bag deployed, and it punched her really hard, right in the face.

When she came to, Alex was driving, or trying to. Everything was pitch-black. Great sheets of lightning tore across the sky and the noise-cancellation phones, amazingly, were still on her head. She was slumped in the passenger seat and drenching wet.

They were in some small town. The town strobed, periodically, into visibility around them, in massive flashes of sky-tearing lightning. Because everything was utterly noisy, everything beneath her headphones was silent. The town was a silent ghost town, under silent artillery bombardment. The town was simply being blown down, blown apart. Walls were being twisted apart, and roofs methodically caved in. But the bare wind was not alone in its work. The wind had brought its friends. Things – projectiles, shrapnel – were randomly smashing the town, smashing anything that stood up, smashing anything that resisted, flying and smashing and crushing and bursting. Flying, wrecking things. Ancient telephone poles from before the wireless days – they were being snapped up clean and picked up and thrust through the sides of multistory buildings. With a weird kind of ease, like someone piercing big blocks of tofu with a breadstick.

Everything was airborne, like a little city churned into a dense aerial mulch. Laundry. Stoplights. Bicycles. Doghouses. Sheets of tin, bending and tumbling and rippling just like big shining sheets of paper. Hills of branches, mountains of leaves. Satellite dishes, multibranched hollow radio and telephone aerials. The town's water tower had fallen over and ruptured like a big metal egg. Dirt. Dirt everywhere. Sudden mean gusts of dirt like a sandblast. Dirt that pierced the skin like ink from a tattoo needle. Dirt and hail, and water that was full of dirt, and water drops that hit her hard as hail.

Alex had twin runnels of blackness streaking down his face and she realized numbly that his nose was bleeding. Her nose too. Her nose hurt; the wreck had really hurt her nose. . . . Alex was driving down the main street of town, rather slowly and clumsily really, and with a lot of pained attention to detail. There were cars turned upside down all over the place, kicked-over cars like a giant child disturbing a convention of turtles.

A quite large brick building gracefully gave up the ghost as they passed it, and it cascaded gently into the street like a sackful of dominoes. Inside it, every object on its walls and floors took flight like liberated pigeons, and its guts spewed great crackling gouts from severed power lines.

Outside the city, they picked up speed again. Jane's head began to hurt a lot, and suddenly she regained full consciousness, and she came to herself. She went at once for the comset, pressed the mike to her lips between two closed hands, and began shouting into the mike. Not that she could hear herself. Not that anyone in the Troupe could hear her, necessarily. But just to bear witness. Just to bear witness to everything, to bear witness as long as she could.

They entered some kind of forest. That seemed like a really bad idea. Charlie began jumping over downed trees in the road, and she could tell from the way his wheels scrunched against the tarmac that this was not at all good for the car. The car was badly damaged. How badly, she couldn't tell.

Trees were whipping back and forth at the roadside like damned souls frantically flagging down a lift. Another great sheet of cloud-to-cloud lightning arc-lit the zenith, and, incidentally, also lit an F-1 that was striding knee-deep through the forest alongside them, not fifty meters away. The spike was just churning along there, spinning like a black cone of wet rubber and methodically tossing a salad of smashed tree. She saw it again, three more times, in three more lightning flashes, until it meandered out of sight.

On the far side of the forest an insane wind gust pounced on them and almost blew them away. Charlie actually leaped into the air like a hooked fish and sort of skipped, leaning and kicking violently against the wind, an odd maneuver dredged up from some subroutine she'd never seen before. Jane said as much, into the mike, for something to say, and then she looked at her lit Trouper cuff.

It was June 16, at two-thirteen in the afternoon.

Then another stronger gust hit them broadside, and Charlie was knocked completely off its wheels, and rolled right over and jumped up. And rolled over and jumped up, and rolled and jumped in yet a third somersault, tumbling in the grip of the wind like an aikido master. Until Charlie fetched up, very hard, with his undercarriage smashing into the unyielding trunk of a tree. And then all maneuvers stopped.

Jane did not pass out. The air bags had deployed again, but without the same slamming gusto they had shown before. She realized from the sharp stink of ozone and the steady buzzing that the superconductive had cracked.

Alex gripped her shoulder – from above, since they were now hanging sideways in their seats, propped against the tree trunk – and he shouted something at her, which of course she could not hear. He shook her and shouted again and shook his narrow, rain-drenched head, and then he climbed out of the top of the vehicle and vanished into the dark.

Jane assumed that Alex had at least some vague idea what he was doing, but she felt very weak and tired, and she had no urge to leave the vehicle. Jane had often imagined herself dying in a wrecked pursuit car, and it was a relatively peaceful and natural idea for her. It certainly seemed more comfortable and decent than stumbling into the woods in a violent rainstorm to hunt for some fresh way to be killed.

She kept on talking. She wiped fresh blood from her upper lip and she kept talking. There were no answers, but she kept talking. Charlie's superconductive blew its last fizzing volt and all the onboard instrumentation crashed. The radio stayed on, though. It had its own battery. She kept talking.

After half an hour Alex showed up again. The wind had begun to slack off in spasms, long glassy moments of weird calm amid the roar. Also, it was not quite so dark. There was a rim of drowned greenish light in the west – the F-6 was moving east. The F-6 was moving past them.

And apparently civilization was not so desperately far away as it seemed from the tilted seat of a smashed car, because Alex, amazingly, was carrying a hooded terry-cloth baby towel, a six-pack of beer in biodegradable cans, and half a loaf of bread.

She tried talking to Alex then, shouting at him over patches in the constant rumble of thunder, but he shook his head and patted one ear. He had gone quite deaf. He'd probably been deaf from the very first instant the F-6 hit. He might, she thought, be deaf forever now.

Worse yet, he looked completely insane. His face was drenched with rain and yet still black with dirt – not just dirt on the skin, but dirt tattooed under his skin, his face stippled with high-speed flying filth.

He offered her a beer. She couldn't think of anything she wanted less at that moment than a beer – especially one from some cheap Oklahoma microbrewery called 'Okie Double-X' – but she was very dry-throated from shock, so she drank some. Then she wiped her bloodied face with the towel, which hurt a lot more than she had expected.

Alex skulked off again. Hunting something, out in the black pitching mess of trees. What on earth was he looking for? An umbrella? Galoshes? A credit card, and working fax machine? What?

Not two minutes later Leo Mulcahey showed up, and rescued her.

LEO ARRIVED IN an aging Texas Ranger riot-control vehicle, a big eight-wheeled urban chugger with a peeling Lone Star over black ceramic armor. What the hell a Texas Ranger vehicle was doing this far out of Texas jurisdiction was a serious puzzle to Jane, but the thing was a bitch to drive and Leo was in a tiny captain's chair looking through some virtuality blocks and wearing a headset. Jane sat slumped in the back in a cramped little webbing chair, shaking very hard. Leo was very occupied by the challenge of driving.

They drove maybe ten kilometers, a lurching, awful trip, pausing half a dozen times to work around or smash their way over downed trees. Then Leo drove the vehicle down a wet concrete slope into an underground garage. A steel garage door slid shut behind them like an airlock, and the torrent of noisy wind ceased quite suddenly, and fluorescents flicked on.

They were in a storm shelter.

A privately owned shelter, but it was a big place. They took stairs down from the garage. A nice place, a regular underground mansion by the look of it. Thick carpeting underfoot, and oil paintings on the walls, and designer lighting and a big superconductive someplace to keep all those lights burning. Outside, hell was raging, but they had just sealed themselves in a big money-lined Oklahoma bank vault.

Leo stepped into a small tiled room with a compost toilet, and opened a pair of overhead cabinet doors, and offered her a thick canary-yellow towel. As if in afterthought, he pulled a pair of foam plugs from his ears, then ran one hand through his disordered hair. 'Well, Juanita,' he told her, smiling at her. 'Janey. Well met at last, Jane!'

Jane rubbed at her hair and face. Filthy. And her nose was still bleeding a little. It seemed a real shame to put blood on such a nice thick dry towel. 'How'd you find me, out there?'

'I heard your distress call! I scarcely dared to leave the shelter, but there came a break in the weather, and you were close to the shelter, and well' – Leo smiled – 'here we are, both safe and sound, so the risk was well worth it.'

'My brother's still out there.'

'Yes' – Leo nodded – 'I did overhear that. A shame your brother – Alex, isn't it? – didn't have the wisdom to stay with the vehicle. When it dies down, maybe we can make a try to find young Alex. All right?'

'Why not rescue him right now?'

'Jane, I'm no meteorologist, but I can read a SESAME report. All hell is breaking loose out there. I'm very sorry, but I won't comb a patch of woods for a missing boy while the landscape swarms with tornadoes. You and I were lucky to get back here alive.'

'I'll go alone, I can drive that thing.'

'Jane, don't be troublesome. I don't own that vehicle.'

'Who owns it, then?'

'The group owns it. I'm not here all alone, you know. I have my friends! Friends who strongly disapproved of my leaving this shelter in the first place. Would you think this through a bit, please ? Consider this from my perspective.'

Jane fell silent. Then she couldn't restrain herself. 'My brother's life is at stake!'

'So is my brother's,' Leo said sternly. 'Do you know how many people have died in this horror already? It's already leveled five towns, and the F-6 is headed right for Oklahoma City! Tens of thousands of people are going to die, not just one person that you happen to know! It's a holocaust out there, and I don't propose to join in it! Get a grip on yourself!' He opened a tall closet. 'Look, here's a bathrobe. Get out of that wet paper, Jane, and try to compose yourself. You're in a storm cellar now, and that's where sane people are supposed to be, during a storm. We're going to stay here now!

we won't be leaving again.'

He shut the door and left her alone in the bathroom. Alone again, she began shaking violently. She glanced at herself in the mirror. The sight of her own face sent a chill through her. She looked terrifying: a madwoman, a bloodied gorgon.

She tried the faucet; a thin trickle of ill-smelling water emerged. Very chlorinated. If you were rich in Oklahoma, you could drill a big hole in the ground and put a mansion inside it, but that still wouldn't get you decent water. She stoppered the sink and rinsed her face, quickly. Then she put a cupped handful of water through her hair. Something like a kilo of rust-colored Oklahoma dirt dripped out of her hair and into the sink. And her paper suit was smeared with wet dust.

She stepped out of the paper suit, and put it into the sink and ran a little water over it, and washed her hands and wrists. Then she pulled the suit out again and wiped it with the towel, and the paper suit was pretty darn clean. It dried out in no time. Good old paper. She stepped back into it and zipped it up.

She opened the bathroom door again. There were distant voices down a sloping corridor. Jane tromped down the corridor in her trail boots. 'Leo?'

'Yes?' He handed her a mug of something hot. Café con leche. It was very good. And very welcome.

'Leo, what on earth are you doing in this place?'

'Interesting question,' Leo admitted. 'It's no accident, of course.'

'I thought not, somehow.'

'Even the blackest cloud has a chrome lining,' Leo offered, with a tentative smile. He led her into an arched bombproof den. There was a sitting area with low, flowing, leather couches in a conversation pit. The walls were stuccoed ceramic and the roof was a thick blastproof stuccoed ceramic dome, like the inside of a roc's egg. A brass chandelier hung on a chain from the top of the dome. The chandelier swayed a little, gently.

There was a media center with a pair of silent televisions on, and an old rosewood liquor cabinet, and a scattering of brass-and-leather hassocks of brown-and-white furred brindled cowhide. There were a pair of Remington bronzes of mustached cowpokes on horseback doing unlikely horsebreaker things, and a pair of awesome octagon-barreled frontier rifles were mounted on the wall.

And there were eight strangers in the shelter, counting Leo. Two women, six men. Two of the men were playing with an onyx Mexican chess set, off at the far end of the conversation pit. Another was gently manipulating a squealing broadband scanner hooked to an antenna feed. The other four were playing some desultory card game on a coffee table, pinochle or poker maybe, and munching from a red lacquered tray of microwaved hors d'oeuvres.

'Well, here she is,' Leo announced. 'Everyone, this is Jane Unger.'

They looked up, mildly curious. No one said much. Jane sipped her warm coffee, holding the mug with both hands.

'Forgive me if I don't make introductions,' Leo said.

'You know what would be a really good idea, Leo?' said one of the chess players, mildly, looking over his rimless glasses. 'It would be a really good idea if you put Ms Unger back outside.'

'All in good time,' Leo said. He turned to the silent televisions. 'Oh dear, just look at that havoc.' He said it in a voice so flat and numbed that Jane was taken aback. She set her coffee mug down. Leo looked at her. She picked the mug back up.

'It's pretty much leveled El Reno,' remarked the other chess player, cheerfully. 'Pretty damn good coverage too.'

'Have they structure-hit that broadcast tower outside Woodward yet?' Leo said.

'Yeah. It came down three minutes ago. A good hit, Leo. Real solid hit. Professional.'

'That's great,' Leo said. 'That's splendid. So, Jane. What would you like? A few spring rolls with hot mustard? You do like Thai food, don't you? I think we have some Thai in the freezer.' He took her elbow and led her to the open kitchenette.

Jane pulled her arm free. 'What the hell are you doing?'

Leo smiled. 'Short explanation, or long explanation?'

'Short. And hurry up.'

'Well,' said Leo, 'shortly, my friends and I are very interested in dead spots. This is a big dead spot, and that's why we're here. We've put ourselves here quite deliberately, just like you and your Troupe did. Because we knew that this area would be the epicenter of damage from my brother's F-6.'

'Leo, I gotta hand it to that brother of yours!' called out the second chess player, with what sounded like real gratitude. 'Personally, I had the gravest doubts about any so-called F-6 tornado, it seemed like a real reach, a real nutcase long shot, but Leo, I admit it now.' The chess player straightened up from his board, lifting one finger. 'Your brother has really delivered. I mean, just look at that coverage!' He pointed briskly at the television. 'This disaster is worldclass!'

'Thanks,' Leo said. 'You see, Jane, there are many places in America where human beings just can't live anymore, but that's not true for our communications technologies. The machines are literally everywhere. In the US – even Alaska! – there's not one square meter left that's not in a satellite footprint, or a radio-navigation triangulation area, or a cellular link, or in packet range of netnode sites or of wireless cable TV . . . "Wireless cable," that's a nasty little oxymoron, isn't it?' Leo shook his head. 'It took a truly warped society to invent *that* terminology . . . '

Leo seemed lost for a moment, then recovered himself. 'Except, Jane, not here, and not now! For one shining moment, not here, not around us! Because we are inside the F-6! The most intense, thorough, widespread devastation that the national communications infrastructure has suffered in modern times. Bigger than a hurricane. Bigger than earthquakes. Far bigger than arson and sabotage, because arson and sabotage on this huge scale would be far too risky, and far too much hard work. And yet here we are, you see? In the silence! And no one can overhear us! No one can monitor us! Not a soul.'

'So that's why you over heard me in my car? My distress call? Because you're paying so much attention to broadcasts?'

'Yes, that's it exactly. We're listening to everything on the spectrum. Hoping, aiming, for perfect silence. Luckily, we have the resources to help the project along a bit – to take out a few crucial relays and especially solid towers, and such. Because God knows, the damned repairmen will all be back in force soon enough! With their cellular emergency phone service, and the emergency radio relays, and even those idiot ham operators with their damned private services out of ham shacks and even their bathroom closets, God help us! But for a little while, a brilliant, perfect silence, and in that moment all things are possible. Everything is possible! Even freedom.'

Someone, lackadaisically, applauded.

Jane swallowed coffee. 'Why do you need that much silence?'

'Do you know what "electronic parole" is?'

'Sure. When they put, like, a government wrist cuff on prisoners. With a tracker and a relay inside. My Trouper cuff is a little like that, actually.' She held up her wrist.

'Exactly. And all of us here, we all have similar devices.'

She was amazed. 'You're all out on parole?'

'Not the common kind. A special kind, rather more sophisticated. It's more accurate to say that my friends and I are all bonded people. We gave our word of bond. But we're in a Troupe, of a sort. A Troupe of people in bondage.'

'Excuse me,' said the man at the broadband scanner. He was a large, hefty, middle-aged man, with short brush-cut hair. 'May I see that device, please?'

'My Trouper cuff?'

'Yes, ma'am.'

Jane unbuckled it and handed it to him.

'Thanks.' The man rose, examining Jane's cuff carefully, then walked into the kitchen. He placed the cuff carefully beside the sink, opened a kitchen drawer, swiftly removed a meat-tenderizing hammer, and smashed Jane's cuff, repeatedly.

'Why are you doing this?' Jane shouted.

'It's a big world,' Leo said, between his friend's precisely judged hammer blows. 'It's an old world, it's a sad and wicked world . . . We in this room, we are definitely people of the world, Jane. We're a very worldly lot!' The radioman carefully ran sink water over Jane's shattered cuff.

'We've done some of the work of the world, in our day,' Leo said. 'But you can't acquire that kind of power without responsibility. Power doesn't come without an obligation, without any account to pay. The people who put these cuffs on us – well, you might say that we all quite voluntarily put them onto one another, really – these bracelets are badges of honor. We thought of them as badges. As fail-safes, as a kind of moral insurance. As talismans of security! But after the years roll on . . . It doesn't ever stop, Jane, time just keeps going on, consequences just keep mounting up.' He lifted his arm and looked at his watch. It looked just like any other watch. Nothing too special about Leo's watch. Just another metal-banded businessman's watch. Except that the skin beneath the watch was very white.

'We've come here to stop being what we are,' Leo said. 'There's no way out of the Game, no way outside the code of silence. Except for death, of course; death always works. So we've found a kind of silence now that's an electronic, virtual death. We're going to cut our bonds away, and we'll die in the world of the networks, and we'll become other people, and we'll leave and vanish for good.'

'Like evacuation freaks?'

One of the poker players burst into laughter. 'Hey! That's a good one! That's dead on. Evacuation freaks. You mean those weird poseurs with no ID who just haunt the camps, right? That's good, that's very good. That's us right to a T.'

'Leo, what have you done that's so horrible? Why do you have to do anything this weird and elaborate?' She looked into his eyes. They were not cruel eyes. They were like Jerry's eyes. They only looked very troubled. 'Leo, why don't you just come to the Troupe camp? We have our own people there, we have resources and ways to get people out of trouble. I can talk to Jerry about it, maybe we can straighten all this out.'

'That's very sweet of you, Jane. It's very good of you. I'm sorry I never had a chance to know you better.' He lifted his voice to the others. 'Did you hear that? What she just offered? I was right to do what I did.' He looked into her face. 'It doesn't matter. In any case, after this meeting you'll never see me again.'

'Why not?'

He gestured at the ceiling – at the storm outside their bank vault. 'Because we are far beneath the disaster now. We're all just empty names now, in the long roll call of the dead and missing from the F-6. Everyone you see here – we all died inside the F-6. We vanished, we were consumed. You'll never see me again; Jerry will never see me again, ever. We're cutting all ties, annihilating our identities, and Jane, we're the kind of people who know how to do that, and are good at doing it. And that's the way it has to be. There's no way out of what I've become, except to stop being what I am. Forever.'

'What on earth have you done?'

'It's impossible to say, really,' one of the women remarked. 'That's the beauty of the scheme.'

'Maybe you'll understand it best this way,' Leo told her. 'When your friend and colleague April Logan was asking the Troupers about when the human race lost all power over its own destiny – '

'Leo, how do you know about that? You weren't there.'

'Oh,' said Leo, surprised. He smiled. 'I'm inside the system in camp. I've always been inside the Troupe's system. No one knows, but, well, there I am. Sorry.'

'Oh.'

'My brother's an academic, academics never pay any real attention to security updates.'

'I'll say,' said another of the shelter people, speaking up for the first time. He was big and dark, and he was wearing a charcoal-gray tailored suit, and Jane noticed for the first time that he was very young. Younger than twenty. Maybe no older than seventeen. How had this boy . . . ? And then she looked at him. He was very young, but his eyes were like two dead things. He had the skin-creeping look of a professional poisoner.

'You see,' said Leo, 'the human race still has a great deal of control over our destiny. Things are by no means so chaotically hopeless as people like to pretend. The governments can't do anything, and our lives are very anarchic, but all that means is that the work that the governments ought to do is shrugged onto vigilantes. There are certain things, certain activities, that transparently require doing. What's more, there are people who recognize the necessity to do them, and who can do them, and are even willing to do those things. The only challenge in the situation is that these necessary things are unbearably horrible and repugnant things to do.'

'Leo,' said the first chess player, in weary exasperation, 'why on earth are you dropping our pants to this woman?'

One of the women spoke up. 'Oh, go ahead and tell her, Leo. I'm enjoying this. It doesn't matter. We're free now. We're inside the big silence. We can talk.'

'That's you all over, Rosina,' said the first chess player in disgust. 'I hate this bullshit! I hate watching people blow all operational security, and spew their guts like some teenage burglar, drunk in a bar. We're professionals, for Christ's sake, and she's just some prole. Don't you have any pride?'

'She's not just anyone,' Leo protested. 'She's family. She's my sister-in-law.'

'No, I'm not,' Jane said. 'I didn't marry him, Leo.'

'Details.' Leo shrugged, irritably. 'Jerry will marry you. I suppose you don't realize that yet, but he'll do it, all right. He'll never let you go, because he's pulled too much of you inside of him now; and besides, you're too useful to him, and he needs you too much. But that's fine, that's fine, I like that idea; you'd never do anything to hurt Jerry, would you? No, I can see that. Of course not. It's all right; it's all just fine.'

'You are being a complete moral idiot,' said the chess player.

'Look,' Leo snapped at him, 'if I wanted to stay in the Great Game, do you think I'd have gone this far? Do you know anybody else who could get that damn cuff off you? Then shut up and listen. It's the last time you'll ever have to hear me out.'

'Have it your way,' the chess player interrupted, with a calm and deadly look. 'Jane Unger, listen to me. I can see that you're a very observant person. Stop watching me so very observantly. I don't like it, and I won't have it. It's boring and clumsy to threaten people, but I'm threatening you, so listen.' He pulled his manicured hands from the chessboard and steepled his fingertips. 'I can commit an act in three seconds that will make you a clinical schizophrenic for eighteen months. You'll hear voices in your head, you'll rave about conspiracies and plots and enemies, you'll paint yourself with your own shit and that can all be done in three seconds with less than three hundred micrograms. Dead men actually do tell tales sometimes . . . but madwomen tell nothing but pathetic lies, and no one believes what madwomen say, about anything, ever. Am I clear? Yes? Good.' He moved a bishop.

Jane sat, weak-kneed, on one of the cowhide hassocks. 'Leo, what are you doing? What have you got into?'

'It wasn't for us. It was never for ourselves. It was for the future.'

The woman spoke up again. 'The delightful part about the Great Game – I mean, the genuinely clever and innovative part – is that we don't even know what we've done! It all takes place through electronic blinds, and cells, and failsafes, and need-to-know, and digital anonymity and encryption. One cell, for instance, will think up five potential direct actions. Then another cell will choose just one candidate action from that list of five, and break the action up into independent pieces. And then, yet other cells will distribute that work into small independent actions, so fragmented as to be meaningless. It's just the way engraved paper and money still meant something.'

'Right,' said the second chess player, nodding. 'So that one year, some theorist predicts how useful it would be to have Bengali cholera decimate some overcrowded hellhole of a city. And eight months later, someone watches some little paper sailboats melting in a reservoir.'

Jane stared. 'Why would any one do that?'

'The best of reasons,' Leo said. 'Survival. Survival of humanity, and of millions of endangered species. A chance for humanity to work its way out of heavy weather into real sunlight and blue skies again. We had a lot of chances to take steps to save our world, and we blew them all, Jane. All of them. We were greedy and stupid and shortsighted, and we threw all our chances away. Not you personally, not me personally, not any of us personally, just our ancestors, of course. No one convenient to blame. But you, and me, and the people here, we are all the children of heavy weather, and we have to live under consequences, and we have to deal with them. And the only real way to deal with them is ugly, just unbearably ugly.'

'But why you, Leo?'

'Because we know! Because we can! For the sake of the survivors, I suppose.' He shrugged. 'There's no global government. There's no formal, deliberate control over the course of events, anywhere. Institutions have given up. Governments have given up. Corporations have given up. But the people in the room, and the many others who are like us and with us, we've never given up. We're the closest thing this planet has to an actual working government.'

Jane looked around the room. They were agreeing with him. It wasn't any joke. He was telling a truth that they all knew and recognized.

'Some of us, most of us, are *in* the government. But there's not any government in the world that can stand up publicly, and say coldly and openly, that the eight billion people on this collapsing planet are at least four billion people too many. Jane, each year, every year, there are enough children born on Earth to equal the entire population of Mexico. That's insanely far too many, and it's been like that for eighty years now. The situation is so desperate that working to solve it is like joining a bomb squad. Every year a bomb explodes, and it's a bomb made of human flesh, and every human splinter in that bomb means extinction and carbon dioxide and toxins and methane and pesticides and clearcutting and garbage and further decline. There were a lot of ways out once, but there are no more alternatives now. Just people who will probably survive, and people who probably won't.'

'Leo's being a bit dramatic, as usual, but that's part of his charm,' said the woman, Rosina, with a fond smile at him. Rosina looked like a schoolteacher might look – a schoolteacher with a taste for platinum jewelry and expensive facial surgery. 'The Great Game is less romantic than it might sound. Basically, it's just another American secret government, and while those are common enough, they never last long. We're very much like the southern resistance during Reconstruction. Like the Invisible Empire – the Ku Klux Klan. For a decade or so, the Ku Klux Klan was a genuine underground government! Where everybody took turns holding the rope for a minute. So nobody really lynched the darkie. You see, the darky just sort of perished.'

She smiled. She said this terrible, heart-freezing thing, and she smiled, because she found it amusing. 'And everybody involved went right back to being a county judge and a policeman and a lawyer and the owner of the hardware store. And next week they rode out in their hoods and masks and they killed again. That's exactly what it's like for us, Jane. It can really happen. It has happened. It's happened in the United States. And it's happened here before, long before networks or encryption, or any of the really easy, safe, convenient ways to facilitate large conspiracies. It's not farfetched at all, it's not even hard. It's quite easy if you work at it sincerely, and it's very real, it's real like this table is real.' She slapped it.

'Just because we few are dropping out of the game doesn't mean that the Great Game will end,' said another poker player. He looked vaguely Asian, with a West Coast accent. There weren't any black people among these people. No Hispanics, either. Jane got the strong impression that ethnic balance hadn't been high on the agenda when they did their recruiting, however people like this did their recruiting. Floating Nietzschean *Ubermensch* IQ tests in obscure corners of networks, maybe. Intriguing intellectual puzzles that only those of a certain cast of mind could win. Little suction spots in the Net where people could slip into the Underground and never, ever come out . . . 'Like AIDS for instance. That bug is a godsend, we might have cured it by now, but there are brave, determined, clever people who will guard every last AIDS variant like a Holy Grail . . . A virus that kills sexually careless people! While at the same time lowering immunity, so that afflicted people become a giant natural reservoir for epidemics. It's thanks mainly to AIDS that new tuberculosis treatments become so useless so quickly . . . If AIDS didn't exist, we'd have been forced to invent it. If it weren't for AIDS, we'd have ten billion people now, not eight.'

'My dear friend Rosina has misled you somewhat with that ancient KKK analogy,' said Leo, gently. 'We're certainly not racists, we're very multicultural; we never aim to exterminate any ethnic group, we simply work consistenly to lower global birthrates and raise global death rates. Really, our activity is no more a lynching than this F-6 is like a lynching. Like the F-6, it's a death remotely traceable to human action, but taking steps to increase the global death rate doesn't make death into murder. An epidemic isn't genocide, it's just another epidemic. Anyway, the vast majority of all our actions are perfectly legal and aboveboard, things that would never raise a second glance! Things such as . . . offering a scholarship to a medical student.'

He poured himself some coffee and added steamed milk. 'Instead of saving thousands of harmful human lives through public-health measures like clean water and sewers, why not train that doctor to do elaborate, costly measures, like neural brain scans? Usually, the heart and soul of a nation's public-health work are a few very lonely, very dedicated people. They are easy to find, and their organization can be structure-hit in a very subtle way. These selfless neurotics don't have to be shot out of hand or lynched by racists, for heaven's sake. Generally, all they need is a few kind words and a little gentle distraction.'

'Yeah, a fad here, a twist there,' said the Asian guy, 'a brief delay in shipping to some hard-hit famine site, or a celebrity scandal to chase off news coverage of some lethal outbreak . . . The current muddled semilegal situation with drugs, for instance, that was a work of genius . . . A great source of finance for anybody's underground, and the people who shoot up heroin are extremely reckless and credulous. Street drugs will almost never be tested for additives, as long as they supply the thrill. There are narco-contraceptives – one shot makes a woman permanently allergic to the lining of her own uterus, something the woman would never notice, except that a fertilized egg will never adhere to her womb.' He nodded sagely. 'That works very well with mass inoculations, too, if you can manage to contaminate the vaccines . . . I suppose you could argue the technique's rather sexist, but we've tried covert sterilization with men, and statistics prove that the cohort of fertile women is the real crux of population expansion; it's all in the womb, that's just the way human reproduction works . . . People willing to take intravenous drugs are already flirting with suicide; there's no real harm in assisting them.'

'Not to mention legalizing euthanasia on demand,' said the second woman, testily. 'And at least that form of suicide tends to be far more male-based.'

'The whole military policy of structure hits was based on destroying enemy infrastructure – avoiding the political embarrass-ment of battlefields deaths so that the enemy populace died of apparently natural causes.' It was the radio guy again, sitting ramrod straight in his chair before the scanner. 'It was Luddism writ large – the first deliberate policy of national Luddism. That the practice of structure hitting quickly leaked into the American civilian populace only indicates the broad base of support for the practice . . . Very much like the CIA and lysergic acid, if you don't mind a favorite analogy of mine.'

Leo sipped his coffee. 'I'm going to miss all of you very much,' he confessed.

'I told you he was sentimental,' said Rosina.

'It seems such a terrible shame that the talents of a group like this should be wasted on entirely clandestine endeavors. That you'll never have your real due. You all deserve so much better.'

'Oh, none of us are any worse off than Alan Turing was,' objected the second chess player. 'Just more deep, dark, digital spooks.'

'Someone will track it down someday,' Rosina told Leo, comfortingly. We ourselves don't know the full extent of Game activities, but there must be tens of thousands of buried traces . . . Someone in the future, the next century maybe, with time on their hands and real resources for once and some proper database investigation, they'd be able to dig us all up and piece the story together.' She smiled. 'And utterly condemn us!'

'That's their privilege. A privilege we're giving to the future. Two great privileges – survival and innocence.'

'That's why we're dead people now,' Rosina said. 'You know what we are, Jane? We are lifeboat cannibals. We did something terrible that had to be done, and now we're sitting here, sitting here on these couches right now in front of you, still smacking our lips on the shreds of meat from a dead baby's thighbones. We've done things that are way past sin and become necessity. We are vile little pale creepy creatures that live deep under the rocks, and we belong by rights with the anonymous dead.' She turned to the man at the scanner. 'How does it look, Red?'

'It looks pretty good,' Red said. 'Real quiet.'

'Then I want to go first. Get this damned thing off me, somebody.' She lifted her left arm. No one moved.

Rosina raised her voice. 'I said I want to go first! I'm volunteering! So who's gonna cut it for me?'

The very young man in the suit stood up. 'You know what the hell of this is?' he said to Jane, his dark eyes like two oysters from a can. 'The hell is that you bust your ass for five years finding some network doods that are truly elite, and then they turn out to be this crowd of middle-aged rich pols and lawyers! People who post way too much about academic political philosophy shit that doesn't mean anything, and then when it finally comes to taking some real action, it's always somebody else's fault, and they end up hiring some bent Mexican cop to do it for them. Jesus Christ!' He sighed. 'Gimme that pneumatic, dood.'

The second chess player reached under the leather couch and handed the young man a pair of pneumatic diamond-edged bolt cutters. 'You want the safety goggles?'

'Do I look like I want fuckin' safety goggles? Wimp!' He hefted the bolt cutters and turned to Rosina. 'Out. Out on the stairs.'

The two of them left.

No one said anything for thirty seconds. They dealt cards, they studied the chessboard, Leo pretended huge interest in the broadband scanner. They were in anguish.

Rosina came back in, her wrist bare. A big bright smile. Like a woman on cocaine.

'It works!' gasped the second chess player. 'Me next!'

The young man came in with the bolt cutters. The armpits of his suit were soaked with sweat.

'Do me next!' said the second chess player.

'Are you kidding?' said the very young man. 'I know statistics. Let somebody else do it this time.'

'I'll do it,' Leo told the chess player. 'If you'll do me afterward.'

'Deal, Leo.' The chess player blinked gratefully. 'You're a straight shooter, Leo. I'm gonna miss you, too, man.'

They went out of the room. A minute passed. They came back in.

'We're real lucky,' said the second chess player. He wiped sweat from his forehead with a canary-yellow washcloth he'd snagged from the bathroom.

'Either that,' the very young man scoffed 'or they're not designed as well as we thought. What'd you do with the dead bracelets?'

'Left 'em in the hall.'

'We'd better detonate 'em later. Wouldn't want anybody reverse-engineering that circuitry.'

'Right,' said Leo, with a glance at Jane. 'You can see now why the Crimson Avenger became so integral to our group! Only nineteen years old – but there's one of those young rascals in every network; it happens to even the best of company.'

'Why did you come here?' Jane asked the Crimson Avenger.

'I been in the Game five years now,' the Crimson Avenger muttered. 'It gets real old.' His face clouded. 'And besides, if I don't clear town but good, I'm gonna have to kill both my lame bitchfucker parents! With a fuckin' shotgun!'

Two of the poker players rose – the Asian guy and the second woman. They exchanged a silent glance heavy with deep personal meaning and the man took the bolt cutters and they left together.

Fifteen seconds later there was a loud explosion. Then, screams.

Everyone went white as paper. The screams dwindled to agonized breathy sobs.

The Crimson Avenger reached inside his jacket and pulled out a snub-nosed ceramic revolver and walked stiff-legged to the door. He yanked it open, leaving it open behind him. There was a brief gabbling wail of anguished terror, and a shot. Then another shot. And then a long, meditative silence. And then another final shot.

The Crimson Avenger came back in, with his suit lightly spattered with blood, flying little droplets of blood on the shins of his charcoal-gray trousers. He had the cutters – the diamond jaws of the device were blackened with impact. 'Hers blew,' he said. 'We don't have to do his now. He's dead too.'

'I think I've changed my mind,' said the first chess player.

Without changing expression, the Crimson Avenger lowered his pistol and pointed it at the bridge of the first chess player's glasses. 'Okay, dood.'

'Never mind, I'm going.' He looked at Red, the radioman. 'Let's do it.'

'I'm going too,' said the Crimson Avenger.

'Why?' said the chess player.

'Because I got left over, and you're gonna do me last. And because if you wimp out and try to run off with that bracelet on, you're gonna do it with my bullet in your head.' He sniffed, and coughed. 'Dood, for a guy with three advanced degrees, *man*, you are fuckin' *slow!*'

They left. And they came back alive.

'I think a twenty-five-percent mortality rate is extraordinarily good under the circumstances,' said Leo.

'Considering the extreme precautions taken to keep us from accomplishing this . . . yes, quite acceptable,' said the second chess player.

The television, which had been showing snow, flickered into life again.

'Look, it's hitting Oklahoma City,' said the first chess player. He turned up the sound a bit, and the six surviving Gamers settled in on the couch, their faces alight with deep interest.

'Look at the way they've networked those urban securicams to catch that first damage wave coming in,' said Red. 'Not only that, but they are the very first back on the air! The staff at Channel 005 are really technically adept.'

'Leave it on 005,' said the second chess player. 'They're definitely the best fast-response storm team in the country.'

'You got it.' Red nodded. 'Not that we have any choice. I think everything else is still down.' He began channel-switching the second set.

'Whoa,' Leo told him. 'Look at that SESAME satellite shot. . . .
. . . That's very odd, people. Oklahoma City seems to be under siege by a giant doughnut.'

Rosina chuckled.

'That's a very odd shape, isn't it, Jane? What does it mean?'

Jane cleared her throat. 'It means . . . it means that Jerry is right. Because I've seen that shape before, in his simulations. That's not a spike, it's a . . . well, it's a giant torus vortex down on the ground. I mean, you think of a tornado . . . and you turn it sideways and you put the tip of it into the top of it, like a snake eating its own tail . . . And it becomes a giant ring, a torus. And it sucks in updraft from all directions outside the ring, and it spews downdraft out the top and sides, and it's stable. And it just gets bigger until all the heat and moisture are gone.'

'What does that imply, exactly?'

Jane felt tears slide thinly down her cheeks. 'I think it means that all my friends are dead.'

'And that Oklahoma City is definitely dog meat,' Rosina added.

'Mega,' said the Crimson Avenger.

Oklahoma City was methodically recording its own destruction. Jane knew immediately that she was seeing history bubble off the screen, an odd and intense kind of history. Like some decadent Roman poet reciting his autogiography as he opened a vein in the bath.

At the touch of the F-6, now in its full fury, Oklahoma City was exploding on television, block by block. It was being sucked up and peeled apart and smashed. Heavily reinforced high-rises were being pulled up bodily out of the ground, like a farmer pulling up carrots. They were very hard and very strong buildings, and when they fell over and started rolling, all their contents would gush out of their windows, in a fountaining slurry of glass and trash and mist. The falling high-rises would rip up big patches of street with them, and when the wind got under the street, things would start fountaining up. There was a lot of room under the earth in Oklahoma City, a lot of room with a lot of human beings in it, and when the wind got into those long shelters it simply blew them like a flute. Manholes blew off the streets and big whale gushes of vapor came out of the pavement, and then a whole pod of whales seemed to surface under the street, because another skyscraper was slowly falling over and it was ripping up the street surface with its internet links and its indestructible ceramic water pipes and its concrete pedestrian subway.

And somebody was putting this vision together, deliberately assembling it. Somebody had broken the screen into compound miniscreens like a bee's eyes: traffic securicams and building securicams and minibank securicams and all the other modern urban securicams that offered no one even the tiniest trace of security. And as the cams were blinked out and smashed and ripped apart and exploded and were blinded and crushed, whoever was at work just kept adding more viewpoints.

One of them was a sudden glimpse of the Troupe. It was Jerry, he had his back half-turned to the camera, he was leaning, half-doubled, into the gusting wind. He was shouting and waving one arm. It was Troupe camp, and all the paper yurts were smashed and torn and writhing in the wind. Jerry turned to the camera suddenly and he held up a broken-winged ornithopter, and his face was alight with comprehension and terror.

And then he vanished.

It didn't look like a machine was doing these viewpoints. It was the sort of montage technique often best left to machine, but Jane had a very strong intuition that someone was doing this work by hand. Human auteurs were putting it together, very deliberately, swiftly, and deftly assembling it with their own busy human fingertips. Doing it, knowing they were going to die at their post.

And the sorrow and pity of the great disaster struck her then, lancing into her right through that busy thicket of interface. And she felt the hurt explode inside of her. And she thought, with greater clarity than she had ever thought of anything before, that if she ever, somehow, managed to escape from this shelter and from these People of the Abyss, then she would learn to love something else. Something new. To learn to love something that didn't stink at its spinning core, of disaster and destruction and despair.

Then the broadcast blinked out.

'Lost transmission again,' said Red. 'I bet it took down the main towers out on Britton Road this time – who wants to bet?'

'That was great,' said Rosina, appreciatively. 'I can't wait till they compile all this coverage and do the definitive disk.'

Red combed channels. 'SESAME's still up.'

'Yeah, the feds keep their weather links down in the old missile silos,' said chess player two. 'Practically unnukable.'

'Where are we exactly?' asked the Crimson Avenger, looking at the SESAME map. Red pointed. 'Well,' Avenger said, 'I don't see any precipitation over us. I think we're in the clear!'

Suddenly there ws a violent series of explosions just outside the door – explosions actually inside the shelter. Leo winced, then suddenly grinned. 'Did you hear that, people! Those were our detonation signals!'

'Close,' said chess player one, and plucked at his lower lip. He had gone quite pale. 'Real close.'

'How'd they squeeze that signal through?' said the second chess player.

'I'd bet autonomously launched drone aircraft,' Red theorized. 'Probably sweeping the whole locale. Of course, if a drone can safely fly over us, that ought to mean that we can leave here safely.'

'Fuck the theory, I'm checkin' this out,' the Crimson Avenger declared. He left.

He was back within a minute, his handsome leather shoes leaving faint smudges of fresh blood on the shelter's thick carpet. 'The sun is out!'

'You're kidding.'

'No way, dood! It's wet, and everything is smashed completely flat, but the sky is blue and the sun is shining and there's not a cloud in the sky, and people, I am out of here.' He walked into the kitchen and pulled a shining ceramic valise off the top of the freezer.

'You won't get far on foot,' said chess player one.

The Crimson Avenger glared at him. 'How stupid do you think I am, Gramps? I don't have to get far. I know exactly where I'm going, and exactly what I'm doing, and my plans don't include you.

Good-bye, doods. Good-bye forever.' He opened the door and stalked away, leaving it ajar behind him.

'He's got a point,' Leo said. 'It's a good idea for us to split up as quickly as possible.'

'You want to ferry us out in the personnel carrier?'

'No,' Leo said. 'It's wiser to stick to Plan A. You leave on foot, and I'll plastique the works here. The cars, the tank, the bikes, the shelter, everything.'

'The bodies,' Rosina pointed out.

'Yeah, okay, I'll put the deceased directly inside the tank before I detonate it.'

'I'll help you, Leo,' the second chess player said. 'I owe you that much, after all this.'

'Good. Time's pretty short, people, let's get moving.'

Leo and his five remaining friends went into the hall. The woman and the Asian man were lying very dead on the sloping floor, the carpet sopping with their blood. The walls were pockmarked with shrapnel from the eight discarded cuffs that had detonated there. It stank of plastique. Rosina, and the older chess player, and Red the radioman picked their ways daintily past the corpses, with their eyes averted.

Jane tarried at the back of the hall. She wasn't too upset by the corpses. She had seen worse corpses. She was far more appalled by the living.

'Wet work,' said the second chess player, sadly.

Leo hesitated. 'I think we'd better use latex and medical paper for this job. That's a lot of body fluid.'

'We don't have time for precautions, Leo. Besides, they were two of us; they're clean!'

'I don't know. I wouldn't put it past Ruby,' Leo said, meditatively. 'Ruby was quite the personal devotee of retrovirus.'

Jane began to walk up the hall. She brushed past the two of them. Her boots squelched moistly on the carpet. She was trembling.

'Jane,' Leo called out.

She broke into a run.

'Jane!'

She broke out through the garage door. There was no wind. The sun was shining. The world smelled like fresh-plowed earth. The sky was blue. She ran for her life.

ALEX WAS SITTING in a tree eating a loaf of bread. It wasn't a fresh loaf, because the smashed home where he'd raided the bread had been abandoned for at least two days. It had been the home of a man and his wife and the man's mother and the couple's two bucktoothed little kids. With a lot of religious stuff inside it; gold-framed devotional prints and evangelical literature and a thoroughly smashed farm truck with bumper stickers reading ETERNITY – WHEN? and AFTER DEATH – WHAT THEN?

It looked like it had been kind of a nice little farmhouse once; it had its own cistern, anyway, and a chicken coop, but it was all shattered now, and being Christians, the occupants would probably act real thankful about it. Alex had been astounded to discover that the inhabitants had a big stack of paper comic books, Christian evangelical comics, the real thing, in English no less, with hand drawings and black ink and real metal staples. A shame they were all torn up and rain-soaked and uncollectible.

Off in the distance, to the north, came an enormous explosion and an uprushing column of filthy smoke. The wind was so calm now, and the damp sweet sky so beautifully blue, that the burning column rose straight up and stood there in the sky and preened itself. It sure looked and sounded like a massive structure hit, but maybe he was being uncharitable. Could have been a detonating natural-gas tank or maybe a broken propane line. These things did happen. Not every mishap in the world was somebody's fault.

Alex chewed more bread and had some carrot joice. The Christian family had been very big on organic whole juices. Except for the dad, presumably, who kept his truly awful Okie Double-X beer hidden under the sink.

Alex's tree was a large and fragrant cedar that had been uprooted and knocked over at an angle. Many of the branches had been twisted off; a passing F-2, showing red heartwood that smelled lovely. He had climbed into the downed tree and was lying on the sun-warmed trunk about four meters up in the air, his back against the underside of one of the thicker limbs. The gray-barked trunk under his paper-clad buttocks was as solid as a bench. His spot wasn't too far from the site of the crash. He could see the dead wreck of Charlie from where he sat.

Juanita was gone, and to judge by the tracks in the fresh mud, she had left with a rescuer in civilian shoes who had some kind of big military truck. That was good news to Alex, because Juanita's eyes had been crossed and glassy in those last hours, and he had her figured for a mild concussion. He felt sure that Juanita, or at least some helpful Trouper, would show up again in pretty short order, somehow, soon. She'd be coming to find him. And even if she didn't want to find him in particular, that car had a lot of data and megabytage in it.

Alex felt rather restful and at peace with himself. He was partially deafened, and his face hurt, and his lungs hurt, and his eyes hurt, and he could taste blood at the back of his tongue. Scrambling through the roadside forest – in a mindless panic, basically – had left him striped with many nasty scratches and a couple of hefty, aching bruises, plus a thick coating of cedar gum and dirt.

But he had seen the F-6. It had been pretty much what he'd been led to expect. It was nice not to be disappointed about something in life. He felt he could put up with dying with a better grace now.

He chewed more bread. It wasn't good bread, but it was better than camp food. There was a gray squirrel running around on the forest floor. It was drinking out of the rain puddle in the roots of the fallen tree. Didn't seem upset in any way. Just another squirrel going about its job.

Vaguely, under the persistent whine of aural aftershock, Alex heard someone calling out. Calling his name. He sat up, put his foot in the smart rope, lowered himself down from the trunk to the ground, and swiftly coiled the rope around his shoulder.

He worked his way through the labyrinth of fallen trees back to the site of the wreck.

And when he glimpsed the rescuer, searching vaguely around the wreckage, Alex fled. He reached the fallen cedar again, cast his rope back up, and yanked himself quickly back into the tree.

'Over here,' he called, standing on the trunk and waving. He couldn't call out too loudly. Shouting really hurt him inside.

Leo Mulcahey walked over, methodically working his way through the maze of fallen limbs. He wore a sturdy felt Stetson and a safari jacket.

He stopped in a small patch of knee-high undergrowth and looked up at Alex. 'Enjoying yourself?' he said.

Alex touched his ears. 'What's that, Leo? Come closer. I'm kind of deaf. Sorry.'

Leo stepped closer to the leaning tree trunk and looked up again. 'I might have known I'd find you much at your ease!'

'You don't have to shout now, that's fine. Where's Juanita?'

'I was going to ask you that, actually. Not that you care.'

Alex narrowed his eyes. 'I know that you took her away, so don't bullshit me. You wouldn't be stupid enough to hurt her, would you, Leo? Not unless you've really got it in for Jerry, as well as me.'

'I have no quarrel with Jerry. Not any longer. That's all in the past now. In fact, I'm going to help Jerry. It's the last act I can commit that will really help my brother.' He pulled a ceramic pistol out of his jacket pocket.

'Oh, that's really good,' Alex scoffed. 'You dumb spook bastard! I've had two tubercular hemorrhages in the past week, and you're coming out here to shoot me and leave me under this tree? You hopeless gringo moron, I just lived through the F-6, I don't need some pissant assassin like you! I can die perfectly well all by myself. Get lost before I lose my temper.'

Leo, astonished, laughed. 'That's very funny! Would you like to be shot up in that tree, where it might be painful or would you like to come down here, where I can make it very efficient and quick?'

'Oh,' said Alex, daintily, 'I prefer being murdered in the most remote, impersonal, and clinical manner possible, thank you.'

'Oh, with you and I, it's personal,' Leo assured him. 'You kept me from telling my brother good-bye, face-to-face. I dearly wanted to see my brother, because I had certain important personal business with him, and I might well have got past his entourage and seen him privately, but you interfered. And then, in the press of business, it became too late.' Leo's brow darkened. 'That's not sufficient reason to kill you, I suppose; but then, there's the money. Juanita has no money left; if you're dead, she gets yours, and Jerry gets hers. So your resources go to environmental science, instead of being squandered on the drug habits of some decrepit weakling. Killing you is genuinely helpful. It'll make the world a better place.'

'That's wonderful, Leo,' Alex said. 'I feel so honored to assuage your delicate feelings in this way. I can only agree with your trenchant assessment of my moral and societal worth. May I point one thing out before you execute me? If the shoe were on the other foot, and I were about to execute you, I'd do it *without the fucking lecture!*'

Leo frowned.

'What's the matter, Leo? An old bullshit artist like you can't bear to let your condemned man have the last word for once?'

Leo raised the pistol. Behind his head, a thin black noose snaked up silently from the forest floor.

'Better kill me now, Leo! Shoot quick!'

Leo took careful aim.

'Too *late!*'

The smart rope hissed around his neck and yanked him backward. He flew off his feet, his neck snapping audibly. Then he leaped up from the forest floor like a puppet on a string as the serpentine coils of the smart rope hissed around the butt of a cedar branch. There was a fragrant stink of burned bark as the body was hauled aloft.

The hanged man swayed there, violently, dangling from the tree. And at length was still.

It took Alex forty-seven hours to get from a smashed forest in Oklahoma to his father's penthouse in Houston. There was a lot of bureaucratic hassle around the federal disaster zone, but the Guard and the cops couldn't stop him from walking, and his luck changed when he got his hands on a motor bicycle. He didn't eat much. He scarcely slept. He had a fever. His lungs hurt very badly, and death was near, death was very near now, not the romantic death this time, not the sweet, drug-addled, transcendent death. Just real death, just death of the cold, old-fashioned variety, death like his mother's death, an absence and a being still, forever. He didn't love death anymore. He didn't even like death anymore. Death was something he was going to have to get over with.

It wasn't easy to get into his father's part of town. The Houston cops had always been mean, tough cops, the kind of cops that had teeth like Dobermans, and heavy weather had not made them kinder. The Houston cops were kind to people like him, when people-like-him looked like people-like-him; but when people-like-him looked the way that he looked now, the Houston cops in 2031 were the kind of cops who collared diseased vagrants off the street and did terrible secret things to them far out in the bayous.

But Alex had his ways. He hadn't grown up in Houston for nothing, and he knew what it meant to have people owe him favors. He got to his father's building without so much as a change of clothes.

And then he had to work his way past his father's own people.

He worked his way into the building. He won his own way with the machine in the elevator. The human receptionist at the penthouse floor let him in; he knew the receptionist. And then he found himself waiting in the usual marble anteroom with the giant Aztec mandalas and the orangutan skulls and the Chinese lamps.

He sat there coughing and shivering on a velvet bench, in his filthy paper suit, with his hands on his knees and his head swimming. He waited patiently. It was always like this with his Papa. There were no alternatives, none. If he waited long enough, some gopher would show up and bring him coffee and sweet English biscuits.

After maybe ten minutes the bronze double doors opened at the far end of the anteroom, and in came one of the most beautiful women he'd ever seen. She was a nineteen-year-old violet-eyed gamine with a sweet little cap of black hair and a short skirt and patterned hose and high heels.

She took a few tentative steps across the inlaid marble floor and looked at him and simpered. 'Are you *him*?' she asked, in Spanish.

'Sorry,' Alex said, 'I don't think I am.'

She switched to English, her eyes widening. 'Do you want . . . to go *shopping*?'

'Not right now, thank you.'

'I could *take* you shopping. I know many nice places in Houston.'

'Maybe another time,' said Alex, and sneezed violently. She looked at him with deep concern, and turned and left, and the doors closed behind her with a tomblike clunk.

Maybe seven minutes later a gopher showed up with the coffee and the biscuits. It was a new gopher – it was pretty much always a new gopher, gopher being the lowest rung in the Unger organization – but the British cookies were really good and the coffee, as always, was Costa Rican and fine. He kept the cookies down and had several cautious sips of the coffee, and he physically recovered to the extent that he really began to hurt. He ordered the gopher off for some aspirin, or better yet, codeine. The gopher never returned.

Then one of the private secretaries arrived. He was one of the older secretaries, Señor Pabst, a family loyalist, a nicely groomed old guy with a Mexican law degree and a well-concealed drinking problem.

Pabst looked him over with genuine pity. Pabst was from Matamoros. There were a lot of Unger family connections in Matamoros. Alex couldn't say that he and Pabst had had actual dealings, but he and Pabst had something akin to an understanding.

'I think you'd better get right to bed, Alejandro.'

'I have to see El Viejo.'

'You're not in any condition to see El Viejo. You're going to do something foolish, something you'll regret. See him tomorrow. It's better.'

'Look, will he see me, or won't he?'

'He wants to see you,' Pabst admitted. 'He always wants to see you, Alejandro. But he won't like to see you like this.'

'I think he's past shock by this time, don't you? Let's get this over with.'

Pabst led Alex to his father.

Guillermo Unger was a tall, slight man in his late fifties, with carefully waved artificial blond hair the very color of the finest-quality creamery butter. He had blue and very watery eyes behind very thick glasses, the unfortunate legacy of a prolonged experiment with computer-assisted perception. Beneath his medicated pancake makeup, the acne from the hormone treatments was flaring up again. He was wearing a tropical linen suit. His mood seemed – not good, you could never call it good – but positive.

'So you're back,' he said.

'I've been staying with Juanita.'

'So I understand.'

'I think she's dead, *papá*.'

'She's not dead,' his father said. 'Dead women don't read their E-mail.' He sighed. 'She's still shacked up with that big dumb bastard of a mathematician! He's taken off her somewhere in New Mexico now. A failed academic, for Christ's sake. A crazy man. She's thrown it all over, she's let him smash her whole career. God only can help her, Alejandro. Because God knows I can't.'

Alex sat down. He put his hands to his head. His eyes filled with tears. 'I'm really glad she's still alive.'

'Alejandro, look at me. Why the paper suit, like a bum off the street? Why the dirt, Alejandro? Why do you come into my office looking this way, couldn't you at least get clean? We're not poor people, we have baths.'

'*Papá*, I'm clean as I'm going to get. I've been inside a big tornado. The dirt lodges deep in your skin. You can't wash it out, you just have to wait till it grows out. Sorry.'

'Were you in Oklahoma City?' his father asked, with real interest.

'No, Dad. We were out where the storm set down at first. We were tracking it and we saw where it started.'

'Oklahoma City was very heavily mediated,' his father said, reflectively. 'That was a rather important event.'

'We weren't inside Oklahoma City. Anyway, they all died there.'

'Not all of them,' his father said. 'Hardly more than half of them.'

'We didn't see that part. We only saw the beginning of the F-6. We – the Troupe – they wanted to track the storm from the beginning, for scientific reasons, to understand it.'

'Understand it, eh? Not very likely! Do they know why the storm stopped so suddenly, right after Oklahoma City?'

'No. I don't know if they understand that. I doubt they understand it.' Alex stared at his father. This was going nowhere. He didn't know what to tell the man. He had nothing left to tell him. Except the ugly news that he was very near death, and someone in the family had to watch him die now. Just for formal reasons, basically. And he didn't want Jane to have to do that. And his father was the only one left.

'Well,' his father said, 'I've been wondering when you'd come back here, back to sense and reason.'

'I'm back, *papá*.'

'I tried to find you. Not much luck there, not with your sister hiding you from me.'

'She, uh . . . Well, I can't defend her, *papá*. Juanita's very stubborn.'

'I had good news for you, that's why I wanted to talk to you. Very good news. Very good medical news, Alex.'

Alex grunted. He slumped back in his chair.

'I don't know how to tell you the details myself, but we've had Dr Kindscher on retainer for some time, so when I heard you had arrived, I called him.' He gestured above a lens inset in his desk.

Dr Kindscher arrived in the office. Alex got the strong impression that Dr Kindscher had been kept waiting for some time. Just a matter of medical etiquette, a way to establish whose time was more important.

'Hello, Alex.'

'Hello, Doctor.'

'We've had new results from Switzerland on your genetic scan.'

'I thought you'd given up that project years ago.'

Dr Kindscher frowned. 'Alex, it's not an easy matter to scan an entire human genome right down to the last few centimorgans. Doing that for a single individual is a very complex business.'

'We have to subcontract that business,' his father said. 'Bits and pieces.'

'And we found a new bit, as Mr Unger has said,' Dr Kindscher said, radiating satisfaction. 'Very unusual. Very!'

'What is it?'

'It's a novel type of mucopolysaccharidosis on chromosome 7-Q-22.'

'Could I have that in English?'

'Sorry, Alex, the original lab report is in French.'

'I meant give me the upshot, Doctor,' Alex croaked. 'Give me the executive report.'

'Well, since your birth, this genetic defect that you suffer from has been periodically blocking proper cellular function in your lungs, proper expression of fluids. A very rare syndrome. Only four other known cases in the world. One in Switzerland – we were quite lucky in that eventuality, I think – and two in California. Yours is the first known in Texas.'

Alex looked at the doctor. Then at his father. Then at the doctor again. It was no joke this time. There wasn't any of the usual hedging and mumbo jumbo and alternate prognoses. They really thought they had it this time. They did. They had it. This time they actually had the truth.

'Why?' he croaked.

'Mutagenic damage to the egg cell,' Dr Kindscher said. 'It's a very rare syndrome, but all five of them diagnosed so far have involved maternal exposure to an industrial solvent, a very particular industrial solvent no longer in use.'

'Chip assembly,' his father said. 'Your mother used to do chip assembly in a border factory, long before you were born.'

'What? That's it, that's all there was to it?'

'She was young,' his father said sadly. 'We lived on the border, and I had just begun the start-up, and your mother and I, we didn't have much money.'

'So that's it, eh? My mother was exposed to a mutagen in a *maquiladora* plant. And all this time I've really been sick.'

'Yes, Alex.' Dr Kindscher nodded. He seemed deeply moved. 'I see.'

'And the best news of all is, there's a treatment.'

'I might have known.'

'Illegal in the U.S.,' his father said. 'And far too advanced for any border *clínica*. But this time it sticks, son. This time they really have the root of it.'

'We have a clinic contacted already, and they're ready to take you, Alex. Genetic repair. Legal in Egypt, Lebanon, and Cyprus.'

'Oh . . . ' Alex groaned. 'Not Egypt, I hope.'

'No, Cyprus,' his father said.

'Good, I heard there's a bad staph strain in Egypt.' Alex stood up and walked, painfully, to the doctor's side. 'You're really sure about it, this time?'

'As sure as I've ever been in my career! Intron scans don't lie, Alex. You can depend on this one. The flaw is written in your genes, obvious to any trained technician, and now that we've spotted the exact position right down to the branch of the chromosome, any lab can verify that for you. I've already verified it twice!' He beamed. 'We've beaten this thing at last, Alex. We're going to cure you!'

'Thanks a lot,' Alex said. 'You son of a bitch.' He hit Dr Kindscher in the face.

The doctor staggered and fell. He scrambled up, amazed, holding his cheek, then turned and fled the office.

'That's going to cost me,' Alex's father observed.

'Sorry,' Alex said. He leaned onto the table, shaking. 'Really sorry.'

'It's all right,' his father said, 'a son of a bitch like that pest, you can't hit him just once.'

Alex began weeping.

'I want to do this for you, Alejandro. Because now I know, it was never your fault, my boy. You were damaged goods right out of the box.'

Alex wiped his tears away. 'Same old *papá*,' he croaked.

'I don't know if things will change when you are no longer a mutant,' his father declared, nobly, 'but maybe you will. Who knows? I'm your father, my boy, I feel I owe you that chance at life.' He frowned. 'But no more foolishness this time! None of these scandals like that shameful business in Nuevo Laredo! Alejandro, those people have lawyers on me! You are going to Cyprus, and you're going right away, and you're going to stay there. No talking, no phone calls, no charge cards, and you do just as you're told! And no more nonsense from you, and especially from your damn fool of a sister.'

'All right,' Alex said. He sat in the chair, half collapsing. 'You win. I give up. Call the ambulance.' He began giggling.

'Don't laugh, Alex. Gene replacement therapy – they tell me it really hurts.'

'It always hurts,' Alex said, laughing. 'It all hurts. Everything hurts. For as long as you can still feel it.'

EPILOGUE

Austin, Texas, had once been called the 'City of the Violet Crown,' back when the city had been small enough to fit within its bowl of hills. That bowl of hills was alleged to serve as protection from local tornadoes. Of course the Violet Crown no longer did that, if in fact it ever had, and even the oldest central section of Austin had been ravaged by an F-2 within the past five years.

The spike had tracked right through the city's oldest northern suburb, an ancient residential district just north of The University of Texas. The area was now part of The University's privately managed, and privately policed, urban demesne. There was not much overt sign left of the spike damage, except for some ancient and now spectacularly crippled trees. Big old pecans mostly; some dead and replaced by saplings, but many of them maimed and left upright.

To Alex's eye, the damage track was easy to spot. You'd be driving under an even canopy of flourishing, pampered, CO_2 glutted streetside giants, and then there would be this tortured Goyaesque mutant breaking out all up and down with scrawny little green sapling limbs, maybe one original crooked branch left as a kind of beckoning finger. He pointed this out to his companion.

'We never have tornadoes in Boston,' she said.

His sister was living in a little crackerbox place. A little brown-and-white shack that looked a hundred years old, if it was a day. Back in the early 2020s, when the practice had been in vogue, somebody had sprayed the outside of the entire building with a weatherproof lacquer. The white housepaint beneath the lacquer looked unnaturally clean and sprightly.

When Alex stepped up to the concrete porch, he could see that the housepaint trapped beneath the lacquer had given up the ghost and shattered into tens of millions of tiny paint flakes no bigger than fine dust. It didn't matter. The dust wasn't going anywhere. That lacquer was there for the ages.

JANE LOOKED THROUGH the security glass at her door and saw a short, plump young blond man in a suit and tie. And a very odd-looking woman. A tiny, witchy-looking boho student type, in a slashed silk dress and striped stockings and red ankle-tyed sandals. Half her face – ear, cheeks, temple – was disfigured by a huge purple tattoo.

They didn't looked armed, though. And not very dangerous. Anyway, there was rarely much civil trouble around The University. Because The University had massive heaps of data and attention, and even some money, and more importantly, it had a large paramilitary phalanx of armed, disciplined, and enthusiastically violent students.

Jane opened the door. 'Hello?'

'Janey?'

'Yeah?'

'It's me.'

Jane stared at him. 'Christ! Alex.'

'This is Sylvia,' Alex said. 'Sylvia Muybridge. She's traveling with me. Sylvia, this is my sister, Jane Unger.'

'How do you do,' Jane said. 'Actually, I go by Jane Mulcahey these days. It's simpler, and besides, it's legal.' She held up her hand with the gold ring.

'Yes,' Alex said, pained, 'I knew you had a married name, but I thought you still networked professionally as Jane Unger.'

'Yeah, well, I'm probably gonna change that too.'

Alex paused. 'Can we come in?'

'Oh hell, yes!' Jane laughed. 'Come on in.'

She knew that the place looked disastrous. It was astrew with printouts, textbooks, and heaps of disks. There was a giant framed multicolored chart on the wall reading UNITED STATES FRE-QUENCY ALLOCATIONS: THE RADIO SPECTRUM.

Jane threw a cat off the couch – a paper-covered futon – and cleared a small space for them to sit. 'Are you still allergic to cats?'

'No. Not anymore,' Alex said.

'How long has it been, Alex?'

'Eleven months,' he said, sitting. 'Almost a year.'

'Damn,' Jane said. 'What can I get y'all?'

Sylvia spoke up for the first time. 'You got any ibogaine?'

'What's that?'

'Never mind, then.'

Jane touched her brother's shoulder. 'They must have been pretty good to you in Cyprus, because you look pretty fine, Alex.'

'Yeah,' Alex said, 'they tore out all my seams and rewove me, in Nicosia. They tell me I'm supposed to be this fat. Metabolically, I mean. Genetically, I'm supposed to be a big fat blond guy, Janey. Of course, I'll never get over being stunted in my youth.' He laughed.

'I'm sorry I didn't recognize you at first. Mostly it was that suit.'

'No,' he said. 'No, I'm completely different now, I know that. Genetics, it's the core of everything, Janey, it's mega witchcraft. Just look at my hands! It was supposed to change my lungs, and it did that, my lungs are like rock now. But look at my hands! They never looked like this.'

Jane held her own hand out and placed it gently against his. 'You're right. They look just like my hands now. They're not all : . . well, they're not all thin.'

'It's simple, really,' Alex said. 'I didn't have a life before they rewove me, and now, after this, after everything I went through, I actually have a life! I'm just like anyone else, now. The curse is lifted. It's been erased, wiped out. I'm probably gonna live a really long time.'

Jane glanced at Alex's girlfriend. She assumed this was a girlfriend. Normally a woman wouldn't dress so provocatively and travel alone with a guy unless there was something happening. Her being here could only mean that Alex was deliberately showing her off.

But then there was that face. That huge blotch on her face. It was really hard to look at. And she'd done something to it too; it wasn't just a giant port-wine-stain birthmark, she'd messed with it too; she'd outlined the edges of it in some kind of very fine and very elaborate stippling. Like dots of rainbow ink, that shimmered. Jane had never seen anything like it. She found it frightening.

'How are the Troupe people doing?'

'Oh, we hear from them sometimes,' Jane said. 'Buzzard, quite a bit. Rudy and Sam and Peter and Rick have their own team up in

Kansas now, they're still chasing. Martha never calls much, but I never got along much with Martha. We see Joe Brasseur socially sometimes, he's got some cushy job in town with the State Water Commission.'

'I never got a chance to tell you how sorry I was about Greg and Carol. And Mickey too.'

'Well,' she said simply. 'Mickey was a good man, and Greg and Carol were my closest friends.'

'How is Ed?'

'Well, Ed's got the use of both his arms again. Not like before, but pretty much. Ellen Mae is a lot better too. She's up in Anadarko now . . . '

'How is Jerry doing? Is Jerry here?'

'No. He's at The University. I'm expecting him.' She glanced at her watch. 'You want some lunch? I'm making tacos, it's easy.'

'I'll help,' Alex said.

THEY DRIFTED INTO Juanita's cramped and ancient kitchen. Sylvia stayed on the couch. Alex winced as he heard her deftly fire up the TV with a remote. She began methodically combing through Austin's eight hundred available channels, with repeated dabs of her thumb.

He moved beside the electric range and watched the taco mix bubbling in a pan. The top of Juanita's stove was liberally spattered with orange grease. Jane shook some garlic salt at the taco mix, as if trying to choke it into submission. His sister had to be the worst cook in the world.

'You gotta make allowances for Sylvia,' he said quietly. 'She's not real good with other people, just kind of shy.'

'I'm just touched that you would bring your girlfriend along to meet me, Alex.'

'I'd kind of like it, if you and she could get along. She's kind of important to me. The most important woman in my life, really.'

'That serious, huh?'

'I don't have a lot of room to judge there,' he said. 'I met her on the nets, in a genetic-disorder support group. Sylvia's good on nets. People like Sylvia and me, people who've been through a lot of sickness when young, it tends to narrow our social skills. She had kind of an autism thing, she's had a hard time of life. But she's all rewoven now, and she's okay underneath.'

'Boy, it really *is* that serious,' Jane said.

'How is Jerry? Are you getting along?'

'You really want to know?'

'Yes, really.'

'He's different. I'm different. We're a lot different than we were a year ago.' She looked at him hard, and he could see it there behind her eyes, waiting to pour out.

'Tell me,' he said.

'Well, it's since the baby . . . Alex, he's really good with the baby. The baby really got through to him, he's so good with his little son. It's like . . . he's really good when he has someone he doesn't have to *reason* with. He's so patient and kind with that little kid, it's really amazing.'

'How about you, though?'

'Us? We get along. We don't even *have* to get along. We're stuck here in this dinky little house, but you wouldn't know it. He's got his little office here with the virching stuff and his university link, and I've got my net-rig in the back in the baby's room, and he does his thing, and I do my thing, and we do our together-thing, and it works out okay, it really does.'

'What are you working on these days, exactly?'

'Net-stuff. The usual. Well, not the usual. Mommy net-stuff. The kind of stuff you can do with one hand, while you're wiping warm spit off your forearm.' Jane laughed, and poked at her taco mix with a wooden spoon. 'Anyway, that data we got – the stuff you recorded when the stream broke down on us? That made it on three final release disks! We got money for that. Pretty good money. We bought this house with it.'

'Oh.'

'Alex, this isn't a big house, I know that, but it's a stand-alone in a really prized area. I've even got a real garden in the backyard, you should see it. And you wouldn't believe the neighborhood politicals here in Austin, they are really fierce. You can walk to campus, and play with your kid right in the parks, anytime day or night, and it's a really pretty area, and it's really safe too. The crime rate is very low here, and you never see a structure hit, never. It's a real enclave here, it's a mega-good place for a little baby to live.'

'Can I *see* the baby?'

'Oh! Sure! Let me turn this down.'

She shut down the stove and led him into the back room. The nursery. The nursery was the first room in the house that actually struck him as a place where Juanita lived. The nursery looked like a room where an intelligent and hyperactive woman with design training had spent a long time thinking hard about exactly how things should look. It was like a big jewel box for a baby, it was like some monster bassinet in shades of fuzzy-cuddly midnight blue. It was the kind of room that created in Alex the instant urge to flee.

Juanita bent over the antique, hand-stripped, repainted wooden crib and looked in on her child. Alex had never seen quite that expression on her face before, but he recognized it. He recognized it as the place where all Juanita's raw ferocity had gone. All that steamy energy she'd always had, had been sucked into that all-encompassing Madonna look.

She was actually talking baby talk to the infant. Genuine oogly-googly sounds without enough consonants in them. Then she lifted the child up in its little trailing baby dress and handed him over.

The kid's hairless little noggin was in a little gray skullcap, kind of like a stuffed baked mushroom. Alex was no connoisseur of infants, but even he could tell that his little nephew – Michael Gregory Mulcahey – was not an attractive child. It was hard to tell, with the baby's squashed, cartilaginous little face, but he seemed to have the worst features of both his parents: Juanita's square jaw and Mulcahey's odd, bull-like forehead.

'Gosh, he's really cute,' Alex said. The child reacted with a fitful look and vigorous kicking. There was nothing wrong with the infant's legs. The kid had legs like a centaur.

'You can't believe it, can you?' Jane said, and smiled.

'No, Not really. I mean, not until now.'

'Neither could I. I think of all the times I almost took that abortifacient thing, you know. I actually put that pill inside my mouth once. I was gonna swallow it, and my period was gonna come back, and Jerry and me were gonna be exactly the same, and everything was going to be extremely lifelike. And if I didn't eat that pill, then the consequences were gonna be unimaginable and extremely grave! And I chose consequences, Alex, I did it all on purpose, just like I knew what I was doing. And now I have this little stranger in my life. Only he's not a little stranger at all. He's my baby.'

'I see.'

'I love my baby, Alex. I don't just sort of love him, I really love my baby, I love him desperately, we both do. We dote on him. I want to have another baby.'

'Really.'

'Childbirth's not that bad. It's really interesting. I kind of liked childbirth actually. It felt really intense and important.'

'I guess it would,' Alex said. 'I want Sylvia to see my nephew.'

JANE FOLLOWED HER back to the living room. He carried the child as if Michael Gregory was a wet bag full of live frogs. The strange girl peeled her reptile gaze from the television, and her eyes shot from the baby, to Alex, to Jane, to the baby again, and then to Jane once more, with a look of such dark and curdled envy and hatred that Jane felt stunned.

'He's really cute,' the girl said.

'Thanks.'

'That's a nice hat he's got too.'

'Thank you, Sylvia.'

'That's okay.' She started watching TV again.

Jane carried the baby back to the nursery and put him down. He'd just had his feeding. The baby was good about being handled. He liked to save his most energetic screamings for about 3 a.m.

'I guess her reaction seemed strange,' Alex said. 'But babies are kind of a funny topic for women with genetic disorders.'

'Oh.'

'She really wanted to see the baby, though. She said she did.'

'It's okay. Sylvia is fine.'

'Did you have the baby scanned for disorders?'

'Alex . . . ' She hesitated. 'That's kind of an expensive proposition.'

'Not for me. I know ways, I have contacts. Really, it's no problem; just slip me a little sample, you know, a frozen scraping off the inside of the cheek, we can get a genome rundown started right away, hit the high points, all the major fault centers. Reasonable rates. You really ought to have him scanned, Jane. His uncle has a disorder.'

'We're not very lucky people, are we, Alex?'

'We're alive. That's lucky.'

'We're not lucky, Alex. This is not a luck time. We're alive, and I'm glad we're alive, but we're people of disaster. We'll never truly be happy or safe, never. Never, ever.'

'No,' he said. He drew a breath. A good, deep breath. 'Jane. I came here to Austin beause I needed to tell you something. I wanted to thank you, Jane. Thank you for saving my life.'

'*De nada.*'

'No, Jane, it was a lot. You could have let me be, like I was telling you to do, and those quacks would have killed me in that black-market *clínica*. But you came after me, and you got me, and you even looked after me. And even though we were close to death, and surrounded by death, and we chased deadly things, we both came out alive. We're survivors, and look, there's another one of us now.'

She grabbed his arm. 'You want to tell me something, Alejandro? All right. Tell me something that I really want to hear.' She tugged him to the side of the baby's crib. 'Tell me that's your family, Alex. Tell me you'll help me look after him, like he was family.'

'Sure he's family. He's my nephew. I'm proud of him.'

'No, not that way. I mean the *real* way. I mean *look after him*, Alex, really care about him, like when I'm dead, and Jerry's dead, and this city is smashed, and everyone is sick and dying, and you don't even personally like him very much. But you still care anyway, and you still save him.'

'Okay, Janey' Alex said slowly. 'That's only fair. It's a bargain.'

'No! Not a bargain, not a money thing, I don't want that from you or anyone. I want a real promise from you, I want you to swear to me so that I'll never doubt you.'

He looked at her. Her face was tight and her eyes were clouded, and he realized, with a strange little jolt of surprise, that his sister was truly afraid. Juanita had come to know and understand real fear. She was more afraid for this little bundle in the crib than she had ever been for herself. Or for her friends, or for her husband, or for anyone. She had a hostage to fortune now. That baby's sweaty little monkey hands had gripped her soul.

'All right,' he said. He raised his right hand, solemnly. 'Juanita Unger Mulcahey, I promise you that I'll look after your son, and all your children. I swear it on our mother's grave. Pe lo juro por la tumba de avestra madre.'

'That's good, Alex.' She relaxed, a little. 'I really believed you when you said it that way.'

Voices came from the front of the house. Jerry had come home.

Alex went to meet him in the front froom.

'This is a pleasant surprise,' Jerry boomed. He and Alex shook hands.

Jerry had lost weight. He'd lost the great heaps of muscle on his shoulders, and his arms and legs were of relatively normal dimensions, and his gut looked like the gut of a family man in his thirties. He'd lost more hair, and the sides of the beard were gone now; he had a professorial Vandyke, and a real haircut. He had a shirt, suit jacket and tie, and a leather valise.

'They must be keeping you busy, Jerry.'

'Oh yes. And you?'

'I'm getting into genetics.'

'Really. That's interesting, Alex.'

'I felt I had to.' He looked hard into Jerry's eyes. Maybe he could, for the first time ever, make some kind of human contact there. 'You see, Jerry, genetic treatment changed me so profoundly, I felt I just had to comprehend it. And I mean really understand it, not just get my hands on it and hack at it, but genuinely understand the science. It's a difficult field, but I think I'm up to the challenge. If I work at it hard, I can really learn it.' He shrugged. 'Of course, I still have to go through all that equivalency nonsense first.'

'Right,' Jerry said, clear-eyed and nodding sympathetically, 'the academic proprieties.' Nothing was wrong, and no one was missing, and there were no ghosts at this banquet, and no deep dark secrets, and for good old brother-in-law Jerry, life was just life.

'Done any storm work lately, Jerry?'

'Of course! The F-6! Extremely well documented. Enough material there for a lifetime.'

Jane spoke up. 'Nobody believed it would happen, even though he said it would. And now he's trying to explain to them why it stopped.'

'That's a real problem,' Jerry said, savoring it. 'A nexus of problems. Nontrivial.'

'The best kind of nexus of problems, I'm sure.'

Jerry laughed. Briefly. 'It's good to see you in such good spirits, Alex. You and your friend should stay for lunch.'

'Tacos,' Jane said.

'Good! My favorite.' Jerry's eyes glazed. 'Just a moment, I've got to look after some things first.' He vanished into his office.

Music burst out through Jerry's closed office door, the insistent squeaking and rattling of a Thai pop tune. It was loud.

'Does he really like that Thai stuff?' Alex asked Juanita.

Juanita shrugged. 'Not really,' she said loudly. 'That's just some of my old college music, but Jerry punches up anything on the box when he works . . . He plays it to drown out the city noise. To drown out the hum, y'know. So he can think.'

The music segued into an elaborate Asian cha-cha. Sylvia made a face.

'Let's go in the backyard and I'll show you my garden. The tacos will keep.'

It was quiet in the backyard. It was a lovely spring day. It was sunny and there were honeysuckles and a birdbath. 'Jerry's always like this when they make him do polynomials,' Jane apologized.

'Always like what? Jerry has always acted just like that.'

'No, not quite like he does now, but . . . well, you don't know him like I do.' She sighed. 'The labcoat people have really got him where they want him now. The seminars, the lecture tours, the peer review committees . . . If he gets tenure and they offer him the chairman-ship, we're gonna have some real problems.'

'What kind of problems?'

'You don't wanna know. Lemme put it this way – when Mommy gets her claws on some real money again, Mommy's gonna buy Daddy a nice endowed chair where he can sit and think quietly, all by himself.' Jane shrugged. 'We've been up to Oklahoma City a couple of times to lecture and do media – Jerry's real popular there . . . It's really weird up there now, that city was just leveled, and they were all completely broke and tragic and desperate, and so they just . . . well, they just threw away all the rule books. And now they're doing the weirdest architecture you can imagine! They're rebuilding everything aboveground, out of dirt-cheap *nothing*, out of paper and software and foam. The new Oklahoma City is just like a giant, smart, wasp's nest. Have you been up there?'

'No! But it sounds really worthwhile,' Alex said.

'Yeah. I think so. I think it's the future, frankly. You can tell it's the future, too, 'cause the plumbing hardly works, and it's crowded, and it smells bad. They got the storm problem whipped, though. God help them if they get a fire.' She looked at her garden: beans, tomatoes. 'I got some special stuff from some Oklahoma agro-engineers during Jerry's last speaking tour. It was kind of a celebrity perk.'

Jane was growing two rows of corn in her backyard. Corn, *Zea mays*, but with the chlorophyll hack. It had taken the human race quite some time to understand chlorophyll, the chemical method by which plants turned light into food, and when the ancient secret finally came out, the secret had turned out to be a really dumb botch. Even after two billion years of practice, plants had an utterly lousy notion of how to turn light into food. Plants were damn near as dumb as rocks, basically, and their lame idea of capturing sunlight was the silliest, most harebrained scheme imaginable.

Serious-minded human beings were working on the chlorophyll problem now, and they hadn't done a lot better yet, but they were doing about fifteen percent better, which was not at all bad, considering. And people might do better yet, if they could get living crops to endure the terrible impact of that much-concentrated human ingenuity. And, in tandem, get the ecosystem to survive the terrible consequences should such a technique ever go feral. Alex was really interested in the chlorophyll hack. He'd read a lot about it, and was following the bigger net-discussions. It was just about the neatest hack he'd ever heard of.

Jane's corn plants were squat and fibrous and ugly, and the ears of corn were about the size and shape of bowling pins. They were splotchy and reptilian green.

'Wow, those are really nice,' said Sylvia.

'Would you like some for yourself? Just a second.' Jane wandered into her backyard garden shed and came out with a drawstring bag. 'You can have some spare seeds if you want.' She shook half a dozen kernels of corn into Sylvia's outstretched palm. The misshapen kernels were the size of rifle cartridges.

'Thank you, Jane,' Sylvia said gratefully. 'These are mega-nice, I really like these.'

'Help yourself,' Jane told her. 'Can't copyright a living organism! Ha-ha-ha.'

Sylvia wrapped the seeds carefully in her silk kerchief and stuffed them, unselfconsciously, into the thigh-high top of her striped stocking.

'Jane, come out in the street for a second,' Alex said, opening the side gate to the front yard.

She followed him. 'What are we doing out here?'

'I want to show you my new car.'

'Okay. Great.'

'I parked it up the street around the corner because I didn't want it associated with your house.'

'Oh.'

The car was sitting where he had left it. He'd had to pay a stiff fee to the university police to bring it inside the district.

'Holy mackerel,' Jane said, 'looks like they didn't even detach the gun mounts.'

'Those are urban antitheft devices. It's licensed for them, too, isn't that great? Technically sublethal.'

Jane's eyes were alight. 'You've put it through its paces already, huh?'

'Yeah. You could say that.'

'What kind of interface is it running?'

'A mega-dog-meat military interface. That's why I want you to have it for a while.'

'Really?'

'Yeah, I want you to have this car as long as you like. It's yours, you run it. I'd even sign over the papers, but I don't think that's a really good idea, legally speaking.'

'Oh?'

'Yeah, and I, uh, wouldn't take it to Hidalgo, Starr, or Zapata counties, or over the border into Reynosa, because it might be slightly hot there.'

Sylvia tugged his sleeve and whispered, *'Hey. We need that car! Don't give her the car!'*

'It's all right, trust me,' Alex assured her, 'Jane's very good with cars, I've never known her to so much as bump a fender.' He smiled.

'You can't just give me a pursuit car, Alex.'

'Sure I can. I just did. Who's gonna stop me? And what's more, I want to see you take it for a spin. Right now. Sylvia and I will do lunch and look after nephew, and I want to see you run this sucker out to Enchanted Rock and tear the hide off of it.'

'I don't think I can do that. Baby needs looking after.'

'Look, Jane, you can't have it both ways. You just made me swear up and down I would guard that child's destiny; you're just gonna have to trust me with him for a couple of hours.'

'Well . . . I'm tempted. I'm really tempted, Alex.'

He leaned toward her, smiling. 'Give in.'

'All right!' Suddenly she embraced him.

It was a solid embrace. It felt surprisingly good to be hugged by one's sister. It was a real gift to have a sister. Not a wife, not a lover, but a woman that you deeply cared about. A friend, a good friend, a powerful ally. An ally against what? Against Nothing, that's what. Against death, against the big empty dark.

He touched his lips to his sister's ear. 'Go and run, sister,' he whispered. 'Go run!'